W9-BGD-933

SHADOW-BOX

SHADOW-BOX

ANTONIA LOGUE

GROVE PRESS
New York

First published by Bloomsbury Publishing Plc, London, in 1999
Printed in the United States of America

FIRST AMERICAN EDITION

Library of Congress Cataloging-in-Publication Data

Logue, Antonia.
Shadow-box / by Antonia Logue.
p. cm.
ISBN 0-8021-1647-7
1. Cravan, Arthur, 1887–1920? Fiction. 2. Johnson, Jack, 1878–1946—Correspondence Fiction. 3. Loy, Mina—Correspondence Fiction. I. Title.
PR6062.O39S53 1999
823'.914—dc21 99-22553

Grove Press
841 Broadway
New York, NY 10003

99 00 01 02 10 9 8 7 6 5 4 3 2 1

For my parents Anne and Hugh,
whose love and faith makes
everything possible. With all my
love and gratitude, always

ACKNOWLEDGEMENTS

I would like to thank my parents and my closest friends, Hugh and Anne, for all their faith and love. For their friendship and suport I would especially like to thank my brothers Christopher and Hugh, along with Fiona McCann, Michelle Woods, Kevin Manning, Mary Burke, Pauline, Christina and Marianne Calderato, Antoin Rodgers, Liz McNamara, and my god-daughter Aine Sandfort. For his love and encouragement throughout, my heartfelt thanks to Eamonn Sweeney, with love.

Of the sources I used in researching this novel, two in particular were outstanding – *Papa Jack* by Randy Roberts (Robson Books), and *Becoming Modern – The Life Of Mina Loy* by Carolyn Burke (FSG). I would also like to acknowledge the help given to me by a number of people – Sam Boyce and Linda Shaughnessy at A.P. Watt, Mary Tomlinson at Bloomsbury, Fabienne's god-daughter Nina Salter at Calmann-Levy, Amy Hundley at Grove Atlantic, the board of the Tyrone Guthrie Centre, the Corporation of Yaddo, and most especially the invaluable contribution of my editor, Liz Calder. My very special thanks to Caradoc King for his enthusiasm and advice.

You must dream your life with great care
Instead of living it merely as amusement.

Arthur Cravan, *Des Paroles*

Everyone, real or invented, deserves the open destiny of life.

Grace Paley

Prologue

You'd dip into Cravan for a day and come out of an acid bath, your body corroding, sinuses so full of poison those inner canals in your ears would hear nothing but a high wasting moan and your balance would be all shot to hell. He strode around Berlin wearing hookers on his shoulders, them tittering and screeching down the Kurfurstendam like they were queens on a float, then leave them back where he found them, all legs and suicide.

Eventually Berlin threw him out, first man ever, they said, for he was too conspicuous. Make sense of that for me, Mina, too conspicuous. They'd never seen anything like him, that was the problem, a white man able to fight like he could without hurting anybody but himself, too much strength and not enough brain to punch with, they said. They didn't read too many of his poems in the places he hung out in that time. Some heard he'd his own magazine back in Paris but the rumours that threaded into the back-bar conversations didn't last if they confused the pimps who brought them, reciting the pillow talk of their girls. Everybody had a history, Mina, nearly every one made up to suit the men who crept through the alleys at night whipping the girls to finish up and get back out under the light. If you didn't fit into the network, you didn't fit in anyplace, and Cravan didn't, Mina, he'd parade the hookers' tired asses on his shoulders two apiece like he was carrying turkey home for Christmas, laughing and teasing and letting them off without ever putting a hand between their legs. And some men don't trust a man like that.

So he came to Barcelona.

Before that we were in Paris together, back in 1914. That was three full years before he crashed into you, Mina, found real love. In Barcelona he was in the same shape as he'd been then, long and broad as the new roads they were building to transport crops that were never coming, already dead in the earth with disease. But Cravan wasn't scabbed or harrowed, he came in, Mina, and I don't think there was a man in Europe I wanted to see more, I just didn't know it.

Weeks went by before he hit me with it, a fight, staged like nothing the Spanish ever saw, better than bullfights, Jack, he said, not a fix, not a real one anyway, I'll stay on my feet long enough to look like I can, then you knock me out, all that money, what about it, Jack? And the bastard would too, I knew it then, he'd let me floor him flat out in front of thousands if it'd get him to America. You knew his ego better than anyone. He would have sold me to the circus, fat Ex-Heavyweight Champion of the World, Any Fight, Name Your Price, if it would get him there.

America was the only thing they talked about, him and his poet buddy Cendrars, two warped missionaries preaching to one of the few men in Spain who couldn't go. I don't think Cendrars even knew about the warrant out on me in the States, I think he reckoned I was in Europe for an easy retirement. Cravan leaned over to me one night over the noise. Come back with us, Jack, he said, we'll get you in again, like I could just climb off that ship and not have the whole damn lot lined up on the docks, sly as pickpockets, me cuffed and sentenced in ninety seconds, with half of America cheering on like it was Willard all over again.

His plan was serious. He'd fight me. Next day he had the posters spread across Barcelona like a pox – *Gran Fiesta De Boxeo, Finalizara el espectaculo con el sensacional encuentro entre el campeon del mundo, Jack Johnson, Negro de 110 kilos y el campeon europeo, Arthur Cravan, Blanco de 105 kilos*. Different fighters, different styles, different successes. All this stuff he had about being European Champion was true, but he'd come to it through a lot of pussy fights, he'd fought two-bit boot boys he'd loom over and intimidate into lying down, but he could fight, he was one of the strongest white men I'd ever seen.

His plan was for me to throw a few, I'd take a couple, and third round I'd put him down gently as I could without looking like his nursemaid. Fifty thousand pesetas between us and 20 per cent of the door each. He knew this nervous wolfhound, Hierro, who set the whole thing up in the old flour mill on the river, a huge sable building shut down after the phloxera hit the wheat three years in a row. I think it was meant for conversion to a steam mill, but it was the same incinerated mess when I came back from Mexico. Everybody sticks to talking in that city.

On the night of the fight it seemed like the whole city had turned out, all around the river was a carnival, people everywhere drinking their throats dry, too many people even for a place that size, but we knew Hierro would get them in. He had strung together a warm-up show out of a bunch of Spanish kids, kids who'd got tough on the streets, ones Hierro had rounded up like some sort of white-flesh battle royal.

The place was dangerous, you knew that the moment you breathed the air inside, over three thousand men packed in on the first floor sweating and singing, play-fighting with blood punches, not a woman in the room, but the hookers had found the riverside, claiming territory in the scrub like they were mapping out a new cartography of body arcs and curves.

Some of these men had worked in this mill at one time, taking the wraps off wheat and pulverising it into flour. Then there were the men from the oldest quarters of the city, separated from money by the Paraleo with its cheap theatres and bars, the dancing halls where wives would forget their hatred for their new hovelled life, without water, without drains, where their children died as newborns in the fetid air. They worked in the new fabric factories as spinners, while their men roamed for work, and the countryside they had abandoned for new lives in the slums continued to rot under the command of an insect half the length of an eyelash.

Danger heaved the room, swelling the floorboards, until even the rafters eighty feet above sweated the tiny balls of flour washed out of the wall by the pores of a thousand men. They tore at the makeshift hoarding nailed across the gap in the back wall where the sacks of flour had once been lowered down on to river barges below and floated downstream to the docks to be loaded on to the trucks and ships; they tore at the thick jabs of nails until they had wrenched open the wide first-floor landing bay, a balcony over the river-bend. This action would save their lives, prevent tragedy where tragedy should have gripped.

Cravan was lucky like that; the little things would go wrong, a shoelace break as he rushed, a missed train, a lightning storm sluicing the countryside as he walked, but he was protected, Mina, his path divined for him so all he had to do was plumb the water. It was as if it was known that he'd be the first of us to go, and he was getting a good ride because it was going to be short. Is that too easy an explanation? I don't know what to say, Mina, this is meant to be a consolation, memories of when he was in my life, but only you know what it is like to lose him properly. It is easy from here, I don't live without him. It doesn't feel as though he is dead these years, he could still be on his honeymoon with you in Mexico. Dead is just a word that gets about in a war. It doesn't fit him; maybe I pretend he's somewhere else, maybe that's what we're doing here, Mina, indulging in a game as if recounting and recounting will displace everything and reinstate him – you can feel he's here with me, and I can believe he's wherever you are. I don't think his luck ran out. I think that night he died things just got bigger than shoelaces and lightning. There was no luck to it.

I didn't need the money like he did. Those fifty thousand pesetas he got off Hierro were his passage to America. The first time he went, he was seventeen and hid in a cargo of untreated cowhides, sailing for weeks as the careless scrags of underside flesh rotted in the hold and he sweltered in the thick unbreathable stench of it. This time he wanted to go properly, not in a cabin or in style, just on top, where the air was. He needed that fight.

I'm not being quaint with age, Mina. God knows, had I found him in the hours and weeks after the fight, I would have beaten him till every drop of sweat and blood and sperm was choked out of him, but after a time I was envious as hell. He didn't care about anything people said, he was never defined by other people's perceptions. I couldn't have got up and done what he did. My ego wouldn't have let me, not then. I was Jack Johnson, in my own head I was Champion of the World for decades after I threw it to Willard. Might have been easier to let go if I'd been beaten, but throwing a fight like that, well, it takes a long time to accept the outcome. I am still unbeaten, that's the way I see it. Cravan understood the real purpose of ego, to keep the real self entire, always challenged, never to let it get slack and dependent on others. You were the only one he changed the rules for. Everything changed for you.

That night, the riot began quick as mercury. I was still in the ring, standing there in my gloves over where he'd fallen while the crowd seethed on to the tarpaulin and I was mauled by the surge. Cravan had disappeared somehow; all of it from start to finish taking just minutes, all the cheers and shouts, the mix of sweat and flour and energy in your mouth when you breathed, everyone trying to touch us as we moved to the ring, bodies all over stripped to the waist, a glisten over everyone as they shouted our names over each other, getting louder and louder, so that by the time we got to the ring all we could hear was a roar of syllables, the musky, high smell of sweat clogging everything then, our throats, our nostrils, our voices, ears, only our eyes still doing their job right in the throb of the crowd, getting us to the ring. It felt like every fight I'd ever won, that same piston knowledge that I would do it, that crowd-spun whirl of certainty as I climbed the ropes into the ring, turning towards the crowd, turning towards

Cravan, the booing as the third man came in – a buzzard trainer Hierro had picked to referee – Cravan looking strong and wicked enough to floor an army corps, staring me straight in the eye with this smile you could read any way you wanted, punching the post in his corner like he was warming up for a massacre. Then we were touching gloves in a handshake for a fair fight, as if that was what the Spanish had packed in for, and then, suddenly, the bell, and Mina, I don't know what happened after that.

I moved in to start sparring, no menace, no attack, just the two of us jabbing high, him dancing round the ring looking tough, the crowd on its feet yelling and shouting for him, then me, then him again just as he powered in with a body blow to my ribs. I got angry, ran a left-right-left uppercut combination at him, all the while talking to him, don't remember what I was saying, just the sound of my voice mingling with the crowd's, and his blood was high now too. He was coming at me hard, both of us pitting ourselves at each other as though this were for real, as though there was the world to prove in who won this, me still shouting at him, teasing him, but his concentration so intense I don't think he knew where he was, Mina, every iota of instinct on the next punch, the next manoeuvre, until suddenly he stopped, realised he was fighting to win and like a switch all the power in his arms was flicked off, he eased off as if his brain had been stung, still looking like he was fighting, but not so much as grazing my jaw, aware now of the crowd, his circumstances, the money he was fighting for. And I got angry, Mina, furious that he was pulling the fight, didn't matter that this was the plan, to me this was for real now, one of us would win, and it had to be me, I had to beat him, had to beat him fairly. I needed to floor him with him coming at me, so I started buffeting him round the ring, trying to square him up, get him going again, but he was having none of it, he was getting ready to go down, and I refused to believe he meant it, that he could be fighting it out with Jack Johnson and not care if he won or not, was able to let it go so easy.

And all round us the noise, men hanging off the ropes, all of them stamping the floorboards in this frenzied hammering, boots hitting wood over and over until all I was aware of was the throb of the pounding and a thousand voices, and suddenly I was swinging back in an arc from my shoulder, deep and true, in a slow dolphin punch that caught the side of his head, knocking him straight to the floor, unconscious. There was maybe two or three seconds before the crowd swelled up, and I realised what had happened, and he was gone when I looked down, disappeared, like I'd punched air. It was Cendrars, he had it all arranged, he had Cravan off the canvas and in under the ring before anyone was even sure Cravan had gone down, the two of them shot down the mill-chute that Hierro had carefully erected the ring over – the one for chuting fresh-filled flour sacks down to the warehouse below – Cendrars dragging Cravan into a car on the river bank to the docks, to the New York ship, unconscious and good as dead he hauled him on, and when Cravan came to he was nine hours nearer America and sore as safari-cull.

They went after me in the ring but I was hauled out while benches and pews were thrown alight, a swarm of bodies whipped up with a crazed energy attacking one another, bare-fisted and raw with ferocity. But the fire from the burning pews had caught angrily in the room now, licking the floorboards alight, reaching high to the rafters and beams until soon the room was ablaze, the heat making everything writhe, bodies, faces, the black metal roof-pins, the iron girders in the stone walls, the men surging towards the open loading bay, leaping blind, until the river bank was a dance of bodies hurling themselves out of the mill fire into the river, men jumping headlong into the spit of it, the water turning black and thick with burning flesh, so many that after the first leaps men jumped on men, limbs and backs and shoulders broken in the panic of chaos, and all the while Cravan sailed on towards America. Towards you.

FABIENNE

It is the heat that makes her laugh, as if she had forgotten it, stepping happily out on to the street with her delicate ivory train draped across her forearm, her other hand seeking out the budding arum lilies that crown her marrying head. He is not here. She has insisted that he meet her at the church, and like a game he throws himself into the novelty of it, and is there, high on the hill, waiting, without a wince of nervousness to furrow his brow. With him the burly figure in the almost immaculate three-piece suit stands perspiring in the Mexican swelter, his mouth tasting like pigswill from all the cigars smoked the night before, and the night before that, and every night this week since Cravan and Mina decided they would marry and asked him to be their witness. His head throbs with envy and drink, only envy because he does not wish away their happiness, merely yearns for it. He has never been jealous of anyone, and at this moment as he sees Mina and Rose, her witness, and their friends come laughing up the hill, Mina translucent in the sun, her hair falling about her face as she turns her head to talk to those behind her, he is jolted back to his own weddings, and he has never felt such love. Not for her, not entirely, and not for anything that has gone before, but for everything he is at the heart of today, this tumbling surging joy that propels him bounding down the hill after Cravan to sweep up the party in his arms and kiss Mina's face. And then at the top of the hill outside the sunswept church they fall into a shambolic order, Cravan and Mina snuggled together laughing as if in a conspiracy all their own, and Jack sent by Rose to unhand the groom and get him to the nave of the church so the wedding can begin.

The dark coolness of the stone disarms Cravan as he and Jack topple into its vastness. He has been inside it before, he has used it often as his sanctuary when he has needed time alone, not away from Mina, simply alone, to decipher the collection of darting notions he keeps in his head and especially the ones that don't dart, the ones that embed themselves and need thinking through, like Mina. He has never loved before this, never been raw with need, never felt his soul halved by a person's absence before now. He never believed she would truly come to him here in Mexico, nor that she would ever want to marry him, that this day would be his for the taking. On the nights he cannot sleep he goes out into the city, into the lulling bustle that seems never to calm. He drinks and wanders, goes to the places his friends do not frequent and gambles insignificant sums, wearies himself of his energies, buys food, talks to himself, imagines he is the new King of France, a sailor on leave, an American spy preparing to oust the Mexican Government, a Mexican general planning his naval attack on the world, a lunatic escaped, a criminal being covert, a carnival owner trying to entice the insomniac city to his paradise.

And then he meanders home and slips into bed beside the most exquisite person he has ever known, leaves breakfast on the table beside her pillow, and looks at her in her slumber, at her silken lashes, her smooth creamy skin soft as he tenderly strokes her sleeping face with his fingertips. With her he can be anything he wants to be, she has no fetters, no ideas of how anything ought to be. They have no oughts, only now, that is what she tells him, and as the shards of stained-glass sunlight cut across his reverie, Jack is turned to him, the padre expectant, the ten or twelve guests scuttling into their seats at Rose's command, and suddenly three voices crack open the air with a single note and 'Ave Maria' ushers the back door to open and from out of a flood of blinding sunlight at the other end of the church Mina walks towards him in her simple ivory silk gown, the bouquet of lilies in her hand, his eyes caught in hers drawing her to his side with every step, her satin train scattering flower petals with every shimmy further down the aisle . . . and they are together now, Jack to one side, Rose to the other, and as they say their vows even the padre is swept along in the force of emotion that fills the small church with this tiny coven of wedding guests clustered at its altar. And then they are all bursting out into the sunlight led by the freshly married couple laughing and giddy all the way down the hill towards the three-day celebrations.

This is my parents' wedding in 1918. This is their start. Within a year I was born, within a year nothing was as it ought to have been, and for my father there was no now. That was how I was told it all along. I am fifty-three now. I live in Aspen, Colorado, an uncomplicated life until a few weeks ago when a parcel came for me, a 'Thank You For Your Sympathy' card slipped in on top of a sheaf of letters from the estate of an Irene Johnson, a woman of whom I had never heard. They are my mother Mina's letters to this woman's husband, Jack, not love letters, not a hint of impropriety in any of them, just her life as she told him. A different life to the one I thought I knew, but she is dead these past six years now, since 1966; it is too late to ask her. I have had his letters to her in my house ever since she moved here before she died, and I left them unread until now. She gave them telling me he had been a great man, had been the only man my father trusted. I don't think I cared enough by then, all the mystery that enveloped everything about this shadow who fathered me, who loved my mother so profoundly that she lived with him in her heart every moment of her life and yet was a fiction to me, a face that stopped ageing at thirty – other people lost their fathers to war, while I lost mine to mythology.

All through my childhood new people turning up to tell my mother he had been seen in some prison or entanglement on the other side of our world, and off she went to search him out, telling me she'd be bringing my father home to me . . . And I, at two, at three, at five, at ten, at twelve, at twenty-seven . . . believing her at first, then inuring myself to all of it, all her fantastic futile treks for someone who always seemed to belong elsewhere, who was never there with us, where my mother so clearly believed he should be. And in between these lost voyages people quietly taking me aside to explain that my father was dead, had died before I was born in a storm at sea, while others excitedly told me that I was the daughter of genius, of a brilliant mother and a spectacular father, a father so exuberant that he had had to disappear off the face of the earth to preserve his legend. I am his legend. I am the only true thing he left behind, the only thing he couldn't counterfeit. It is me. Perhaps that is why I now must find him, my mother's obsession passed on to me by proxy, through ragged letters twenty-six years old. One specific ragged letter that starts me on his path again, like a family affliction. But like her, I must know. I must.

I go to Mexico this evening. I will see the place where they married, where they lived, where I was conceived, from where he disappeared, where he is now if there is anything to find. But I will trace his routes, and find him, whatever has become of him, it is my legacy, for there is no one else alive any more who can.

Jack

Chicago, January 1946

Dearest Mina,

I did not know you were alive, and there you are this morning in my newspaper, 'ENGLISH POET NATURALIZED' – living in New York all this time. Nearly thirty years older than the last time I saw you, but beautiful as ever. You always were the most exquisite woman I ever saw, Mina Loy. I was jealous as hell of Cravan when he showed me your pictures, but it was nothing to what I felt when you came to Mexico and I saw you properly. A little late then, me being best man at your wedding at the time.

This letter is a long time coming, Mina, I'm sorry for that. I wrote to you when Cravan disappeared to see if there was anything I could do, if you wanted to come and stay with us in Chicago, but when I never heard back I reckoned you'd gone back to Europe or else you just wanted left alone. But I should have tried harder to keep in touch, I guess I just lost track. Seeing your face in the paper this morning, hell, it was strange, it brought me back through so much. I had to write to you, chase you up. How are you? Guess you're an American now. Write to me, tell me everything. What you're at, what you've done these past twenty-eight years, tell me all about your life, Mina, everything. It's like we've got a second chance now, time to fill in the gaps, reacquaint each other with the lives we've lived. Without seeing you in the paper I would never have done it, would have pinned you in the scrapbook as part of something past, such great memories. Now we can make up for lost time.

Write, Mina, I'd love to hear from you.

Take care,

Jack

Mina

New York, January 1946

Dearest Jack,

Thank you so much for the newspaper cutting – there were a few others, but I am rather forgotten these days. Even in my own days I was hardly besieged – that tall eccentric Englishwoman obsessed by sex and poetry and home-made hats, that was me. It's odd how others see you, don't you think? All the subtleties disappear. I wasn't obsessed by any of those things, of course. Now after playing at being American for so long, I finally am. It is strange. Fabian would laugh at me. I don't think he applied for nationality anywhere in the world – he merely chose the most appropriate when he needed to and forged the necessary papers. My identity was never so easily sloughed as his.

It is astonishing to hear from you. If being naturalised has only this renewed contact to offer as its reward, it has been worth it. How are you? Back in Chicago – so you did go home after Mexico. What have you done all this time? I feel such fondness at having you back in my life after all these years, but when I tried to explain to my daughter what you had meant to Fabian, I didn't have the words. Facts, details, stories of the wedding, of the bullfight, the boxing Academy . . . but to her they were merely nostalgic reveries I indulged in. It is magical to have you back in contact, Jack, you are right, we have so much to catch up on, to discover.

It is odd to see you write his name as 'Cravan'. I haven't thought of him that way for years. But he was Arthur Cravan to the whole world who knew him, everyone but me. He was introduced to me as Arthur Cravan, but on that first night he told me his real name, told me he could steal mine. He was right, and he did – Mina Loy, Fabian Lloyd. I have signed myself Mina Lloyd for twenty-eight years, Jack, since he disappeared – I have never stopped being his wife. I named our daughter Fabienne after him, but he never got to see her. She is his longevity, wherever he is. But he was always Cravan to you, don't change that.

I'll never forget you at our wedding, as nervous as if it were your own. It was a happy wedding, wasn't it, so gay and full of love. That was what Mexico was to us, just an absolute immersion in the purest form of happiness.

We had such silly days too. Do you remember that bullfight? I had arrived just a few days and there you both were, like children with a sandcastle at your Academy, all proud and eager to show off. That summer was chaos. It was everything that I wanted from Mexico. I wish we had photographs of the wedding, of the church, the view beneath it, the three of us and the padre, us all excited because we'd done it, after all our plots and his escapes, all my concern and uncertainty about coming to Mexico. I was there, we were together again, married, just as we said we would be, and it was the best adventure either of us had ever known. Oh Jack, I was so in love that day, so happy, and so glad you were there, that finally we met and you bore witness to what we'd done. It was a wonderful week the three of us spent together, filled with a strange elation that floated us up over everything, brought us joy in the oddest ways, for the oddest reasons. And then you were gone, we awoke one morning and you had skipped away down the coast to go back to Europe. A few days later people came looking for you, but oh how we hoped you'd got passage by then. And now you are back in my life again, to remember all your stories as if we were sitting on a wall in the sun planning the bullfight together the three of us, looking down on the city and all this had never happened.

You were to be the daring fearless matadors before all those people in that huge amphitheatre, pitting yourselves against the bulls as though you were toilet-training poodles for French ladies for the afternoon. The two of you half drunk in the sun. I expected carnage, I suppose. I probably should have tried to convince Fabian not to throw himself into things like that, to risk being beaten bloody by something out of his control, himself sometimes, in the bar brawls that were his lunacy or street fights or ring fights or those ludicrous exhibition matches where all anyone ever wants is a bit of uncontrolled savagery. But he'd have talked me calm, and he'd have been right, he'd come out the victor. That was against men. Against an irate animal the size of a tank, what were his hopes? Or yours. And I settled there with my fan and water jug and my cartwheel hat, sitting in the curved seats of the stadium watching the dusty space in front of me while the thousands in the crowd spat away the dryness in their mouths and yelled towards the small gate in the wall for you both to come on. It was such a game to the pair of you behind there – let's have a bullfight, let us show these Mexicans how the Spanish matadors would sweep the bulls around an arena, because we are invincible.

It was such a time for us, the war losing steam, the Mexican insurrection brewing, and we there painting ourselves into it all. You were nearly killed that day, the pair of you, some of the women screaming in horror if the bull weaved towards you at all, then fainting when it charged. Me reviving strangers, with my eyes on Fabian as he darted in and out of the bull's path and yours, waving his cloak as though it were armour and not a limp piece of red embroidered sackcloth with sequins. You went down first, then he, you were gored beneath your right arm. A wound as nasty as any I'd seen until we cleaned it, and yet after all it was just a flesh wound, needing nothing more than stitches and some flamboyant bandaging to keep up the myth. But Fabian seemed to get it worse than that, he got it in the thigh, a gash in his leg as he leapt just a fraction too late, the bull with the taste for blood after you, and he limped around the whole of the next three weeks as if a hero, bandaged underneath his suit at his wedding, when all along it was a skin wound too. We dressed it just like yours, as though it were semi-fatal, and he played it up just to glamorise the stupidity of the two of you, such foolish half-wits thinking you were tough and nimble enough to take on bulls that the Mexicans themselves wouldn't touch.

I spent so long searching for him, you know, years trawling jails and chasing rumours for a truth I couldn't have borne had I found it. You made more choices than me, you chose who warmed your bed at night and who to expel. I haven't given myself that choice since he disappeared, all these as-ifs I fumble around with, answerless ones.

We talked of such frivolous things then, all of Mexico a novelty to me, the excitement over the wedding . . . I wish we had talked then of the things you tell me now. That would have really made something of us, made me come to you for the intimacy I needed when he disappeared, a person who truly knew him who could talk me out of my worst fears. I needed someone so desperately then, someone who was both his and mine, who loved him for all the things I loved him for, who brought those things out. We three spent such a short time together in Mexico, just those few weeks, whole lives and pasts we just forgot to mention, were ashamed to. Whatever the reason.

Fabienne is all I have left of him, and she is a near compensation. She is a woman now, almost twenty-seven years old, beautiful, married but with a whole world of choices yet. She has never needed a father, yet she needs him to befriend her as he did me, shock her as he did me, make her think and explode and earn that dynamism he gave to me. I love her for all there is of him in her – her mouth, her eyes wide and blue, the shape of her face, her joyful wickedness, that lacerating intelligence. She is my fourth child, and the only one to bear his spirit. I am not good on motherhood, Jack, not good on children. I have lost two already. Two kept. I seem to spend my life wedged between grieving paths, the widow, the distraught mother, that lunatic grief I'm afflicted with, and yet this is not how I see my life at all. I look on it as you do, as something done and the world better for its doing. My world at least.

You want to know everything. What is there to tell you? Everything is a lot, and there are things I am unable to tell anyone, even now. It is easier to talk of the years before I met him, they seem more neutral, a separate life. It is a shock, though a pleasant one, to hear from you like this after so long. Twenty-eight years, Jack. You used to tease me in Mexico for being as often married as you, but even then I think we were both embarking on our second outing. For me, it was the last. And you? How many Mrs Johnsons did you carry over the threshold, Jack? More than two, I'd wager. Even in Mexico you were game-hunting. I could never imagine you falling in love. But you were funny then, the way you teased me about my first husband Stephen, about my lack of wifeliness. Everything . . . I will start with Stephen, with the life I led before I met Fabian, before you knew me, back when wifeliness seemed to be my only attribute.

I think perhaps I was never really meant to bring Stephen's blood into the world. Of my four children, the two who have survived everything that I have thrown at them have been Fabienne and Joella; Stephen's could not survive me. No one will carry his name or his lineage or all the other things he values so; no one will carry anything that we were, there will be no record of all that inert confusion and quiet battery.

My infant Oda was the reason we became anything at all. I had known Stephen in Paris as I faltered along amongst all the foppery and tortured Wildean wit of the court, the crowd that gathered in the cafés close to my art school. We girls of the college lined ourselves up inadvertently every day we woke up and chose to dress and go and learn how to etch and stipple and sculpt; our mannerisms, our speech, our composure, our profile, our appeal all jimmied together over conversations held by the court in the cafés. Then invitations came, tests, were we up to them? No. It went without saying. But the court's entertainment derived from watching us try. I was so naive then, Jack. Things got past me that my daughters wouldn't have swallowed at the age of six. But foolishness makes you wiser and I indulged in a lot of it in those days. Innocent of all the innuendo and expectations, I accepted an invitation to Aleister Crowley's studio, an end-of-term party, and when I arrived there was the court, circled in armchairs and seats around trays of bottles and drinks. I suppose I was lucky. They simply stared at me, and when I went to introduce myself, a short, sallow, horn-faced man informed me I had been chosen for my beauty, not my brains, and they had already eavesdropped on too much of my dull drivel to be interested in anything I had to say, told to keep my beautiful mouth shut. So I left.

A few months later a girl I knew asked me a favour. A friend of hers was very depressed, very lonely and in need of bringing out of himself. He was looking for a model for a portrait – would I sit for him? He was very gentle and funny, from an old English family, a much-talked about young artist whose company I would love. Perhaps I would have, had it not been foisted on me for over ten years. When I appeared at the stranger's studio to do my duty, it was the horn-nosed Stephen Haweis, and when I turned to go, he charmed me with his begging and his contrition and his obvious lack of anything threatening when out of a crowd. Perhaps magnanimity is the worst sort of graciousness, that assumption of superior moral kindness. It is my only explanation for the friendship that began. Gradually he commandeered all my time, painting me endlessly in the dark studio he lived in at the end of a small cobbled courtyard filled with equally earnest talentless artists painting equally stupid, uncertain women. I got to know them all – my life was run for me from that courtyard. When I would arrange to meet friends, Stephen would arrive breathless to join us, then break away in a sulk if I didn't abandon them for him. He borrowed most of my money and yet spent hours explaining the aristocratic links his family enjoyed, showing me his heirlooms, all the antiques and valuable books he owned that filled the small studio. He physically repulsed me with his crouched posture and vast nose, with the array of small teeth that sat like yellowed maggots in the folds of his mouth when he smiled his ingratiating nervous smile. And yet somehow he wore me down with his attempts to woo me until one morning I awoke naked under the canopy of his studio bed, with him sitting like a smug urchin looking down on me. I don't remember how it happened. I remember his arm draped on my shoulder as we talked on the sofa, I remember an awareness of something beginning to happen, I remember waking up in his bed. I was brought up in a house where my mother's Victorian values hardened her arteries with every breath she took, and I was still such a fool then that Stephen was my first. Perhaps I do remember. Perhaps I simply don't want to.

I was his at that, trapped, and he was sincerely proud of his conquest. I was his. As if by a sinister spell he had passed into my life and when I knew I was pregnant there was nothing else to do. Oh to have the chance to show courage, to have those days now, when I am me, not some light-headed *ingénue* who could be bundled into marriage like that. But without the mess that was my marriage to Stephen, without those weak-minded years, who else would I have been? To have been that wise at twenty was a tall order for the girl I was then. I think there comes a time when you make up who you want to be. You wake up sure of how you want to live, of what it is you want to do. But from the second you are born the drops are falling slowly, little events, changes, lessons, all falling to make that stalagtite you can grasp and break off when you are ready to redefine everything you are. That moment came for me when I went to New York, Jack, but everything, Stephen, Oda, London, Paris, Italy . . . my whole life until I went to America and met Fabian, was a series of drops falling from the roof of the cave until I was able to break them off and escape. It is the rationale I have explained to my daughters, that even the bad works for the good in the end. They have dismissed it, called it glib, but it is true of everything I have done: without the bad, the good would never have come about.

Stephen was definitely the bad. He was brought to meet my family in London, who, not knowing the circumstance of our engagement, thought Stephen charming and the ideal man to take their spinster daughter of twenty off their hands. At least in name. All Stephen had to his well-connected name were heirlooms, none of which he would sell as their sentimental value, he maintained, was priceless. And so my father provided us with a stipend to help Stephen establish his career, and an income for our new life. This was all contingent on the marriage's success. Were it to fail, my father explained, I would be cut off, for it would be my fault as obviously Stephen would never attract any other female in the world besides me.

We married on New Year's Eve, 1903. In May I gave birth to Oda. Stephen was belying my father's prophecy, wheezing on top of his mistress while I squealed and bellowed Oda into the world. We chose the name together, for no reason other than we liked how it sounded, and while Stephen pontificated over which paintings to submit to the Salon d'Automne, I went about learning motherhood from an infant.

It was a gentle time in its way. I had hours and hours while Oda slept or while we walked in the Luxembourg Gardens to think of the situation I had brought upon myself, the horror of sidling through your own life to avoid the company and touch of a man you despise. I would think these things and bring myself to the verge of insanity with my resentment and helplessness, when Oda would wake or gurgle or smile at me as she pointed to a dog or a spider or a butterfly, and she rescued me over and over. Her demands, the endless cycle of feeding and washing and wheeling, her crying and falling and clapping, all fused into something that occupied me with a happiness that drained Stephen out of my system like a lance. I was tired but by late summer Oda slept well enough for me to resume painting in the afternoons, and in August I submitted some of my work to the Salon, not as Mrs Mina Haweis, nor as Stephen's pet-name Dusie Haweis, nor even in my maiden name of Lowy. I decided to rename myself, not to be the Victorian daughter or charming Stephen Haweis's art-dabbling wife. It was simple enough. I just dropped the 'w' and became Loy, Lowy to Loy, Mina Loy. Mina Loy. I have lived with it so long now, it feels odd thinking I ever had another name. As if before was nothing greater than an elongated pretence.

The Salon responded by choosing six of my paintings and four of Stephen's. His were nearly all of me anyhow, so the victory seemed complete from all angles. He had long professed his desire for my name to be as greatly regarded as his, but when the moment came he didn't have the grace. He pouted and postulated a great deal about the enormous importance of the newly established portrait section of the Salon where his work was to be shown, and left me to myself mainly, no special supper in the Closerie or dancing. I dressed up fantastically for that opening, a Poiret dress and a hat I designed myself, and everyone spoke of me as the most elegant and exquisite woman there. Of course they were also telling each other that Stephen couldn't abide the attentions of his wife any longer and that his mistress's home was where he now received his visitors, poor talented man.

The poor talented man came home infrequently, mainly when he did to reassure himself that motherhood continued to distract me from taking a lover or becoming too prolific at the easel. Oda was learning to walk and we tumbled around in the parks together taking centimetre steps and trying to drown the ducks. For her first birthday I made Stephen join us. By nightfall he had gone and Oda was running a fever. All that night and the following day she screamed incessantly, and was covered all over in a hot rash I had never seen before, as if her little body was imploding helplessly. The physician came three times before he would accept it was more than a mere reaction to the cold. The next morning at 5 a.m. she died in my arms, her small limbs rigid within hours. She had contracted meningitis, the doctor too blasé to think my daughter could be dying in front of us as he prodded her little one-year, two-day-old body for proof of a cold.

I lost interest in most things after Oda's death. I despised my husband and had consigned myself to a fate utterly foreign to the one I had dreamt of, but what Oda's dying taught me was the irrelevance of reasons. It didn't matter that the princess life had not come about, nor that I had married hastily and excruciatingly. No. None of that bore any significance when real life crushed your spine as it had in killing my child. The background to events didn't matter. It was the events and their consequences that I had, finally, to deal with through Oda's death, and I never relied on anyone again after it. Not until Fabian. He unfurled the sails again.

All this is so clearly discernible now, all these years later, but in the days and months after her death I thought of suicide so often. Perhaps there is a something in us that allows us to act on these thoughts. I didn't have it. I certainly didn't want my life, but when it came down to it, I certainly didn't want to be dead either. For four months I folded and refolded her clothes. I tried to paint. Stephen said I haunted the studio by sheer force of will. He got me a doctor, a different one to Oda's, and had me diagnosed as having neurasthenia. Womanly nerve disease, as Stephen referred to it.

Perhaps to enliven me, probably because they were no good, he sent some of the attempts I'd been making in the studio to the Salon d'Automne that year. We had been married less than two years and already were playing the kind of savaging games that scarify a marriage. He had six works accepted that year, while four delicate little pictures of women I had sketched in ennui were to be shown too.

They were ignored. Stephen was lauded all over Paris, spoken about – as if his dull mind had produced anything original in its twenty-five years of trying. Someone else made an impact too, a scandalous one, an unknown boy called Henri Matisse. Imagine, Jack, wandering into a gallery to confirm your own brown art hangs straight and being besieged by all those colours, that imagination. I was so overwhelmed I went each day until the exhibition ended. Stephen would not hear of us buying a painting. He had tried his hand as Rodin's official photographer after the sculptor saw some of his photographs and proclaimed him a talent, but the business had lasted just months. We were being forced to move out of the studio into Montparnasse, and the luxury of new art was not one Stephen would countenance. Besides, he said, aren't our friends amongst the most talented in Paris? But they weren't. Like Stephen, they were painting their way into a life, into a world where their college-taught skill and ability to emulate gave them a gilded credence, enough, when matched with their arrogance, to be accepted as artists, as a fresh sheaf of talent. And so our new apartment was adorned with the same genius as the old – impeccable Whistler replicas, perfect Beardsley-style water-colours, Pre-Raphaelite 'interpretations' – while on the other side of the city hung the chaotic originality of Matisse.

But then I was the great success of the next Salon d'Automne. Stephen was still its golden aesthete, but almost all of my cynical paintings were singled out by critics, and I was celebrated as a great new talent, which delighted Stephen, for now his wife was Somebody. I had, he told me, a 'reputation', I was a part of Paris properly now. His glee was short-lived – when the Salon closed that winter, the Committee invited me to become a permanent member, a Sociétaire. I was, they said, its youngest member, but my work was so arresting and I so enchanting that they would be honoured if I would accept my place. I was to be part of the glorious accepted elite and Stephen was not. But having seen Matisse and the Fauves, I had also seen my worth. I was never going to storm anyone's imagination with my painting, and that it bothered me so little to relinquish my ambitions made me understand how close I had come to Stephen's reasoning, to painting to be talked about at tea-parties.

Stephen's reaction to my becoming a Sociétaire was typically one of pettiness and jealousy. We had barely managed civility of late, and he decided one day in a temper that we would separate. I was joyous. He moved all his clothes and books into his mistress's home, and informed me it was not to be regarded as the basis for divorce. We would not divorce. We each needed an income, and my father's stipend was our only consistent means of supporting ourselves. My father must not know of our separation. Stephen meanwhile would continue to receive the money into his bank and would visit me monthly with an allowance. I was to be paid alimony from my own parents' bank, fed pocket-money like an aristocratic suckling, and not even afforded the freedom of divorce. But it took Stephen out of my life, took his sweating upper lip out of my sight when I awoke in the morning, his infantile demands and paranoias and neuroses switched into the care of some woman who thought him wonderful, spending my money on buying her dinner each night. It was as close to freedom as I had had. The respectability of the married woman yet freedom to do as I wished in my own days.

Stephen told me many years later that he had loved me for my beauty. For my beauty and my elegance and my vulnerability, as if the attention they attracted might lure me into worlds I was not fit for, and he could protect me. What he had not accounted for, he said, was the way in which that vulnerability would change, dipping down into neediness, dependency, depression, and then eventually cresting upwards into the antithesis of each, into haughtiness, independence, uncontrollable vivacity. What he did not see was that that same beauty lured me into a world I was not fit for, his. Escaping it took such time, Jack.

With him finally out of my life in all but name, with Oda no longer connecting us, you would imagine I lived gaily, visiting friends, galleries, going to concerts and parties and laughing until my eyes dried out, but no. I discovered, when he had gone and I had no child at the centre of my world, something circumstance had hidden from me up to now. I had no real friends. I had not gone to a party in someone else's home since before I married, all I had were unimpressive connections and a shabby apartment filled with useless things. So I slipped yet again into that wearing depression that is a mixture of real sadnesses and abject self-pity, the worst kind.

My new freedom was like being hoisted up on one stilt, leaning on a wall while you searched out the second. The second was closer than I thought. The more people I met, the more I yearned for that great glorious romance that pervaded Paris then, people putting love before propriety everywhere except in my small life. I wanted to be wooed and thought wonderful, to have secrets and assignations and be worshipped like all those around me seemed to be, to make up for the past. That was the stilt I needed to give me the happiness I sought.

I've been lucky with all the lovers I have chosen. I've been very coveted, loved even, in some cases; something has always come of them. I was a fumbling seductress at first, anxious and malleable and excessive all at once, wanting to seem bright and witty without putting him off. I could be such a fool back then. I've met a few girls since who remind me enormously of the scattered eager demoiselle I was then – I have taken them under my wing, brought out the madnesses in them, not the responsibilities. There was no one there to awaken me, however, and I tripped along like a debutante in the months after Stephen left me, Oda always somewhere in my mind as I threw back my head and tinkled with wit and charm. I genuinely thought these were the things I exhibited, when probably I seemed more like a slightly crazed semi-divorcee whose child had just died.

People were kind. Most of all my doctor, Henri Joel Le Savoureux, coming at first to my apartment to lift my depression with all the tricks of his trade, bleeding me with leeches once because I begged him to. He believed in a new medicine, thought all that mere witch-doctory, and he was right, for here I am now kept alive by the very things he aspired to, so magnificently preserved they say I have another decade in me at least. He was young, Stephen's age, just a few years older than I and very dashing. It was as if when I opened the door to him he was shirtless or wore just one shoe. His hair was very dark, very soft when it brushed your face or breast, and it fell into his eyes each time he bent his head.

I think we both understood the vacuity of a diagnosis such as neurasthenia. It simply covered the pantheon of unsettled mentalities, feminine ones – everything from grief to inexplicable elation was put down to neurasthenia. So when Henri came to treat me each week we talked and I sketched him, and we gave each other a kind of attention that was new to us both. At first he came in his capacity as my personal physician, paid for by my father via Stephen, but almost immediately he refused to be paid for his attentions, and instead we would go walking in the parks where I once took Oda. He listened to me talk of her, things I had never said to Stephen while she was alive for he was never there, and all the feelings of loss I had harboured gradually drained away until my mourning ceased to orchestrate my mind like a bullying conductor, and I felt able again.

It was Henri who encouraged me in my submissions to the Salon, who took me out when I was made a Sociétaire, who took me to the Bal Bullier club where, a few years later after I had gone, Fabian would make his name. Perhaps I fell in love, perhaps at twenty-three I found my first love, but I think I just found in Henri a man who made me feel certain of myself again, took me dancing and to the country and into new worlds, new circles, at a time when my own strangled me and took all the air from my brain. He rejuvenated my spirit, I suppose. And he gave me Joella.

When we first discovered I was pregnant, there was a curious but complete lack of anxiety. I felt he knew Oda from all our early conversations about her, and that he would give me a new child, albeit so unexpectedly, seemed as natural as the revelatory pleasure I now found in the very act that had planted the seed. Sex with Stephen would have been the most harrowing experience of my life had I not had to live with him at the time too, but with Henri it was a new world, gentle, erotic, ferocious. It established a taste that I never abandoned.

Stephen's reaction was less gallant. Everyone, he said, was talking about my new lover and what a scarlet shame I was to my husband and the memory of my dead child. This in the city where wives and mistresses shared their men happily, where women lived openly with their female lovers, where boudoirs received more visitors than dining-rooms. But to Stephen the slight was very real, and no doubt too the myth that he was the victim of a flagrantly unfaithful wife who slept with her lover while he sat at home, cuckolded, yearning for his lost love.

When Henri asked me to come away with him, for a few dizzy moments I knew exactly what I wanted to do. I would have my child on my own, I would abandon them both and trust my own instincts for a change. This conviction lasted a week at best. I had a husband, a lover, and my belly swelling all the time. I had no income, no independent source I could depend on, and my father had been quite clear on my options were I to leave Stephen. I could not risk being cast off, not with a child. Paris depended on fathers and mothers and patrons to fund its budding geniuses, all an amalgam of stipended talents delaying the moment they would enter a working life. There were exceptions. I was not one.

Stephen appeared gleefully at my door one afternoon. He could forgive me, he said, eventually; despite my appalling infidelity, he would have me back. He had forgiven me. Forgiven. My hatred for him in that moment was complete.

It is easy now to see that there was no need for me to return to Stephen, that my life was fortified enough by then for me to have left him and have had Joella with Henri, to have made a new life out of what had been a restitutional affair, transient. But I didn't take the risk. I responded to an argument made up of responsibility, finance, propriety . . . I was a wife; I had become pregnant through an affair; my husband was now willing to recognise the child; there was only one conclusion in 1907, Jack, and that was what became of me. Stephen left his mistress and I left Henri, and we put Paris behind us. Within weeks we had left the city I had finally begun to make my own, and were living on the side of a Tuscan hill in a villa with gardens and a cook, and a ready-made community of foreigners fleeing their pasts, just like us.

I missed Henri so much. I missed the attention, the joy of someone else being responsible for my happiness. Sometimes in Italy I wondered what it would have been like to have stayed in Paris, being a doctor's wife, being part of a respectable elite, though tinged with enough scandal all the same to be feared ever so slightly. I would have been a real wife, depended on, listened to, needed. And yet it would have wizened me, Jack, dried me out in a year. I see that now, of course. Then it seemed blessed compared to life with Stephen. But I hadn't got the courage to forfeit my wifely bond with Stephen. And I did not love Henri enough in the end.

I don't know how you are with regret, Jack. There is a gift in our rediscovering each other after such a time; I want to know you, want to compensate for the years in between when we should have been friends. I would like to have had you to rely on, Jack, or rather, to be unreliable with, just every so often, to retread the past a little. We have all the time we need now for that.

Write to me soon, I will look forward so much to hearing from you again, and thank you, Jack, for this fresh connection. It makes me very happy to fall asleep at night knowing you are there with the past curled up in your head just like me.

With affection,

Mina

Jack

Chicago, February 1946

Dear Mina,

I was worried you might not write back – I'm glad you wrote back so fast. You're right in what you said. All the stuff we know about each other and we don't really know a damned thing, not about the past, or what we've been at since those few days in Mexico. I hope I didn't offend you joking like that about you getting married all the time. I knew the story. Happened to me too, wrong person, bad time in my life. I've got a woman I care a lot about now, but we don't have what you two had, you and Cravan. Luckily we don't have what you and that Stephen had either – that was not a sane life for anyone. How long did you stick with him? I can't match the woman I used to know with who you were when you were married to him, not at all. What changed you, Mina, was it Cravan? As for me, well, you could say things have been fairly eventful for me all round, though they've been quiet as a morgue these past few years.

I lost the title – well, you guessed that, it'd be some fighter held on to it for forty years. Makes more sense to start with – all the stuff before Mexico really, how it all got wheels. How I got to be the Champion, why I lost it, how Cravan and I got together – do you mind if I keep calling him that, Mina, it's just a bit strange using his real name, the name Fabian just isn't real to me. You seem to miss him even now – he's about the only one I do miss. I wish there was someone I could say I was still in love with, someone I'd do anything for even now, but there's not. Just ghosts and wives and situations. Maybe it isn't the wisest thing stirring up all this stuff again, but I didn't know he hadn't told you about my past much. Not even how I got the title? How I lost it? He must have said something about that, Mina, he must have done. I thought I knew a lot about you, he'd talk all the time about you, but I guess not. Not like I thought.

It doesn't take many mistakes to bring the self-righteous and the bigots out these days. All I had to do was win a title and hold on to it for seven years, no matter how much they wanted me to hand it back. For those seven years, Mina, I got treated like I stole that championship, like I won it at poker and wouldn't give it back when the croupier explained it was all a joke. Took me long enough to get the chance to fight for it too. But the reasons they hated me had not very much to do with boxing, it was all in the other stuff – white women were my taste, the money I got, the way I flashed it around, didn't just sit on the stoop and count it out once a week for the neighbours. It was the money, but mainly it was the women. Belle got to me, Lucille got to them, and Etta just got it. It wasn't my fault what happened to her, but they were looking for the rope to lynch me. Well, it took them long enough trying, and they never did do it, no matter how much rope I tickled them with under their fat chins all these years. But Etta was always the one they used against me, proof that I was a bad bastard, no matter how much I flashed a smile in their direction. Always Etta.

She was shallow, a stupid girl, without anything to centralise her but me. She moved from her mother's house into mine, a shift in geography, a new place to suck her thumb and invite her friends. Now they say it was me who killed her, but if she'd started lolling naked down the street with flowers in her hair, they'd have said that was me too. I gave her what she wanted – she wanted me to cut back, and I did, she wanted marriage, I gave it, she wanted more nights to wear out her jewellery, and I took her. I wasn't a backstreet mechanic who suddenly fools around to everyone's surprise. She knew me. You can't love a person based on what you'll make of them. You take the package, you open it, and if that's what you've always wanted, that's what you take home. But Etta was the kind of woman who buys a dress because with a bit of letting out and taking in and doing up, it's exactly what she wants. Whereas Belle just waited till she saw it on the hanger.

But Belle came later, she was the woman I should have married, I guess. But I never really thought marriage through, and that was the tragedy for me in being at your wedding. You and Cravan in Mexico, that was how it should always be, with everybody there feeling like they're part of something amazing, something so full of magic it seems like everybody's drunk. But hell, that was real love, the kind that only ever happens to a lucky bastard like Cravan. My standards didn't reach the sky like his, Mina. I met Etta, and I had stuff to be sorry to her about, so I decided to give her the ring on her finger so she'd know I meant it and not make me feel guilty. Easy as that. Getting married got me out of a hole. But maybe Belle was the woman for me after all. Put me in exile, that's what that two-bit hooker did, but she'd more brains than all of them, never took her eye off the ball. Unlike Etta.

I met Etta in the most glorious of the glory days, when I had my club in Chicago and my title and was the man to know. A magnificent club, Mina, with eighty-seven bolts of claret silk on the walls and the chairs, soft gilded lights and my Rembrandts hung in the ballroom being stung with cigar smoke and all the perfumed body-heat of dancing, but being seen, being looked at. Poker rooms and billiards, all the way from England, and in the smaller rooms Lucille and the girls were there giving us a reputation of supremacy, folded over chair-backs with legs splayed, taken from behind like an accidental photograph. Sofas swathed in velvet and Etta upstairs in the apartment. Sometimes she would come downstairs and we'd dine in the restaurant at the back of the club, duck and burgundy if she was there, best meal in America.

It was loud in the club that night, no fights or tantrums yet, but shouting, success in the poker room, Sig Hart set up to win but still believing in his skill, set up for days of guaranteed losing on the strength of tonight's win. I was eating with some guys from the racetrack who were setting up a syndicate for a fix, but I called her from one of the downstairs booths around eight to tell her some of her friends were in dancing with their excitable husbands. She was having a bath and I'd see her later, she said. After nine I saw there was a panic behind the bar, Mattie the barman looking like he was on fire as he ran to get Lucille, then he raced over and told me. I ran up those stairs as fast as I could,

It looked like she was drunk on the floor, Mina. I still see her like it was just last night, her hair all loosed from its pins, but I knelt beside her then, drew it off her face, and there wasn't one, just a pulp of tissue and blood and cartilage, raw as carcass. The bullet had shattered the browbone over her right eye and taken everything with it, her cheekbone, her nose, her brain, her headaches, her depressions, her winking violet-blue eye that would look up from under half a lid and speak slowly as if what it was saying was far too complex for her mouth to bother with. It was a fool who called it a lazy eye. I was static with fear, I didn't know what of, death maybe, her death, the absolution in the room as if she regretted nothing, and most of all the panic of accusation in the corpse, this is your solution, this blood, this repulsive smell of singed hair and shit clogging your nose, this is your contrivance. And the room full now, people looking at me to see what was happening to my face, if I was crying, howling, grief-stricken, if I was swallowing the urge to retch as they were, if I was going to lift the mess and carry her into the bedroom, was I stunned or still in the realm of shock, God help us, was I jocular and soothing. Then a ripple as Lucille the deathknell leans in and shrieks that Etta is breathing. This same woman who declared my wife dead ten minutes earlier and had me sent for revises her opinion in the face of everything and so phantom breaths from a dead heart get Etta trundled into the ambulance and we trail behind to the hospital in what we know, all of us, is a cortège, but for my sake they all pretend there is hope and are devastated, loudly, when the news is broken to me that she never came to. And Etta was dead.

The first time I knew what my life would be like I was standing on sewage watching a white man pack a wicker suitcase with a worn-out blue linen suit. Forty thousand people were shouting coon-boy and nigger-shit and a man called Jack London was sitting five feet away from me telling me to get my black ass back to Georgia. I'm from Texas. A few years later Belle bought me a whole shopful of his books and that black ass has never been warmed with such satisfaction. It was supposed to be Hughie McIntosh's night – he was the man who'd finally agreed to shut the black boy up once and for all and let the people pay to see Jack Johnson put in his grave. Hughie's idea of making money was to pay his own guy the full pocket, pay the contender, me, not a dollar, and make himself referee so his man didn't lose the title. Sydney didn't have anywhere that suited Hughie, so in ten days he had Rushcutter's Bay Stadium built. It frightened some people, but forty thousand good Australians were game enough to climb in and shout abuse at five dollars a head. Hughie had it built in the open air on thirty-foot stilts over the municipal swamp so, while the city's sewage sludge fermented underneath us, Tommy Burns and I were saying our hellos to our welcoming crowds.

Burns was a good fighter, and that is what people like to forget now. Burns had a low right uppercut that if it got the solar plexus it could take the fight out of a man long enough to dose him with a punch that floored him. He understood how to distract an opponent with only half of what was coming. He was on to the instalment plan. But he was small and loved to drink, and not all the eight-mile runs and sparring bouts could tighten up the softness in his belly that would lure him into a bar to souse himself. So I was careful to be seen drinking in twice as many bars as he was, but only Jim Fitzpatrick knew what was in my glass. Back then I was like a gored bull about getting that title, and in 1908 it was Tommy Burns who gave it to me. That and a lot more besides. Just to give it an extra sharpness it poured torrents on Christmas Eve, so when we all got to the stadium the next morning the stench was ripe as a plague corpse. It added atmosphere, McIntosh said. He'd taken to lugging round a piece of lead pipe wrapped in a shirt, to kill that black bastard when he jumps me in an alley, he said. If winning the World Championship wasn't enough, that it wiped out McIntosh a few years later made it a glory even greater.

Something happened at that fight that spun me right around, and left me ready for anything. I could take abuse, shouts, insults, easy hatred, all of that fired me up, the more of it I got the more focused I got, tens of thousands of mouths opening and closing round you yelling 'Coon' . . . but that day when I came out of the tunnel shack they got me, for a split second they got me. They went silent. They all sat back, forty thousand bad bastards, and eyeballed me, stared out at the sky, looked at the ring, as if seized by a maniacal fury that had soldered their vocal chords, tonsils, lips. Just a few shouts, less than thirty or forty spread all across the stadium making the silence even more acute. Designed to put fear in me, and if not fear they scored momentary shock. From then on I depended on nothing, not even the surest thing. But of course Belle was to get me on that one.

The silence lasted maybe a minute, far longer than felt human, while I kept strolling towards the ring as if they were cheering me their hero, as if deafened by the bawl of them, jarred inside but not for even a second in my gait, in what was visible to them. So I had them, arms up high above my head as if acknowledging their rapture, and about four hundred feet from the ring they exhaled in a long hard bellow of 'Nigger bastard', faces contorted with the violence of getting the words out loud as they could, the objects coming at me, newspapers rolled tight, beer bottles . . . but I was in the ring blowing kisses and grinning like it was my birthday, until they got so fired up they didn't even notice Burns at the mouth of the tunnel shack waiting for a space in the noise to make his entrance. Then McIntosh shoved him in the back to get him going and they all erupted all over again, Tommy jogging down to the ring like a paper-boy, all grins and dimples and triumph, bashful as a virgin, all this for me? And all of us looking at him like he is an imbecile just escaped, for Tommy is head to toe in a three-piece suit in pale-blue linen, hands all bandaged and looking as if he's ready for an honest day's work.

I jog on the spot, spar the air, flex my hands in readiness for the compression of the gloves while Tommy climbs in the ring and starts a rigorous striptease that shows just how many real ones he's missed. With the concentration of a coal miner testing a shaft in the dark, he takes off first the jacket, then the waistcoat, then the ruffled shirt . . . and folds each piece immaculately and places it in a wicker suitcase resting on McIntosh's knee, raising his arms to the crowd's roar with each garment, while our impartial referee looks up at him with a thrill on his face like it's a strip club. I feel like I'm at a cabaret, and as the crowd tire of Tommy and remember why they're here, I jog around the ring punching air with a glaze on my eyes as if I don't see them, and I understand this is how it will be. Absolute hatred everywhere, cured in an instant of the naivety that the way I fight, the power of it, would level things, would make titles seem my due, earned glory. That day in Australia I get the first full force of how things are to be, knowing as I punch the stench that I'm walking away with the Championship of the World in a matter of minutes, and the short little boy-scout packing his case, and all his clan, have no idea of the impact I am about to have on their world. I am about to punch my way into history, and not one of them will ever stop me.

In the end it was majestic. Tommy had drawn out the prelims even further by checking my hands for hard tape eight or nine times, then covering his elbows in the stuff so we'd a wrangle over that for near on ten minutes. McIntosh knew the crowd was restless so he just pulled the tape off Tommy himself. Then we were tied into our gloves and the bell rang out for history. I was pretty sharp even for me. I reckoned it would be short and I wanted to lull him, so I measured the distance with a few flick punches, then drew back and let him come to me. I let him have the centre of the ring and danced around him telling him to come and get it. My legs were able for it, and I knew they wouldn't have to last up any distance, so he thought he was on the up, that he had me doing the side-steps while he reigned confident on the centre spot. Then I cuffed him.

I was after a knock-out. I wanted absolute humiliation, so I eased up on him, rebounded a few open-handed, facing the palms of my gloves in close to his face so he thought he was getting me on the defensive, reflecting his blows. Then he lunged, but I stepped aside, and when he came back at me, I feinted a long left-hook, could even see his eyes follow it, and I dipped down with my right, took a step in closer and came up from the shoulder with a right uppercut that rammed his jaw up into his nose. He was still following the left, leaning into the right to evade it, leaning into the right so it caught him like a speeding car. And that was it. McIntosh might have been able to turn a blind eye to fouls or over-ruled my corner, but there's not much protection you can give to your assets when they're lying in a stupor looking at the Sydney sky like it's about to fill with angels. You can't disallow a knock-out like that, you just kick the sorry bastard who fell for it.

Burns was tough. Not to beat, that was easy, but tough to humiliate because he kept coming back for more. I'd busted his eyes and cut up his mouth but he still kept throwing these big swaying punches at my belly, like I hadn't watched him, hadn't learnt everything there was to know about the World Champion in those three years I'd chased him round the world for these moments. I'd earned him, earned the right to frighten them, so he could aim at my solar plexus all he liked. That was the key. It wasn't in the fists. It was in the head. I saw a lot of guys who had it in the fists, not as good as me but close enough if they'd stayed at it, but nothing in the head. So Burns there was swiping at me like a dog-catcher and couldn't work it out when I was never there to take the blow. I gashed all over his face with everything from light warning grazes to granite power-punches that started a foot back from the shoulder, ones where you felt your muscles tighten and quiver like an overtuned cello string when the punch landed, but up Tommy bobbed, no matter what. It was the Chinese-torture routine, and all the small gashes together spewed so much blood it trickled thickly down Tommy's neck and on to his chest, splattered McIntosh and all the ringside hacks when he took a blow. There were parts of the canvas that became part of the strategy for us, places where the blood made it hard to keep afoot for sliding. Now and again he'd hit a good punch and I'd taunt him with it, challenge him to better it, to make it hurt, to draw blood, tease him for his natty suit all folded up, offer to teach him how to fight when we got home, grinning at him like I'd just won the Pennant, congratulating him when he managed to stand straight, complimenting him on his lovely wife. I laughed like I was at the vaudeville when he'd try and shout back at me, telling me I was a dirty dawg, a nigger bastard, a coon cur, telling me to fight like a white man. If I had ever in my life fought like a white man I'd never have got out of the Galveston dockyards. And the more of that nigger shit he threw at me and the crowd roared at me, the less of a knock-out I wanted, the passion boiling in me for a big long drawn-out bastard of a fight.

Burns' jaw was hanging off him like dribble by the eighth

round, the blood flowing out of one eye so much I was sure they'd row in and pull him out, but they kept slapping champagne on his face between rounds like it was a miracle healer, so for a few seconds at the start of each round the molecules of sweat and dried blood would be coated in a tight champagne glaze. He looked ready for the oven. His legs were from a comedy show, wobbling every time I touched him as if his own weight was too much to bear, and it was now him having to dance around the outside while I stood centred turning this way and that, confusing him, and still the blood came out of that eye and still they refused to acknowledge the humiliation, so in the fourteenth I just threw a power right-cross at his left cheekbone, and when he hit the canvas the cops crowded in and scraped him off, Tommy screaming like a kid sent to bed that he was still good, he'd still beat that nigger, he could still win it. And around him there was the hush of embarrassment, a shock more real than anything electric, a stunned, frightened, silenced crowd of forty thousand brains slowly understanding that Tommy beat meant the black man had won. Their nigger coon was Heavyweight Champion of the World. And there was nothing they could have done to have stopped it.

Jeffries was twenty pounds out of shape when they first got on his back to come out and flatten me. It was London who started it, writing all this mindless gallery-playing stuff about battering the golden smile off my face, rescuing the white race, finding the Great White Hope. I let them at it. I was Champion now, I had them scared but it didn't matter too much then, it was being Champion that woke me up at night just out of sheer hammered excitement, this curl in my belly that gave me the runs sometimes it'd get so away with itself when I thought about it all. Which was all the time.

The parties and the parades weren't too hectic when I got back from Australia. You'd have thought they'd all have gone mad but word got out that I kept in with white women and didn't pay much heed to the ones who thought I'd do a better job keeping in with my own. Did I care. They'd had all this palaver lined up in Galveston – I was to come up the river on a great boat and there'd be bands and classy hoopla on the docks and a big cavalcade, but then, even before we'd left Australia, we got a telegram asking who was this Hattie McStay woman and was it true she was a white woman. Well, that was that. Mind their own damn business. Truth was, I was bored with Hattie, she'd taken the edge off the newness of Australia for me, but she talked a lot, idiot talk most of the time. But I kept her by my side every time we went out after I got back to Chicago, every time I saw a photographer I'd kiss her or take her hand and lay it on my thigh. And then I met Belle.

The Everleigh Club was the smartest of its kind in America. When I opened my own place, I modelled that side of things on what I'd heard the Everleigh sisters had done in their club. Pure class. Of course, the problems in my life more or less started that March night I got turned away from it, when this gorgeous piece of tight laughing ass called Belle Schreiber came out into the light with a customer and I moved in on him right there on the doorstep. She was a good judge of circumstances, Belle, though I sure as hell wasn't where she was concerned. Nothing would be the same for me after Belle.

Cravan asked me one day if I hated her. If I blamed her. I said damn right I did, two-bit whore, and he laughed at me and said that was all bullshit. She was the only woman I'd ever loved, he said. He had this cynicism about love that he had decided would stop him from ever finding it. He believed in it like some philosophy about death that you would live your life by and then be thrown down a hole in a wooden box the day you actually knew if you were right about it all. It was all in the head to him. Love was something he had worked out the same as his fuel-to-speed ratio and his acceleration potential on a wet road. It could be rationalised and understood, aspired to and controlled, dealt with as a fact. I didn't think anyone would ever crack him. But then I was wrong.

And he was wrong about Belle. I never loved her. I don't think I have it in me. I used to assume I had, but then your wedding in Mexico made me appreciate that whatever it's been that's got me in and out of people's lives all these years, it has never been that. Not even now – and I love Irene – do I use the word like it was invented to be used. It buys affection, it fills in gaps, it offers you a bond with someone you have time for, someone you might lust after or want to get into bed for every kind of reason you can think of, even spite, it puts someone at the other end of the phone when you want to talk late at night on the road, it seduces loyalty, it gives you a sense of spontaneity and purpose. It does all those things. But my kind of love doesn't bring calm, it doesn't make the lines in your head stop leaping around and settle into shapes, it doesn't fill that sense in yourself that whatever you have done you are missing an instinct, a way of waking up and filling your heart with somebody else, somebody not you, somebody whose angle you never need to work out because it isn't there. Someone you want to fill yourself so full of that you forget about yourself more often than you remember. Someone to change for. And I've never found that.

Back then Cravan could think that my hatred of Belle was unrepentant love, but back then, Mina, he knew just about as much about it as I did. He didn't know you.

After Australia, I needed money. You'd have thought they'd have been throwing it at me, boxing promoters all over the place wanting to get in with the Champion of the World and set up his fights, name his price, take their cut . . . but not with me they weren't. Not yet. I'd ditched Jim Fitzpatrick back in Australia – he had more of a problem with the white women than anyone, kept leaping at me about it, he kept dancing this word propriety around. Sex embarrassed him, he'd think up the dirtiest moves in the game for you, but outside of training he was pure prude. And the fact was, I liked sex a lot. I liked the excitement and the anticipation, and yeah, I liked the authority, the ways of getting a woman to do whatever you wanted. More than anything, it was fun, always different, always mutinous. All those reasons explained the prostitutes, and the fact was, I got on well with those women, and I never saw marriage as anything to tighten up for. I didn't have any wives at that point anyway. Fitzpatrick's logic was just down to jealousy at me being mad for sex, and always being able to get it. Then this whole white-women business began and he started in on me, said I was only doing it to stir trouble, that to me it all had the same result anyway, no matter what colour the woman, so why couldn't I just keep it all quiet, keep it to my own. Jim didn't last long after that. I never fired him, it wasn't like that, he just got sick of me, and I got sick of the sight of him, so we agreed to make our separate ways back to America. And that was that. A World Champion without a manager and not a vulture in miles looking to swoop.

The real problem was that there was no one good enough for me. Anyone up to staying a few rounds, I'd already fought, because they were black men – Sam Langford, Joe Jeanette, Ed Martin, Peter Jackson, Sam McVey – and I didn't see much point in fighting them again. I was the one who made it to the title, and I was the one who broke the white hold on it. They could have made their chance just like I did. They just didn't want it like I did, weren't up to it, not in the fists or in the dream of it. You can do anything if you want it badly enough, and I wasn't backtracking to the old days for anyone. Anyhow, nobody paid to see a pair of black men fight, even if one of them was World Champion. The money was in luring the white prey in, playing on all that hatred till it made me rich. It had to be a white challenge, and they didn't have one. They all had their heads tucked under their arms in a huddle in New York, while I kept the pressure up by telling every reporter I knew that I was out to pulverise Ketchel, Kaufman and Jeffries. But not a word came back.

I needed some easy money, so I decided to set something up myself. I had a look around at some of the fading has-beens who'd go up against me just to keep their name in lights, the ones who were past being noticed by the big guns in New York. Philadelphia Jack O'Brien got picked to do the job. He was only about a hundred and sixty-five pounds but he'd been the Light Heavyweight Champion once, and he'd been fairly hot in his day, a bit of a looker who liked to dress up and act the debonair. A man I could like. Of course he was same as all the rest of them, saying to reporters that he was only taking the fight on to belt the nigger back into the pit he belonged in. It was a slow cup of coffee the morning I read that. I had a bit of fun with him though, being World Champion and all that, I made him come to Pittsburgh right into the back room of the dirtiest shabbiest bar in the coloured district to sign for the fight. It belonged to a guy I knew, and I was fond of it, but just like we planned, O'Brien was disgusted and held his nose on the way in like some silly wife crossing a puddle. The fight wasn't much better for him.

I went on the beer the night before – how could you train to fight Jack O'Brien – and so we had a bit of a dance inside the ropes. I roughed him up a bit, put in six rounds like the contract said, and went out on the town with the five-thousand-dollar purse that night. Didn't make for much of a spectacle, but it did make it on to film, and the idea was to get the New York boys all complacent about me so they'd set up a fight with one of the big guns so I'd be looking at a mega-buck title fight by the year's end. I got myself a fairly great diamond ring and the nicest little speed roadster I could find. That just about cleaned me of that purse, so we were on for another one, as many as they wanted to see until temptation got too much for them. I did in Tony Ross next, an Italian who decided he'd hit the big time a lot sooner if he ditched the Italian and went for a solid Irish name. Didn't do poor old Antonio much good. I broke his nose with the first punch I laid on him, busted his lip with near on the second. I went easy to make it last the six rounds in the contract, just like before, but there wasn't much to it. More money.

Eventually the bait got bit. First up was young Kaufman. He was up for nothing, so that got disposed of easily enough, a lot of blood and craziness. But a month later the big goods arrived in the shape of the Assassin Stanley Ketchel. He was a mean bastard. When he was a kid he'd found his father in a barn with his throat slit, and a couple of months later his mother went the same way. Ketchel didn't hang about much. He traipsed around the country working on the logging rivers and watching his back, winding up Middleweight Champion for the things he learnt on the way. He had a taste for blood, boxed like a stunned crazed fox in a chicken coop, tearing flesh and pounding open wounds till they pumped blood on to his gloves, going for ribs like he was hatcheting at an eighty-foot tree.

I did a deal. I knew I'd finish him in two rounds, which was giving him his dues and a bit of space for leeway, and no promoter wants a film with a couple of rounds on it. The money at the gate was beer money compared to the film potential on a fight like this. Here was the nigger they all loved to think had climbed down off a tree in some jungle out Galveston way, and here was a savage bastard of a fighter whom everyone knew hated me like I'd killed his father myself. Fight films were the hottest thing in the business, they got screened in theatres all round the country with more deference than newsreels. And Sunny Jim Coffroth who was putting the fight together hadn't fallen for those stunts on O'Brien and Ross. He knew how good I was, and he sure as hell wasn't going to have me flatten Ketchel in two rounds. No. So we sat down and talked. I got a big fat percentage of the film revenue on top of forty thousand dollars if I kept it going for twenty rounds. If not, I took twenty-five thousand dollars. Either way, poor little Stanley got eighteen thousand dollars and a beating. It happened in a place called Colma, just outside San Francisco. Belle came with me to the training camp, and juiced me up for the fight. She'd have been about twenty-four around the time of the Ketchel fight, and more beautiful than any other woman I'd ever seen. She knew what to make of that. She had this platinum hair all curled up at her shoulder and she'd wear these suits that caught her waist like a pinch of the ass and made her legs seem like they went on for miles, ankles that could make me go hard just seeing them twirl gently at the top of her heel, all wrapped in silk like the rest of those legs. The day of that fight she wore a little hat with a veil and a tweed suit, I remember the roughness of it against my face when she came in as I was sitting getting my hands bandaged ready to go out. They hadn't let her in to the dressing-rooms at first, thought this elegant blonde was all confused, thought she'd got lost trying to find her seat or her husband. She got through by flicking her heels into their calves, told them she was my wife and I suppose she was the nearest I had to it at the time. Maybe if I'd married her she'd have kept her mouth shut, but you'd never get a girl like Belle to change. Others, sure, like Lucille, but not Belle.

Ketchel was such a bad bastard his trick was to come out and act like the crowds weren't there, ignore them, fight, leave. But this one wasn't about Ketchel, it was about demolishing me, so the crowds were wild, they cheered for him and yelled for him and applauded him and roared for him and when he came out to all that noise he burst out crying, these big wet softman tears pouring down his face like he'd just given birth to a healthy baby boy, this big tough bastard of a fighter blubbing at the emotion of so much damn support and will for him to win. That was the only surprise of the night. I was wearing my lucky belt, the US flag, and they hissed at me all the way down to the ring, spat, all the usual. I smiled back like I was being introduced to the lifers in an asylum all trussed up in their strait-jackets, forty-eight thousand of them. And me with my arms free, swinging them back and forth over my shoulders to loosen up. I just kept smiling at them. Stanley had got his nose wiped and his eyes dried for him, even after the gloves went on his corner kept popping out to wipe up his nose because he was fumbling about with a bit of cotton with the big thug gloves on him trying to do it himself like a geriatric. Then he pulled himself together and marched slowly round the ring close to the ropes, locked into a world of his own, head down, staring out the bugs on the canvas, getting his concentration back, pretending the noise wasn't there and psyching up every bit of ruthless bastardness he had in him. I knew what he was at. Everyone does it, the key was to do it on your own, to come out and face them with your head hard and resolute, not to need the last moments before the bell to draw in your strength. It's too late by then.

It started slow because I had to draw him out twenty rounds. I'd give him a pounding every now and again to make it look like there was somebody else in the ring with me, but most of the time in those early rounds I'd dip out of easy flooring punches, try to close up the spaces Ketchel made so it didn't look like I was too obviously avoiding good chances, covering up his mistakes where I could have cleaned him out with an uppercut to the side of his head. I feinted a lot, sent him round the ring after punches that never came, had him flailing around like a windmill after me, but I'd just stand back and laugh when that caper got going. I had his nose running again but red now, and his mouth too, but the ribs and the gut and the brains were all still fairly intact by the time we hit the twelfth.

I came out of the corner when the bell went and sauntered over to him with a left jab under the chin, a tickle almost. This got him mad but he let in another before Rudy Maxwell his trainer yelled at him '*Now, Stanley*', and next thing he landed a meteor on the skullbone behind my left ear and I stumbled back with the force of it, using my right hand to break the fall, which could have been the stupidest thing I ever did but no damage was done and the second my ass grazed the canvas I was up again, the referee suspended mid-breath with his finger in the air ready to guillotine the seconds. Stanley thought he had me, that I was still recovering from the punch, so he raced at me ready to pound me back on to the canvas. Stupid Stanley. He ran from one side of the ring straight into my volley of punchbag blows rhythmic as a set-dance, and then one fast hard right uppercut that he opened his mouth for, so when I pulled back my hand the leather was all torn with these two yellow-white pearls embedded in the stuffing, while Ketchel fell back like he'd been harpooned, hitting the canvas a dead weight. I was sure I'd killed him, the whiteness of him, the lifelessness, the way everyone was rushing around him, round the referee who was counting him out, while I stood to the side and watched over, wishing the bastard would just wake up. They dragged him over to his corner and started with the smelling salts and the rum until poor old Stanley fluttered open his eyes like a Southern coquette, and realising what had happened just closed them again and got ready in his head to walk the walk of shame out through the crowd. He turned out to be all right after that. Sunny Coffroth had cut him into the film deal too, a tenth of what he promised me, but still, enough so Stanley thought he'd got one over on me, and I never told him different. We went gambling that night, the pair of us, and I let him win one thousand one hundred dollars off me at craps. A year later he got caught screwing the wrong girl and her husband came and ripped out his heart with a single bullet. And that was Stanley. Poor stupid Stanley, fodder for the big fight and the saddest man I ever met.

I met Etta shortly after the fight, at the racetrack at Saratoga. She was kind. Giving. Me and Belle had celebrated the Ketchel victory right across the country – we'd crashed cars and ridden trains and in every town we stopped in there'd be parties for the Champion. Me. Parties for me, and with me came Belle and Sig Hart and Jack Curley and Lillian St Clair and all the other variables who fell off the bandwagon a few towns on, but we snaked our way from San Francisco to New York like some hoopla circus that'd let the animals loose to roam. So I was tired when the party slowed and tired of Belle, tired of all the gaiety in her, the whims that took you tottering around with her giddy entourage, the now-now-nowness of Belle's life, a revelation when you're on the up and looking to be heroic in damn near everyone's eyes, and a pain in the ass after two months on the road and the fighting and the hassles and the shit. I wanted to be calm for a bit. Rested. Soberer. And loved quietly, not in lights with feather boas and pearls wrapped round my neck by a girl who never seemed to think much before she raced on and on into her life like she'd only rented it. So I thought I wanted Etta.

Belle and I had settled in New York for a bit and one Sunday up at the races I was introduced to this bird-like woman with the softest skin and gentlest eyes. She walked into my life, and for the rest of hers it was me there at the centre, me who was loved pathologically, me who was blamed when it all rose up and fell on her. Etta, ex-wife of a glorified chancer, thick and serious and frantic even then, but that was it. I wanted to fall in love and I did. This little woman with big eyes hooked me, and only reliving the circumstances could ever make clear why I decided that of all of them she was the one, the first real, official Mrs Jack. I married her in a rush one day and have been blamed for it ever since.

Fools pay. Before we married Etta moved in with me in New York – Belle had headed back to Chicago for a bit, but she'd come back every few weeks or so. Of course she wasn't too happy to find Etta settled in wearing the jewellery I'd given her and sleeping in the bed she'd pegged as half hers, but Belle was ever the professional, she adapted to circumstance. Eventually so too Etta – but that was a wrangle I wouldn't want to go through again. Thing is, it all comes down to need. Who needs more than the other. Did Etta believe I couldn't do without her, didn't want a life that didn't include her? I had fifty things going on in my life every day, and Etta was there but in the way that Sig Hart was there and the cars and the bets and the training and the insanity of all of it, caught up but not too distinguishable, and not necessary. Training helped me keep nimble – but I'd have floored every one of them just as hard if I'd eased up on it. All my things in life had substitutes and Etta assumed my declarations gave her an edge, that she was beyond that, special. And she was, but not indispensable nor irreplaceable. Belle knew the story – if Etta had followed Belle's example sooner there would not have been walk-outs and cars sent in the night to vacant hotels. And she did follow, and life settled for a short time into a calm happy freedom we all enjoyed.

I suppose the change started towards the end of that year, invisible then, just another sequence of events, another dawdle towards something vague. That's the beauty of retrospect, everything is clear and judged. First thing that happened was I got a big contract with Barney Gerard. For one thousand three hundred dollars a week Barney paid me to star in his vaudeville show – the Atlantic Carnival, he called it. I signed up round December and we went on the road in the New Year, me, Etta, Belle, Sig, Jack Curley. The idea was I'd go on stage last, after the memory man and the dwarfs and the high-voiced quintet and the clowns and the carousel dancers and the sad-faced My-Sweetheart-Lies-Under-a-Tree-singers who changed with nearly every town as Gerard tried to find himself a star attraction in the girl department. All this would yelp up the crowd and then I would come on shadow-boxing, lights fixed so it looked like I was fighting my own giant on the back wall of the stage, all dressed for the ring and throwing punches like a true Champion. Then I'd don my robe and walk around the stage telling stories, describing fights, big stories where I'd act out all the voices, do all the actions, use my whole body to make them laugh then hit them with the punchline.

It felt good making all those people laugh, that size of noise is better than a fight if you're in a certain mood. Spontaneous, it just opens out this great raw deep bellowing of eight hundred odd people throwing back their heads, clapping you on, elbowing each other at the punchline as if to say, Did you see that! Ain't he great! and urging you on to the next one, joining in with their own jokes, Did you hear this one, Jack?. Coming up on stage sometimes if a lady said she could sing or a kid wanted to show off a trick, and I'd bring them all in on it, keeping the air in under all the sketches, mine and theirs, so my turn floated along all light and fun. Then at the end they'd shout me back on and I'd do another few minutes and fight my shadow some more and wave and that'd be their memory of the great Jack Johnson planted there in their heads for ever, and the next time some wise piece of shit put me down in front of any one of them, they'd say, Hey, hold on a minute, I saw Jack Johnson, he's the greatest, and tell all about the time they came and saw me in the Barney Gerard Atlantic Carnival, Jack Johnson, Star of the Stage.

Etta of course didn't see it that way. She saw it that I was always off with other people, always entertaining everyone but her, she didn't see that it came with the job and you don't get paid one thousand three hundred dollars a week to take your girlfriend out for supper every night after the show. She hated the gypsy life we had in those months, a new town every three or four days, but mostly she just hated Belle, and Belle of course played up to it until on one train ride to Cleveland Etta launched herself on to Belle's fur coat with Belle still in it and started biting big clumps of mink and pinning Belle to the floor with the knuckles of one hand forcing down on her forehead. You don't keep Belle anywhere she doesn't want to be, and in seconds they were rolling around on the carriage floor like big hairy tomcats in silk stockings. I was impressed with Etta, I'd have preferred if she'd won, it being such a big deal for her to fight anyone like that, but when Barney Gerard came into the carriage and pulled them apart Belle was pretty much in charge, had Etta's hair all uncoiled and in her hands and pulling pretty hard as well as kicking Etta's calves. After that I just sent the pair of them back, Etta to New York and Belle to Chicago, and kept

Hattie on with me. Queen of Dullness, but a quiet girl had a lot going for her when the options were Etta and Belle.

One thing Belle was right about though was the way I got treated on that tour. She'd never leave off it, always listing all the reasons that I had to quit, to demand fair treatment, to ask for more money. Thing was, she was pretty much right. Out on the stage I was a hero but in most of the theatres I was just the nigger-act once I was off it. Every night Belle would sniff out the situation ahead of me, and every night give me a dressing-down for being a soft chicken-shit coward for taking their crap. Not in what they said, I was always above that, but the other things, the same damp basement storage room in every theatre with the bad light and no heat, the way people walked around me rather than touched me as they brushed past, the refusal of anyone backstage to have a drink with me, all the praise, the Hey, Jack, great performance and then not a soul to touch a bottle with, all segregating their precious asses from mine. The contract Gerard drew up even declared that I was forbidden to hang around with any of the girls in the show. Belle couldn't let it go, the instincts were there in me, but not the anger, not at the start, but even after she left for Chicago she kept on at me over it. I stuck it out for a long while, I didn't want them to believe they were affecting me in any way, and the money I was getting was double everyone else's anyway. Let them have their cosy spots and little whisky nights, it was me who was being paid a star's wage.

Then Gerard did something he shouldn't have. He loaned me out to Frank Rose – Michigan it seemed was big Jack Johnson territory and Rose wanted me to headline his touring show for a week. We had a ball that week, Rose treating me like I was royal, but a few days after I caught up with Gerard again, Belle telegrammed me. A kid who worked on the Rose show had surfaced in the bar a friend of hers worked out of and was telling everyone how Jack Johnson was being duped like a cheated wife, that everybody had a take on the great Jack Johnson, Vaudeville Star. Belle got the kid roughed up till he told her what the scene was. Gerard it seemed had told Frank Rose that I was a greedy nigger who wouldn't move from the Atlantic Carnival Tour to do the Michigan week for anything less than two thousand five hundred dollars, and there was nothing he could do to move me on it. He threw in that I'd beat him stupid if he didn't come back with that kind of money for me. Then Gerard came to me with the contract for the week, paid me my one thousand three hundred dollars as usual, and pocketed the difference.

Problem was, he couldn't keep his mouth shut, and every bootboy and usherette in the state knew of the scam, except me. It was that in the end that turned it. I'd been conned, taken advantage of, screwed around . . . yes, I was furious, but that every whore and retrograde in sight had known before me, that I was a public fool, that placed me beyond anger. I went after the little shit and demanded the full two thousand five hundred dollars. He denied it had happened, but eventually agreed it was true and after a bit of gentle force offered to pay me the one thousand-two hundred-dollar profit he'd cleared, call it a day and get on with the show as normal. In the end after a bit more persuasion he handed over two thousand five hundred dollars and I quit, got the next train to Chicago and was with Belle by nightfall. The little shit cancelled the tour then and there because they'd lost their main attraction, and sued me for loss of earnings, reneging on a contract, and physical intimidation. A little bit more of the latter, by proxy, cleared the whole thing up in a matter of days. And that was the end of Barney Gerard's Atlantic Carnival.

It was the stories you heard about Jim Jeffries that made the bastard seem like a story himself, one that a father would make up to make his children feel secure. Don't worry, baby, you are safe here in your cot from big bad Jeffries, now close your little eyes and I'll protect you. Except in wonderful white America it wasn't quite like that. Big bad Jeffries was in fact the great hulking good fairy who was going to fly in from retirement and hit nasty black Jack with his wand and magic himself World Champion. That's what children fell asleep to, and that's what their parents prayed for. It was Jeffries, Jeffries, Jeffries every way you turned in 1909, no matter that I actually owned the Championship at the time, it was an obsessive march towards getting Jeffries up and at me as soon as he'd agree. Which of course he did, all that ego and money not going to waste. We signed for it at the end of that year, just after I'd signed up to Barney Gerard, and it was scheduled for 4 July 1910.

Some wisecrack thought of that. Actually getting a promoter was a different thing altogether. Not that we were stuck for choice – every pro in the business wanted a cut of this – but because there was so much trouble getting it arranged. The original idea was that the secret bids were to be opened in great ceremony at the Hotel Albany in New York. Then as the whole fanfare was ready to go, the cops came in and bust it up like it was a low-rent backroom gambling joint, not a massive luxury-hotel meeting room that every soul in America knew all about if they read their papers, listened to the radio, paid attention to their friends. But boxing and the promotion of boxing were still officially illegal in New York, and so the circus was sped to New Jersey. All the heads were there in some shape or form. Most sent their brightest stooges as if getting down in the muck of the deal was above them. The two big San Franciscan bosses, Tuxedo Eddie and Sunny Jim Coffroth, had their men in along with Phil King who was Hughie McIntosh's guy. That pair wanted to bring it back to Australia. A stadium as fine as Rushcutter's Bay couldn't go to waste, it seemed. Uncle Tom McCarey was trying to swing it towards Los Angeles, but even though McCarey had taken care of me in a lot of the early fights, it was a new guy, Tex Rickard, that I liked the look of. A mean bastard, hard as granite when it came to business, and supposed to be good at his word if he was on your side. If not, his word meant jackshit. The only interests Tex looked out for were his own. Luckily for both of us, our interests were intertwined after all the bids were opened, handsome all of them, but none more so than that of Tex Rickard, promoter of the finest, proudest fight ever contested by Jack Johnson, Champion of the World.

Rickard won the right to promote the fight because he put up the best money. He offered a hundred and one thousand dollars for the purse, with ten thousand dollars each to both Jeffries and myself for turning up and putting our name on the contract in front of the press. The winner got 75 per cent of the purse, and a severe stake in the film money. There was no loser, not in financial terms. But for this one the money just separated the chancers and the main man, Rickard. The money didn't mean a damn thing when it all came down to it. And the reason I liked Rickard was that he saw that from the day the idea germinated in his head, something that the Hughie McIntoshes of this world didn't have the clarity or ruthlessness to see. The other promoters wanted fame and cash in their pockets for life. Tex Rickard wanted a winner, and from the outset, based coldly on form and talent, he wanted me to win.

There was a lot of fuss about the money. The *New York Evening Sun* kept writing articles about how we were changing the face of boxing by wagering this amount of money on a single fight. They reckoned the sport would never recover and there'd be payouts like ours going on into infinity, bigger and bigger money till it lost all sense. They said we were proof that civilisation wasn't too lucrative, that it was the Stone Age characters like me and Jeffries who were the real winners in this life. That opened out the path for endless takes on the same cartoon, Jeffries in his cave rubbing sticks or stones or hunting bison, or doing something to help mankind progress towards civilisation while I hung by my six-foot arms from a banana tree and looked savage and dangerous. Who cared? Anyone who did was on Jeffries' side, and they'd get taught the second I laid my first glove on their man. All the rest were my guys and they had faith that I'd do the job like a World Champion should. Majestically. Rickard didn't have the cash himself, but he had a backer who thought the sun shone out his ass, which was the same thing, without the risk. It was a goldmine millionaire who put his money behind Rickard's instincts. The cleverest thing about this was that Tex was a rich man. He was also writing the contract, along with Jack Gleason who weighed in for Jeffries in case Rickard proved impartial. You could see the paranoia set in early in the Jeffries camp, something that always gets to the fighter one way or another. So Tex was writing in his terms, his percentages, his cut, and not a cent of it was his to lose. Nor mine.

He was a cold bastard though, friendless, and, as far as I could tell, by choice. He looked like he'd escaped from these Wild West shows they'd had a few years before, the tall, white, tanned cowboy in his lumberjack shirt and leather waistcoat, all stubble and macho gruffness. Stories filtered out about him, but he didn't talk much, at least not about himself or his past or his plans for life. But the stories came down from the places he'd worked at, stories of how he'd lost his parents when he was ten in a fight for land that the James brothers reckoned they owned. Not people anyone messes with, but tell that to the old Rickards now and you wouldn't get much of an answer. Tex it seemed moved to Texas as a kid and picked up the accent there, and in their wit somebody bright called him Tex. He worked as a horse wrangler, got married and settled down young with his wife, working as a frontier marshal, Mr Respectable, a man you could have brought to the Governor's house for afternoon tea.

Then his wife got pregnant and both her and the kid died after she got kicked by a horse in the belly. Tex left Texas and drifted a while, ended up in Alaska in the gold rush and made himself some money, got bored and drifted off to South Africa to the gold mines there, got even richer and came home. He put his money into the Northern Saloon in Goldfield,

Nevada, where, naturally, there was another gold rush in full flow. That's where he got into boxing, promoting fights so that even more attention came Goldfield's way. He had an eye. He spotted young Joe Gans on a trip to Baltimore, and set the black kid up against Battling Nelson, one of the nastiest, toughest fighters I've ever encountered in my life. A bastard. He put them at each other for forty-two rounds, a mauling fight, and in the end Nelson went down, hit by the rule book when he planted a left-hook in Gans's balls and the poor little bastard doubled up and fell over with the pain and shock of it. It didn't matter a damn that it hadn't gone the distance – that fight made Goldfield famous, and made a promoter out of Tex Rickard. After that his ambition was ruthless and he came straight for the biggest catch of all, Jack Johnson, Heavyweight Champion of the World, against Jim Jeffries, the Great White Hope. The biggest catch of all.

America knows how to fête its famous. It was one reason the vaudeville show had been sold out everywhere we turned up, for I'd signed the contract for the fight in December and worked the vaudeville circuit till the middle of March. But once I was freed of that commitment, the attention hit me like one of my own right-hooks. Everywhere I went, everything I said, every club I visited, every woman I brought out, every hotel I stayed in . . . every last detail appeared in the captions under huge photographs of me. Belle started keeping every article and photograph inside this big cookery book some client had given her, must have been an in-joke or something, but it had hard covers and she kept them all in there laid out pristine and flat. She probably has it still, much use as it'll be to her at this point in her life. She'd be over sixty now, Mina, old. Sure, I'm older, but I made my money a long time ago. She never had a cent in her life except what she earned or what I gave her, and I stopped giving a long time ago. I'd say the earnings went the same way not long after. Twenty-five is old in her game. Sixty's antique. After the trial she'd have been popular for a bit, but she'd have had to do to every one of her clients what she did to me if she planned on staying in the limelight for more than a few weeks. Short memories, Mina, nobody remembers unless you make them.

Every paper and magazine in America had Jeffries on to demolish the coon. Or to restore white honour. It depended which papers and magazines you got. Not even baseball commentators or racing coverage could keep their noses out – it was time Johnson was taught and hero Jeffries was gallantly coming out of retirement at the age of thirty-five to ram the Golden Smile down Jack Johnson's Golden Throat. It was as if there had never been anything this important in American history, as if our trade links and federal government and the quality of our bourbon all depended on Jeffries beating me to a pulp. Which was fine if you were all wrapped up believing this, but if you were the one man on earth who knew it was all a load of delusional hoopla designed to draw attention away from a government screwing the country out of its head, then it all just seemed insane. I'd pulverise him, anyone who'd seen me fight knew I'd pulverise him, you only had to ask Stanley Ketchel. Which they did, and he said Johnson'll pulverise him, but then he went and got shot and people could say he was nuts all along.

The reason everyone believed in Jeffries, aside from an unmentionable pathological fear of him losing, was the reputation. Jeffries became a myth in the way you do if you retire at the top of your form. It is part of the consolation package that you are revered as a god, a fighting hero whose true genius remains a great intangible unknown. The best is always ahead of you if you retire at the top, the heroism of success glorified until you are safely too old for anyone genuinely to expect you to prove it, and so you age and die a deity.

Jim Jeffries never made it that far. He was a fool, a couple of years of being the graceful hero had duped him into believing he was filled with genius and natural instincts like nobody who'd ever gone before him. As if he could beat me. He believed his own stories, that he'd beaten a class heavyweight while hobbling around the ring with a freshly broken leg, that he'd set fire to himself to prove a bet that it wasn't fatal if it got your hair, that he'd cured himself of pneumonia by skulling a case of whisky in thirty-two hours. It was a case of external assurances of invincibility, nothing core. It is something you know. You know your worth. You know the fights when you made mistakes, when you win because the other guy is weak, when you tire too fast, misjudge the distance, bust an eye and can't hold concentration. You know these things. These tell you how strong and able you are, not leggy girl reporters who come so close you can smell their scent and their perfume, telling you that you are the strongest toughest man in the whole wide world. You don't believe a race of people who need you to win for their idea of honour, and you don't believe men who write about a sport they've never removed their linen suits to fight in. You believe your bones, how they hurt when you spar, when old wounds are belted, when your liver throbs fit to burst when you take a low hit. Your body guides your head when you are as good as Jeffries had been, because getting to be that good means it has taken all those punches for you, taken them better than anyone prepared to fight you, that you are the best. Just as your body guides your head when you are young, when you are at your peak and your head tells you not to risk a rally on your ribcage just so you can lure the bastard in and then savage him, but you do it anyhow because your body says to, it says it'll stand up to whatever comes in, just get the head ready to recognise when the space is right to throw the punches and the bastard can be floored. What is in your head is influenced by talk and ego and desire, and that is what happened to Jeffries. He listened to parts of himself that he'd lost control over the minute he retired, and didn't listen to the part of him that had to go into the ring with me, the part that still had to be standing when that victory bell went. And while all their dancing parades went on to celebrate the hero's return, I knew this, as every true fighter looking on knew it, and when the papers asked was I scared, I just smiled and said I sure as hell hadn't seen much to be scared of.

The fight was set for 4 July in San Francisco. Towards the end of April, after I got away from Barney Gerard, I headed out to the training camp at Seal Beach that Sig Hart had set up for me. Jeffries was holed up in the Santa Cruz Mountains, all two hundred and fifty pounds of him. The stories left his camp and came to mine via the press, and left mine and went to his the same way. Dud stories. So when we heard that he had syphilis, was in detox, wasn't able to sweat much, couldn't keep the weight off . . . we acted like we'd heard he'd just had his second coming and was back to peak form. The newspaper guys were obsessed with us, with how black and lazy I was, with how pure-hearted and white Jeffries was. Then the rumour came that wouldn't disappear, that I had been paid to lie down, that Jeffries had the fight in the bag, that I was only going through the motions of training to fool the press. They were so busy trying to let everyone know that nobody could fool them that I don't think they realised that their set-up conspiracies made their guy look all the worse if he lost and diluted the glory if he won. Which they all still believed he would, by a knock-out. They couldn't have put more pressure on Jeffries had they laid the Rock of Gibraltar on his back. Suited me fine. I was the enemy, the pretender to the crown of Champion, as if they'd loaned me the damn thing while Jeffries took his kids to the beach for the day and I'd got in a sulk and hadn't given it back. I won that title, and I'd kept it in the face of every white guy they threw at me. How anyone watching my form and watching Jeffries' could think he'd have a hope beats me still. It didn't take genius to see the differences. Still, I would win and they could make all the fuss they liked about white honour and black honour.

The more fuss they made about their Great White Hope restoring glory to America, the more angry I got, the more determined to bury Jeffries, to put every last little lynching bastard in their place. We all went out on the beach one night at the end of May, me, Etta, Sig, Tex, Eva the cook, all the staff from the training compound, and watched Halley's Comet streak across the sky like a finger painting. Holding Etta there I felt conviction, angry conviction that I had to do it, that I would not let it go when I'd won, that I'd go on beating them all – every one they threw into the ring with me. I felt a softer conviction too, a loyalty to the people I'd gathered, to Etta, to my mother, to Belle, the ones who looked out for me, no matter how awful I was, how unloving and callous. I felt a gentleness in me that I never got back, Mina – whatever magic was in that apparition of a comet never came back. I went away and started all of it again, all the violence and coldness and selfishness, all the old characteristics, and lost that gentleness. It was a good thing to lose then, a focusing that prepared me for the fight, but I know it gave Etta false hope to see me as she'd always tried to cast me. Maybe that night I did love her. In an inconsequential way perhaps I did. But it passed, as these things do, and I got back to what mattered, to concentration on the fight. Whatever else happened that was always the most important, that was the something that had to be done.

We'd all chugged out to California because it was the location of the fight, but while I was star-gazing and driving too fast along the coast roads, the moral righteous mobs of America had sent out a million postcards to California's Governor Gillett to have the fight stopped. They laid a whole load of Holy Joe pressure on, which he shrugged off, so they got some heavyweight congressmen in to explain that the Panama-Pacific Exposition San Francisco wanted to hold in 1913 might go elsewhere if such a morally corrupting event as an inter-racial title fight happened in their precious state. So Gillett decided that California could stage an exhibition fight but not a prize fight, and we were told to move our asses out of California. It was only two weeks till the fight. Tex worked quick though, and we all moved out to Reno where they'd promised they'd build Tex a twenty-thousand-seater stadium in time for it. Didn't bother me. Did bother Jeffries though. He was a nasty piece of work, Jeffries, gave out shit to everybody and never took the blame for his own mistakes. A grumpy bastard too.

He was all shook up about the change, complained it unbalanced his head, was bad for his rhythm, and screwed up his mental preparations for beating the nigger. It was all self-indulgent junk. I trained hard enough towards the end. I'd done a lot more than I let on to the press, but I didn't bust myself too hard. I'd taken to learning the bull fiddle so I'd do shows for the gang, for the journalists when they were around, played baseball, read a good bit, listened to the phonograph. At a certain point of fitness you can ease up on yourself, overdoing it makes the muscles too nervy, too tight and twitchy. With me when I trained too hard the muscles in my arms would want to stretch out on their own when I'd be only punching out to pull in again immediately and punch out a little lower on the spar. It slowed me down to be trained too tight, so I'd just go for a run, maybe spar a little. I probably spent more time with Etta then than I ever did. Which isn't much preparation for anything really, but it wound me down a lot. The moral crusaders hit on Nevada soon enough, but they got nowhere. They called for the state to be taken out of the Union on the grounds that it was a moral menace, and the pulpits were crowded all around America as the WASPs got their drawers in a twist over the appalling notion that a black man should fight a white one on equal terms. It was all fuel for the fire to my mind. Every article or story or joke I'd hear about just made me harder and calmer.

When we got to Reno the party had started. It had fifteen thousand people in it usually, but over forty thousand had piled in to see if it really was the hardest drinking town in

America. It had seventy saloons, and legal gambling, and was the divorce centre of the world as far as I could tell, and I played craps every night in a different bar up till the fight. Some nights I felt I'd found my ideal there in the middle of that desert. Etta hated it. Sig loved it. Tex loved it and loosened up a bit more at the craps table. Every sportswriter in the world seemed to have got away from his wife to come to Reno and cover the fight, over seven hundred of them, more than had ever attended any sporting event in history. Jack London was there sliming about in the alleyways and mouthing off about how white dignity would be returned to America on Independence Day 1910, how America would never forget that date. Damn right. Fool.

They'd got everybody writing about it, every boxer who'd ever fought pro had mutated into a journalist for the fight, half of them had signed their contracts with a big scrawled X, but that didn't seem to worry any of the editors. John Sullivan, Jim Corbett, Battling Nelson – even Tommy Burns was there to send back his articles, telling everyone who'd listen that Jeffries would finish where he'd left off. That I'd finished him off seemed to get forgotten. There I was, Heavyweight Champion of the World, and I was the one going in to win the title.

The town was like nothing I'd ever seen before. Everyone was drunk or happy, excited as if they'd inherited a fortune, each of them, and had only weeks left to spend it, rich with giddiness and a strange edgy danger. The Sundance Kid was in town, and every decent gangster in the country had come to pay their respects and bet a few thousand dollars. All the big money was going on Jeffries. There weren't enough hotels or places to eat – everywhere you went people were taking it in turns to sleep in the parks and streets and alleyways, even through the daytime. There were three-block lines everywhere, at cafés, restaurants, hotdog stands, at people's houses where they were setting up money-spinner cookhouses in their front yards. Everywhere was dollar bills and wagers, drinking and gambling and eating and getting sleep where you fell. I've never been in a place so full of life, Mina – there was none of that New York weariness, no sense of people having lives less than carefree.

Nonetheless there was a sense of acute menace running all along the belly of it – our camp was like a fortress, just like Jeffries'. I slept with a shotgun by the bed and a pistol under a pillow. I didn't show it though, that awareness of danger. Like I say, all it does is harden your heart all the more. I had the original marble heart by the time the fight swung around. I was going to murder that big bastard and I'd do it right in front of them, right where they'd placed him. At my mercy.

The betting had Jeffries with the fight all wrapped up from the first few rounds. Everybody had him to win. Even boxers my own colour, men I'd fought maybe twenty times like Joe Jeanette and Sam Langford, said Jeffries would annihilate me. People took to writing how Jeffries' breeding and education would turn me into a snivelling wreck once I got in the ring. Who the hell fights with calculus? At least I knew who my father was which was more than most of them could say. In Kansas the Colored Holiness Church held special services for me to try and attract divine intervention so I'd win. Then some Midwest minister started the same game for Jeffries. You couldn't walk to the end of your nose without being asked to declare your side. The whole world seemed to be watching me, watching to see if I'd lie down or just get pulped of my own free will and Jeffries' all-round greatness. All America was standing by waiting for the ticker tape and wires to bring them the news. That morning I woke up and felt I was getting up to go out and save the world. It still feels like I did.

Jim Corbett kept popping up like some sort of evil Jeffries troll, appearing in the street as I walked, in alleys, in shop-fronts, spitting at me and shouting 'Da Nigger's Goin' Down, Blackboy, You's Goin' Down' like he was auditioning for vaudeville down South. Corbett was the man, Mina, once upon a time he had it like nobody had, beat Sullivan, seemed like he was going to be the greatest, but a few solid years of bad women and the usual drinking and he was living on his own and taking photos of naked women for a magazine a friend of his put out. All in the fist. Then Jeffries found him and gave him some money to be his trainer, and help run his camp. Corbett's idea of support was to run round Reno after me, and buy as many guns as he could lay his hands on in case the camp was overrun. Corbett hated me. Really hated me. If the choice had been to kill himself or save me, he'd have got out his knife and slit his jugular, no question. He couldn't wait for this fight, this was the one, I'd be killed in public, and with maximum humiliation. Did you know, Tex was offered bids for my corpse after the fight. They were going to chop me in public, lynch me, even though I was dead already, and bonfire me. Guess who started that ball rolling. Tex took their money and split it with me. He knew I'd win and wanted to screw the bastards. A few of them chased the money afterwards, but most were too stunned. It's so hard to tell you now, Mina, now when me winning is in the annals and it is all history, how sure they all were, everyone in America, that I'd get crucified in that ring. That Jeffries was God and Hercules and Zeus all in one man, and I was the fake, I'd be shown my place.

They served lemonade at the fight, so worse than thirty thousand drunk swaying fanatics, the stadium held in its treachery over thirty thousand sober ones, about a hundred of them backing me. Drunks fall down, mumble, laugh and shout abuse. Sober drunks whine a lot and shout louder and clearer and in sentences. It could have mattered, but of course it didn't, it was all part of the mentality, and by the time it came to fighting Jeffries, to the one fight I ever fought that mattered, I had trained myself to take abuse like it was a jammed car horn, loud but easily ignored if you didn't listen out for it. It even spurred me on if I was in the mood. And that day, I was very definitely in the mood.

It was the strangest, most fearsome raging crowd I'd fought

amongst yet. Belle wasn't there, she had stayed in Chicago and listened for news with thousands of others outside the offices of the *Tribune*. Etta was, prim and important, Mrs Jack Johnson to anyone that asked, and plenty did, until Tex whisked her out front to the ringside to bat her eyelids because she was driving me mad with her stories of what people had said to her, the spittings, the death threats, the dead racoon parcelled up and left for her at the hotel. Maybe I was mad with outrage and anger, but probably more just plain fury that she was still talking about herself on this day of all days. So what if she'd got death threats, we got them everywhere we went, and the spitting, and the violence. When she walked along the street on my arm all of this circus began, had done since the very first day we'd gone out in public. It was like her coming and talking for three hours about my driving too fast or why the hotel food was so bad, pointless self-indulgent prattle, a conversation we could have had any time, not minutes before I took on the biggest fight of my life. I threw her out, or got Tex to do it. Later she told me it had been Sig Hart's idea to send her in. Sig had reckoned I'd get so mad at hearing her so upset I'd want to go out and murder someone, preferably Jeffries. Sig was usually wiser than that. He also spent most of his waking hours with me and should have known it was hardly a novelty to have Etta whining in my ear about what a hard life she had with me.

Reno had done Tex proud with the stadium. It was strong and solid and plenty able for throngs. Cops were lined up everywhere, it felt like we'd hired a baseball ground, they were making everyone hand in their weapons at the gate, frisking them down and up as everyone massed through the four tunnels into the stadium. It was the finest place I'd ever fought, and it was a shock to people, most of them were used to the grime and filth and darkness of the illegal boxing joints in the cities, or ramshackle firetraps built on the cheap. So was I. But this was a stadium fit for a title fight, fit for a fight with everything at stake, fit for a Champion like me.

It was a fiercely hot day, a desert day, with the kind of sun you feel is going to lift the skin right off your face when it beams on you. We went drinking in town for a week but then three nights before the fight we had our last jaunt, and then Sig Hart and Tex and all the other wet-nurses locked me up in the compound to dry out for the fight and get my head cleared.

Physically, Mina, I was in my prime, two hundred pounds of pure fighting muscle, and all I needed was solitude to ready my mind. I never felt any pressure, which appears strange now when the intensity of what the fight meant seems suffocating, but I always had the mental strength to remember that, whatever else was around it, what I did in that ring each time I took on a fight, even a spar, was win. That was what I had to do – a fighter can be as good as he wants in the gym but it's your ass out there and nobody else can do it for you. It is between you and the binds and the leather they strap to your fists and the rawness of the space between you and the fight in front of you, and not crowds or noise or panic or fear can ever get in the way of that space. It is yours to close, to manipulate and force, and for all the money in the world there is no one else there but you and him, the blindness of power, of pain. It is a mental fight, one of you will let go, will wilt and be the first to take a half-step back instead of going deeper in to plant the grounding punch, the one that establishes your invincibility. And there is always one, a moment when there is a choice made in a millionth of a second to hit or pull back, to think or do, and that is the moment, the fear is allocated. And if in that half-step it is you who brings it away, you will lose; for every moment of brilliance you perform from then on is caught within the limit of fear and you are broken by it when the moment comes again, senses set like a clock to back down when the danger overloads you again. And you know none of this as you're fighting, you have no time to calculate fear, it is an instinct, but this is what is in your head as you are wiped down and watered between each round – did I reach it yet, when will I force it, and when you sit on that stool having conquered that moment, you feel invincible, all it takes is the purest faith in your talent, your strength, your right to be Champion of the World. And that is how men who live for boxing can know in a second who will win, no matter who it swings for and against in the balance of pain and punches, how near the end or the start it turns out to be, they will see that moment where the fight breaks, see it and know. That is why you cannot take your eyes off a fight. Why you need to go in with your head as taut and blinkered as your body is strong, why a fight is won and lost in the preparation.

In the heat and sun the crowd climbed high into the pinewood pews, and when those were full they squeezed their bodies around pillars and sat on the boundary walls and in the aisles, and the sweat of them made the delicate women, not that there were many, pout their noses into handkerchiefs or just pass out for the drama of it. Sig ran in and out like a telegram man to regale us with details and descriptions of the world unfolding beyond us in the sun as I lay in the dressing-room being pummelled and loosened and advised. But I didn't need advice. I'd seen Jeffries fight, and I knew where to get him, what he depended on to gain control, how he saved certain tricks for when he tired. I knew his style like it was my own, and like I say, how anybody could seriously believe he could carry that title away confounds me.

Some smart-ass sent a coffin round to the entrance of my dressing-room the morning of the fight, so we turned it over and played craps for a while, once I was as loose as I could be without falling asleep. I would skip on a piece of rope in between turns, as much to piss the others off and knock them off their game as anything else. The energy was building though, I just wanted to get out there and do it. Mentally I was sharper than I'd ever been. I felt like all the slackness in my head, all the parts which had women and drinking and speeding, had been tightened up with a screwdriver, and I was a powerhouse. I felt invincible as I went through the final stages before going out, felt such callous pity for the crowds swarming out there singing 'Hey Ho Dixie' loud as they could, as if I'd just seen their children in a boxcar crash and then met them on their way to a lynching and thought, Nah, wait till they get home. No, pity wasn't what it was. Hatred really, but not profound, because you only ever profoundly hate something you've decided is worth it. And they weren't. They didn't deserve my respect.

There was an electricity in the stadium, in the country, that day, the kind that comes from knowing, from the great exuberant anticipating knowledge that the ultimate happiness is about to happen to you if you can bear to sit and wait for it. In the minds of most Americans that Independence Day, Jim Jeffries was about to make them all feel like they'd just had the best sex of their lives, gone out and hit the winning homer in the World Series and come home to find they'd inherited a gold rush. There were no calculated silences, it was a celebration, a day to spend money and laugh and go beyond all your usuals in life, to sleep around if you were faithful, to get drunk even if you were in detox and never touched a drop, talk to every stranger round you if you were shy, turn legit if you were a crook. Just for today, just to acknowledge America's hero was out of retirement and ready to pound the nigger into the canvas and you had a ticket to watch it, a radio to hear it, a party to wait for it, the news, that Jeffries killed him, Jeffries got the coon. Oh but if they knew. All those drinks bought in, all those friends come round, all those dollars spent, all to herald the greatest wake in America's sporting history. People would turn from each other in the street because they were there, together, when the news came in, Johnson won, Johnson won it, that Jeffries is beat.

And it was this in my head as I came down the ramp in my silk robe and shorts, belted with the American flag, to all the boos and spits and hollers, the brass band climbing in the ring as I neared it and striking up 'All Coons Look Alike to Me', daring me to climb in with them as they reprised the chorus over and over, and my face soft and smiling as if it was Buddy Bolden himself in there on the trumpet playing me in. And then Jeffries coming in the other side, cheered like he was the President, like he was the King of England, the great exotic hero there with his thick belly and dirty hair, chewing gum out of the side of his mouth and trying to get me to notice he was glaring me down, but I kept smiling like I was at my own wedding and watched the whole of it through the corner of my eye as I jogged around outside the ring waiting for the damn band to finish clambering out, the force of thirty thousand yelling voices roaring 'JEFFRIES'. I wouldn't look at Jeffries as I moved around, I was taking in the whole scene through the corner of my eye as I limbered up in the ring, seeming glazed and miles away but absorbing it all, the vastness of the voices yelling me down, yelling him up. The vengeful triumphalism of the shouting men, falling on top of each other in the stepped seating as they tried to shout louder, waving scrolls of newspapers like conducting wands as they bellowed, the smell of thirty thousand people sweating in slept-in clothes rising into the windless heat, the panic of the journalists all circling the ring, petrified of not being ready, the radio men and their equipment at the ringside, the sense of the ring being closed in upon, a tiny space in mayhem . . . all this folded in upon me and I stared as if glassy-eyed at the sky while being tied into my gloves.

And I was ready. Relaxed, ready to play. They decided my refusing to look near Jeffries was a sure sign I was frantic with fear and started yelling at me to look at him, daring me to, but I just laughed and acted like I was hiding behind Sig Hart, hiding behind the white man. Oh but if they knew. Then they started the chant, a slow pocket of them spreading the words along through the rows right around the stadium until it seemed even the ushers in the aisles had stopped to shape the words 'Die, Coon, Die, Coon, Die, Coon, Die, Coon' – a sinister malice-laden monotone that rose to meet me then fell away, a silence in the split-second rhythm that was the most evil sound I'd ever witnessed. Tex was panicked, the first and last time I saw him so – he could see the turn in the crowd, the shift from happy expectation and the standard insult to a chilling unreal danger as the voices continued in almost perfect unison. I acted deaf, facing into the centre of the ring and punching air, sprightly in my apparent inability to notice that thirty thousand voices were willing me dead, but Tex was unnerved. Jeffries came centre-ring looking nervous as a whippet and cautiously raised his arms above his head as the crowd went wild, stamping the ground, banging set banks and pews, whistling, hollering, screaming for God, and for them, there he was, every blubbery inch of him right in front of them.

There was no sort of contact at all, not even a handshake, which suited me fine, for they could call whatever tune they liked on the symbolic touches, it was the ones that were out of their control that counted. And the sooner they began the better. Everyone cleared out of the ring and for a second the crowd dimmed their noise to allow us to start, but the second the bell went the madness reached a new intensity. I could have made it quick, shaken him up and broken him almost immediately, but it was a power I wanted to wield, all that hatred and this was where it came to in the end, four fists and these square feet, and I wanted it to be torture, torture for them to watch, torture for Jeffries to endure, torture for everyone who had ever treated Jack Johnson like a jumped-up fool who dared believe he was higher than the dirt beneath his feet just because he walked on it.

I had thought through how I'd do him, how I'd manipulate his strengths, slowly, always giving him reason to think he might just swing a good one, then every time punish him for trying. Forty-five rounds, and he would fell them each one without respite, a humiliation far more complete and irrevocable than a delicate battering and a big punch knock-out. If I floored him early they'd have some reason why I'd taken advantage of God – he had a shadow in his eye, sun up his nose, gloves on his hands, something. Some explanation why I'd been able to floor him besides the fact that I'd hit him to the ground with the force of a blow. So it was going to be tailored for them, a stage-show of a beating, hard, ferocious, beyond all excuses. The bastards were going to see me slowly scarify their precious hope of a white champion, they were going to see what I could do to them, right there, right in that ring.

So Jeffries came into me in the first round, head-first like he was crazed, and that meant I had no work to do at all, just go at him straight, left, right, left, right, left, impact punches that dizzied his head and his feet. But the moment came, and I forced it. He came in at me all furrowed and fierce with a right jab and I held it back with my left arm and came in fast with my right, an uppercut aimed at his jaw, and the eyes connected, the fear threshold right there in the space between my fist and his jaw, and he pulled back, half a step, mid-punch, and I grazed his shoulder, no damage done as far as anyone watching could see, but the fight was lost and won in that moment – the time it took to lose a punch and walk out of another was the time it took Jim Jeffries to lose the fight he had been born to conquer. I had broken him and better than anything that came later was the look in him that recognised it, the look as our eyes locked and his foot went back, the fear and knowing as he saw he'd been beat before even the first round had rung out.

He responded with balls though, went immediately into one of those Jeffries things, clinching like a frightened monkey on the attack, arms wrapped around me punching my sides frantically, and I'd seen him do it before where his opponent got stricken by the inability to move, panicked, pulled himself and Jeffries around the ring with Jeffries pummelling the shit out of him until the other guy went weak at the knees and Jeffries roared in with a floor-punch, bang, on to the canvas, victory. That was them. When he tried this shit on me I peeled him off with a left uppercut to the chest, using his armpit for leverage, and up, back he'd go, legs jangling. I'd talk to him while I was doing it, play with his concentration, tell him it was a great way to spend an afternoon, far too hot to be indoors at a craps table, told him I'd go on like this all afternoon if he liked, dared him to come in closer, dared him to hurt me, told him to take the old bones easy, not to rush himself. He reacted like a rabid bulldog, rushing in, arms swinging and mouth chomping, doing more damage to himself than I could, though I did anyway, hard fast uppercuts to his liver and head. In the fourth he threw a left that cut open a training cut from a few days before, but the crowd thought he'd busted me open, all they saw was the blood, the nigger cut, and went crazy as if the last three rounds hadn't really happened at all, as if this was all you had to do, split a lip and somebody would wander in and declare you Champion. They were yelling 'FIRST BLOOD! FIRST BLOOD TO JEFFRIES!' but it died down soon enough when he went up against the ropes within seconds of drawing blood, all the triumph gone out of his face, trying to protect himself with the clinching and a few thrusts in my direction.

All the while Corbett was sitting like a nancy-boy on a high stool behind Jeffries' corner shouting 'Kill the nigger, kill the coon, Jim', and then shouting directly at me, screaming insults till he was purple and gripping the ropes to hold himself up so he could rage some more. He had this theory, well known round the place, that black fighters went weak and daisy-like if you said nasty things to us. All Corbett reckoned he had to do was yell as viciously and loudly and as close to my ear as possible and I'd keel over. There was a rhythm to the shouts though that calmed me even more than I was. With Corbett so close and loud I could focus on one voice full of hate rather than the blurry head of noise from the crowd, and it kept my thinking pure and absolute. Also made me laugh a little, him there telling me at the first bell that he'd rile me up so I'd not be able to stand, and there he was by the tenth with a face like a horse in a heatwave ready to explode and stain all the stuffed shirts' claret. By the twelfth I'd busted Jeffries' mouth so bad it looked like he'd been pulled head-first through a bear-trap. All the hard punches I'd thrown at his mouth had cut inside it raw on his own teeth, and on the outside he was mashed up all over, his nose broken by a pounding in the eighth, pouring blood all down my back when he clung to me to keep on his feet, bruises settling into their colours all over his face and body, both his eyes busted pretty bad. I'd planned a slower massacre, but he wasn't fighting, he wasn't up to me in any way, worse than I'd expected, so it had come in on both of us, him getting roughed up quicker, me having to carry him slightly to make it linger.

He came out at the thirteenth looking depressing, chewing gum in some excruciating attempt to seem casual about everything, that mauled-up savage bloodied face moving agonisingly as the slow motions of his jaw twisted around the piece of gum, wounds which had temporarily sealed up torn open again by the stretching of the skin as the chewing continued, on and on. He came in the second the bell went and clinched me in a tight hug, hunched into me trying to battle with my solar plexus from up close like a man trying to light a match in a gale. I came in hard on his side with my left and then blew him off me with a right uppercut to his jaw. He tumbled back, and I heard Corbett bleating 'Kill the coon' in my left ear as I followed Jeffries across the ring, held him steady at the shoulder at my right hand and belted three sharp blows to his face and then swung him away, a door on a hinge, with a flying uppercut under the chin. He tottered, eyes closed, and I went gentler knowing how close he was to being floored and wanting to drag it out, brand this humiliation into the memories of every sorry evil little bastard out there in the crowd, in that town, in this great country of ours, who had hollered and whooped about the nigger getting killed, the coon being taught how to eat shit the American way. Well, this was the American way and it was my way and Jim Jeffries would eat it for them, for every last one of them. Every cut on his face was aimed for like a target shot, every bit of flesh beaten raw – in front of them all I made Jim Jeffries as broken and derelict as a human being could be, just as they'd tried to do to me, humiliated, lifeless in all but heartbeat. And when the fourteenth started I went at him the same, heavy then light, not letting him escape to the canvas but bringing him with me, his arms so dead they hung loose in their sockets, every blow asking if he was liking it, if he wanted hit with a left or a right, in his belly or his face, asking if it hurt enough, if I could help him walk into any more punchbag volleys, and he just stood like a sack of wool, one knock and ready to topple.

Then in the fifteenth he came in crouching, following about the ring behind me like he was a drunk playing hide-and-seek, being right there stationary every time my fist went deep, me bent double half the time to make them land, then him standing up and coming at me, walking right into my fists, and I just played them on his face like a drum roll, forcing him back with a series of left and right uppercuts till he was leaning against the ropes again, and this time I went for him, dragged him up to his feet from the left shoulder and volleyed twenty odd punches in formation on his head and face, my gloves slick with blood, pounding each blow harder than the last till his legs buckled under him and he swayed and, for the first time in his life, Jim Jeffries hit the canvas. I stood over him, waiting, but got pulled back by Tex, who was counting him out, but didn't the bastard struggle up at the count of nine and stand there in front of me, the crowd going crazy like I wasn't going to do just the same again, which I did, and down he went to his knees and up again at the count of nine. Everyone at ringside yelling for it to be stopped, to pull Jeffries out while he was alive, the crowd panic-stricken and chanting and bellowing for it to be stopped, and still Jeffries at the count of nine standing there, until I put a left then a right and then a left on him, a full-powered murderous thunderbolt combination that threw him through the ropes leaving him flailed out over the ring, legs caught up in the lower rope while his arms and torso hung limp in the laps of the journalists as he hung like the bloodied piece of white meat he was. At the count of seven Corbett ran in to pick him up and the fight was stopped, all over, the Great White Hope left for dead in front of them, glory days a dream again. A fantasy, Mina, pure fantasy.

That was the greatest day of my life. You never know it at the time. You think, This is how it's gonna be, all your life will be this moment extended, this achievement part of every fibre that twists and weaves to make up your life from here on in. It's not like that. But God has sense, Mina, if you had half a notion that this was it, this was the ultimate hour of glory and all the rest was just reverberations and flutterings, you'd pack it in then and there, you'd never settle for the come-down, for the cruelty of it all. I guess you have to be strong, and if you aren't strong, you live out your supposed glory days propping up a bar getting bitter till your liver gives up on you. I wasn't interested in that. I didn't know that day in Reno was going to be the best of my life, but no matter what, it sure as hell would have been worth anything to have it. But I was able to keep strong, Mina.

Write to me soon again, tell me more about you, about your life. It's so damn good to hear from you, Mina, you've no idea.

Take care of yourself,

Until later,

Jack

Mina

New York, March 1946

Dear Jack,

We are busy at the moment preparing a surprise for Fabienne – it is her birthday in ten days, on April 5th, but really it is a farewell, I suppose, an excuse to gather all her friends, and Joella's. It will give them a chance to say goodbye, for my daughters are moving to Colorado shortly. Not for another three months, but proper farewells are never done when they are delayed to the last moment. Joella is helping me, but what she doesn't know is that I have been inviting her friends in secret, and so it will really be her surprise too. It is a nice excuse to make a fuss of Fabi, to give her a cheerful birthday. Their nanny Giulia did all these things when they were children – occasionally I get around to compensating as best I can. It is not much, but I don't think anyone particularly cares any more. We are all adults now.

They want to drag me to Colorado with them. It is not for me, not at all, I like tranquillity in my head, in my room, but when I open the window I want to feel other people's energy, Jack, not a glacial Aspen chill. They insist it will be perfect for me there, an idyll of peace and inspiration. But I've had idylls before, and they're not what they're cracked up to be at all.

The Italian idyll was picture perfect, but of course it didn't last long. Wherever we went, however inexpensive and spacious and peaceful, it was still Stephen and I. The countryside round Florence was populated in that period by all sorts of fakes and jewels, I was told, but the latter didn't make themselves known. Instead Stephen attracted all kinds of dreadfulness – an English dowager who knew his tedious family, some terrible artists from southern England, an Oscar Wilde impersonator who thought himself outrageous for his daring . . . all of whom thought Stephen the most charming, entertaining, amenable man they had ever encountered, and his wife a sullen pregnant bore. It was a direct bargain. They would invite us to their villa or castle or estate and pour us tea into their best porcelain, serve us aperitifs in crystal glasses from polished silver trays, and have us sit on their heirlooms. For this pleasure we were to elaborate on every detail of our family history, explain every aspect of our marriage, and justify our decision to move into their world. Stephen was beside himself with the rapture of it all. Comparisons made between their Queen Anne chairs and his Queen Anne footstool, their Louis XV armoire and Stephen's Louis XV writing desk. I bowed out using my pregnancy to gain a few hours each day without Stephen hovering over me demanding was I happy here and could I not show it then. Truth was, I missed Henri, missed the relaxation of being loved by someone whom you delight and who encourages some of the lunacy in your spirit. He wrote often, but my answer was always the same.

Joella was born that July, and her birth was both the most harrowing time since the night Oda had died, and the most balming. There was no confusion. I held her and loved her completely, not for replacing Oda, but for everything she hinted at and became – vibrant, gentle, sweet-natured, a laughing child. Giulia, the sister of our cook Estere, came to live with us then as Joella's nurse, and I was happy for a time. I converted the little tower adjacent to the villa into a studio, and I painted there, and spent the rest of my time with the baby. With every cough and tickle in her throat, every dullness I spotted in her eyes, I called the physician, until gradually Giulia weaned me away from my paranoia and allowed me to trust that Joella would not die unnoticed as Oda had.

There was even a sense of harmony between Stephen and me, and we began sleeping together once again. I can admit it now, but I got through those nights by thinking of Henri. Within a year I had a son. I allowed Stephen to choose his name, for I had not allowed him any say in the choice of Joella's name. I had wanted her to carry a connection to her father. Stephen chose John Stephen Giles Musgrove Haweis. We called him Giles.

After Giles my body went unscourged by Stephen. He had dalliances in every pocket of the area, I heard stories but never cared enough to ask. By now Henri was a fondness in my head. I learnt he had married eventually, but not to whom, and I surprised myself with my lack of regret. Meanwhile I made my first friend in Florence, and I probably owe my sanity to her, for, had she not adopted me, my mind might have imploded with inertia.

She was called Mabel Dodge and had bought a Medici palace for herself and her husband Edwin. They lived a few kilometres above us in the mountains, and Mabel's reputation as an eccentric and an intellectual was unassailable. It is hard to know which the sewing-circle set feared more. Of all the names and reputations and affairs Stephen brought home in his gossip, Mabel was the only one who interested me. It was said she had been the first to collect Picassos, loaned young writers money, was Gertrude Stein's closest friend. So much hearsay clung to her she had become myth, and I scarcely believed she existed until one day she soared down on us from her hilltop palace with an energy that swept us away. She told us stories of friends in America who seemed impossibly glamorous and alive, and all this I loved, for it fed my sense of expectation of the world.

She also saw that Stephen was a fool, declared to me that my husband was without talent or integrity or humour. She was the only other person in the world to see it. That made me warm to her immediately. From the first she had seen how he ran me, how he pummelled our lives into his own shape, and she could not abide it. Nor could she abide her own husband. She had learnt that the only way to gain freedom was by developing his talents for him, so that he became so absorbed he ignored her, she was not noticed at all. What she did went unnoticed, what she said, where she went, and, most importantly, who she saw. Stephen had minor preoccupations, slight affairs. He needed an obsession, and a great love. That way, she said, I would be free. Now, looking back, there seems such stupidity in all she said and did, and yes, Jack, of course I did feel very resentful that the nature of my marriage was so obvious, my mind so easily dissected, and Stephen and I so imbecilic we needed intervention from an American eccentric with too much free time. But Mabel became an ally when I was feeling very rejected. I was looking for someone to blame, and I couldn't find anyone. Stephen was too tired a target, my resentment too ordinary by now to have any salving power, and I hadn't the sense to deposit it upon the only person responsible. Me. That was reserved for self-pity, not for any rational dynamic approach as to how I would change things. What Mabel did was enter my life and insist I see things sensibly, and apply all my energy into bettering them, not continue to lounge around wearing my put-upon face as though it defined me. She gave me sense. And optimism.

I met a world of Mabel Dodges when I went to New York, whole lives lived around philanthropy, around a parasitical fascination with the genius of others. Their money crowned that genius, chose it, fed it, bought what it produced. Without it all manner of talent would never have found the attention it deserved in its lifetime, but it was a rasping overinvolved gratuitous indulgence nonetheless. Who could commandeer the best table at the Waldorf and the most prestigious bohemian company to escort there – entire circles of fatuous lives were led around such things. As though philanthropy were the art and all the effort and discipline and doubting went into that, and the art itself was merely an inheritance that needed spending in a tax-efficient way.

It was years before I would see this. Back in Italy, all I saw was a lifebelt, someone to take me out of myself and my depression and my crucifying self-pity. With my silly home-made hats and Poiret dresses and curious dwarf-like husband I was simply another pendant for her to display around her neck when her friends came that summer from all around the world. She teased me for my beauty, for my body, my taste in clothes, the poets I admired like Rossetti and Yeats, and she did it publicly in front of people who intrigued me. So I learnt to defend myself in those salons, to explain my opinions, my reasons for liking and disliking certain people, books, artists, religions, politics . . . I learnt all the things I ought to have learnt from marriage as I had dreamt it, marriage to a man my equal who challenged and provoked and stirred my mind. I grew up under Mabel Dodge, grew into someone clever and alert, someone I would want to know intimately. I woke up, Jack, all those years of false epiphanies believing that Oda was my salvation, separation from Stephen, Paris, Henri, my new daughter, my new Italian world, my son . . . all, all false. I did not change. I simply adapted. Then through the ministrations of a squat, not very bright American with too much money and a lame husband, I woke up.

It was then that my fixation on getting to America took root, and the dirt it ploughed up with its unrelenting vehemence muddied everything that surrounded me in Florence. I wove the most exuberant fantasies about life in exotic New York, about the people Mabel spoke of, the names I had heard, all the Europeans who were sailing out daily to be glorified there, Marcel Duchamp, Isadora Duncan, Robert Delaunay . . . it seemed fantastic, unreal, some kind of luminous chandelier with an ever-glowing light that shone as far from me as was geographically possible. It was everything I wanted.

And then guilt would erode all the fantastic illusions. It had taken such a time to claw past that lingering grief, diluting it with substitution, with distractions and a new country. But it had not been assuaged by Joella, nor even Giles, and only now was I beginning to awaken and not want to go through Oda's last hours over and over. All that time, and now here I had two loving, interested, intelligent, gentle, mesmerising children, my funny little son and my wise little daughter, whom I wanted to abandon, to leave with a nurse and a cook. To leave them, Jack, as Oda had left me, bereft.

Or would they be? Giulia was their mother, their father, their sister, their grandparents. She spoilt them, fed them, educated them, washed them, admonished them, hugged them, smacked them, played with them, loved them. Stephen and I were houseguests in their lives. We were the ones who argued, who slammed doors and went out at night in silk hats and long velvet coats, who worked in the untidy rooms in the tower where they were not allowed, whose names were spoken of as though we were foreign countries that could be glimpsed from a height on a clear day. They were my children and I missed their illnesses unless I was told, read only the schoolwork I was shown, played only when it suited me. I had a life via Mabel's world, but merely an existence with them and Stephen.

How arrogance consumes us when our lives become inescapable. Retrospect clears your mind like an arctic wind. I can hear that in you too, Jack, that sense of clarity now that nothing can be done about it all. It was about then that Stephen had a revelation all of his own – he was going to go off and search out the South Sea Islands for any natives Gauguin might have missed. Gauguin was his hero then, he had replaced Whistler. Gauguin was divine and holy and was calling him with his art, luring Stephen to follow his example and give up everything in the pursuit of the savage genius soul. There was the marginal difference in that Gauguin was a savage genius soul, an original one, and one whose art transfixed me, yet I didn't want to paddle warm oceans replicating his vision. But imitation truly was the sincerest form of flattery to Stephen and once he had sold some of his allegedly unsaleable antiques, off he went from Naples Bay, kissing the children goodbye while he secreted away their Christmas presents so he could educate the natives with their extraordinary religious significance.

I was desperately in need of money when Stephen left – he had graciously rerouted over half my income from my father to subsidise his South Seas adventures, forgetting I had a nurse, a cook and all the running costs of the villa to maintain. I was able for nothing, perfectly trained if I had needed to sketch some light and shade into a picture of our lives, but utterly unable actually to support us. Getting married was to do that, that swap of independence for financial security, but then Stephen was hardly a husband in any guise, never mind as the stoic breadwinner.

It was Mabel who came up with the solution. She knew of a young New York heiress whose passion for art was bringing her to Italy to study. Her family would not hear of it unless she lived with a chaperone.

Ostensibly I was perfect. A young married mother of two with a large villa in the hills, a Sociétaire with connections in the art world – ideal as a role model for a naive young painter leaving home for the first time. But Frances Stevens was no young *ingénue*, Jack. When she arrived she was fresh and energetic and racing to find all there was to uncover in this anglophilic region of so beautiful a country. She grew fond of Mabel, but to her all the rest were merely diluted versions of the aristocracy of Upper East Side, New York, and she dismissed them out of hand. She could not have been more perfect as a substitute for Stephen – his antithesis dressed in a silk shift dress.

I should have been jealous of Frances. She was twenty years old and already living the life it had taken me ten years to weave for myself, living it to order without the constraints of marriage and children and financial suffocation. She had not yet made a single mistake in her life, Jack; at her age I had been poised to commit my worst. It was within my sights to prevent her repeating my nonsense, and I would not see her rush into anything serious but her art – one life stalled by carelessness was one too many.

This could have made for the dreariest time of my up-to-then dreary life. But it didn't. That sense of adventure that had been coiled in my gut unfurled itself when Frances and her big ideas arrived.

I had some of my own. A new art movement was developing in Italy at the time, one that captivated me with its ideas, the little I had heard of them through newspapers and journals. It seemed so vibrant, so exciting, and they called it Futurism. I told her everything I knew of it, and she was entranced, wanted to see it all for herself. I knew after a matter of days that, despite her wealth and the ease of her passage through life, she was not the kind of woman who had notions about these sorts of things. She chose carefully and intelligently in everything, whimsy was not in her nature. In all the years I knew her I don't think she ever made an important decision rashly. Unlike me. Perhaps she was my chaperone after all, and I played the faux guru. I enjoyed female admiration when it was hers. It was so different to that arduous lust that shirked behind flattery from men.

She was very beautiful, blonde and tall, with a regal grace. I gave her the little apartment in the tower adjacent to the house so she could enjoy her autonomy. We would have lunch together on the verandah each day, and work in the afternoons. Around five I would take her to the Giubbe Rosse, the local café, and it was there that we met an assortment of Futurists trying to impress us with their daring in addressing a married woman and her female companion. I merely thought them a group of indolent men swinging their rural egos on the Futurist bandwagon. I was steadfastly unimpressed.

One though was different. We held a party, Frances and I, one evening in late summer that year, 1913. I was in the yard near the chicken coop when he came, this stranger. He didn't see me at first, he was transfixed by the sight of Joella and Giles playing with the chickens. I knew him immediately. All of Italy knew him. He intrigued me more than any man I had ever heard of, Filippo Tommaso Marinetti, the thorn in Italy's side, this restless madman whose nation's politics he had wrapped up in an art movement and sold across the world as the only way forward. Futurism began and ended in him, Jack, it was his mind that made it, and destroyed it. But in that warm Italian dusk in 1913 he was still the hero, still the visionary.

The children were chasing each other around the coop, trying to catch the unfortunate birds as they went. He watched, gripped by the pantomime of it, suddenly embarrassed when he saw me, shaking himself out of it as he raised himself to his full height, his gaze unwavering as he held my eyes. He smiled as if to charm me, but I knew his reputation and however much he fascinated me I was not prepared to wilt in the evening sun like some delicate flower. I did not blink, merely called the children to my side and swept inside, not a flicker of recognition on my face.

No one had known he was coming. One of the Giubbe Rosse gang had invited him in a fit of sycophancy, but had never expected the leader to show. He took advantage of the element of awe his presence created. All the zealots flocked to him, stunned that this small Florentine soirée should interest him in any way.

It was hot in the rooms of Frances's little tower that night. We had been waiting for a thunderstorm to break for days. I slipped out often to the gardens. Marinetti watched me like a jealous husband – as I circulated the room I could feel my back riven with the stigmata of his gaze. I manipulated his attention, of course, every gesture, every disappearance and reemergence, every casual movement, spontaneous joke, whisper in an ear were all predestined for Marinetti's evolving notion of Mina, as though I had been planning his seduction. I had great selfishness then, Jack, it was the newly developed ego in me. I wanted to be like everybody round me, and be their hemlocked opposite too, poisoning their gang mentality, their collectiveness, their herding instinct that made them little more than overbred litters propagated from the few originals in their midst. And in Marinetti I saw my like. A new version. I saw the fearlessness I was yearning for, and the ability to burn like acid through anyone else's opinion. He did not care about anything.

He was not used to being ignored, I could tell from the boredom with which he dealt with his fawning acolytes. He circled me, watched me in the garden from the balcony, stared at me, and waited. Waited for me to ask to be introduced, waited for me to approach him, waited for someone to proffer an introduction, for me to offer him wine, to act as demi-hostess, to make my bid for the attention so patently up for auction. But my price was not found that night. I enjoyed the game, the obvious infantility of swatting flirtations on a hot evening, of feigning disregard. But that was all. It was entertainment on a dull night. And so I grew bored, I disappeared to my villa, to sleep.

The next morning it was Frances not Giulia who brought me my coffee, and she was as excited as if she had just invented oil paint. She dragged me out of bed to peer around the shutters and there striding below on my verandah was the tanned and vain Marinetti holding his face up to the sun as though it were a rarity in Italy, as though he was on his own, unspied upon. Neither of us had a notion of why he was there, only that he had come directly to the villa and not gone near Frances's apartment. She had seen his arrival from her bathroom. When I went down he was sitting having coffee with Joella. She was describing the sea to him. Giles was playing in the garden, his breakfast untouched, while Giulia hovered in the house, appraising herself of my latest supposed shenanigans. He stood.

'Mrs Haweis, alone with stokers feeding the hellish fires of great ships, alone with the black spectres who grope in the red-hot bellies of locomotives launched on their crazy courses, alone with drunkards reeling like wounded birds along the city walls, alone, it is you that I have come for Mrs Haweis, you alone.'

And then he sat down and poured me coffee.

Unfortunately for him I was not the frustrated *hausfrau* he suspected. Equally unfortunately, part of my captivation with the movement had led me to translate the Futurist manifestos. This insane tirade had been published on the front page of *Le Figaro*, and was part of the rhetoric that had fired the bandwagoners so much that they had written themselves into Marinetti's one-man cause. The hellish fires and red-hot bellies did not therefore have the desired effect of me thinking him a fabulous genius come to sweep me to bed. No. Merely a flatulent egotist with more pomposity than a Victorian judge. I called Joella to me, turned on my heel, and left. After trying to follow me, and having Giulia to deal with for his efforts, he marched out to his large car and drove off in a sulk. And that, we thought, was that.

The Teatro Verdi was thronged when I arrived. Frances came out to meet me, brought me in through the stage door, while at the front almost three thousand people seethed and heaved towards the closed doors, trying to get in. All around scuffles and fights and overloud voices bullied their way into an artistic crowd's idea of a riot. The event had been much heralded, it was the Futurists' turn to perform for the public, enough of Dante recitals and Puccini operas, enough archaism. This was the banter in the Giubbe. Let us take over a theatre ourselves and make trouble, tell them what we think of war and history. Kicking Italy into the new century was their prime target, and though it is easy for me to be dismissive now, Jack, I honestly thought it was the first really exhilarating idea they'd conjured up. I thought it was wonderful. Frances and I had designed posters and we had raced around Florence putting up all our respective creations.

We hadn't had any idea of the interest the word of mouth stirred, an almost maniacal desire to reject everything old, everything caught up in the cobwebs of museums, everything tying Italy to her past. But inside they had prepared for it, anticipated it. The doors opened and bodies rushed in from every aperture, shouting and laughing. This was no night at the opera. I was still sceptical of Futurism, still not sure that it wasn't merely a panoply of half-witted intellectuals looking for a cause. I suppose I condescended to involve myself, then got swept away by its force. Up until the Teatro, I was still condescending.

As the crowds elbowed and forced their way through the foyer into the theatre itself, I saw Frances and others I did not recognise take baskets of rotting fruit and eggs from behind pillars, statues, from consoles and cubby-holes, and leave them prominently at the back of aisles, on seats, all over the theatre. I was completely mesmerised. Then, with just over half the crowd in the auditorium, the lights went out, all but those spotlighting the stage where the curtain was slowly rising to reveal a lurid red podium, then two trousered legs, higher, until there stood Marinetti silhouetted against an astounding array of huge coloured canvases.

The crowd was in uproar at the lights going out, falling over themselves in the dark, shrieking and bellowing, but as the curtain rose they too slowly became silent, their eyes pivoting round their heads as they took in the strange eerie quality of the stage, of the sculptures of industrial parts, the frightening coldness of the canvases. This was exaggerated by the noise still shaking the foyer as everyone bustled and squeezed their presence into the dark theatre so that an arc of hysteria crooked itself around the entrances along the back of the auditorium.

There suddenly was Marinetti on the podium, the centre of all this, behind him the untold hideousness of a savage transfixing vision, a cruel callousness in the art there that I had never seen before, nor since, not in all my experiences at the Salons, in Paris, in London, in art school. No one taught you how to take a scalpel to humanity, to pare away at human organs still thumping, to take out all the redemption and faith and put a metallic disenchanted barbarism in its place.

He was shouting now, and I shook myself to hear him, to listen as he began exhorting the assembly to abandon everything they knew, to go out and find a true originality, to make an enemy of imitation, to rail against the tyranny of good taste and art critics, to innovate using all the weapons of modernity, steel, speed . . . on and on, feverishly, all semblance of coolness, of sternness, gone. Rejoice in being called mad if that is how it falls, rejoice in nature, in burning canons, in decimating the contents of galleries, museums, libraries, churches, in destroying the national infatuation with all that has gone before. Obliterate the obsession with the past, and replace it with cynicism, with war, with truth, with dynamism. His presence affected the crowd with an overpowering energy. Such noise and electrification.

When he had come on to that stage I saw that this was what he was, pomposity and arrogance was simply what he amounted to. In everyday life it was misplaced and awkward, but on this stage it was a gift to him, it allowed him to awe and communicate at the same time, to stir in people the desire both to placate him and be him, to rile and to do.

The crowd's hostility would have petrified a weaker man. Not Marinetti. In the plush comfort of the dark they roared at him, yelling obscenities, telling him he was a disgrace, unfit to be Italian, an embarrassment to his nation, an animal, a rapist, a murdering fool, and he simply shouted louder, and with the help of a vast megaphone he told them Italy would crumble under them, denounced them as archaic purveyors of passeism with no idea of the industrial world that was gnashing its steel jaws, seeking out conservative fodder like them to bankrupt, to spit over its shoulder back into the last century. Telling them Florence was nothing greater than a city of parasitic snobs, ancient and cobwebbed; his voice bellowed over the insults, the chants, the abuse, until it became almost affectionate, this manic fevered litany of insult and diatribe.

I stood at the back squeezed in amongst the demons, watching unfold this perplexing exchange between three thousand people and one illuminated figure – this was Futurism? This, this barrage of abuse? Why had they thronged, why come and rail against something hated, why waste all that energy? And now Marinetti was shouting at their stupidity, telling them Futurism would clean out their foolish minds, would rid Italy of her allegiance to the dead, the stuffed, the worm-ridden, until slowly the whole theatre was clapping him home, clapping him triumphant. Then the fruit began to be hurled at the stage, and the eggs, but he raised his hand and caught an egg, intact, unbroken in the palm of his hand, and he played out the drama as though it were scripted, which it was, right down to the egg as he folded his fingers around it and squeezed the yolk on to the stage.

'Let's break out of the horrible shell of wisdom and throw ourselves like pride-ripened fruit into the wide contorted mouth of the wind,' he roared at them. 'Let's give ourselves utterly to the Unknown, not in desperation but only to replenish the deep wells of the Absurd.'

And the same men who had accused him of raping Italy began pulling out seats and throwing them onstage in agreement, cheering him and throwing fruit as though he were a vaudeville act, earning his supper causing riots in music-halls.

'Live for speed, live for explosions and dynamism, live for war, for it is the world's only hygiene, live for patriotism and destructive gestures, for beautiful ideas, and fight moralism, fight those who push cowardice and feminism on you, who extol cemetery logic, who want to make Italy a dealer in second-hand clothes, who fill abattoirs with antiquities and call them museums, fight this, fight the old who will choke you to death with their archaism! Fight! Seek out war and win!'

And for the next three hours that was what the crowd did, they started with fruit and by the time the *carabinieri* arrived they had stripped the Teatro Verdi of all her archaism: her archaic gilded gas-lights, her archaic velvet seats, her archaic cornices and archaic orchestra pit.

We escaped, Marinetti appearing suddenly from the maelstrom and rescuing me, almost mobbed as he did, bringing me to the café where one by one in all states of undress and disarray the core arrived from the Teatro. He was untouched by anything as foul as rotten pears even though there had been nothing more than a podium between him and the initial onslaught. Most of the gang smelt like an orchard floor in a heatwave. They were very excited, asking over and over what I thought, was I shocked, had I heard him, did I believe in what I had heard tonight, questions, questions, questions, until my thoughts bled from the frenzy and I sat down. Marinetti leaned across to me and poured wine. 'Well?' he said. 'Converted?' as though an evening of riotous giddy bravado would make me think suddenly that women really were an inferior race; but I was convinced of things I had dismissed as foppery before, convinced that a war was needed now to clean out Italy, that the past truly did possess more dangers than the future possibly could hold.

That night, in Marinetti's triumphalism, I was swept up in something larger than anything I had known, an overpowering optimism, a hatred for my glorified past and the events that marked it. I was elated by a searing excitement for everything that was to come, my whole life ahead of me, and I wasn't thirty-two and trapped in a terrible marriage with two children and a hellish depression. I was about to start anew, and while this might have been ludicrous nonsense, there was enough in the passions it aroused for me to want more, to want involvement. I turned to him. 'Yes,' I said. 'Converted.'

I was on fire after the Teatro Verdi. As if my puritanism had been slaughtered and even my scepticism, its replacement, was being put out to graze. Not altogether, however. I still retained my cynicism, for the movement still seemed vacuous enough in some pockets, with an almost juvenile desire to stick out silly tongues at blind men. That was for the zealots. What interested me was not the imbecilic leaping around decrying women and authority and lust. No. For me all the power lay in the intellectual complexities Marinetti was setting up around him, the abandoning of old strait-jackets in pursuit of a modernity and newness that was waiting to be crafted by whoever chose. It felt like a religion, a vocation that seemed as unlikely as the call of God in a young girl's ear, but it revelled in one thing – absolute rejection of the past. Was there anything more suited to my life at that time, Jack, than an intellectual excuse to give up haunting old slights and mismanaged manoeuvres, a whole movement wrapped around discovering and inventing and changing. I thought I could turn a blind eye to his pontificating about the general uselessness of women and the great need for art to change the world.

Art wouldn't do that. War would, and that appealed, that sense of annihilation and indulging futility. That is the most wonderful thing about wisdom and retrospect, it allows you to see your shrieking youthful stupidity and pass on over it. War to me now is an evil, an appalling destructive force. But in 1913 I was still playing the Italian princess, beautiful and deserted high in her hills, waiting to fuel her mind with great things and be adored by great men. I lived in a fantasy then, with Frances my handmaiden and my future merely perilous rocks for Dorigen to set as a task for her suitors. I was a child for so long, longer than even my children, and my life a series of short-term masterplans that would elevate us all to glory. But it doesn't work like that, Jack, you understand it as well as I now, those fights, the immediacy of achievement . . . it takes so much effort to hoist yourself above the easy choices. You had to fight for yours, and so did I, but mainly I was fighting myself. In the end that is really what it is, fighting all the characteristics that will render you as plain as flour if you do not condemn them through your actions. And those times with Stephen when I plunged into deep depressions were because I had the self-knowledge to condemn those parts of me that ceded to him.

Marinetti was as much a child as I was. He called at the villa the day after the Teatro, the impresario in him recognising opportune timing, and sure enough I was still in thrall to the excitement I had witnessed the night before. I was also still deeply suspicious of him, and though this time I let him breakfast with me, it was only to relive the night before, to use him to work out what had happened to have gripped me so. And it was simple. It was energy. I sat in my turreted villa and dreamt up ways of escaping my marriage and running off to New York, growing stale and wise, when all this dynamism was exploding in the valleys and hills and towns, this passion for war and industry and progress and life. Life, what I was mulling over, grasping at. A few giddy coffees with Frances and some ribald gossip with Mabel did not add up to the same thing at all.

Marinetti was delighted with himself, visiting me at every opportunity, attributing my change from hauteur to enchantment to his magnetism and genius. He was put clear on that. It had been the crowd's electrified sanity that had turned on itself, become madness. The idea of chaos. Is there anything more attractive to an undecided, dulling mind than chaos? No, not to me, it was the lever that prised me open. It takes just one thing in a life, Jack. In mine, that was all it took. A twist of madness.

He came often, and I did not care. He arrived later and later in the day, stayed later and later in the evenings, dined with the children, played with them, took them off my hands when I had things to see to. I took tremendous pleasure in turning the great Marinetti into my child-minder, and great umbrage when one twilight on the verandah he blew out the oil-lamp and placed his head on my lap, his arm encircling my waist. Yet I did not lead him on this merry dance any longer than suited me, and one evening stopped the playful spurning and brought him to my bedroom instead, for I felt sure enough now to embrace every desire I encountered.

Something else did happen immediately after the Teatro, Jack. I began to write. At first it was prose, long confused assessments of all that was in my head, intensely involved, ramblings at best. Exorcisms perhaps, though that is being kind to myself. I grew bored with them, but not with the effect of the words. And on the balcony one afternoon a few weeks after the Teatro I found what I had been yearning for amidst all the oil paint and sketching lead. I wrote my first poem, a prose poem, a hybrid. Perhaps that could have been the defining moment of my life, the one act that shaped the immortality of the play, but it was not. That moment came four years later, that moment was Fabian, Jack.

I sent that first poem to Mabel; she started everything for me. She was back in New York primping her social set for the journey to Italy, and playing lady of letters every time Gertrude Stein came into view. The poem was published in a magazine in New York, *Camera Work*. I was desperately excited. She wrote and asked for more, and soon I spent every day writing, the pent-up stupidities coming out clear as a bell, a lucidity with my pen in hand that I had never possessed in my most eloquent moments. I found myself awaking each morning eager to discover what I could do with my ideas, and I grew fascinated by reading again, read everything, writing things out of my body that had not been purged since Oda's death. These poems I didn't send away. These I kept for my children when they were old enough to understand. But like all detritus, they got lost in the panic and abandonment of subsequent years.

I began looking for a big idea to impose my experiments

on, something litanous and grand. Meanwhile I sent more and more poems to Mabel and began to get letters from all kinds of editors and writers and fans – fans, Jack! All these people writing to me, discussing my ideas, asking questions, wondering how I had come to this conclusion, or written in such a way . . . letters forwarded by Mabel from people like Gertrude Stein asking for more work, for the honour of publishing my poems.

So elated was I by the idea that the frenzy surrounding me in Italy was producing something that would bring me into another new world, into literary New York, into a different medium and way of life. I suppose in part it was arrogance – to think that people were aware of you in a place so distant.

My mind was forming and murdering new infallibles continuously. I felt like a blunted knife-blade rubbing against a pumice stone, sharpening for action. It was strange – I was the pumice stone and I was the knife. The parts of my brain that had grown numb or had been suffocated by the things I had succumbed to in marriage were sentient again, made sharp by the understanding that there were madnesses out there that fired people, and I had these things in me. I seemed constantly to think at a new depth, not merely when I read or painted or walked. And all the thinking was coming together in a piece of writing I put body and soul into, my own aphorisms on Futurism, my idea of what was vital in it, worth spreading. It was this I sent to New York, all my beliefs for a new modern Futurist world. My conversion tablet.

Marinetti was less brittle now – I had accepted him, accepted his interest in me, indulged it. He had nothing to dance for now that he was in my life, albeit peripherally, nothing to be heroic about, or loud. We argued a lot, not about each other, but about all the ideas and concepts that were anathema to the other. Neither of us believed that everybody was entitled to an opinion – there was a wrong way and a right way, and unfortunately each of us was convinced of our own righteousness. Our battles grew fierce.

I was asked to show my work, my newest dabbles since the Teatro, in Rome, as part of the First Free Futurist Exhibition. I was to represent England. It was prestige, it was a coming out, an honoured request. It was an invitation to irresponsibility, for I would travel as Marinetti's lover and all of Italy would know of the married English woman seducing their lunatic *bête noire*. I would be in all the papers, for Marinetti was as famous as Michelangelo then, Jack, notorious for his rallies, his exhortations to war, for the political movement he had made from art, for the speeches and addresses he gave all over the country, for his swagger and fervour and handsomeness. I was to disclose myself to the world as a scarlet woman. It was seduction in itself.

I came back to Florence revived, as if I had taken a cure, as if I was meant for Mabel's life of scandalous insouciance rather than my adopted one of playing everything straight. My very public affair was selfish and indulgent and exactly the opposite of what a mother of two young children should be doing while her husband dashed around the South Seas pursuing his muse. I felt unspeakably alive.

The effect quadrupled when on returning to the villa I received a parcel from Mabel with all my poems published together in a small volume, with a livid red-silk cover and my name in silver. She had, she said, arranged with Alfred Steiglitz to print three hundred copies and this was the first. The others she told me had almost all been sold through the effect of the magazines I had been published in and the word that was escaping about this mysterious English poet writing in her Italian castle. Mabel had the art of embellishment perfected.

Oh Jack, it was one of the most glorious moments I have ever known, being published like this, my mind communicating at last with a world outside the perimeters of children and Stephen and balconies, and Frances and Europe and Mrs Mina Haweis. New York knew who I was. People there who thought like I did, to whom such things mattered, were opening up my book and seeing my ideas there, in their untouched form, the form I had given them, to read on the train, to read aloud or to themselves. People were going around Manhattan carrying my aphorisms in their head, maybe trying to make sense of them in the context of their own New York lives, maybe confused by them, maybe understanding completely, maybe being entranced by what they read, or disgusted, repelled. But reacting. All over New York, people reacting to my ideas.

Of course now I know how it works, know how there are so few who have an interest, who would go out and read poetry. It mattered, yes, but all over New York, as I discovered, people were darting to their jobs, their lives, crawling around on hot-air vents under newspapers, climbing carpeted steps into ballrooms, buying tomatoes and selling pretzels, not lusting after the latest edition of a little literary magazine. I knew that then too, could have imagined it at least, but the excitement of seeing my ideas there in print overwhelmed me. I thought the world was mine for the taking.

I was working on a bolder task now, on my *Feminist Manifesto*. I had begun it before our jaunt to Rome, and now, with Marinetti off to England to convert the innocent, I went at it day and night, taking out my red-silk collection every few hours to remind myself how much could be said if it was shouted through a megaphone to a screaming crowd. Or to a group of literary bandits, but the idea was the same.

Things were changing in the world. Word was coming through of tensions between Serbia and Austria, but I absorbed the information with only the slightest of concentration, for Mabel was back with her wealthy band of lovers and acolytes to brighten up an Italian summer. We had written to each other about the idea of taking a large villa in the distant mountains to avoid the summer heat, her entourage and mine. Hers being filled with fascinating company and mine with two squabbling children and an irritably dutiful nurse. So we packed up and trundled towards Vallombrosa in the hills above, vaguely aware that somewhere trouble was brewing, but far too self-absorbed to pay much attention.

Mabel was fascinated by my sexual intrigues in her absence. She loved the idea of Marinetti, of his striding about the place looking for ways to seduce me. Mabel liked to flirt. Were she Marinetti, she said, she would have let me burn right through him. When a letter arrived from Marinetti in London saying he would come to the mountains as soon as possible, Mabel was more excited than I'd yet seen her.

Her attitude was one of an African explorer doing a sideline in exporting savage exotic beasts. Capturing a real live Futurist in her enclave, well, who knew what he'd do. He'd most likely be violent before long, but that was manageable, and it gave her the chance to be the consoling companion. Of course he would shout a lot, bellow instructions at her servants, but that could be quite titillating, and certainly would keep them on their toes. He might steal some *objets d'art* despite his wealth, given that he hated the idea of art being collected, but it was a holiday villa, and none of the treasures were hers. And of course he would consistently attempt to get her alone and ravage her, but she would be disgusted at his disloyalty the first few times, and then, amidst seductive protestations and gruff endearments, she would relinquish her qualms and enjoy covert rambunctious sex in outbuildings.

When he did come at the end of July, he had more on his mind than a simpleton New York view of his movement. I was delighted to see him, but he refused even to come into the villa, he was almost quivering with the excitement of what he knew. He drove me higher up the mountains to a *pensione*, and told me of the soldiers swarming the railway stations in Paris, Narbonne, Lille . . . how war seeped out of every crevice and industrial cranny in France. He ached for it. He believed, and I with him then, that war rooted out the evil, purged those countries it stirred in of their poisonous hypocrisy, made men of childish adults, created absolute power through the truest democracy, battle. Together we yearned for war that night, going through in our minds all the possibilities for action. Of course, we were almost completely wrong in all our predictions, but two days later one came right. Germany declared war on Russia and the next day on 3 August they invaded Belgium. As he prepared to leave me to Vallombrosa and hurtle towards his acolytes to work out their plan when Italy entered the action, Italy declared her neutrality. He was furious, ashamed; his anger that France, England and Russia should enter a war Italy was too cowardly to fight in was more fierce and unabating than any I had seen before, as though all the energy invested in Futurism had been a mere rehearsal for the business of war.

He left me at the Vallombrosa villa, and darted down the mountain in his great black rat of a car, much to Mabel's dismay. She had hoped for some Futurist intervention in enabling her to make sense of the events that had occurred in the days since I had left. But he had in his mind the idea of rallying his troops and forming a battalion of his own, one that would do battle where Italy would not. And still, amidst his shame at his country's cowardice, he had strong hopes for her embrace of bravery, that Italy would not let him down. His foreign legion would be prepared for all manner of evil, but it would most likely go unused as true Italians answered the inevitable call to war that would come soon. But it did not.

So Mabel entertained and flirted while Marinetti skipped back and forth between playing war with his own mini-legion and coming back to woo me, to take me up to the *pensione* and have long, fiercely argued dinners, churning through all our thoughts and options and ideas about the war developments since last we met.

It was as though he saved every thought for me, Jack, his opinions like the fontanelle on an infant's skull, almost completely formed yet intimately vulnerable, and he made me feel that it was my input, my thrashing around with the contradictions and impracticalities of his theories, that constituted the protective love that sealed the vulnerability, made his mind intact. I realised that what had begun as a game, as a conquest, had for him become intensely important, I had become intensely important, I had been worked into the fabric of his life just as much as the oratory and international converting . . . that he was falling very much in love with me. I could not reciprocate with the same intensity.

He showed me an unlimited tenderness and this was a revelation. The man who strode Russia and England and France bellowing to audiences of Futurism's forthcoming world-dominance was more concerned about the fate of my children should war fall on us than Mabel or Frances, or Stephen, whose correspondence had stopped months before. Yet while we argued about many things, there was only one that divided us in a manner which made me constantly wonder what I was doing with him. He believed, with a passion that was insurmountable, that all power was masculine, all courage, creativity, all, all masculine. *Disprezzo della donna* was his phrase for it, it covered all arguments on the subject. There he was in London supporting the suffragette movement, declaring it the embodiment of the Futurist ethos, while explaining carefully to me the futility of women seeking the vote for we had not the brains to do anything with it. Scorn For Women. He preached it everywhere alongside his exhortations to war. For womanly things softened a man, love and desire and gentleness and giddiness and patience. This was what we were. These things made a man weak, made him consider his actions at precisely the moment thoughts killed the dynamic of his deed. And women brought out the most debilitating trait of all in a man. Lust. The most virile man in Italy suggesting it was a sign of cowardice in a man if he could not resist a woman's body. The most cowardly man in Italy it was then who raced up mountains to make love to me over and over, with such careful loving attention, and raced away to shout his manifesto in a hundred thousand more ears until he returned again. And that was us there, this confusion of contradictions, him believing profoundly in everything he declared to the world, yet breaking off his rallies to go to a woman up in the hills. And I, I overcame my outrage and ignored the anxious gnawing within me that tried to justify my relationship with a man who so despised women. I overcame it because it suited me. Retrospect made a mess of all my reasoning, but retrospect was not at hand to lure me away with its logic then. I wanted him, Jack. Or more correctly, I wanted the distraction and devotion and intelligence he offered me, the separate world he enticed me into, far more interesting than anything I had dabbled in before.

I overcame my qualms because he gave me the means to do it. He told me I could not be included, that I was outside all such theory, too intelligent and sharp-witted to count as a woman at all. Remarkably, I allowed this to work. It fitted my sense of being separate from the rest of the world, of being the only one of my kind. Maybe the word is ego. Maybe I was simply ludicrously easy to flatter. But it would have to be more than that. More to allow me to remain in the heart and bed of a man who was a sworn enemy of my own sex. The *Feminist Manifesto* was my way of working around the contradiction; in my own individuality as the excepted woman, I could say and stand up for all the things that my conscience denied me in his company.

Marinetti did not like it at all when I showed him my *Manifesto*. He said it belittled me, and all he had believed good in me, all that was forceful and able. High in the mountains in our little *pensione*, he told me it was a weak and squalid little mind that believed women were fit to hold power over any man. I was his exception, for I, it seemed, was simply a beautiful woman with a man's mind. I was a man in all but body, he declared, and this was why he loved me, for my combination of femininity and genius. He said many things that day. I laughed. His inanity was astounding, and I found I despised him for it. I knew he loved me, at least with his idea of love, and knew equally that the feeling was not in me. He stirred many things in me, but nothing to make me linger against my own advice. I threw him out and shouted at him that our relationship was over, such as it had been.

He did not believe me. He stormed away in his car and for days and weeks the war-polluted postal service chugged out missives from Florence, Rome, Paris, Toulouse, Milan, Naples insisting I explain myself, retract my foolishness, declaring love, fidelity, apology, until finally asking if I would bear his child, wanting me to carry the progeny of genius, a dual genius. And it was there the letters ended, trailing off as the replies went unwritten, and perhaps there were more but I do not know, for we moved down into the city, and I never saw him again in my life. That last day seemed so final in my mind, but face to face it felt so inconclusive; to end something just like that, and not be believed. I would have liked to have seen him again, a few years on perhaps, in New York with Fabian or in Mexico with you, but that was it. I never saw him wither, and he never saw my hair turn white. Because of the vanity that propelled us, I am sure that was the best way for each of us. And that was the end of my affair with Marinetti.

I needed a new distraction after that. I left Giulia and the children in Vallombrosa while I settled in Florence and volunteered as a nurse. They were recruiting frantically, so I suspected Marinetti was close to triumph in his bid for intervention. Meanwhile Mabel and Frances deserted me for the safer territory of America. I yearned to join them, to explore another world, but Giulia made it quite clear that, were I to go to America alone, she would not continue her surrogate mothering of my children. I was to take them, or stay in Italy. Working as a nurse in Florence was my perfect alibi as far as securing Giulia's continued service was concerned. I had a whole new freedom again.

My poems were still being published in New York, new ones that Mabel had taken back with her, and the letters continued to be forwarded to me, letters of admiration, encouragement, repulsion. I was having an effect. I answered each one carefully and enthusiastically, but with each one the frustration grew. I had a dreadful sense of my life starting elsewhere without me, of a whole sequence of events defining who I was, while I wrote poems alone in my shoddy apartment, as if serving penance for having children, for having dared have an affair. A whole world thrived over there where books and art and dancing and conversation made up each day of some people's lives. If I lived there I now would be 'some people'.

I would love to think that, after my harping after war, after the whining hankering I indulged in with Marinetti and the Giubbe gang as a whole, my life was made perfect by the bloody slaughter of innocent Italian youths on battlefields when eventually Italy did join in. But Italy merely grew more depressing. My eyes were very clearly focused on a different world now. America.

The war trudged on and on. I did not make it to any battlefields, but instead joined the Red Cross and graduated to sewing flesh wounds. I was floundering. I had had enough of being the martyr, staying behind while Stephen floated around the world, playing mother to my children like a hollow doll. We all deserved better. Now I see my selfishness, I know that I could have justified murder if it eased my conscience and allowed me to travel to New York.

And so I began the careful process of selling Stephen's much admired heirlooms and antiquities to all the Anglo-moronic aristocracy embedded in the Tuscan hills. Of course they all asked after him, and said it must be a sad day for Stephen to part with all his mother's treasures. I said it most certainly was. I brought the children back from Vallombrosa and settled them as boarders in a new school, left Giulia money to run the villa and to keep the children during weekends and holidays, and booked passage on a ship leaving Naples for New York.

The day of my departure came. I said farewell to no one. Only my children and their nurse were there to cut the binds and free me of my responsibilities. I would earn money in New York selling my paintings and publishing poems, I would design dresses and covers for *Vogue*, take photographs and write articles for prestigious, well-paying newspapers. These were my plans, Jack. Within a term, I told Joella and Giles, I would send for them and we would all know the excitement of America together. Until then I would write every week and tell them my adventures. They hugged me and cried and let me go. My mind was too drunk with the reality of departing for New York for me to feel an ache at the parting, only elation at the prospect of my arrival. As I embarked upon that ship, they were just my son and daughter, seven and nine, too young to understand that I was going any further than the mountains without them. This was how I consoled my conscience. And it would only be for a few months, and then they could come and share it with me, all that America had to offer two excited children. Stephen would visit, they would be enthralled with their new life, and happy in my absence with their schoolfriends and Giulia and Estere and the house that they knew. But it would be three years before I would return for them. By then my son would be living on a different continent, his young body silently, unwittingly dying. Giddy with adventure, I waved from deck until my wrists throbbed and as the ship pulled away I blew kisses over and over. I would never see my son again.

Such is life, Jack,

With affection,

Mina

Jack

Chicago, April 1946

My dear Mina,

You don't seem too surprised to hear from me. It's like you were expecting it. It doesn't feel like a long time, and then you go telling me your life and now I'm going telling you mine, and suddenly it seems like we should be pushing each other round the park all day talking to the grass. I like this exchanging of lives, Mina, it makes me realise I've lived. Things are so damn quiet these days I need reminding. Not that there's anything wrong with a quiet life, there's just not a lot right with it either.

You'd sure lived plenty by the time I met you. I reckon I'd have shot that guy Marinetti myself. You pick them, don't you? You and Cravan always seemed right, but there was a bit of the princess and the jester to the pair of you too. That doesn't seem so surprising any more – the less ordinary the better, from what I can see. I think I went the other way. The more they pretended like they had balls, the easier it was to pay no heed to them – Etta, Lucille . . . they'd whimper a bit, moan about not seeing me enough, but they took it. In their own ways of course; hell, Etta's way nearly sank me, but that was all in her head, that paranoia and screeching. I wasn't at anything special at all, nothing she didn't know about when she married me. I thought Belle fitted nicely in the pattern, less demanding maybe, and far more fun. She never acted like she needed me, as if her whole world would collapse if I wasn't there at the centre of it. No clinging, no insisting. Then when we were together she'd still make me feel regal, but we both knew she'd never expect a damn thing. That way she got more. In the end, I couldn't have got her more wrong, Mina. She wanted more than all the others put together. She wanted my balls on a plate.

We celebrated for near on two weeks after Reno. I wanted Belle with me, I had Etta, but it was Belle I wanted. I telegrammed the result to her first, and she came quickly. It wasn't love that made me want her there, nothing romantic, I just felt right with her in that time, I wanted her to share in the glory and madness we threw ourselves into after the chaos of the fight and the aftermath of it.

There's only one thing that's ever thrown me in my life, and it was Tommy Austin. We didn't hear about it for days. When I was around nine or so back in Galveston they would blindfold us and put us in a ring, seven or eight of us, and make us fight one another. Last kid left standing got the money. Tommy and I met at one of these Battle Royals and we learned a way of looking out for one another, taking it in turns to be the one who backed into a corner in the ring and punched everyone who came near, while the other would roll on the ground catching ankles and pulling the other kids down to make it harder to get hurt. Most times the whites would try and stop it but then they'd get into the idea of us bringing each other down, and by the time we perfected it, I was the puncher and he was the skittle, I'd be left standing and he'd hardly have a mark on him and we'd split the money. Galveston was an evil place for a black kid then, you were the lowest form of life in their eyes. Tommy and I used to empty the cargo ships on Galveston docks and when I got ready to box my first proper fight with Joe Choynski, Tommy was my spar and my trainer, and when me and Choynski got arrested in the ring for fighting in an illegal bout and got put in jail, it was Tommy's wage that bailed me out twenty-four days later when the judge let him. Every cent he could lay his hands on to get me out.

I fought on and on and, when I'd run out of Galveston fighters, I moved to California, drifted east, drifted west, got a reputation. Tommy stayed and made some money rebuilding houses after the flood in 1900 washed the town flat, got married, had some kids . . . came and saw me fight Ketchel that time too.

We found out through my mother, through a telegram. A lousy way to find out anything. Tommy and everyone had been yelping it up, celebrating the win, drinking, and ended up in a fight with some whites over it all. Blood was up everywhere, and everywhere blacks were getting happy and triumphant and not staying dumb to protect anyone's feelings, shouting I'd won to everyone, and the whites in Galveston didn't like this too much. They picked on Tommy's gang, a fierce fight, they say, and two whites ended up stabbed, said Tommy did it. I'd believe it. Not killed or anything, cut up a bit but breathing and alive, but the fight intensified and got nastier and more people got sliced. Nasty, but it ended, as these things do.

The next day they found Tommy's seven year old hanging in the woods. They'd sought her out and lynched her. And as we dealt with that it came in from all over, riots and lynchings and death across America just because I'd beaten Jeffries. In Georgia a gang of whites hit on a construction camp with rifles and chased the men into the woods, killed three of them because they were black. Same in Louisiana, three killed. In Delaware it was a white guy and in revenge the numbers gathered and lynched two black men. Two white guys knifed to death in DC. In Virginia, a gang of sailors went on the rampage looking for black men to do in, just as people did in LA and Baltimore and New Orleans, all around America the blood vessels burst and ruptured tragedy round the nation. My fault, they said. My fault.

We buried Tommy's kid then came back to Chicago, and

what could I do? Was it because of me that we were fighting back, feeling strong and in control and not ready to take the shit any more? Course not. It was way deeper, way more complicated, and it all landed at my door because they said I gave off the example, I didn't show respect, didn't stay in my place and be grateful about it. Damn right I didn't. I'd have respect when they put a white man in the ring with me that could beat me. Till then I'd be triumphant as I felt like, enjoy all the glory, the worship, the crowds of twenty thousand people who met my train into Chicago and followed me home to Wabash Avenue like a conquering hero, like I was the best thing ever entered their lives. And I was, I am, Mina, I am Jack Johnson and they will never undo what I did that day in Reno, in that ring, in front of all those people, never tell any of us we are the weaker, lesser people after that. I gave something that day that cannot be made cheap by riots and lynchings and dying, that wasn't me, that was reaction, and what I did I would never undo, even if it would have saved Tommy's kid, and all those people. Because it wasn't about me and Jeffries, it was about what happens inside people when they get humiliated, angry, looking for someone to blame, and they all got me, but I wasn't, I'm not, their great big bully-boy ready to take the blame. I did my bit, I floored him, and I will never never wish for any of it to be different. Anything I did in that ring I did right. All the wrong started far, far away from it. And far away from me.

But it went on and on. Some black tenement houses were locked and barricaded and then set on fire, women and kids inside, and white gangs chased down every black kid they could see and beat the life out of them. All over people dying, fingers all over America pointed at me. What I'd done was prove that you can be black and be the best in the world, but the bigwigs saw it as chaos, as a celebration of lunacy, of the idea that there could be anything equal about a coloured man and a white one.

They decided there would be a black rebellion and I would

be to blame. Blame? Hell, that was one thing they could pin on me and I'd be the proudest man in America for it. Nobody had to ask permission to do anything, and there they were blaming me for it, saying that just because I was the best in the world every black person round the country would get ideas in their head they could do the same. Well, damn me. I'd shaken the nest, hell, I'd tumbled it out of the tree, eggs and all, and started building my own, and did they hate that. Wasn't in the rules. Even the people you'd think would be on my side, the intelligent men like Du Bois and Booker T. Washington who were cracking the system with words, got on my back over it, said I should keep my mouth shut and go off quietly, not have a white wife and white women round me, not splash out with my money and drink lots and have fun. No. What I was meant to do was fight the fight in the ring, take my money, and go home to Galveston, buy a little poky house, marry some woman my own colour, raise a few kids and pretend the world was just hunky-dory, just me and my vegetables and a few memories of the day I was let off the leash for a few fighting hours. Put me back in my box.

Like hell.

But that is where the close-down started. I was to be hunted some way and the race started the second that punch connected and Jeffries fell through the ropes. First they wanted to do it in a roundabout way. They wanted to ban boxing. Abolish it for ever, make it a crime in every state. Never let what had happened in Reno ever happen again. Well, there was forward thinking for you. Papers were told not to cover it. Theodore Roosevelt, who'd always up to then been a boxer's man, jumped out of the shadows and said he hoped that the fight in Reno would be the last ever to take place in the United States, get it all banned as soon as possible. It took off, this ban-boxing palaver. But that was too general, not a sharp enough weapon to scrape me. So they had to find another one, Mina, each one failing to cut as they grasped and fumbled to get me, but I just wasn't out to be got.

They thought they'd found out when the film of the fight was ready to go. I'd make a good amount of money if it was released and there was a manic level of interest in it, all those people who had to rely on newspaper reports to explain what had happened, and for a few cents they could go in and take a seat and have it all unfold in front of them, like it was happening all over again. Not just a black audience – interest all round, people wanting to see for themselves how Jeffries had managed to lose, how I'd managed to beat him. But the do-gooders had mutated into a perverse cast of governors, mayors, ministers and somebody's idea of educationalists and they lobbied to get it banned. It would make black people feel unnaturally superior all over again, would rile us into believing ourselves more worthy than the white men we worked for if they saw me beating Jeffries to a pulp in theatres around the nation. And the more intensive the interest in the fight, theatres all over baying to get it, the more they twisted their little lace handkerchiefs in a knot and held tea-parties to plan how to stop it.

They lost. The film got shown everywhere, and I was a hero all over again, and not a riot or shooting or death happened in those later weeks and months. Just the tribe out on my warpath, out to show me I could only win the little battles. Like flooring Jim Jeffries. I'd have liked to see them do it. In Chicago, they said it, exactly it – better for Jack Johnson to win and a few blacks die in body than for Jack Johnson to lose and all blacks be killed in spirit. And that was it, Mina, that was it.

We celebrated for a long time though, and Tommy Austin's kid was the only thing really on my mind that wasn't buoyant and upbeat. I got mobbed everywhere I travelled, in Chicago, in Philadelphia, in New Orleans, San Francisco, Cleveland . . . but when I hit New York, hit the heart of the place with Grand Central Station thick with people, thousands of them with banners and signs and a band to guide me to my hotel on Herald Square, a whole cavalcade of automobiles honking their horns and sending off fireworks into the night – that's when it hit me how important what I'd done was, how I could have made the same money whipping some factory worker's ass to make my company rich, but who could buy this? Who could buy being a hero, being a god to this many people? It was frightening, like I was being trusted with everyone's savings, but not all the dollar bills in the world would have bought that sensation, like driving faster than is humanly possible and you're there doing it, you've the wind round you and the speedometer telling you and you just know there's never been a feeling like it ever before in the world.

I thought that all this would make me prime meat for vaudeville, that all the crowds coming to cheer me in every city would mean there'd be managers queuing round the block to have Jack Johnson, Heavyweight Champion of the World, starring on their bill, but it was like coming back from Australia all over again. The reason, they said, was that there would be riots at all the theatres I showed up in and nobody could risk getting their place torn apart for the sake of a few dollars' extra revenue. They told me to go away and take a rest, spend my money, and come back when the heat was off. Getting treated like that, rejected like that, when you had just taken on the world and stuffed it, it makes you angry.

It was a hard time then, when things were cooling down and people's lives getting back into shape, everyone's but mine. All the people I'd lived with in the training camp like Kid Cotton and Doc Furey and Sig Hart went back to their wives and kids and girlfriends, to their real lives, but I was still living mine there in some great big hole. I had nothing to do except take a casual stroll down a street I'd be recognised in and sign autographs and play with kids and drive too fast from New York to nowhere in particular and back again. I kept getting tickets and summons and trouble, but with the kind of money I had, they were sorted out easy enough. Etta was driving me mad, always there, always looking to be taken somewhere, shown something, spoiled . . . as if being free with my time made me her personal dream-maker. It came to a head when Nat Fleischer stopped by to do an interview, and I brought him up to the hotel suite I always had when I was in New York. But I hadn't sent a maid or a bell-boy or a winged goddess up to Etta in advance to warn her, as if I ever did, and when we walked into the suite she came out butt-naked into the room, and Nat stood there covering his eyes with his hat and Etta screeching and running to cover up and then coming back in a robe and lifting a chair, delicate little Etta, and flinging it into my back. I fell down, hurt, Nat helping me up into a chair, and it was sore, Mina, so damn painful I thought I'd broken half the bones in my back, and I was so angry.

I went to Atlantic City. I telegrammed Belle in Chicago to come and meet me, and she was there the next day, told Miss Painter, her boss, that she'd a sick uncle there who she had to see. After a few days I was bored with Belle and moved her to another hotel. I got a guy I knew there to line up a selection, and he'd bring them to me night after night, day after day, and I felt divine for those days, drinking and being treated like a god in the sunshine, and I got some of the old gang to come and join me there. We didn't do much, drank, played craps, had the women, and it was fun, like the old days before things became too complicated and hard to keep a balance on. But it got too much like a gang of diehards sitting chewing tobacco and getting old in their heads before their bodies had even caved in, it got boring. Word came from New York that the vaudeville might get going in a bit if I wanted to go on the road. I suppose I did. You know when you're restless, when nothing seems to settle you, and so I signed up and spent the next few months playing the bull-fiddle and telling my stories and calming down either Belle, who was still around, or Etta, who'd come after me and made up.

Now it was Belle who was driving me nuts. That too came to a head. She had this stupid runt of a dog somebody had given me as a present that I'd told her to get rid of but she'd decided to keep it and spent most days ordering room-service for a squirming flea-ridden animal a circus wouldn't have taken. We'd fought over it endlessly and fought over everything else too. Etta, money, how she thought I treated her. It was building. That night, as her voice got shriller and her face more twisted and filled with hate for me, I hit her hard across the face, then again across the mouth, and pulled her corset off, her stockings, garter belt, and hit her hard on her legs and breasts, the fury of her hating me, judging me, her a two-bit hooker I'd given the high-life to, an identity, a place in the world by my side. Her maid started screaming and I left, sick with the emptiness of all of it, of what it came down to, me always being something for everybody and giving it all and then just being seen for a fool at the end of it, seen for somebody you could yell at over a dog, always something to turn them, always a tiny thing to make them betray you. How was I to know how far Belle would turn, how far she'd go. It was more than a fight, it was a point where it all folds in on you, and she had been there, it had been her. It could have been anyone. Then maybe it was always going to be her. I went back to Etta, and told her it was over for good with Belle. We got gentle. I felt like taking care of her, like she was mine to protect, just for a while. But like always there's something comes along and catches you in its spokes.

I got guilty about Belle. I felt low that I'd lured her away from her job to be with me and got her fired. I sent her some money and told her to meet me in Chicago. She'd forgiven me, I'd thought. I didn't like the way she depended on others all the time to take her in, other people's brothels she earned for. I thought it'd be a good idea if I got her an apartment of her own to work from, and so we went looking and got a nice enough place in the Levee District in a place good enough to work but not so good that the neighbours would kick up a fuss and have her cleared out. We got new mattresses and easy-chairs, and some picturesque lady-screens, and two friends came in with her. They got a guy to supply them with beer, and in a couple of days she had her own little saloon and brothel all in one. It cost me a few thousand dollars, but it made me feel good, made me feel I was giving back something, all the times I'd gone too far and she'd stuck with me, it was a way of balancing our lives out, what they were at the time.

Etta and I got on well when I arrived back in New York. In thinking I had given Belle up for her, she felt more sure of me, I think, more able to be funny and strong rather than the screaming demanding troll she'd become when Belle was around. One thing Etta and I always shared was a passion for driving fast, too fast, the danger of speed as the unknown we would push automobiles into. I could always come home after crashing another new roadster and know she would care only for me, my safety, my nerve. Then we'd buy another one and test it together, go out at dawn on the roads, winding around the city, and push the car as fast as we could. It never seemed fast enough. She hated her sidecar element, seeing the rabbit and roadrunners we felled, whereas I saw nothing but the road ahead. What were they called before roads were built, that was a typical Etta question. But I couldn't let her drive and she never asked, not directly.

I challenged Barney Oldfield to a race that fall, and she was so excited as if she would be driving in it herself. Oldfield was the fastest driver in the world then, fearless and composed, and had never yet lost his nerve in any race. He had that ability to break the road the way I had to break a fighter, pushing past that conscious fear and into the next realm. I'd dreamt of racing him, and when it came up as a joke one day over craps, he said sure. Second word got out the American Automobile Association, his father and mother in most senses, said they'd throw him out if he dared race me, big coloured troublesome me, and Barney just laughed, announced there'd be three five-milers, best of three. I don't know if they ever did throw him out. For the AAA to kick out Barney Oldfield was a bit like those film people turfing out Mary Pickford. There was no Association if you took Barney out of the picture.

I trained and practised every day, switching between roadsters to find the fastest, and took them out on the track at Sheepshead Bay on Coney Island. Every day I raced myself round and round, every night I stood up and shadow-boxed again, played the fiddle, acted the dandy for them all. It was a groggy month, all wind and rain and danger for the driver, so we really discovered what those machines could do. Henry Ford should've hired me to test his engines – I knew more about what his cars could do than he did. I decided though on a big shiny red 90 HP Thompson Flyer for the race, and Oldfield got himself into a 60 HP Knox. My machine was far better than his, which put me in confident mood, and over five thousand people turned up to see it. Unfortunately. He got me on the turns in the first race, beat me by near on half a mile. Four minutes and forty-four seconds. Embarrassingly, he slowed a lot for the second race and still kicked my ass. I dawdled home compared to him, able for the speed but not the bends. I kind of felt sorry for myself after, felt a bit like a guy I'd pulverised in the ring, but we went out drinking after it and had a blast for three days. Oldfield was a very solid guy, fun and loose and mad, but always within himself a man of deep thought, I found. Whatever about me in the ring, on the road I was just another madman with big ideas. And as I always said to Etta, there can never be enough of those in any sport.

Things seemed to be going well for us then, but like always, it was a matter of when the mania began, and it did begin, harshly. On Christmas night that year I put Etta in hospital, a beating so bad I thought I'd killed her. Glass and a table-leg and pure blind anger, again over Belle, over me lying that I'd stopped seeing her. Sometimes I feel I'm the wrong man to be this strong, as if God made a mistake, gave me a power to feel such rage, and a power to orchestrate it, to do everything with it, even beat women I loved. After I took her to the hospital, I drove straight through the night to Belle, I had to see her, but she wasn't too pleased about it, and started in on me about being the number two, always the one in reserve, in the shoddy hotel, the worst room. I bundled her into the car and drove right back, took her into that hospital and showed her a worse room, a worse hotel. Etta, unconscious, wrapped and bandaged and tubed, and Belle understood. There was nothing worse or better than being with me, but if pushed the anger did dangerous things. I didn't want to hurt her. I could control the anger outside when the taunts and insults barraged me, when the hatred came – all the while I'd smile and wave and smile some more and act above it all, but at home it couldn't be like that, not always. Things happened in me, a rage only part connected to the irritation the women fired up. And Etta was proof of it. Belle was warned.

Etta forgave me. It might have been the stupidest thing she ever did, given what happened, but I took her on holiday, told her how I loved her, and when we came to Pittsburgh we got married. A fit of fun and a way of giving her what she wanted, I thought. Who knows what Etta was thinking, she didn't look like she did that much of it, but something must have gone on behind those big tragic eyes. Mrs Jack, the very first.

A few months after I married her I decided we would go to England, see what kind of fighters they had there. I was in strange form, wanting to fight but wanting to sit back and enjoy the money, the attention and the supremacy I'd fought all those years to get. But I kept getting into trouble, got put in jail for a month after me and an automobile guy had a race through Golden Gate Park and they did me for reckless driving. Got the pair of us going at 62 m.p.h. Seems crazy now. All those tanks and super engines and me in jail for a speeding offence. Sure they let my meals come from the hotel, and Etta got in a few nights a week, but it felt like I was being held up by amateurs and still couldn't break free. We all knew it was a trumped-up charge, and there was plenty more to follow. Got done for having the wrong licence plate in the wrong state, for driving too slow, driving too fast, for not paying some two-bit artist who'd decided I'd asked him to do a sculpture of me. They did me for everything and anything, even trying to pin underage sex on me, with some dancer in one of the vaudeville shows. Hell, I had so many of them, they were part of the job, half of them lying about their age to get work in the shows. But that upset Etta, and the cops upset me, so we decided we'd sail to England and have a long trip away from it all.

We took two of the cars, and some people to drive them, a couple more to spar with, to take care of things for us, but really it was an adventure for me and Etta, a honeymoon, I guess. There was a king to be crowned, and we liked the idea of a bit of real pomp and ceremony. So we sailed in time for the Coronation of King George, and in my head I planned to crown another one, to fight the famous Bombardier Wells in London and make my name resonate both sides of the ocean. We had plans . . . Monte Carlo, Paris, Venice, Rome . . . to take it all as we found it and have a majestic time of it. We couldn't have imagined a place so empty and fickle, unworthy of everything thought of it in America, the glory and culture, the grace of the people, their intelligence – all absolute garbage. Coarse, thick fools, well, most of them. The ones in power.

It started off a dream. I was booked into the Oxford Music-Hall and the critics went into raptures at how witty and modest and entertaining I was. I just did the usual, the shadow-boxing, the stories, a few songs, some jokes about Americans to ease them up a bit.

The Jeffries fight had been huge news in Britain – everywhere I went in the early weeks people stopped me in the street to shake my hand, to measure themselves up against me, to compliment me on my beautiful wife. I was more popular than King George for a bit. Parties and balls and country houses, even the ex-King of Portugal came to watch me spar and chat and tell me how much he admired my strength of character. People said that a lot. Great strength of character,

Mr Johnson, to survive such malice. You know how they are. Sorry, I forget, you're English. But you don't count, Mina, you aren't like them in any way.

So, on the surface everything seemed pretty good. I announced that any fighter in Europe who could put up thirty thousand dollars could fight me. Bombardier Wells didn't let me down. He was up for it, for a big loud title fight, and we both started training, invited in the press to watch and take photographs and talk and set the fire going round England. Oh and it blazed. Too, too hot, all the attention on the fight between a black man and a white. I was the downfall of crisp old aristocratic Britain, me, I had my eye on tearing down the great society of knowing one's place that made Britain great. I was scum, I was to be stopped, the fight stopped, footage of all my fights stopped. Britain wore white lace gloves and there I was going to soil them. Oh it got me angry. Jeffries all over again, only even more inane, even more reactionary and ignorant, and hell, I just felt above it all, I hadn't gone through all that shit over Jeffries and kept my head high to come to some foreign country and entertain them just to get this sort of a run-in. They got churchmen and Parliament guys and high-school teachers and aristocrats and parents to put more and more pressure on the Government to get it cancelled. It would only go getting us negroes passionate, that was the story they had, we'd want to think for ourselves and stop tying other people's shoelaces for a living. Well, hell. America nearly seemed welcoming for a minute or two.

All this over two grown men having an organised official title fight. It hit the desk of the guy in charge, and he got scared and ran off to Scotland to avoid making a decision. There we were, me and Wells, training up for this fight while he cowered in some grand estate, but the bastards went crazy, chased the guy down from Scotland, got him to sign their bit of paper and that was it, we were banned from fighting. Banned. First and last time that's ever happened in that country of yours, Mina. Never again did they give a shit who fought who, except when Jack Johnson came to town. And you know the name of that coward who signed away our rights? Winston Churchill. The big hero, the visionary, the man, he was on his way up to the job then, almost there, Home Secretary, on his way to fame and posterity and all the praise a man is fit to hear in his lifetime, and there he was, too scared to stand up for what was right. We went to court over it, and I knew who'd win it but it had to go on the record, and I told them why. Why it was racism and fear and crazy hypocrisy that had our fight banned, why these people were the destroyers, not the builders, why I had earned that right, the right to travel to their country a World Champion and expect to fight the best guy they had to offer. Fear, Mina, such fear. They saw what I did to America, how I showed kids what happens when you don't take the shit but get up and go after something. I inspired fear, and you know I think long-term I got more satisfaction out of that. Me. Screw England. They sure as hell weren't going to call my tune.

The English lost the gleam in their eye because I wasn't Mister Hey Ho Have A Laugh, all jokes and modesty. No. I was mad as hell and saying so all round me. Couldn't wait for me to leave was how the papers put it, and believe me, Mina, I sure as hell didn't want to stay. I know exactly why you got out. We shipped out in time for Christmas, six months of glory and worship and ugly politics, but I stood my ground, and came back with my head held high as ever. Banning fights was nothing new. It'd take a hell of a lot more than that. How was I to know that was exactly what America had in store for me? When we got back I was bored. I wanted fights. I wanted to show why I was the Champion, to quit this pussyfooting around and get in the ring. Nobody was fit to get in with me though, they tried to find anyone big and able to take me on, but one man had kept pulping the hopefuls while I was away, until eventually some bright spark suggested he be the one to take me on himself. And that was how I came to fight Jim Flynn.

While Flynn was getting his name about for the title, the authorities were back on my case. I'd got Etta this diamond necklace back in London, a beauty that cost me six thousand dollars, and she'd stored it in her jewellery case and said nothing more about it to the import guys when we sailed into New York. There were a lot of the crowd out to get me, ones who thought, that year, maybe I was a bit uppity and loud for a black guy, all I did was throw a few punches for a living.

Generally they were guys whose wives I'd slept with or who I'd punched about when I got drunk, or poked fun at. The ones who thought they were delicate and put-upon and reckoned one call to the Treasury Department would put me back in my box. Well, it turns out there were a few calls made and suddenly the necklace was swiped by the officials, I was told to pay up nine thousand six hundred dollars in duty and then, then me and Etta were indicted for smuggling. Something was up. Before anything came of it though, I'd be allowed to fight Flynn. As if Jim Flynn would get in the way of anything.

Flynn was short, fat, and mean as they came. Things got so nasty in his camp that his trainer Tommy Ryan threw in the towel and said Flynn wasn't training to fight, he was training to foul. We all knew we weren't in the same class, and this time out nobody even pretended we were, but he was as close as they could bring to a contender so there we had him, old Jim Flynn training how to hit a man in the balls and get away with it instead of how to break down my defence. How could you take him seriously?

The papers that supported me started calling Flynn the Titanic, saying he'd go down just like that big unsinkable white-man ship had done less than two months before. If I'd been white with this much money and free time, I'd have been on that ship, Mina. No doubt. Right up my alley, a thing like that. They were writing songs about me and naming babies after me, and there was Flynn scampering about asking that he be shot in the head if he lost to me. If. I'd have done it for him if he'd asked.

I wasn't in shape, London and Paris had their effect and I really hadn't been inclined to undo it for the sake of Jimmy Flynn. It didn't make much difference. On the day, 4 July 1912, another Independence Day, he flailed about and swung like a mill-wheel, arms going mad, body rigid and squat, and I beat him like I was some sick father attacking his small fat son for not helping out around the house. You could see his mouth was ripped open inside and he was drinking his own blood like he had a siphon open in his gullet. I pushed out my belly and asked him did he want to compare, mine was so flat and smooth and hard, did he want to show me his? And he belted away at my belly-button and I stood over him laughing to the crowd. What there was of one. Jeffries had taught them that you had to be something else to lay a glove on me, and whatever else Flynn was as he fluffed away on my belly, he wasn't something else. Something maybe. So the crowds had stayed away, not wanting to encourage me in a fight that the whole world knew I couldn't lose. As if showing up would sway it in any way.

It was less than three-quarters full, the least exciting fight in the history of boxing, I'd guess. So I'd chat away idly to Sig Hart and Etta and the ringsiders and all the while Flynn was bent double trying to beat my stomach into submission. He got more and more frustrated, swearing and trying to jut his head in under my chin like a lunatic ram and then jump up into the air, ideally hitting my jaw with his skull. Gorgeous move. Unfortunately I wasn't that stupid, nor the referee that dumb. The referee was Ed Smith, a man you stay on the good side of, and when he started warning Flynn to fight clean or be disqualified, Flynn spun round and launched in on him how I was holding him, how I'd clamped my fist on his shoulder like this, and proceeded to demonstrate the whole fictitious thing on Smith's shoulder. Never touch a referee. Smith started to smoulder. I stood back laughing, and Flynn got more and more het up. It was the stupidest fight in boxing. Smith ordered that the fight continue, and I just kept on thumping

Flynn, he kept on bleeding, and it all ran along like a dependable train. Etta got excited. By the eighth Flynn had been warned six times by Smith to fight fair, but still he kept up his big lumpen pirouetting to try and shake me, jumping two feet in the air to smack me on the top of my head and fighting slapstick. I just kept jabbing, kept landing the uppercuts and catching him on the solar plexus as he came down, making him bloodier and more savaged-looking after every punch.

In the ninth he caught my jaw in a misfired headbutt, and Smith stood looking confused till a guy shot in the air and climbed in the ring and stopped the fight. Of course, officially, he had no right at all, but this was boxing. He got Flynn out of there, and lifted my arm up and Smith just stood there like he thought the shot had been aimed at him while everybody in the crowd either booed or, occasionally, cheered for me, and in an hour we were in a bar drinking bourbon like the fight had never happened. Flynn had stitches sewn in just about every bit of gum and cheek he'd bared for me, and never really fought a fight that big again in his life, just slid slowly downwards till he finally retired, broken and broke.

Of course the fact that hardly anyone had showed up to watch it didn't stop everyone in sight having an opinion on it. I'd deliberately disfigured Flynn, they said, deliberately roughed him up. Well, hell, like he'd been out for a stroll and ended up by accident in a World Heavyweight title fight. As if boxing was about who could wear the prettiest trunks. But they went after me all over again, and this time they scored, just slightly. They got Congress to ban the transportation of fight films interstate just so no one could get to see me duffing up another precious white man, another pounding. So we didn't get a whole lot of money for that film, but by then there were worse things happening, things that change lives, and end them.

They delayed the diamond trial. That would come later. After Etta, before Belle had started her party tricks. The real effort had begun to get me, to nail Jack Johnson, Heavyweight Champion of the World, with something stronger than the force of fists. The law.

Did I care. As far as I was concerned it was all speeding tickets and a diamond necklace. I was on a high. I'd shown London, come home, gone headlong into a title fight, kicked Flynn's ass, and I was the indisputable Champion of the World, rich and with time on my hands. I nailed the bastards who'd shopped me to the tax authorities, then settled down with my real friends and we planned ourselves the biggest, grandest, most luxurious club in the land, a place a man could come and eat the finest food, drink the finest wine, have the best brandy, see the best musicians play, and come like a thoroughbred. The Café du Champion, a place for heroes.

By then I had two jealous wives, one legal and one Belle. Maybe I should have married her instead of Etta. It didn't matter much, from both I got the same incessant carping, each about the other. So I got a new steady woman, one who was working right under their noses. Lucille genteel Cameron, a pleasant-looking girl from the club. So there we had Etta on the top floor, in our apartment, Lucille on the ground floor in the club, and Belle in Pittsburgh for any time, often, I felt like getting in my cars and racing away for a while. I had Etta and Belle so irritated by each other I don't think it occurred to them that I might have other trees planted too.

It wasn't life though. It was this routine of game-playing, of being the loud character able to tell stories and relive the fights. There was such an absence that not the club or Etta nor Belle nor Lucille nor the cars filled. I'd wake hungry and then have nothing to go and feast on, no fight to prepare for, nothing to focus my head and rally it, enrage it.

All the usual barrage of death threats and insult came and went every day, but there was no payback, no way of getting out there, getting at them all. I fought too much, with friends, with unwary customers, with suppliers, with Etta. I was a businessman now, a proud profile of how to use your money to realise your dreams, and your talent to realise your money. I was idolised, and so, so bored, Mina, so desperate for a shake-up, a fight, a new thing, anything, something to put passion and energy and hope into. I was ready for the world more completely than at any time in my life, and the world didn't seem to give a damn. So I did the things a person does when they are bored. I got Lucille, I drove too fast, got more cops on my back, I travelled a lot to see Belle, I beat up people I shouldn't have, I bought things I didn't particularly want, I drank a lot, I just got more and more bored trying to avoid boredom. It was bound to erupt.

When that bullet shattered the browbone over her right eye, took everything with it, Mina, none of the glory mattered a damn to anyone after that. Or if it did, it mattered the wrong way. America turned on me after Etta, this great country you've just signed up for, hell, it knows how to spit on its own far better than it knows how to fête them. Don't get comfortable, she'll turn on you like a vengeful snake if you do her wrong. I don't suppose you will though. Nor me any more. Our time is up on all that. And thing is, Mina, I love this damn country despite all the shit it's thrown at me. I pretend like exile was the best time I ever had, but it was here I wanted to be the whole time. It was Cravan who got me through. Hadn't been for him, I might have gone back with my tail between my legs. Then again, I couldn't have done that, couldn't have given the Feds the satisfaction.

At least you only have two marriages down, and one of those was the real thing. Here I am on number three and counting. I do love Irene, she's a great woman, and for the moment everything is rolling along just fine, but we'll see. I've had the stupidest reasons for marrying, mainly because who I married pissed folk off mightily. Lucille was the one that really got them. They even kept her in jail so she wouldn't be able to run away with me.

When Etta died, Lucille comforted me, spent a lot of time with me. She was fun. Nothing seemed to ruffle her, and in a girl of nineteen, that is a rare quality. She wasn't giddy like the others, she stood her ground, but always knew how to make you feel in charge, even when you knew she had you round her little finger. I liked being with her. It was as simple as that.

Then some wise-guy reporter put it in that Jack Johnson's grief was as hollow as you'd expect from a murdering nigger cheat, that it was an open secret that I was bedding a prostitute called Lucille Cameron, and I had been since before Etta's body went cold. That's the sort of shit I was always getting. It stung, of course it did, but in the end anybody I cared about knew it for the horse-shit it was. All the rest didn't matter a damn.

But one person it did matter to was Mrs F. Cameron-Falconer. She showed up one day at the club screeching for her daughter to come out this instant. When Lucille went out to her, the madwoman tried to force her into a waiting car and drive away with her. Fortunately she failed, or maybe unfortunately, the trouble that old crone started on me. She hadn't been very well acquainted with what her daughter did for a living, believing Lucille's sweet little letters about the trials of a young stenographer's lot. As far as Lucille was concerned, she was sending home money. How she got it was none of her mother's business. Then mama went and read the paper. If she was horrified to read of her daughter's profession, it was nothing in comparison to the photograph they printed of Lucille on my arm. Her precious child with a black man? How dare they. So she came to mount the rescue operation.

Some mothers might have been placated with a few large brandies, a look inside their daughter's secretarial bureau, a tour of the club and a good dinner. Not Mrs F. Cameron-Falconer. I had lured, nay duped, her precious virgin into evil and perverse ways. I must be made to pay.

Which is how, two days later, I came to be served with a warrant for my arrest on the grounds of abduction, brought by the alleged abductee's mother. I got taken to the station, and three hours later was out on an eight hundred-dollar cash bond. It was as familiar to me as the smell of sweat, after all the speeding charges, the traffic violations, the accusations of brawling, the bending of the licensing laws, the gaming laws, you name it. It was procedure. But this procedure was to wreck my life for ever and I had not a clue.

From the second that the Bureau of Investigation had got wind of the claims being made by Lucille's mother, they began to loop the noose. They smelt the Mann Act, thought they had a tidy violation that would enable them to collar me once and for all. The Mann Act is the most ludicrous reactionary moralising law in legal history. You might even get a few lawyers to agree with me, for it is the law of the self-righteous. They decided they could use Lucille to do me under it. What I had basically done was drive Lucille places I was going to. I had driven her in my car. What the Mann Act said a man could not do was to transport a woman interstate 'for the purpose of prostitution or debauchery, or for any other immoral purpose'. That meant any man who took any woman who was not his wife across interstate lines and had sex with her was up for arrest, trial and sentencing. Half the damn country was up for it. But they only wanted to pick on one person, Mina, me.

The law was so stupid it was only used to curtail pimps from moving their operations into different states, and stop them thinking they had the better of the government. You had to be a pretty big viceroy to get done for the Mann. Or else you had to be a black man, with a penchant for white women and big fat world titles. When Lucille's mother hit the scene, they thought all their pay-days had come at once.

When it rocketed into the press that I had been arrested for violation of the Mann Act, every lowlife in America crawled out of hibernation. They'd had nothing much to do after I won the title, and Etta's suicide had only brought out the reactionaries. The hardcore stayed at home. Driving home from the club one night after I was released on bond, I hit into a mob who were burning a stuffed sack effigy of me on a long pole. They thronged the car, surged forward with the bastard thing blazing, but I was able to turn as I saw them and drive well away. Still, it shook me. All over the city people were doing the same, celebrating the news that Jack Johnson was going down. Everywhere friends asked was it true, had they got me, and I laughed it off. But the bastards were out and I should have seen it coming. Something massive was up.

Lucille was a revelation. I liked her a lot, but in the way I had liked many others before her. Certainly there was more between Belle and me than there ever was between myself and Lucille, but it was she who stood by me. They took her away from the Café, and held her in Rockford prison as a witness, prevented from speaking to friends or newsmen, and most of all, to me. Her mother and all the papers were spreading these great stories that Lucille had been an innocent thumb-sucking farm girl who had come to the big smoke to become a stenographer, meet a good man, and settle down as a mother and wife. Then she had met me. I had gotten her drunk, absolved her of her virginity, and besmirched her reputation for ever. In doing so, I had infringed the Mann Act, taking her from Chicago to Minneapolis purely to impose my perversions on her innocence. For this I must go to prison.

When Lucille took the stand, she knew she was about to blow them out of the water. They asked her with great big grins on their faces if she could please tell the court of how she had been purloined by Mr Johnson's pimps and brought to his club where she was forced to do unspeakable things and, degraded, had allowed herself to be coerced into a life of prostitution and ruin. She smiled sweetly and detailed how she had been a prostitute since she was sixteen years old, had worked out of the oldest brothel in Minneapolis, had come to Chicago and worked in several houses before moving to the Café de Champion a few months earlier because the treatment was regal and the pay was fair. She explained in detail about the letters she had been sending home filled with news of her life as a stenographer, and apologised to her mother for lying. However, she said, she had fallen in love with me the moment she saw me, and loved me very deeply. I had never done her any harm, and had shown her only kindness. I was, she said, still in profound mourning for my first wife and was the most loving man she had ever encountered. At that she began crying and eventually had to be carried out of court in a hysterical fit. I was bowled over in admiration.

They took her back to Rockford to maintain the pretence of a case, but there was none. She was utterly useless to them. They had known they were going after me on trumped-up charges, but so zealous had they been when Lucille's mother had shown up, they had neglected that small detail of building a case. And so, they had gone to court, before a Grand Jury, and been left for fools.

In any other circumstance they would have conceded defeat and walked away. Not with me. The public thought Jack Johnson was going down, and they would not react very happily to the idea that I in fact had got the better of them all, and was going no further than my vacation. So the Bureau decided to trawl every last detail of my past. All my sexual history, all the travelling I'd ever done, reckoning that somewhere along the line the Mann Act must have been trampled on just a little bit.

Two things I loved – women and fast cars – were the two things that, with a bit of interstate mileage, combined to do me. While the Bureau went about gathering a new case, I lobbied to get Lucille out of prison. She was there for no other reason than her mother and the law thought that it would prevent her from returning to me. But they continued to keep her. Still smitten by her loyalty, and in the mood to annoy the whole damn lot of them, I let it be known that the minute she got out, I was going to marry her. Mrs Lucille Johnson. That riled the entire country. Doing it once was an outrage, but making a second white woman my wife? There had to be laws about that. So they kept Lucille away and Congress went all out to make it illegal for interracial marriages in every state it was allowed, including Illinois. The shit was well and truly rising to the top.

But Lucille was their decoy. In all their stone-turning they'd come up with the real gold. Belle. They'd heard all about her from Sig Hart, my old manager, and, I thought, one of my oldest friends. He'd been around in some form or other from the start, from before Tommy Burns. Now he'd turned snitch. Me in my ignorance had him round to the big party I threw when Lucille had stumped the Feds. He got so drunk he ended up sleeping where Lucille was supposed to, me there on the other side not even realising when I woke up next day that I was lying beside the little bastard who would bring me down. Up he got, came over with the rest of the people fallen round the house, helped me open up the club, and sat at the free bar all day long. All day long, Mina, and there he was watching and spying and stealing my friendship like he was in a jewel heist. Well, he told them all about Belle. How she was my regular woman for the past few years, how I depended on her, how I'd gotten her out of a bad brothel and set her up on her own, how she travelled almost everywhere I did, either in the car beside me, or by railcar to meet me, with money I'd wire to her. Sig did most of the wiring for me. Most of the calls to her too if I had to go on stage or fight, or entertain, but would want her there to talk to later. That was the thing. Sex was there, of course it was, and she was good, but it was the way Belle's mind worked, that powerful lack of need, always sure of what she thought, scared of nothing I did, anyone did, an absolute piece of granite when it came to sentiment, but as sharp as flint. She had such a brain, Mina, you would have liked her, not at first, you would have sized each other up and seen there was no getting past either of you, but with time you'd have seen what was so great about her. Anybody can be good at sex if they're a pro. Lucille was great. But when I'd be in my dressing-room ready to go and jazz it up for the vaudeville crew, I wanted Belle there when I came off. And most times, thanks to Sig, she'd be there.

They tracked her down to a brothel in Washington on D Street. Sig was with them. He told her the story, all about Lucille's testimony, how they wanted me done. But there was no need to convince her of anything. She had been waiting for them. She read the papers, she knew all about it. And knew all about my declaration of love for Lucille. If I was going to marry Lucille Cameron, she was going to testify to anything they wanted to hear. And that was when the noose first started getting tight.

There I was thinking there was nothing to get worked up about. I'd been up on charges from the day I was legal, and since I'd had money there was nothing that couldn't be arranged, or unarranged as the case may be. Then word came down about Sig. Then Belle. Sig was cut loose by the Feds, and disappeared. If I'd tried, I'd have found him, but I'd more on my mind. I've a feeling some of the others looked him up and gave him a going over, but it was a story that never came out of the same mouth twice, or sober.

Belle was protected. Every time we got a handle on where she was, they'd move her. We put word out that there was a ten thousand-dollar reward for finding her, but the Feds moved her round like a dolly-cart – Washington, Baltimore, New York, Chicago. I found out afterwards that the whole time I had my eye focused on getting Lucille out, a good month before I heard about Sig or Belle, Belle was secretly brought before a Grand Jury and made to tell her stories about life with me.

I've seen the testimony, Mina, I got it smuggled out when I got back to America and was still obsessed with the case. Did she do a job on me – every single occasion we had ever met, she listed. Towns I'd forgotten I'd been to, hotels I couldn't remember staying in, fights I didn't even remember her being at, training camps I thought I'd had Etta at, but it was all true.

She'd told them every intimate detail, my preferences in bed, the times when I had more than one woman in bed with me, the times I had hit her, every second of pleasure we had enjoyed, every dress I bought her, every drink, every meal, every journey we took together.

And it was that that did me. She could remember every single journey we had gone on together. As if I would take Belle, or anyone I was sleeping with, into a different state purely to have sex with her. It was by the by, like saying I had driven her from Illinois to Minneapolis just to have dinner with her, just to walk next to her, to have a drink with her. Foolishness.

But it was enough. They only needed one incident, and Belle gave them a thousand. The one they chose I couldn't even remember, a trip we made from Pittsburgh to Chicago. She'd stayed with me for four days, then got a railcar home, she said. The reason for her journey was, she testified, precisely for the purposes of prostitution. And so they hooked me.

They arrested me on 7 November 1912. A few of the guys were there with me and tried to rough them up, but in the end I went quietly enough. I still reckoned a few well-placed dollars would sort the whole thing out, so I called Sol Lewinsohn, a bondsman who could both bail me out and arrange for some envelopes to pass hands.

They asked me did I know Belle. I said most men I knew did. So they asked me again, and I said sure I did. It was after midnight before I got out, but the next day came the hearing, and after that they put me in jail. The judge hated me, told me as much, which was why they changed their minds on bail. That prison was a filthy place. Second I was brought down all the other five hundred prisoners started yelling 'Lynch the nigger, Lynch the nigger' till there was a near riot with metal food bowls banging on the bars and the wardens unable to put any sort of calm on it. So they moved me into the hospital wing.

I got out after a week. Once I got out, they had to let Lucille go too, as it was pretty obvious with Belle in the witness box that there was no need for her any longer. I married Lucille two days later at the house in Chicago. My mother was there, though you can bet hers wasn't. At the time I did love her. I liked her company, and she had a good spirit, fun and loyal and interested in everything that went on around her. She also didn't care about money the way Belle and Etta had. She appreciated presents, rather than expected them. It was an attractive characteristic in a life where everybody seemed to want a piece of you for free.

Of course when word got out that I'd gone ahead and married Lucille, the country went into uproar. Nothing I wasn't used to. The lowlifes had stayed out above ground and were ready to attack. They tried it in a hundred different ways. First of all, my licence was taken off me for the club. That made it illegal to sell a drop of alcohol. If it had happened a year before, I'd have kept on going and put the necessary faces in the pay-off frame, but now things were different. Now I was on bail. The boards went up on the club three weeks later, the Rembrandts put in store along with the crystal and the chandeliers and the velvet sofas. To my mind it was temporary, till this thing blew over, but that was the end of the club. It was the thing in my life that had given me most pride, and most happiness, after boxing. That it was where Etta had shot herself did not matter. It broke my heart to close it.

In Congress the fire went up in the Southern politicians, with that old fool Rodenberry insisting that a constitutional amendment be introduced that forbade white women from being 'corrupted by a strain of kinky-headed blood', and said that the laws that allowed me to marry white women if I wanted were pure villainous. This was the level bastards like Rodenberry worked from. And it did nearly work, Mina. After I married Lucille, twenty-one bills were introduced to Congress to try and ban interracial marriage. Twenty-one. In ten of the states where it wasn't already illegal, they tried to overturn the law and make miscegenation a crime. Lord knows how, none of them became law, but they were really out to get me, to get at this great big symbol they'd turned me into.

I was angry that I wasn't able just to get on with being Jack Johnson the Champion of the World, I had to be Jack Johnson the anti-Christ. Every damn thing that went wrong had to be my fault somehow. And to prove it they were going to send me to jail, not for actually doing anything, just because they decided they'd found a law that let them. They built their case.

After the club was closed, I decided I'd had enough. I wanted to escape. I trusted almost no one by then, the Sig Hart thing had made me sharp, but I did trust Lucille, and I did trust my valet Joe Levy. I got Joe to get three first-class tickets to Toronto, and to ship two of my best cars on ahead across the border under a different name. One night that January we got the midnight train to Battle Creek, Michigan, where the Toronto train was scheduled to stop around 3 a.m. By 5 a.m. the bastards had me in jail. There had been a tip-off at the Chicago end.

Now I decided I could trust nobody. Well, Lucille, but nobody else. I didn't really believe it had been Joe, but I couldn't risk it again. I decided to keep my head down, arouse no suspicion, and see what happened at the trial.

It made a joke of American justice from start to finish. The jury was a lovely combination of white Republicans, white Episcopalians, white picket-fence businessmen, white teetotallers, white anti-sportsmen. All male. It was a handpicked jury, a total whitewash of faces that made the Feds wet their pants in glee. The Fed lawyer came in and in his opening statement told everybody I was a sodomising, wifebeating bastard who deserved to at least be put in jail for ever before I inflicted myself on any other unfortunate white women. Or words to that effect. He said I'd lured Belle from Pittsburgh to Chicago for utterly immoral purposes, and that I had to go down as I had clearly broken the terms of the Mann Act.

Then my guy came on. Useless damn defence lawyer, the most expensive I could get, and useless for it. His argument was that sure I'd had a lot of sex with the woman, hell, she was a prostitute, wasn't she? A man like me attracted a lot of women – thank God Lucille wasn't in court to hear this – and Belle was known to have a fondness for negro men. Yet the Mann Act had come into effect on 1 July 1910, and by then the affair was entirely over. Legally speaking I had not broken the law for the law did not exist at the time of my relationship with Belle.

This is what I mean about him being a horse-shit lawyer, Mina. There he had it in a nutshell, the perfect argument. Yes, officially Mr Johnson did bring Miss Schreiber over state lines and have frequent intercourse with her, but the Mann Act did not exist at the time he was doing it, so he did nothing whatsoever that was illegal. End of story. But not my guy. A little strong-arm stuff from Parkin, the Fed lawyer, and Bachrach, my guy, was fluttering all over the place picking up whatever crumbs of an argument he could find. Every time Parkin got on a roll, Bachrach would leap up and shout 'Objection', have it overruled and turn to me proudly like he'd just flummoxed the courtroom with his brilliance.

The brilliance was on the other side. From a dead-end position after Lucille had crumbled their case, they had put together an amazing final show in the long-running series Jack Johnson is a Bad Bastard. Up popped Mervin my old chauffeur to say not only had he driven me and Belle interstate, he'd seen us having sex in the back of the car through his wing mirror. The hard-faced old bitch Belle had worked for before she met me came on and said that I had forced Belle out of her employ where she had been house favourite, and made her come to Chicago to work for me. Such crap. She'd begged me to get her out and I'd sent her money to come and stay, then gone off and got her her own place for her and her friends to work from. So then they pulled in the guy who had been Belle's landlord at the apartment who testified that all the rent was paid in from my account like clockwork, and she was obviously working for me.

Then on came the queen herself, all dressed in red silk, done up like royalty. She wouldn't look down at me, not even on the side of the courtroom where I was sitting, her chin up like she was announcing the winner of a presidential vote. I might as well have been in China for all it registered in her. She had given as evidence the great big cookery book full of every press cutting ever featuring Mr Jack Johnson and friend, companion Ms Belle Schreiber, every photograph ever published, as if I was denying I knew the damn woman, when in fact my point was that half of Pittsburgh and the municipal borough of Chicago knew her just as well as I did, and paid well for her company.

She sat there answering the most intimate details about us, where and how and how often we had made love, when I had hit her, what gratified me most in bed, what abuse I had inflicted on her, how I had forced her to leave Pittsburgh and move into an apartment so I could have her all to myself. How I got into jealous rages, how I told stories about how I'd beaten up my wife, boasted to her, taken her to see Etta in hospital after I'd put her there. It went on and on, with Bachrach bouncing up and down every few seconds shouting 'Objection' until the judge, the Feds, the crowd, the twelve members of the jury and even me, rolled our eyes every time he stood up.

Then they let her down off the stand, and as she walked past the bench she looked right at me and with her thumb and forefinger made a ring around her wedding finger. Then she smiled and sauntered on, content in the knowledge that whatever my guilt, that jury would damn me for so much as knowing a woman as filthy as Belle. To think that marrying her was all it would have taken to prevent it all. It wouldn't have been much of a hardship either, though if I found her these days it'd probably be because I tripped over her in the street wrapped in a dirty blanket, that is, if syphilis didn't catch her first. And yet she was all it took to bring a great man down in the eyes of the world. One bright, pox-ridden prostitute with a grudge to bear. She was all it took.

They ran a few more faces past the jury, Belle's maid Julia who'd been there when I lost my temper at Belle and tore off her undergarments, and who'd picked up the money each time I wired it. Hattie, who'd been in on it all for a while as well, a few other women I'd had passing acquaintance with. Not a lot more was needed after Belle's sparkling character witness. When it came to my turn to take the stand, I was calm. I knew it was a lost cause, so there was nothing they could say to me that I couldn't answer with my full dignity. They asked me about my affairs, and the women I consorted with. I explained that it came with a fighter's territory. When Parkin tried to insinuate I had been involved in faked fights, and had dived, I suggested that, having not lost a single fight since a fluke punch hit me back in 1905, he could tell me exactly when these dives were supposed to have taken place. That shut him up for a minute.

Then he bounced back asking about Etta. It was overruled. About my wife-beating. I said all fighters were labelled wife-beaters as if they couldn't leave their work at the office like everybody else. But you can't, Mr Johnson, he said gleefully, you don't have one. So I asked him did he go home each night and interrogate his wife, did he shout 'Objection' at his children when they played too loudly, and he laughed and moved on, but I said, No, Mr Parkin, do you interrogate your wife each evening about her day? Of course not, he said. And I do not go twenty rounds with my wife, I said. The questioning ended there.

The jury were sent out at 10 p.m. At ten-fifty they returned with an eight/four verdict in favour of my conviction. The judge sent them back. Twenty minutes later, probably in a bid to get to bed for the night, they came back with the same verdict, expecting to be sent to a hotel until morning. But they were sent back. At eleven forty-five they came back with the verdict. Unanimous. 'We the jury, find the defendant, John Arthur Johnson, guilty as charged in the indictment.' Well, hell, what a surprise.

Pandemonium broke out as journalists raced to file their copy and hold the front page. Parkin started his press conference while the jury foreman exhaled the last syllable of the judgement. He said it was my 'misfortune' to be the foremost example of the evil that was interracial marriage, and this victory would reverberate world-wide and would force the banning of interracial marriages such as mine. I lifted my cane from the desk and walked through his entourage, knocking over two journalists and a prosecution clerk as I did, but on he went, how I would have been so much better off if I stayed penniless and happy rather than trying to be the big guy, needing to win. I gave out hell on the courthouse steps, how it was a disgrace and my legal team would ensure it was overturned, and then I went home to the woman they thought was my greatest sin. She was crying, the house already full of gloaters pretending to commiserate, journalists looking for the defiant talk, the pictures of me and Lucille, trading stories about the case as if they were in the newsroom and I was the cleaner. I got rid of all of them. But first I gave them the defiant talk, the pictures of me and my beautiful white wife, said I was far from beat, even played along with the frauds who were pretending to be my friends, not one of which I could trust any more. Then I broke down with Lucille and my mother, and tried to think of how the hell I could get myself out of this one.

I didn't show I was shook to anyone else. I drove around too fast like I always did, ran lights, bought drinks, ate out every night. I did this for a month until the day of sentencing came. When it did no one was happy. The maximum was five years and/or a ten thousand-dollar fine. What he gave me was one year and one day, and a one thousand-dollar fine. To the Feds it was leniency, to the judge an example had been made of me.

To me it was the final straw. I had had enough. One year in prison for daring to marry who I wished, fight who I wished, spend my money as I wished. Do you remember I told you they threw Cravan out of Berlin because they said he was too conspicuous? Well, that was exactly what they did me for. If I'd just shut-up and stayed broke and patronised, I'd have been all right. But I had to go and become Champion of the World. I had to go and beat them.

I wasn't going to let them put me away for it. No matter the cost. I set up four escape routes and leaked three of them through my 'friends'. While trains were being searched and highways scoured, I was driving calmly through Canada. I left five days earlier than I'd leaked in the other plans, with two tickets to Le Havre via Montreal. That way, even though my conviction was non-extraditable, the Canadians couldn't be persuaded to hand me over under that discreetly vague catch-all of 'undesirable citizen'. I was merely an alien crossing Canada *en route* to France. My ticket proved it. I was free.

It was only when the ship docked in France and we disembarked that I really believed it. I truly was free. But for the privilege I was now an exile from my own country. I had had no time to think of the consequences, only that if I escaped I would not go to prison. There had been nothing else to consider as far as I could see. But what was I coming to? What was here? A few casual acquaintances and a language I couldn't speak? I was panicked so badly in those first days, Lucille had to take care of me so well. Then I decided to quit the self-pity and enjoy myself. The trial cost me a hundred and thirty-eight thousand dollars, but I reckoned I was still rich.

We'd get a nice house in Paris and start hitting society. Whatever I was, I was still Champion of the World. And that was all there was to it.

Write soon,

Jack

CRAVAN

Mexico, November 1945

Jack, how many years? I expect you heard all that happened, how I drowned, well, disappeared . . . I have wanted to surprise you all this time but it seemed indecent to break the spell. I would surely be caught. I am dead, utterly dead to the world, I do not exist. Arthur Cravan drowned in Mexico, did you not hear? Fabian Lloyd went with him. All my lives sank out there in that ocean with its sharks and squalls and tempests, no greater alibi than nature.

Are you surprised to hear from me again? Surely you knew I wasn't fool enough to sink myself. Nor kill myself, which is the other theory, that I came to my worthy conclusion. What fools, to think death as choice could be carried out in anyone with the spirit to live for ever. I have been through many things and they have not yet got me – dunking my lungs in the Caribbean is hardly part of the inspired game-plan.

I am back in Mexico. You meet not one sane person here, Jack, everyone is mad and raving. I am here only weeks and already I know it is catching. How are you? Is lunacy contagious yet in those hot states you thrive in? Come and rescue me, I am in desperate need of a little sanity and logic. Do. I need a man like you to trundle in and raise the roof a little. Everywhere here there are animals. I forgot about all the beasts there would be, things that rustle and squawk when you get out of bed and stand on them, everywhere, Jack, and not a sensible mind in the vicinity that understands how they drive me mad. Come.

I came here out of instinct, out of panic. I needed to be far from Europe, near something I could remember for only good reasons, back to where I was happiest. And it was here, it was with you and the Academy and the bullfight and the boxing, but most of all it was her, where we married, where she came to be with me, trusted me, loved me, where I was happier than I have ever been. I dreamt of this country these past years, activated every memory of Mexico I possessed as though they were a legion of soldiers I could conscript and march out to battle against all the poisons in my head. And they were well-armed, Jack, it would surprise you how effective they were. So I had to come. Now I need you, and most of all her, I need Mina, I need her to come and rescue me.

I don't know if you will understand why I left, Jack. It's that feeling within you when you're one punch away from victory, and then you remember the man you are in the ring with is your brother. You are blinded by the speed and the ferocity of the fight, of his moves. Do you leave down your fist when you understand who it is you will be knocking unconscious, who it is you are conquering, or does that selfish need for the feeling of the final punch, that blow which floors him, the power surging all the way through to the ends of your fist . . . is it that which wins and when you shake out of yourself suddenly you are watching people mob around your brother there dead to the world on the canvas where you have just put him?

That's how it felt, Jack. One minute I was away, away, away, off to seek our fortune, off to test our little schooner on the waves, and the next I was battling for my life in a hurricane wind, the storm tossing the boat every way but upside-down, and when it was all over the very fact of being alive inebriated me so much I decided to have an adventure. I knew I was dead if I wanted to be, could adopt whatever alias I chose and live it, and that, Jack, is what I did. I died. I sank my boat two miles from the Guatemalan coast and swam off into my adventure. One year, that was all I was taking, one year while the war busied itself with the world and Mina with the baby, then I was coming back. Except I didn't. Not until now.

I am in a different part of the country, further south, away from anglophones and tourists and mercenaries, away from all opportunity of being recaptured and hauled back to old ways. I have done this many times without regret of any kind – of all people you have been the one to share more metamorphoses than anyone: Paris, Spain, Mexico . . . and the one who understands most too. But it is almost thirty years and two wars on. I am more sensible now, I suppose, I yearn for those old ways in a manner alien to me all this time, I have remorse. You know that I left Mina there on the banks waiting for me, burgeoning with our child, a savagery urging me further and further out to sea, away from her. I didn't even leave her in a country she knew, instead one I had enticed her to with my promises of love, of need and passion. All true, even now they are true, and I believed then that I was able, for all that, to give her the love she deserved, that it was her that I wanted for always, to marry and travel with, explore the world through her eyes and mine together, through that love.

I bolted from that, from all that Mina gave me, as though it were my right. As though all our happiness was courtesy of a pawnbroker and the ticket was mine. I retrieved my anonymity, my freedom, a whole new life at her expense. Yet it is only now, after the atrocity that has been this second war, that I feel the savagery of abject remorse, the kind that gnaws and prevents everything else finding shape or sense. You are the only other human being in this world capable of such selfishness, Jack, of that absolute clarity of need and self. Without it you would never have got to Tommy Burns, never have beaten Jeffries, would still be sitting bitter in Galveston, fantasising. You used it to turn your life into something, while I ruined lives, destroyed anyone who gave me anything. I didn't destroy Mina, I know she will have survived it all. I dream constantly of finding her, of turning up to see her. She may be dead by now. I don't even know about my child, if it survived, if the shock of abandonment killed the child inside Mina.

I am not a fool, I know I cannot waltz into lives I deserted, cannot hope to retrieve Mina. If she is alive she will be married again to another, a woman of her genius and depth of love does not sit idle and lonely. He will be a great man, a man to stir jealousy with his talent and his beautiful talented sublime wife, his adopted child perhaps, his happiness . . . All that was mine, it stood and waved me off and I abandoned it utterly. Abandoned her.

I did not suffer from regret, Jack, and that enabled me to desert guiltlessly all responsibilities, all situations, every sort of entrapment. I have retained my freedom in all ways, all my life. I had an instability in my balance that had me falling when I stood straight in society – I needed to chase my own tail like a distempered dog, to run away incessantly, as though all of it were merely a ludicrous game I was bound to by habit.

But everything has changed, Jack. I have come back to Mexico, back to the point of desertion, and everything robust and fearless in me has evaporated in the heat, in the strength of memory, of loss. I am besieged by it, besieged by memories of her smell, her voice, her laugh, her frowning concentration, her hats, her wicked cackle of glee when suddenly happy; the feel on my fingertips of her silken sculpted back, the half-smile she wore when dreaming, when utterly lost in thought, the way she understood me in my darkest moments, would hold me, never tore at me for the sake of a simple explanation, never apologised for anything she did; her delirious arrogance, her confidence as she walked, as she sat in the sun talking to our unborn infant, her certainty that everything in life happened for a reason, that logic had no part in happiness.

I miss her with a force stronger than any other desire I have known, even the interminable need to reinvent myself. All the things that have driven my life, Jack, the urges and needs that moved me on, defined my next move, all these things seem as fatuous and infantile as Manhattan socialites. I understand why they dominated my past. Why has it taken me thirty years? What I want now is to reclaim what I lost, if she'll let me. She will be married, her poetry will have made her famous, she will have other children, she will have all the good in her life that I bereaved her of, but she will have that love for me still, she must do, even if it is coated thickly with bitterness and anger and hatred of me – our love was not like others. It was untarnishable, even after thirty years of desertion, its rawness will live in her yet as it does in me. I know that. I have faith in her as I have faith in no other thing, alive, dead, real, spiritual, false . . . she is my faith. I must find her.

I understand, Jack, if it is something you would prefer to keep distant from. If you feel that way, write to me, my name here is Ernesto Guavez, and in a few weeks your letter will reach me here. What I am asking of you is if you will find her for me, find out if she is alive, if our child survived, was it a boy or girl, what he or she does now if alive, what Mina has done these thirty years without me, if she is happy, if she is remarried, if, Jack, there is any space for me to return to her, to explain and reclaim contact with her. I need her, Jack, she is nothing that is ordinary, and I need to know she is alive, or where she is buried, I need to regain her soul as she has mine.

If you will search for her, I have only my thanks, I have nothing else. I always loved listening to you together, there is a kindred disdain for order and piety in each of you, an energy shared. But politics got in the way before. Now perhaps there is a chance of regaining that, if she is alive, if she will allow me back. I know there is such arrogance in believing she will, but Mina is unlike anyone. And she loves me. All I have is that hope. We three will meet, will come together as though thirty years were thirty days and it is us that matter, not circumstance, nor even betrayal.

I don't know where to start. She had family in England, but they would be dead by now . . . though perhaps not her sisters . . . New York, perhaps, where we met, she and I, there are many people there who may know her. But she cannot know I am alive. Not yet. Please, find her, and tell her nothing, say only that you were thinking back to old days, reminiscing, and thought of me, of how she must be. Say simply that you were going over your life and thought of her, yes, say that you thought to see how time had evolved for her in my absence. That you wanted to resume contact, see if she was happy . . . She will not be suspicious of you, will not think I am alive, it has a rationale she will understand. Hers was a life replete with strange contact. Find if there is any way she continues to think of me, to love me, if her new husband or lover is everything she wants, or if I stir anything in her yet. If she loves me still. The fate of our child. New York is the place to search for her, a man there called Walter Arensberg, or Duchamp if he has not returned to Paris by now. She will have kept these people close to her. I will enclose with this all the addresses I remember for them, though I am sure they are changed, they were not people who allowed habits to form. Still, they may lead to other addresses, or to people who will hear you are looking for her and give you her address . . . I know, Jack, the enormity of what I ask. You are the only one. Only you could understand what propels a man to turn upon what he loves in pursuit of something savage in him that he must act on, live for. That selfishness. We each had it. You used it to conquer the world, and I to demolish mine.

Jack, she is everything now. She will not want me at first, but we will be together, our love is not the kind destroyed by the turns of life, only tested. No other woman in the world would understand. Mina will, eventually, she will. She cannot know yet, there is so much to be done, to discover, before I can approach her. She cannot know, Jack, she must believe in your power to reminisce, believe in your desire to find out her fate, how she survived my death. I am still unsure what I will do if she is alive, if you find her . . . everything in me wants to take her in my arms and explain, but I know there are some things best left raw, and this is one of them. Whether I can leave it so is different entirely. I cannot know my action until I know what has become of her. I will do nothing unless I hear from you. If she is dead, if she does not want to see me, if our child is dead . . . even if these things are real, write and tell me. I will not act unless you write.

I have a great many things to explain, I know that, and I will, I will write again and explain all this time, all these years. But for now, Jack, find her for me, please.

Write to me here, I will be waiting eagerly for your word.

Cravan

FABIENNE

He sees Mina waving from the shore and is delighted with his prowess, his skill at turning this volatile tub into an ocean-worthy yacht. He turns her around and around in the mouth of the bay, using the wind to show his wife what he can do with this piece of junk they chose in the salvage yard as the project that would get him out of Mexico and on to Chile. It is 1918. He has made this unsailable wreck float, made it curl in the wind like a shy debutante, made it rise and fall on the waves with the breeze in its sails, this sinking chamber-pot his friends had laughed at so knowingly saying he couldn't bluff his way on to the water like he did with everything else. But Mina knew. She knew he would make it sail if it was going to bring him down the coast and past the borders that held them in, if it would unite them and their unborn child in Chile. He sashays around the bay like a fop at charades, knowing she is laughing at the shapes he is making in his rescued boat.

And suddenly the wind picks up as he is facing away from the beach Mina waves from, the boat's momentum picking up, and he grows excited at the prospect of speed, of bouncing across the waves seeing what his creation is able for. He decides to navigate his way out to sea, to start the journey now that he is due to make in a few days anyway, up to Puerto Angel to trade this coquette for something stronger still, something that will brave hardier waters. The light is strong, he works out his points, pleased that the winds are gaining strength,so absorbed in the exhilaration of this new-found vitesse that he fails to notice the menace that creeps into the strong breeze, the way the sails no longer contain the winds but cede to their force. Out on the open sea the novice sailor does not appreciate the imperceptible change of course the rising winds impinge upon his passage, that he is losing sight of ever seeing Puerto Angel and is instead blown south-westwards. He is only taking his boat out into the bay to show his wife that it truly sails, and now, well, now he is indulging his weeks of work, the efforts he has made, to realise these moments fresh, at sea, free. Free. That is what he loves most, that is what is flying through his head as he skirts the waves and delights in the wind, the freedom of it, you could go on for ever and never be caught, and a thrill rises in him unlike any he has known before. Only then does he notice the sinister black of the sky that is sucking out his precious light, but this does not alert him, for he thinks it is night closing in and relishes the prospect of reading the stars, of applying all he has read of them since infancy towards guiding his voyage to Puerto Angel.

The dark sky is immense against the open sea, and as the winds become gales he finds he is unable to control the boat, unable to turn her or ease her into any other direction than that of the storm he is facing into. He battles hard as the rains begin hitting him in sheets, scraping his face with their pelting sting, and he is no longer an amateur out on a jaunt, he is fighting to stay afloat in the dark heart of a hurricane, every drop of blood in his veins circulating his body a hundred times faster as he keeps her from keeling, his arms and fingers almost black with cold, the boat racing ever faster as she stays true to the wind. He lunges the boat sideways to stop the sail from ripping, smashing into waves that seem as big as Mexico as they hurl him across the deck, the rain blinding him as he scrabbles to his knees at the wheel just as the great sail rends in two and he is knocked unconscious as the masthead loosens and swings round battering the side of his head.

When he comes to it is as if he dreamt the tempest, the skies above him glaringly bright and pure blue, the waters peaceable, land visible. For the initial seconds his eyes are open he feels nothing but pain circuiting his head, then sees the skies, the waters, the land, and feels a surge of elation, of strength at being alive. He struggles to his feet and begins to guide the boat towards the glimpsed coastline, thinking all the time, I should be dead, I should be dead, I should be dead . . . Then he realises that he is, to all intents and purposes, he is. His boat should not have survived that storm, nor should he, this naive sailor in an over-sized rowing boat, he should be drowned, sunk by the torrents, swept overboard, his boat lying deep on the ocean bed, both powerless against the waves and gales. He stops his efforts to sail her towards the inlet, thinks how it would be to be dead, not for ever, just long enough to reappear like an illusionist's elaborate trick, this ultimate act of forgery, to take your own life and not die . . . if he could pull it off, fool them all, what a coup, what a scandal, what a challenge . . . And could he?

It seems difficult to him, and all the more seductive for it. He knows he is on the right continent to start it off, has the perfect alibi, the ocean. Mina is on the beach waiting, he thinks, but then he thinks of her voyage in just a few days, first to Chile, then onward to have her baby. She doesn't need him in the way at the moment anyhow, she said so herself as he fussed and prattled around her on the beach just two days before. She will go back to New York and he will find her there soon, see his child, settle then with her. This part of him that plots his escape from the world is the part she loves most, she has always said it, the spontaneous element that cannot settle without adventure, she would understand. So sure is he of her that a burst of love explodes in him that he should have her love, the love of a woman unlike any other, with freedom and gaiety in her every pore. She will understand him, and as for everyone else, he does not care. He will find her in New York.

Mina

New York, April 1946

Dearest Jack,

We had our party a few nights ago, all surprises and gaiety and even more urgings, tearful ones, that I should join Joella and Fabi in their new life in Colorado. They have other responsibilities, Jack, and in Joella's case, children. Why would I substitute a life that makes me happy in order to satisfy the unnecessary guilt of my children? It is ironic, is it not, that they should care so while I abandoned them so blithely. But they have more sense than I. Or perhaps less.

Did you like Paris? It grows on you so much, you think you have your grip and then you lose it . . . always surprising you. I moved back to Paris after I gave up seeking him, brought Joella and Fabi and Giulia and Estere and pretended we were a family. It was a tough time, Jack, his absence was so acute. No one could understand – to Joella he was simply a stranger I spoke about all the time, father to her new little sister Fabi, while to Fabienne herself he was her glorious absent father, the man I filled her head with stories and tales about, her father from the photographs, as much a fiction to her as the fables I read to her each night. We had a strange life in Paris then.

I can't think what Paris would have made of you, Jack. I suppose it would have been enraptured after a fashion, appreciated all the grandness and jollity in you. It is not the easiest place to settle anew. Mind you, nor is New York. When I first arrived off the steamship from Europe I thought New York might swamp me. It seemed impossible that I should be able to negotiate it at any level, never mind one of my own choosing. The tables turned and I moved in with Frances in the beginning, and then a few weeks later I found my own apartment on West 57th Street. It was small, but it was bright and it was all my own. No husbands or children or nurses or suitors or egos anywhere to clog up my time, my thinking, my day-dreaming . . . it was magical, Jack.

At first I was awestruck. Florence for its beauty was an old world, a place that thrived on artefact and legend. In New York, old seemed to be something that happened last week. I wanted Marinetti there to see what the world really looked like when you threw out the old in favour of the new, but had he arrived in New York I would have stayed hidden. This was my new life. Eventually the children would join me, but I had freedom until then to craft an existence that fulfilled me. All the latent energy and enthusiasm I had brought with me to Paris all those years before, hijacked by my own stupidity and Stephen, were free to express themselves at will now, as they had begun to in Italy. I had my children, but it was as if I had been made a single woman again, with all my choices ahead of me. As if my mistakes had been erased.

I barely saw the apartment at first, such was the tizzy of welcome put on by New York. I had not realised, sequestered in my idle Italian world, that the poems I had sent had caused outrage, that I had acquired a spectacular notoriety. I had never known the extent of the effect I was having on literary New York – I had assumed Mabel had been exaggerating and diluted everything she told me by at least half. It was very gratifying to hear she had been telling the truth. My poem 'Pig Cupid' had caused uproar. How on earth could a woman write such sexually graphic poetry, if it was poetry at all, how could she write of genitalia and desire, of a woman's deeply private sexual thoughts, her secrets? I was denounced in

Christian journals, in all the right-wing newspapers, slated as a harlot, without morals, shame, dignity or sense. It was magnificent. When it was known that I lived in New York now, one magazine called for my deportation on the grounds of obscenity. Journalists came to interview me, to take pictures. I, they decided, was the personification of the daring Modern Woman. Mina Loy the Modernist.

The joy of upsetting a false standard with my work was invigorating, it made me passionate for writing again, for working hard at voicing all the ideas in my head. But as ever the backlash was nastier than I could ever have anticipated. Amy Lowell and Marianne Moore both declared against me, said I was not fit to publish. Lowell threatened to abandon her patronage of one of the literary magazines unless they undertook never to publish me again. They did, and retained her support, through great diplomacy, I assume. It became fashionable in literary salons to declare one way or the other on the subject of my dreadfulness/splendidness.

Whatever it was, it was exciting. It was so much better than sitting alone in cafés and restaurants hoping that one of my three New York friends would take pity on me and include me in their plans. I had had quite enough of solitude. Instant notoriety was far more pleasing.

Being a *cause célèbre*, for at least a week, was an astounding way to meet people I had heard about, whose lives I had heard Mabel describe, whose lives I had admired from Italy for their glamour. In the flesh they were very different, vaguely tannic and sour in their approach to newcomers. They were also the people whose money paid for everything, the magazines, the balls, the dinners, the cocktails. They were a grand-scale New York City version of Mabel, but without her humour and self-deprecation, and her genuine interest in all the things she supported. They were bored socialites, in effect. Later, I would learn to my cost what getting involved with them did to you, when Peggy Guggenheim decided she wanted to back me. As I had learnt with Marinetti, anything approached out of boredom tends to become boring in the end. I was determined not to allow that to happen to me.

One couple were different. Frances introduced them to me, and with my stupid arrogance I assumed they were the same as others she had introduced me to, those who had treated me as though I were a particularly controversial, if talkative, sculpture. But they were not. I had heard a lot about the Arensbergs. Their salon was the most famous, and they were the most talked about in terms of the company they kept. Half of what was allegedly bohemian New York (that was supposed to include Amy Lowell and the dreadful Marianne Moore) looked down on the Arensbergs' salon for being unruly and attracting unvouchable types from Europe and beyond. The other half craved to be included, but the couple were known for their idiosyncratic judgement. There were no rules or criteria. With the Arensbergs, you were simply invited, or not.

Luckily, I was, and I found in each of them the energy and wide-eyed wonder at life that had drawn me to New York. Their apartment was ten blocks from mine, but it was a different universe. They were millionaires, and their penthouse with its vast sweeping staircase, deep velvet sofas, *chaise-longues* exuded an undiluted air of opulence. But one thing prevented it from being another Mabelesque cavern of wealth. On every wall, sometimes four or five high, hung the most phenomenal display of modern art I had ever, have ever, seen. It was like a fantasy art gallery, all the artists you ever wanted to see, there before you: Monet, Picasso, Van Dongen, Picabia, Man Ray, and there in all its glory Duchamp's *Nude Descending a Staircase*. I was awed to see so much all at a glance within one room. On alabaster podiums and in alcoves sat sculptures I recognised as by Brancusi and Stephen's former ally, Rodin. Envy and astonishment and elation darted inside me like electrified eels. Everything I wanted in my life seemed attainable from that evening on.

I was glad that Frances had accompanied me. She told me

to stop staring. Had all this been in a gallery, I would have been very excited by it; that it was in a private apartment stunned me. I was sure they thought me a fool, but of course everyone who walked in for the first time, no matter what they were told in advance, reacted with the same awe. It was beyond all imaginings.

The first night was fun. I met a lot of people who would remain friends all my life. That was the night I met Marcel Duchamp. He signed the death certificate, you know, Jack. His testimony to the police gave us all at least the sense that officially, legally, no one believed Fabian might still be alive.

Marcel had given Walter Arensberg *Nude Descending a Staircase* as a gift. Walter and Louise had been paying the rent on an apartment down the hall for Marcel, which, contrary to theirs, had the air of being recently ransacked. At one end was a collapsible bed and a small gas ring, while the rest of the space was filled with objects, pieces of automobiles, scrap iron, bedsteads, with large canvases leaning against walls and windowsills. With the exception of the mass of apparent scrap, it was much the same as any studio I had been in before, with one other exception. It was in one of the best apartment blocks in America, the kind of place that heiresses queued to move into when their husbands' wills were read out. The reason for this luxury was its proximity to his patrons; it enabled their cook to bring him meals. Lou Arensberg insisted.

They took the pain out of living, the Arensbergs, but Marcel could not be anaesthetised by mere domesticity. Still, here it was, one of New York's most elite addresses, with its dado rails and cornices and wall-to-wall carpet going utterly to waste as Marcel stockpiled his carefully scavenged hoard. It seemed a world I could only look in on. At the time I could not see a place for me anywhere within it. But Walter and Lou did.

After a few visits I settled in, for the crowd formed a core with all types coming in and out as they passed through town. I felt like a New Yorker. The Arensbergs arranged readings for me at salons and recital rooms, at 'events' they organised around me. They were thronged, every one, thanks to the attentions of different magazines that photographed me, sent cartoonists to sketch me, wrote articles about me, published my poetry, blazed against me, and gave me an unpurchasable notoriety that attracted the oddest numbers to my readings. Life at the Arensbergs became a refuge, fun though this all was. My poems were celebrated in the salon with a fervency and gusto I had never imagined.

I started spending long periods of time with Marcel. At first he sought out my company, mainly, I think, because, of the ten or twelve people there each evening, only three of us could speak his language. He had only a little English when I knew him then, though in later years it was more than passable, and so he depended on French-speakers for conversation. We became friends out of pragmatism. But it was more than that – we had each turned our backs on Europe, on European ways, thinking, approaches, had made the decision, for much the same reasons, to cast away from the lives we had there, the progress we had enjoyed, the antique schemes that were meant to make Europe modern. We didn't want to be a part of the failure. America had the aura of opportunity, the breadth of mind and disrespect for tradition that allowed us to be fearless. For him, Paris had come to be his trap. For me, Italy. The Arensbergs' apartment became our springboard.

The other francophones were Frances and a man I knew for weeks simply as Bill. He seemed to be treated with enormous respect, and wrote poetry, but it seemed a hobby for he had a doctor's practice upstate somewhere from which he drove most evenings to join us. Frances was in thrall to Louise Norton then, and spent less and less time with us, and so Marcel, the doctor and I began an alternating chess tournament with deeply confusing counter-rules. Marcel won flat-out each time. We decided it was because the rules were of his devising. We became known as the Parisian corner, for the three of us tended to gather in the same part of the apartment as a matter of course, underneath the large penthouse window that overlooked Manhattan, squashed in on the deep blood-satin feather sofa. We squeezed into it and talked for hours about our lives, our mistakes, our appetites, the fraud of marriage, about poetry and art, and how we would use them to change everything, as though we were an army advancing on propriety and righteousness.

Walter Arensberg dined out on the story for months when I asked him who was this sweet-natured doctor everyone treated with such easygoing admiration. Bill Williams, he said, as though I were stupid. Williams, he repeated, and started laughing at my blank face as though he were going to choke on his asparagus, William Carlos Williams. I felt such a fool the next night I went over to the apartment. Luckily Walter had gone to Philadelphia for a few days and my obtuseness didn't come out for another week or so. It didn't change a thing when it did. Why should it have, I suppose, but I did feel a terrible idiot.

There was a curious harshness to the salon, for all the décor and bonhomie. A need to retreat from all the softness of routine and order provided each night without fail. The friendships were, in the main, true, but a catty pettiness thrived amidst all the respect and talk of sex and art and how to change the world. Marcel especially had a tremendous capacity for being an absolute bastard when the mood took him. While very fond of the Arensbergs, and most people in the group, some irritated him enormously, as Louise Norton found to her cost. Louise would have been an intelligent socialite had she had the money, so instead she opted for being intelligent and name-dropping. She thought herself very glamorous and erudite, and wafted her cigarette smoke around the room as though it were the trail to the most kissable lips in New York. She flirted coquettishly with Marcel, though it was well known that he regarded relationships as time-consuming distractions that clogged up his working time. The way he saw it, casual flings meant interesting sex; for interesting company and conversation all he had to do was walk down the hall at ten o'clock each evening and there it was, the best of all worlds. But Louise Norton thought she would be the one to change him. Her plan was clear. Flirt until he was at the point of seduction, then back off. Do this incessantly. Once he made a move to seduce her, reject him. Repeat endlessly, until he became so enraptured that he was in love, wanting all of her, not merely her sexual proclivity, and they would begin living together. Quite what her husband made of it I don't know, but the rest of us thought it excruciating to watch. Whatever anyone thought of Marcel, no one had any illusions about his dedication to his work. If he had decided that love obstructed it, then out went love. Especially if Louise Norton was its object.

So I was surprised one evening to find her sitting where I usually sat, deep in conversation with Marcel. Bill came over to me and explained Marcel was teaching her French. Maybe I was peeved, she was just such a simpleton I felt slightly aggrieved that he had given in to her barrage of female manoeuvres. But Bill brought me within earshot, as though we were simply leaning on the other arm of the sofa as we talked, and whispered in my ear to listen to Marcel.

He was certainly teaching her French. She asked how to say 'It is a pleasure to make your acquaintance'. In the most charming and plausible of voices he told her how to say 'I have the most beautiful vagina in the world' in absolutely perfect French. I got a fit of giggles when she repeated it back to him with the utmost concentration, announcing it delicately over and over, asking him to correct her pronunciation. Bill made me stop, said that she would get suspicious, though he was stifling his own laughter as he said it. 'May I see the menu, please?' – her favourite Midtown restaurant was French – and dutifully and attentively Marcel got her to repeat 'I desire your manhood enormously, young man'. And so it went on. Louise learnt to ask for the washroom, order a starter, request the bill, and say she was a great art-lover in impeccably obscene French, managing to give her sexual history, covert desires and a full description of her body as she did so.

A few days later a note arrived from Marcel asking me to join him for lunch with Frances, Bill, Lou and Walter, and Louise Norton. I was to join them at the Brevoort Hotel, a frequent lunching place for us, famous for its aloof French staff. We were thrown out before our aperitifs even reached us. The drinks waiter was asked would he mind if we copulated in the cloakroom when Louise confidently asked for an ashtray. Women were not generally allowed to smoke in public, even then, and so when he went off shocked and harrumphing, Louise laughed at how staid and fusty they were at the Brevoort. The manager came to smooth things out, thinking his waiter mad when he saw his regular lunch troupe sitting elegantly talking to each other. Louise looked at Marcel, who gave her the nod, and so she made motions as if to say, Leave this to me. Lou and Walter weren't very certain what was up, Frances was squirming nervously in her chair, and Bill and I were covering our mouths to stop laughing. 'I desire your manhood enormously, young man,' Louise said brightly. Within forty seconds we were collectively out on the street, our coats thrown after us. Louise could not understand why a request for menus had caused such umbrage. Frances walked off in disgust at Marcel, Bill explained it to the Arensbergs who both thought it hysterical, while I watched Marcel explain to Louise what she had said. She stormed off. We five went and had lunch down the street.

Frances harangued me over it. She said if I had meant anything I had said in my *Feminist Manifesto*, I would be repudiated by the demeaning of Louise. It was my duty as a woman, no matter my view of Louise, to defend her, and prevent a man degrading her so in public, when I had it in me to stop it. I couldn't agree at all. It was Louise's vanity, arrogance, and stupidity that had made the endeavour funny, not the fact that she was a woman. I told Frances she took everything too literally. I never saw her at the Arensbergs' again, nor Louise Norton. I went to see Frances and made up with her, but she adamantly refused to return to the group of people she had introduced me to. She said I was made for such company, and she was not. Already things were changing.

I had only been in New York a few months and yet already it felt more of a home than any I had known. Marcel and I felt war was following us, for he too had come to escape it and start anew. His interest in me had deepened a great deal, and I sensed that I was next on his predatory list, which was ironic in that half the people we knew seemed to think an affair had been going on for some time. But I was not Louise Norton. I had no illusions about converting him into a monogamous devotee, nor did I want one. I was enjoying the company at the Arensbergs', the sedate consumption of enormous quantities of alcohol, the hot chocolate and *pâtisserie* Lou wheeled out at midnight, the conversations and games and seductions and scandals presented just before dawn, after which we lurched home to sleep, waking to put into action some of the ideas so grandly acclaimed, before starting the whole thing again a few hours later. It made me feel alive. I wrote with such energy in the afternoons and early evenings, I didn't think I could be happier. I was alone when I chose to be, never afflicted with the loneliness that haunted me in Florence, nor the sense of desperation and claustrophobia. It was not that I was averse to a casual affair with Marcel. It was simply that I felt no need for the complexities of any kind of involvement. What I had filled me to the brim.

One night Alfred Kreymborg asked if I would read something for him, give him my opinion. It wasn't unusual for people to swap manuscripts, in fact it was as regular as Lou's midnight trolley service. It was a play, *Lima Beans*, he called it, and it was a wonderful satire on the exigencies of marriage, the husband and wife acting as though marionettes on string, commandeered by another force as they bicker and rile. I loved it. It was comic and silly and serious all at once. Then he told me he had written it for me. He had written it having heard me send up my marriage, and wanted me to take the role of the wife. If it was all right with me he would be asking Bill Williams to take the husband's role. I was deeply flattered.

Neither Bill nor I had acted before, but we had such fun trying. We rehearsed for four weeks and then as the Provincetown Players we performed our little endeavour with much vigour and amateurism. People hated it. Reviewers, audiences – they said that we were not espousing the serious concerns of the real world, that we were satirising decent beliefs. Fools. All it was was a bit of harmless clever fun. Piety was everywhere as the war encroached. Everyone was losing their sense of make-believe. Not at the Arensbergs', though. Perhaps that was why when the world of prisons and poverty and isolation came when he disappeared I was so unprepared for it, Jack. I truly felt inured to the badness of the world, even in Mexico when we hadn't a sou, as if my decision to start anew in America was all it took to ward off the dangers of sentience.

This was all ahead of me, bound up in the fate of a man I hadn't yet met, but the process of his discovery was beginning. There was dissent at the Arensbergs', frustration at the rhythm and order of the art shows, with their committees for choosing the pictures, committees for deciding what hung where, next to what, committees for deciding the committees, the sub-committees, and who spread what rumour about the old committees. It was the European system, the one that over a decade before I had been so proud to be a part of. That was Paris. That was a twenty-three year old's pride. In New York we wanted away from old habits, and by now everything was old, even the motivations of the year before when the Arensbergers had held a vast exhibition of their own devising in the old State Armory. But things were different again now. We were chasing change.

It was Marcel who was most frustrated with the process of judging the work. We talked more fervently now, his depressions coming back to skewer him with greater frequency, his need for frivolity matched equally with a desire to talk long into the night about our pasts, and our decisions to abandon them. He was intrigued by Joella and Giles, by the idea I should leave them behind, and it gave him understanding as to why I would never truly desert all I had been before. For a short while he thought he wanted a child, but the responsibility passed. So too his mood, and when he emerged from his melancholic pensiveness it was with aplomb. His spirit was leaping around looking for trouble, and a cause. He decided a new Society of Independent Artists would do the trick, and along with Walter Arensberg and me, and all the other Arensbergers, we laid plans for the first truly independent exhibition New York had ever seen.

The idea was to circumvent the judgement process. If you were an artist and had the confidence to submit your work, then you paid six dollars and we hung it. Marcel was in a rage against everything that spring as the war caught up with America, U-boats sinking ships indiscriminately, xenophobia catching the country by the oxters and lifting it into a new realm of distaste for anyone who spoke in an accent other than American.

I don't know about it now, Jack, some of the things I invested my energy in as my collision with Fabian grew closer and closer seem so redundant, childish. But at the time they were more important than anything else, this world of ours the only conduit for expression that we had. It was Marcel who took the reins in all the dealings the new Independents manoeuvred. It transformed his career, allowed him to express his disdain for the New York art world, art in general, life in general. There was wickedness in him, but not just the mischievous kind, a malaise lingered too, one that made him seem hungry for something that was always beyond his reach. He and Fabian did not always get on, a clash of egos perhaps more than anything, but each had in them a sense of unfulfilled havoc and disruption, and it affected all our lives.

Marcel was adamant that there would be no system of judging of any kind – to arrange an exhibition freed from taste and variable concepts of talent, of art itself. As a result we received works that I wouldn't have used as bedding for my cat, but the freedom also meant the most startling, wonderful canvases and sculptures arrived at the Arensbergs' for us to unpack, pieces that reaffirmed our belief in what we were doing.

As Walter, Marcel and I prepared to hang the two thousand five hundred entries that had arrived in all shapes and packages over spring 1917, we realised that in setting aside certain pictures to hang together, certain sculptures to inform each other, we were in fact doing what we'd set out to rupture, we were classifying, judging what belonged where and with what. Marcel came up with the solution. We arranged the work alphabetically, a logical progression through the exhibition rather than a curated one. To prevent the A's and B's and C's from gaining undue precedence, we put twenty-six letters in a bowl and took out one at random. It was R. That was where we'd start, we would place all the artists whose name began with R at the entrance, followed by S, then T, and so on, all the way round to Q. Democratic as it was, having a name beginning with L didn't do my own contribution, I called it *Making Lampshades*, many favours. Francis Picabia had a worse deal again, while Man Ray was flying.

I have fond memories of that exhibition, it was a time when I felt alive amongst the people I knew, not the ennui I feel now. Perhaps it was the sense of a new beginning, that I was capable of anything and surrounded by people I knew thought the same. Or perhaps events wizen the spirit no matter how hard you fight their effect.

I have not had a day when I do not think of Fabian a hundred times, Jack, he is in me as though his soul had been injected into every cell in my body. There are days still when I have to blank out all senses and ignore the proof that the world doesn't stop in loss, people still fall in love, men become husbands, girls wives, lonely people in their small worlds go out one day and are saved from the path of a speeding car by the person who is their destiny, children are born, Venice still floods in rainfall, earthquakes still shake Peru, someone else walks into the path of that car because their destiny was not to be loved. I want to be oblivious to it all. Other days I simply dream of the past, concentrating my thoughts on our days in Mexico, reliving our conversations.

My affection for the time in New York is more than nostalgia. Certainly it was to lead to the happiest period I have ever known, for it held such adventure and fascination. The exhibition was bait to the conservatives, all of them lined up for war, and they came at it with their tongues erect and their sensibilities irreparably sundered. Marcel was filled with unvented rage, volatile and liable to turn on any one of us as easily as on those he pegged as fools. Only chess truly calmed him, and he and Walter would sit and play for hours. Other days he would arrive at my apartment and we would go walking through Brooklyn and Queens, into the European quarters, exploring the modern labyrinth for ourselves. He was so convinced that a hair's breadth of fate separated him and his comfortable patronaged life from those off the same kind of boats that had brought us, the people we saw on our walks, standing outside cobblers' in aprons awaiting trade, or pushing pretzel carts to their pitches. He was never sure of his right to any of it, of our right as a group, to the luxury and elitism of the world that we had woven on a spindle around us, brittle and fragile as sugar threads. Never sure that art was a job, merely a vocation, something to do well but in thrall to those who earned a living. Now we talk sometimes of those walks, of his mind then, and he is unchanged. The prices his art fetches pass him by. He takes the money, but his respect for those who pay it is negligible, eroded by the sense that all he was doing was showing the futility of art for art's sake. But any time we talk of it now he gets irritable and goes home. I don't think we were meant to age and live to think over the things done for the moment. At least Fabian has that on us, the freedom of timelessness.

Marcel was especially sickened by what he saw as the hypocrisy of the Independents themselves, the great organising dynamic that was making this elaborate alphabetical art democracy possible. This of course included ourselves, but he had found a niggling conservatism amongst some of the self-confessed radicals in the group when he had put forward his alphabetising scheme. He wanted to rout out the dead wood, and cause a stir. He had a plan.

A few days before the opening he and Walter went out to a plumbing showroom, the Mott Iron Works, and there Marcel searched out the urinals until he found one he liked, in white porcelain. He imprinted the name R. Mutt, after the Mutt and Jeff cartoon, and, along with an address in Philadelphia and his six dollars, entered it into the Independents for exhibition, under the title *Fountain*.

When it arrived, he was there, as if by accident, hanging pictures and unwrapping the slow stream of late-entries. He unpackaged it and he and Walter set about installing it on an alabaster stand in the section just after my own. I was having a late look at the hanging of my own picture, and I began to laugh when I saw it. I knew of his plan, devised in the early hours of the previous morning, but when executed it seemed even more absurd, and very very funny. But others were not so amused. George Bellows, who did that wonderful painting of you and Tommy Burns (see, Jack, I did know about you before I met Fabian), well, he and a couple of Marcel's friends were members of our new society and they came into the Grand Central Palace and saw *Fountain* in all its imposing glory. They summoned an emergency meeting. This was a ludicrous battle of wills, with every conservative-blooded mammal in the building appearing to cast their vote in favour of this R. Mutt character's expulsion from the exhibition with a reimbursement of his fee. Marcel, Walter and I argued fiercely against that, for in the end it was an example of exactly what we had set out to undo, to have arbiters of taste and artistic merit judge the suitability of something an artist had created. But therein lay the problem – how, they argued, could you 'create' something already created? Marcel said if the artist thought it art, then who were we to argue? Walter and I said that the piece had an intrinsic aesthetic value, it had been shown to be a rather shapely piece of porcelain. But it went to a vote, and the mysterious Philadelphian's urinal disappeared off to the Arensbergs' apartment while Marcel, Walter and I resigned from the Society's board in protest. It was months before Marcel's involvement became widely known, and that meant war in the circle, for many of the Arensbergers felt miffed at having been left out in the cold.

It corroborated the myth that Marcel and I were engaged in a tempestuous affair. Why else would he have let me in on it? People were certain of it now, but I had rebuffed him gently twice, once when he was very drunk in his apartment, and once in mine a few days later when, sober, he came to apologise. Marcel expected more from me than I gave for a long time, and what finally convinced him that I would never fall for him was when he saw how I fell for Fabian. He told me here in this apartment just a few years ago, when I first arrived back from France, that he had always been in awe of what Fabian and I shared. He had wondered why he and I had not had the same. But then Marcel had flirtation down to an art far grander than any he placed on his ready-mades, and it was a performance art between us. It still is, and we are well beyond any inklings or stirrings now.

There was more going on in the world than battles over urinals. Three days before the exhibition opened, war was declared and the country went headlong into tumult. I knew so few who went to war that first time, I inhabited an enclave of conscientious objection. All my pontificating in Italy, my ardent espousal of a grand lumbering war machine ready to hoist itself into battle for the sake of its people's dignity . . . what absolute frippery I believed then, such naive exuberance. And dangerous. But in America all that sort of murderous foolishness was lauded, and those of us who refused to indulge in it – ironic given my Italian leanings – were branded with suspicion and treated as undesirable foreigners. My English accent had mutated slightly, but it was nonetheless recognisable as that of an ally. But Marcel did not fare so well, his broken English spiked through with his French accent sounding desperately foreign to warmongering Americans. He was put on a surveillance list, as were we all in the end. Paranoia fell on America like a veil and obscured her view for many years. Everything went awry with war.

It was Marcel who brought me a copy of a magazine one day and opened it out on the picture of a broad-shouldered, light-haired man in a pale suit and dark speckled socks and tie, sitting on a sofa with his handkerchief stuffed hurriedly in his left breast pocket, and two black-faced sable Siamese cats curled lazily on his lap. I have gazed over this photograph almost every day of my life since, in anger, hatred, frustration, confusion, yearning, grief, but most of all in love. Besides his letters, it is almost all I have of him. This, said Marcel, is the man I have been telling you about. This is Arthur Cravan.

I looked at the picture of the manic Frenchman Marcel had known in Paris, now freshly arrived in New York and already causing havoc. But he had no interest in Marcel's friends, was contented, it seemed, to roam at liberty through New York, and could not be enticed to the Arensbergs'. He was however coming to the Blind Man's Ball. I looked again at the picture. Homosexual, I said to Marcel, and he laughed at me. Not quite, was what he said, and I took it to mean I was almost right, but I was wrong. What he meant was that Fabian was a Lothario, as far from attracted to men as he could be. His subsequent fidelity to me was all the more remarkable for his past, but on that day he was merely an unusual-looking man holding Siamese cats and looking somewhat homosexual in his perfect clothes. I felt nothing.

He was, according to Marcel, France's most infamous critic, who had been imprisoned for the bluntness with which he executed his attacks on the more famous names in Paris in his magazine *Maintenant*. I had heard of it certainly, and I suppose of him too, but in all these years of trying to crystallize those half-formed memories of his name, I have none. All I knew of him was that Marinetti had been apoplectic about him for a time, but I had paid no attention at all to it, not even when they wrote of him in *Lacerba*. They had a new iconoclast, a new model Futurist every time they came back from abroad. How I wish I had listened; those years could have been employed in Paris, discovering Fabian. We could have gone to Spain together, I would have met you, would have seen you fight together, it would have been I who spirited him off to the *Montserrat* that night, and I whose arms held him as he awoke in the dawn of America.

Everything changed the first time we met. Did he ever tell you about it? I had been involved in starting up a new magazine with Walter and some others in the group. We called it *The Blind Man*, and held a ball to celebrate its launch and to milk money from New York *debonaires* who professed an interest in artistic endeavours. We wanted it to be a gay affair, as much for our own as for their delectation, and we ordained it a fancy-dress evening. Not of the paltry kind seen at Hallowe'en, no, we wanted a lavish and splendid ball that would be the talk of the town, with a glorious ballroom and an orchestra and exquisitely imaginative, unusual costumes with cocktails to match.

We practised our cocktails at a 'pre-ball reception' in Walter's apartment – that was what had been calligraphed on select invitations, but really it was just an opportunity for us to convene and eye up one another's costumes and start the delicate process of drinking too much and falling over, before climbing into carriages and prancing down Fifth Avenue to our Blind Man's Ball. The apartment was giddy with elation at the success of the exhibition, a feeling amongst all of us that we had truly undone the regiment and given artists the chance to free themselves of all the old strictures. We didn't really change things at all. Marcel did, separately. We as the Independents didn't really unleash art from the binds of biased judgement, from panels and committees and elites. We were the ultimate elite at the time. How else could we have wielded our power? How else do you change things?

But at that time we were certain of our brilliance, flushed with exhortations of new great things we could achieve together as long as the group stayed strong and true. I was abuzz with such a fearsome sense of belonging, of finally having found a place I could unfurl and be lauded for it, not put into context and passed over as had happened in Italy, in Paris, in London. New York was my home, I was so sure of it that night, and I resolved to live there for ever, come what may. It was like the ideal love, anything could be put back together if it fell apart in such partial surroundings. We were all dressed quite absurdly, as steam radiators, lampshades, hard-boiled eggs, cornets, panthers, newspapers . . . not the glamour expected of us, but certainly the unpredictability.

We were aflame that evening in a way that did not occur on all our other cerebral brandy-drinking, chess-playing, discursive soirées at the apartment. All pomposity was in the things we wore and the poses we struck rather than in anything we voiced. There were also far more of us, the basic core of twelve swollen eightfold as the Arensbergs invited all who interested them, as though for us to try them out without any commitment to purchase their company again. The callousness within the group at times made me thankful for the notoriety accorded my poetry in advance of my arrival in New York. How would I have fared had I been on the Perhaps list?

It was Marcel's invitation that had the door open and reveal my nemesis. There he stood in the portal like a Greek sculpture, his height such that he bowed to escape the architrave, and when he stood upright again in the light of the hallway it shone on his cheekbones and made his face seem cold as marble. He was wearing nothing but a grubby tassled bedcover, a self-styled toga, his legs muscled and brown with slight blond hairs in chaos across them, a shoulder bare, and on his head, framing his magnificent face, a towel, wrapped with flourish in a pillar as though a turban. It was as if he had hastily swathed the gold-threaded coverlet around his muscled torso, reached for a towel in which to ensconce his head, and loped towards the Arensbergs' fit for a Ball. He took our breath away – me, Lou, Beatrice Wood, Clara Tice – every woman who saw him turned despite herself to drink him in, to absorb his gait, his strong thighs and remarkable visage. He looked princely – not regal, he seemed too irresponsible for that, but as though a regent, coolly taking in the scene before him: the vast apartment beyond the hall where we all stood, drinks in hand, the walls covered in the art I had been so astounded by, his eye casting lightly over the Brancusis and Rodins in the alcoves all along the passageway to the main room, not an eyebrow or crease of wonder raised. Lou, ordinarily so lithe and welcoming in her soft manner, stood as though a guest at a wedding, afraid to say anything in case she broke the spell, and so he moved past her with a smile and went towards Duchamp who in turn leapt across two feathered birds of prey in diamanté heels when he saw him.

I shook myself alert. I had been wrong in my appraisal. There was not a single homosexual tinge to this man. But he had the unforgivable air of unbesiegable confidence, and I found myself disliking him immediately. He seemed a physical presence of undeniable power, but uncomfortably certain of his right to be here, his right to do as he was doing now, holding a conversation with Bill Williams and Marcel and Walter as though it were his apartment, his hands prefiguring his voice, hunching his shoulders as he spoke in such a way that it was part of whatever he was saying because when he straightened the others fell about laughing, he with them. He had no awe. Even his bedcover and towel were remarked upon, Bill and Marcel gesturing at them as though they showed absolute daring and wit. Marcel saw me watching and I turned away, angry at being caught, but he shouted my name and came to bring me over to meet this man, this Cravan, this life-changing embodiment of everything I would come to love most about being alive, but whom I regarded at that moment as an arrogant usurper.

He knew my name. Mina Loy? he said, before Marcel could do it for him, and when I said, Indeed, he fished in his toga, brought out a folded piece of paper, and pressed it into my hand. The others looked on curiously. I unfolded it. It was a letter, from an apparent amour of his, angrily accusing him of spending the night of the opening with 'that tall, mad poet-woman Loy'. It informed him that she would not see him again, and would not answer his letters when he wrote. I was desperately bemused but I pretended to be deeply offended by the insinuation, so much so that he began explaining he had long desired to meet me, had noted my address, the names of the poems he had read, which friends we had in common . . . and the jealous woman had found the notebook and assumed me his mistress.

Now, he said, You are responsible for me.

And I was. It began in that flickering evening, all that was different and vivid about him struck itself alight like sulphur on granite amidst those staid and ordinary souls. There were exceptions, of course, Marcel and Bill and even Frances to a degree, but none compared to him. No one ever would after that night, but you do not know these things at the time, it is nostalgia and things unsaid that make you certain that you knew it all along. But I didn't, Jack, I knew only that he was unlike anyone I had ever met, and I disapproved intensely of his effect on everyone around him. I did not want someone else to unbalance our inner court. I wanted to be the last to make a difference, for the doors to shut behind me. I did not want him in my world.

I was of course immensely flattered that I had acquired an admirer of such dedication. I used it to my advantage while I worked him out, treating him with an hauteur and disregard that perplexed Marcel, who caught me as we drove to the Ball and asked me why I was being so unnecessarily rude. To Marcel my behaviour was wicked substance for a nice dramatic falling out, if my dislike for this Cravan character were to boil over into an outburst. Consequently, despite having asked me to accompany him to the Ball, Marcel danced with every other woman in the room and began a cloyingly repulsive seduction of an appalling heiress as he sat beside me. The reason was to stir trouble, as he was bored, for despite all our excitement about the Ball we had all drunk far too many cocktails in our familiar surroundings and were really not fit as a group to venture anywhere until sober, never mind to a mammoth full-length Ball of our own organisation. It was thronged, mostly with acolytes we barely knew, society faces, art critics, curious New York aristocracy loath to miss out on any new dalliance.

Fabian collapsed in the chair next to me as I batted away an overdressed trumpet-player who wanted to dance. Fabian was amorous and draped a vast brown arm across my bare shoulders as he began to talk. My superiority was awakened, and I de-draped him, and shrugged myself away from his grasp. When he stood up I saw he was wearing nothing more than a pair of tight white boxing trunks, as though ready to fight, his swaddling clothes having been discarded, lying in a heap by the orchestra pit. He looked obscene, a vast bulging purse of hardened flesh as clear to view through the thin fabric as the hairs on his bare chest. My coldness eventually saw him move away into the dancing crowd, and that was all I saw of him for the evening until the end when he crashed in on me as I walked to the lobby with Bill, a fistful of ladies' telephone numbers in his hand. He asked me for mine, then saw it was I and said, Aha! The mystery lady with eyes, I may call, but I will not . . . and he darted into the crowd again, gone.

I fell asleep at Marcel's that night. We had breakfast together and I went home to sleep more. I knew of Fabian's lecture that evening, it was to be a grand affair, but truly I was too tired to dress up and be lively, I simply wanted rest and a quiet meal and to reply to Joella whose letters came every third or fourth day. He intrigued me, yes, had attracted me, amused me . . . but I often think now that some higher power must have guided our fate, for in those hours after our meeting there was nothing more than curiosity and bemusement in my regard for him. Nothing aflame, nothing to suggest the world I was about to enter, eyes wide and soul in hand.

His lecture was the final event in a fortnight that had begun with the declaration of war, continued with the fracas over Marcel's *Fountain*, the grand opening of the exhibition, the party in Lou and Walter's, the Ball, and now, to bring it all back to source, this talk on 'The Independent Artists in Europe and America' by France's leading critic Arthur Cravan, editor, columnist, lead reviewer and owner of French art journal *Maintenant*. And nephew of Oscar Wilde.

All of this had been spewing forth from Marcel, whose idea the lecture was, for weeks. The last thing he had said after breakfast was an attempt to urge me to come to it, and such was his harping that I said I would. I had no intention. Picabia was also involved in organising it, and together they filled the Grand Central Palace with all of the Upper East Side's grandest art-loving philanthropists, their wives, their daughters, all the doyens of the literary dining circuit, society princesses in preparation for their coming out, chaperoned to this elucidating lecture on European art by the preened women who would present them to New York society, matrons who professed to be 'artistic' though only through their purses . . . And to the common viewer, why not? What was wrong with inviting the wealth of New York's stupidity, superiority and self-delusion to a talk on the art of two continents, given by an expert, a proponent, a poet and critic? What indeed.

My door bell rang at five o'clock that morning. It was Walter. He had, it seemed, arrived at the Grand Central Palace an hour and forty minutes late, to a bristling audience who, with pursed lips and shoulders erect in righteousness, had stayed in their seats at Marcel's urging that it would be a memorable lecture and worthy of their patience. In lurched Fabian in a three-piece cream linen suit, absolutely polluted with drink, with a shabby leather bag in his hand. He strolled drunkenly to the podium and planted his bag on the table, opened it, and brought out a small crystal tumbler and a bottle of clear liquid, which he ceremoniously opened, still without uttering a single word, and walked to the ladies in the front row, wafting the bottle under their nostrils. They recoiled dramatically, partly from the smell of the liquid, partly, according to a delighted Marcel, from the disgust at being manhandled by an inebriated stranger. 'This,' Fabian declared at the top of his voice, 'is my final performance,' his drunkenness apparently sobered in a second.

'You are my chosen few, before you all I shall pour from this bottle into this glass the fatal arsenic absinthe mixture and drink from it, and I will die here before ye.' He proceeded to pour the stuff into him.

Marcel said the crowd went into consternation, but of a babbling inactive sort, not the kind that dissuades a man from killing himself before you. Marcel of course assumed it was a joke, and stood merrily by along with Bill Williams and Walter, who thought it equally amusing. By this time Fabian had begun loosening his tie and unbuttoning his waistcoat, all the while shouting at the audience for all the whores-in-waiting to sit on the left and whores-on-the-slide on the right, please, all the while disrobing, throwing his shirt in the air towards them with one hand, his tie with the other, bare-chested now, taking off his socks and tossing them away as if sweet-scented bouquets, as he exhorted them to steam-ship their way to France in the morning and see the real world, see what women of the streets really looked like, to repaint their faces, unsheath their clothes, while he himself began unbelting his trousers as he shouted, the ladies squealing in horror and outrage, screeching for the police to be fetched, for this Cravan to be arrested, but on he went, the absinthe coursing through him, until he stood naked before the desk on the podium and delicately rested his genitalia on the table. Now, he said, The Independent Artists in Europe and America . . .

But by now the grand hall was in pandemonium, women fainting and being revived, smelling salts and umbrellas being waved, over a thousand gentle, over-privileged souls in shock at what had just gone on before them, the hall dethronged as the women flocked out on to the street, their minds unable to grasp the fullness of what they had just witnessed, only a few remaining as the police rushed in and pinned Fabian to the floor, his rhetoric still flowing in a calm, even tone, Fauvism his subject, as Marcel and Walter and Picabia raced across to stop the arrest, Bill Williams gathering his clothes while one of the police battered Fabian across the head with his truncheon to shut him up. But still the litany of detail and art criticism came forth, by now both Picabia and Walter urging him to stop, and Marcel beside himself with glee at the outrage of the entire affair, laughing as though he were at the vaudeville.

Walter told me everything that had happened, and that Fabian had been taken to prison. All attempts to bail him out had been useless. Wives of senior politicians, daughters of prominent families, nieces of New York aristocrats . . . Marcel had lured the lot, and their husbands, fathers and uncles were raging furiously at the Police Commissioner to ensure that the full force of the law came down on Fabian. He was soberer now, and utterly unapologetic, according to Walter. He also refused to speak to anyone. Except me. They had left him there, and were all now in the apartment. Would I go to him?

And I did. I don't know why – pity maybe, a tinge of admiration, but something beyond that made me accede, dress, allow myself to be escorted to the prison by Walter and Marcel as dawn broke over the city, and go in and speak to a man I had no connection with in the world but for a few flimsy sentences uttered at a party.

The prison was intimidating, a compound of iron gates and barred entrances that had to be crossed before we gained access to the room in which they were holding him. He was shabbily reclothed, a crumpled shirt and cream trousers thrown on him, and he seemed drawn. He was smoking a thin cigar when I went in past the guard, and had the air of someone just woken up. He stood when he saw me, and enveloped me in a hug with his vast body. 'You came,' was all he said, and began sobbing on my shoulder, his neck crooked downwards. 'You came . . .'

I was shunted out ten minutes later, but in those minutes everything between us was conceived, Jack, all the tenets that bound us together through all of it. I wanted to know why he had insisted it be me that came to him, and he offered no explanation really, simply saying over and over, It had to be you, It had to be you . . . He had no explanation for the lecture either. He just shrugged his wide shoulders when I asked, and when, later, Walter and Marcel and Picabia pressed him for the story behind his strip-tease, he did the same. But the absurdity of our situation, of me being at a prison at the calling of a man I barely knew, a man arrested for obscenity and public disorder, of us there together with the guard staring off into another universe, it superseded all the usual conventions of courtship, all the tiptoeing flirtation, the tedium of irrelevant information gleaned to establish contact, a personal ground for both to stand on and walk around coyly . . . all of this was passed long before, when he invited my presence and I agreed to come. The irrationality that led us to that cold, damp, ill-lit room was the basis for everything that was ahead of us.

When he let go and sat down with me he seemed vaguely unaware of where he was, or why. He focused singly on my presence, asked me why I had not come to the lecture, asked if I knew how long he had waited to have five minutes alone with me, asked if he could come to my apartment the following day and show me some of the things he had written, if he could take me to the country, if I knew Leon Trotsky, and told me they had become friends on the *Montserrat*, asked if I was in love with Marcel like all the others, asked would I take care of him, did I know that he lived at Penn Station, on the roof. He talked in a low, urgent voice that rolled along without taking breaths and it was then that I remembered what Walter had beseeched me to find out from him. I asked him. He smiled, and asked had they all truly believed it, so I asked again and he said that he had taken a little for effect, but that it had been diluted. Then he told me something I have wrangled with for almost thirty years, Jack. 'When I commit suicide,' he said, 'I will do it very quietly, and I will do it just when they least expect it.' And then the guards came and made me leave.

He was there for fifteen days, and I went to him on each of them. Why? It made sense to me. All the others were busy pasting the clippings of the fiasco on to a large hexagonal board, the story of France's perverted art critic who shamed his nation, Europe and his trade with his obscenity and disrespect. Distressed young débutantes who had been present were pictured alongside angry quotes from their fathers who called for Fabian's deportation, regardless of the German U-boats and the war. Marcel was obnoxious, going around saying it was the most educational, interesting, innovative lecture he had ever been to, and a triumph of genius over propriety. He began claiming Fabian as his closest friend, saying that in Europe they had been in each other's company every night of the week, and that he had discovered the genius of Arthur Cravan long before the rest of Europe saw it in *Maintenant*. But he didn't venture back to the jail. Only I did that.

People were curious as to why he had asked for me. Talk began of a secret affair we were supposed to have had in Paris and in Italy, that I was in fact his wife, his sister, his mistress. The fascination with him began in earnest in those earliest days I knew him. He developed overnight a reputation for daring, for being an unpredictable genius who had no time for any convention or law. That was the start of the mythologising about him. It lives with me still, in the people Marcel meets who ask if they can be introduced to the great Arthur Cravan's widow, but they are pall-bearers, carrying to his death a legendary Fabian, a manic Dadaist hero upon whose life they impose whole creeds and worshipful ideologies. You knew him, Jack, everything he did was because it occurred to him seconds before. There was no great master-plan, no art-induced, poetry-inspired mantra before he raced off to execute some new idea he'd had. He would have hated, just as I do, this imposition of Dada heroics on what he did. They say he was the original Dadaist. They say he was a critical genius. They say he abandoned me because he grew bored. They say that he was possessed by madness – all fatuous, self-aggrandising opinion. You knew him. Would he have aligned himself to anything that was bigger than he was? Of course not. He lived for himself, and then we each lived for each other. The bigger picture bored him. It demanded too much rationale.

But it didn't prevent Marcel and Walter and Picabia and all the Arensbergers from putting him on a pedestal, trying to stir him into drunken rages, searching out his opinions on almost everything and everyone. He was too bright for them. He barely spoke when sober, and when drunk he spoke nonsense, deliberate nonsense, abusing everyone around him, challenging them to fight him, even women.

On one of my visits to Sing-Sing he told me that he had always loved me, from the moment of his birth he had been spiralling down a helix that had me at its foot. Every single defence mechanism within me came down like a portcullis when he said it, this strange accidental man who had elected me to the role of soulmate before he even knew me. I had been tripping along happily in my new life, writing and acting, involved with things and people who stirred my mind, took it out of its Italian somnolence – I certainly was not seeking a complication, someone to consume my attentions, turn even my most casual thoughts into ruminations about his eyes, his mouth, his newest thoughts, his capacity for love, his mind. But of course that had already started.

And so I kept my distance, in my head if in no other way, was cautious in those initial weeks, sceptical. I did not trust myself. It had taken such efforts to liberate myself from all the confusions of my marriage, of my affair with Marinetti. I did not trust him. There was a suspicious remarkability about his feelings for me, so sudden and so apparently strong, followed from an impossible juncture. He could not possibly know me, and his talk of destined love was very seductive to a weaker heart, but not one as under-valued as my own.

And yet. Why did I respond to his request for me to come to a prison at 5 a.m. when a retinue of respondents were offering themselves to him, Marcel, Walter, Picabia? Would I have done it for any one of them if the others were there to deal with it, and they my friends? No. Had Marcel rung and said Walter wanted no one but me, had been arrested and desperately needed me, I would have told him to have sense and deal with him himself. It was Fabian's apparition out of nowhere, the strangled connection made while he stood dressed in a toga and me as a lampshade. Whatever had passed between us then brought me to Sing-Sing. I did not squirm when he held me and sobbed with tiredness and frustration, I did not wonder at his interest – I trusted something to make sense of it all eventually. There was so much that was physical about it. I silently admired his strong limbs, his broad chest, his perfectly sculpted bones, the wide expressive eyes that darted from doleful to mischievous in a glint, the exquisite fullness of his wide mouth. I doubt, Jack, that you would have had the patience for any of it, there were no signposts anywhere to show us where we would be led.

When he got out of prison, he would come to my apartment each morning and we would go adventuring in New York. Neither of us had any money, though I was rich in comparison to him. He wasn't joking about living on Penn Station. He showed me. He lived in a space on the roof, an advertising sign he pointed to with tidebreaker-type fence around three sides, and forming the ceiling, he said. One misjudged flail in a nightmare and he was flying over commuting Manhattan. It was a rat-hole, the size of two double mattresses, according to him, and he slept there with the books he had gathered and journals and magazines, and, before me, with as many women as he could entice into climbing the scaffolds and fire escapes outside that served as his entry. I think most of his affairs were conducted in the apartments of those he picked up – he was very loquacious about the number of women he had slept with in New York, in the world. I saw his eyrie with Walter Arensberg's binoculars one day when Fabian and I decided to go bird-watching in the country, and we side-tracked.

We visited a lot of exhibitions, galleries, spent long hours in Central Park. After a few weeks he began coming to the Arensbergs' with me, and there, after initial attempts to make a hero of him as the first art critic in America to be jailed for giving a lecture, he and I took to commandeering the largest armchair, and there we squeezed in night after night and read to each other and told each other our lives, how we had orbited one another in Paris and Florence without ever knowing it.

I knew and he knew that what was between us had only one direction, absolute consumption of each into the other's life, but, fifteen years too late, I decided that I was unable to trust anything I felt and I would not fall in love again. He would get irritated at being out of control, of not being the hand that conducted his life – that he did not possess me fully enough yet and each of us knew it.

In some ways our earliest weeks were the least romantic imaginable, and in some they were the most interesting, erotic, gentle weeks of my life. That is not nostalgia, Jack, we were falling deeply in love and yet admitting none of it, coming at each other without precedent, without any idea as to why we were as we were. Well, I was. He was quite sure why we had met, why we had fallen into each other's lives with such alacrity. He believed we had been on course for one another from the second we were conceived in our mothers' wombs, that we were each the other's fate. He had no cynicism when it came to love, to us. I had enough for each of us. For all his pontificating about the legion of other women he could have if he wasn't with me, all of whom I told him he was free to go to, the expressions of love came thicker than hot wax, the gentleness in him at the fore of almost everything he did.

Our first night together was the tenderest I've ever known. In the early days after he disappeared I would relive it over and over, wish with such fervency that I was back there with him, that none of the chaos around me was real. He asked one day if he could come home with me, said he yearned for a big hot bath. We had come from walking through Brooklyn, he showed me the boxing clubs he had fought in when he first came to New York off the *Montserrat*. It was a hot day, close in that stultifying New York way, and we each were very warm. I said he could. In the apartment he became entranced by my bookcases, all the writing I had bought with such excitement in my months there, writers I had heard so much about and been unable to find in the paralysis of Italy. They were my greatest luxury. I left him on the floor reading through them, and went to run a bath for him, and to change my blouse, to cool down a little with some cold water.

As I stood dabbing the back of my neck, my breasts and shoulders bare, I felt his arms come around me from behind, pulling me close to his chest, kissing my shoulders at first, then turning me to him and kissing my breasts, my earlobes, my lips, and as we made love it was as though there had never been another soul in our lives. He tore away at the last remnants of my inhibition, and from the moment he entered my body, we were possessed by one another. We felt it always, in crowds, in bookshops, in cafés, in markets, this silent sexual intensity electrified by the simple touch of each other's hand, in an elevator, on a train . . . this glorious eroticism that made everything an adventure between us, even just walking down the street.

Later that first evening as we bathed together, we completed the catapult into each other's lives with a passion we had not known existed. How could I want another man now, Jack? It is not loyalty, nor guilt, nor a strange sense of honour, it is simply that in him I had all the love I could ever want, and another man's body would seem as sensual as caressing cold bronze. I am aglow with the remembrances, with the sensations that come back to me when I think of how we were in each other's arms. I miss him, Jack, I miss him so.

He and I traversed Manhattan a hundred times in those days, and the Bronx, and Queens. He took me to watch boxing, explaining why someone was good, or bad, or lazy. All you say about your fights, your career – it brings those days back with a drunken clarity, as though I were looking at photographs and convincing myself I was there. He said things that you say, would tell me how a fight is won inside a man's head, and that the fists are the part that you can train, but not the mind. He spoke often of you. He confessed the truth about your fight in Barcelona, how he had disappeared when you knocked him out.

It was difficult for him to say it – so much of his hard-edged image was bled into the fact that he had fought you, and had stood his ground, that you had been in that ring as equals. He told me it one evening walking over Brooklyn Bridge in the twilight. He said he had let you down badly, had cheated the only person he thought worth a damn in this world.

Then he retracted that, said that, until he had found me, there had been no one in this world he thought his equal but you. You and Jack, he said, could be King and Queen of America in the new monarchal universe. He would be our jester. He would be happy we're back in contact again. I know he would be.

It wasn't as though he moved in, he had no belongings to speak of, he simply forgot to leave, and I neglected to ask him. He was intrigued by my children. My apartment was full of photographs taken by Stephen when they were young, and by myself and Frances when they were older. He was awestruck by their physical perfection, by their purity and innocence, and could not understand why I had left them. It was our only true source of discord in those early months. I became resentful of his enrapture with the children, feeling that a suggestion of my selfishness in leaving them lay within his praise. Over and over he would ask what age they were when they each first walked, spoke, sat up on their own, how quickly their personalities became apparent, when they opened their eyes first. He seemed to regard newborn babies as infant mice or kittens, as though they would soon stop being pink-skinned and helpless, would grow fur, ferret out their own food and be making their own beds within ten weeks of leaving the womb. He thought Giles and Joella the most wonderful inventions on the planet because they went to school on their own and read books. He was determined we should bring them to New York.

But of course the war prevented that. I wrote regularly to them, and received reports from Giulia and their headmistress as to their progress. Stephen had moved to the Bahamas to live, and the pettiness and oneupmanship between us had finally dissipated. I was free of all the mistakes of the past. Only Oda could not be undone. There was so much to Fabian that I would wake next to him each morning with a flutter in my stomach that we had the day ahead just for each other. My money from the sale of Stephen's heirlooms and antiques had lasted just over a year with careful spending and through making my own clothes, but it was a dwindling resource, and I began thinking of how I would survive when it was gone.

But other things came down on us first. The American government brought in that act, the Selective Service one, that conscripted all able-bodied men between the age of twenty-one and thirty-one, and being foreign did not matter one bit. We had barely been together two months and already the impossibilities were encroaching on our carefully concealed lair. He had managed not to serve in the war so far by escaping first from England, then Germany, then France, and of course Spain, the moment conscription was announced, using all sorts of faked papers. He could have escaped from anywhere. Don't think that hasn't been trawled across my mind a hundred thousand times, for it obsessed me for three years after I came back from the prisons and the trail went so cold. I do mean obsessed, Jack. I could think of absolutely nothing else but how he could have done it. I looked at maps, got tide reports, detailed accounts of the hurricane that hit his bearings over the first two days he was gone, worked out what papers he would have needed. I lived as a deserted wife in my head for those early years of Fabienne's childhood, while outwardly feigning the conviction that I believed him dead. It was one thing, you see, for me to believe it, search out the possibility, test my most fearsome suspicions, but another for others to do it, to treat it as a genuine option. It was my grief, my bereavement, and my life that had to be lived without him. I investigated the possibilities until I was certain that there was no way a boat of that size could have survived a storm of such destruction on an ocean like that. He would not have had time to sail down the coast and disembark, for all the places within the time before the storm were too close to count as an escape. A tall European of his build would have been noted in an instant, and we checked every port-town and harbour for seventy miles, Jack.

There was no other fate. For all his prowess with compasses and forged papers, not even my gentle Fabian could vanquish a hurricane on the open sea. And what everyone forgets is that I knew him better than all of them, it was I who loved him and was loved by him, he would not leave me, and he would not leave our child in my womb, unborn and unseen by him. A child of our own was his greatest wish, his dream for Joella and Giles to join us, to give each other and all the children all the love we had in us. That dream drowned with him. It was not stolen.

He had a gift for forgery that was a greater talent than that of most of the artist-types whom Stephen hung around with in Paris. It itched in him as the war effort began in earnest. The recruiting bureaux squatted like sinister news-stands on prominent street corners across the city, while jingoistic mania thrived like a malignant fungus in the stultifying heat of war.

Foreigners of any sort were now treated as though we had single-handedly started the war, and were only in America to spy. Fabian had made a great deal of high-profile, powerful enemies when he outraged upper-class New York's femininity. Walter warned us that Fabian ran the risk of being arrested unless he either joined up or disappeared. We didn't take it altogether seriously – it seemed to make sense for him to get out of New York, but not to escape abroad, not yet. Picabia's wife Gabrielle arranged for him to travel upstate to Saratoga Springs (wasn't that where the races were held, at which you met Etta?) to work there as a translator for an elderly professor of literature. He wanted someone both to proof-read his French translation of *The Divine Comedy*, and to translate into French a scatter of poems by Catullus and Livy. Fabian, for all his vagabondery, had been given a classical education, up until the age of fifteen, when he ran off to Paris and America first, and his letters to me from Saratoga Springs were filled with a delirious calm. Walter told me that, three months before, no one would have dared recommend Fabian as so much as a window-cleaner. The idea of sending him away to engage in academic conference with a respected intellect in leafy sedation up-state would have been unthinkable. Thanks to me, he was a new man.

There was never any specific point when I fell out with Walter and the Arensbergers generally, but I grew weary of such patronisation. Marcel had grown cold towards me, as though I had betrayed him in falling in love with the Greek sculpture instead of maintaining offence and outrage. Bill too. He was short with me now in the way he had always been with the others, as if he had retracted my special dispensation as his confidante. He did not like Fabian, he thought him uncouth and lacking in respect. He, like Lou and Gabi, took me aside to ask if I knew what I was doing with Fabian. He told me I was a beautiful, elegant, talented woman, and deserved someone who appreciated all these things. He became offended when I said that I already had found such a man.

They all seemed to think Fabian heroic in his disregard for virtually everything the world held sacred, but only at a distance. Falling in love with one of their own was not allowed. Their coldness was my punishment for daring to look outside the fold for my fulfilment, rather than sleeping around behind each other's backs as they did.

I was tempted to go to Saratoga with him, for us both to escape. Fabian would try and persuade me every morning in the week before he left, until it became such a joke that I wasn't going that I forgot I still could. I yearned for him in his absence. All my cynicism and doubtfulness disappeared entirely in those weeks. Without him I felt as though I had awoken too early, as if I was waiting for the hour when I could get up and go about my life, that only the most practical things were setting up their dawn stalls while my real world still slept.

Soon he was back, his sojourn simply a distraction of weeks, not months. We dallied between declaring everything to each other and protecting our hearts. Protection won, the tension between us building daily until we each indulged our frustration utterly. We argued over small indiscriminate things, easy decisions for people operating on even ground, but the tumult within us was heaving up everything we stood on together.

I loved him. I knew it with all my heart. I knew it with a fearsome certainty that petrified me. I knew that everything before, all my artifice around Marinetti, was a reprisal of loneliness, of a neglected soul and intellect. Of boredom. With Fabian nothing was obvious, nothing easily dissected – everything seemed to change arbitrarily as soon as it had settled into place. I was afraid to cede. I had withstood the attentions of others, of Bill, of Marcel, of Walter in his gentle way. Clear attentions. With Fabian, the signals were never replicated. He had told me he loved me, that I was spectacular, beautiful, stellar in intellect . . . and yet other women arrived at my apartment looking for him with a steadiness that did not trickle to a close with the increasing fervency of his proclamations of love. It seemed I was the only one for him but while I made up my mind about reciprocating, he would flirt at will, probably worse. On the one occasion I confided in someone, it was to Marcel, a gesture that depended on the vestiges of our past friendship, if not our current one. But to him it was merely a chance to punish me for choosing beyond him. He laughed at me, said I was the only one in New York who did not know of Fabian's reputation.

I drew away from Fabian, and he felt it. We each protected ourselves as best we could by turning our manic implosion of love, all the memories of our early weeks without the self-consciousness of time apart, into something that had to be hidden, preserved. Things became unbearable in that temperature of unsated love. His declarations became more and more fervent, as though he were trying to hypnotise me into reciprocating his ardency. I recoiled. The visits, he said, were a follow-on from his past, from the man he was the night I had first met him, the night of the Ball. His friend Frost had been his message-taker – he was merely passing his new address on to all those who called. But it all seemed too easy, too explicable. I doubted him, and in that mood of distrust we careered carelessly between such passionate conversations and nights in each other's arms to terse fraught days when I barely acknowledged his presence.

Yet it is those days that I yearn for most, the ones where I had no faith in our discovery of each other, when my past, against all my self-proclaimed abandonment of it, coloured all I had found in Fabian. I refused to be made vulnerable again. If I could have him now I would go back to those earliest feet-finding weeks and love him unconditionally, let myself go utterly, trust all that he gave me and give back with every ounce of love in me.

But that is the exquisite torture of hindsight. All fantasy and impotence. Instead we pushed each other further from what was in us to say – or rather, he tried endlessly to explain what I meant to him and I smiled and held him and said nothing in return, nothing of consequence, only what I thought were a series of staving-off compliments. But they were not. They were, and he saw it long, long before I did, all the reasons why I was falling in love with him, cast-off sentences that accrued in his heart over a period of months and gave him every reason in the world to understand how desperately I loved him.

And yet one evening we had a ferocious argument, his patience thwarted and his anger overbearing as he told me I had no regard for him at all, wanted nothing more upsetting to my perfect life than a casual love, was too weak to deal with one that actually had a future, a rare and powerful future. He threw all his belongings in his bag and left, still ranting and spitting with anger and disgust at what he called my obtuseness. I was equally enraged, but when he had left and the apartment gone silent, the rage dissipated and I broke down completely. I knew what I had lost, for the first time clearly I saw it.

I waited for him to return that evening. I stayed awake all night waiting for his drunken slur to come through the door telling me he loved me, that he was sorry we had fought. I could not sleep for yearning. The next morning I walked to where he had shown me he lived, but there was no evidence of him there. I walked to places he had pointed out on our walks, places he said he had slept. Eventually I walked to the coffee shop I had left as a meeting-place in a note for him, had he come home, keyless, in my absence. And then I went home, tasting in those hours the fate I now imbibe each morning as though it were a long-life potion, my curse.

That afternoon I thought of his closest friend in New York, Frost. I went to the building and was shown to his floor by a liveried concierge. There, as she invited me into his opulent apartment, his maid told me he had left that morning for Canada with a friend, but he would be back in time for Christmas, and if I was one of his lady-friends did I care to leave a note for when he returned. I was stricken. I pressed her for details of his friend. A tall man, she said, fairish brown hair, very strong to look at. It was him, I had no doubt. He had deserted me.

Those days that followed were worse than all my years with Stephen. I went through the months Fabian and I had spent together as though writing a diary in my head that would serve as evidence in a trial. Every nuance, every unsaid heartfelt thing rang in my head as I reclaimed all the glorious, epiphanic moments we had known together, and the gentle, unaware ones which I held even more closely. I realised I understood him as I had understood no other person. He fitted in me like a wick in a candle, as much a part of everything good in me as I was to him. And I realised with a shock that I loved him more than my children, than those two tender, funny, sweet-natured infants I had left to fend for themselves in Italy, armed only with the spiritual sustenance of a nurse to guide them as they broke through the surface water of the world around them. I wanted to see him more than them, I wanted him with me more than them. And worse. I wanted this and felt only guilt, that it was perfectly right to want him more, guilty at the logic of it rather than the shamefulness. Four days later a postcard came from upstate New York, though not Saratoga. It was short, and in his favourite language. *Chère amie, As-tu bien dormi?*

It was signed with his full-blooded flourish. At first I was so incensed I stormed around the three square feet of the apartment shouting at the walls and mirrors and bathroom tiles, shouting at him, having exactly the scene we would have had had he been there, but with the frustrating dissatisfaction of him being several hundred miles upstate.

When I calmed I went out to the Brevoort Hotel, the scene of Louise Norton's débâcle, and had an anonymous supper on my own while thinking things through. I had the postcard inside my novel, but I didn't look at it again. It was still rather unseemly for a lady to dine alone but in between the waiters' fuss and attention I came clear. It was not a taunt. He was angry, certainly, but he wasn't malicious, not to me. He was not like other men. His vanity was of a thinking sort, restricted to appreciation of his mind, not his sentiments. My refusal to fall headlong had bruised an ego, yes, but his desertion was not petulance. His words were not a sneering gloat. If I was to deal with this man on the terms I had come to understand in his absence – that I loved him above all others and wanted him passionately – I had to bleach my mind of all memories of the past. I could not appropriate hurts and slights and any sense of rejection from my time in Italy, or Paris. This had only itself to thrive on, and no collection of confusions and losses and failures from a previous existence would enable me to take Fabian for all he was and love him for it truly. I had to slough off all skins. I had to walk naked. Two days later a letter came, apologising for his temper, his disappearance, our dreadful fight. He told me he loved me deeply, but could no longer live with me on the premise that I might one day love him. He would be back in New York in four days and needed to see me.

In fact it was the following day that he came, thanks to the timing of the postal service. He arrived at the apartment sheepishly, as though he was the one in error, and acting as though he were only stopping by to say hello *en route* to Frost's. We didn't leave the apartment for five days. Everything I felt came out in a rush, a great turbulent surge of love unlike any I'd known, or heard of. All my gnomic silences, my half-smiled non-reciprocations, my luring him into explaining why he loved me without saying a thing back . . . I had months of those to fill in during those days together. I think his shock was genuine, he truly never expected to hear me say them. He knew what I felt better than I. For five days we talked nakedly and honestly by the fire or in bed. He wanted to be with me for the rest of his life, he said. I wanted to be with him. In effect we decided that we would bind our lives together always. That, I suppose, is exactly what we have done.

Then everything was thwarted. Frost arrived. Fabian's name had appeared on a list of foreigners who were to be conscripted under a new provision. He was already late for reporting for recruitment. Frost too had been conscripted, though as an American. That, it seemed, was the reason for the sudden trip upstate, though Fabian had convinced him to come home, purely, as far as I could tell, for his own good, rather than Frost's. But when he was also up for being sent to war, things changed.

It was a difficult one to work out, I thought. But the mastermind had no such doubts. He would leave immediately, and they would escape to Canada, and from Canada go to a country whose neutrality looked tenable. There they would settle, and I would follow on. What did I think?

I was aghast. All the fireside longing, the decision never to be apart again, the intensity of our conversation, of our love-making, of the feeling within us that seemed so utterly inviolable, the raw outpouring of disclosures and confidences that comes when defences are abandoned and anything less than searing honesty seems like a lie.

'Ingenious,' I said. 'Perfect.' And so the plan rolled onward.

Within hours he was gone. I was so caught up in performing my nonchalance at his apparently permanent departure that I had no time to prepare myself for the fact of his leaving, for the fact that I was far from being gaily nonplussed by his desertion. I fell apart when he left, in a day swinging from the most effusive elation I had ever known to a perplexed and deeply hurt cynicism. Everything to nothing in one solitary day.

He thought war a fool's game and had absolutely no interest in dying while defending ideology. There was no question of him becoming a conscientious objector either – it wasn't that he objected one bit, indeed as far as he was concerned everyone could all march off into the trenches and slaughter indefinitely. No. He had no sense of the savagery of war, the barbaric lunacy of it. It was a failing, I think, a lack of comprehension of the intricacies of humanity, its power. At the time I did not think him wrong, merely that my own previously passionate espousal of war made me particularly fervent in my disgust with it. It was I whom I thought unusual. He seemed to fit a matrix already made that had been spinning through the Arensbergers for months, collecting new pseudo-pacifists with every turn like a half-sucked lozenge falling on carpet.

But there was an almost entrepreneurial gusto in the way he adapted to circumstance, and after two years of darting battle in Europe, he regarded American involvement as little more than an irritating circumstance to change one's plans for. If I was a part of those original plans, then I too must suffer the change. There was a pragmatism to him, Jack, that you experienced as much as I. If escaping the fight through a knock-out and absconding with the purse was something he had justified in his desperation, then so too was leaving me behind in New York with our promises not yet dry in our mouths. He truly did not believe the effect of tricking you or running off to save himself from war could ever undermine the relationship he had with each of us. He was an under-writer in so many ways, weighing up the effect of desperation over bonds, and always always risking the bond. I suppose he saw more clearly than you or I the depths we had reached in our relationship with him. He knew he had us.

And so his escape began in earnest. So too his letters. For all of that September I got a letter every second or third day with the post office of the next town he expected to arrive in soldered on in large letters. But I did not write.

I was in a deeply frustrating position. I knew I loved him, that all I felt in the days after our argument was non-retractable, that those emotions were the sum of everything I had in me to love with, and it was him, above all others, for his spontaneity, his breadth of knowledge, that urgent auto-didacticism in him that pushed his mind further and further, always teasing its limitless curiosity . . . for these things and his tender, questioning openness I loved him, and I knew that I was captured. I would never find any other man's conversation, body, laughter, interest in me anything more than something politely to take note of. I wanted so desperately to reject him outright, to say I had no need for him and go back to the life I had before him, to the Arensbergs', to Marcel, to late-night chess-playing with Bill, to writing to my children and worrying about my poetry, writing it, going to exhibitions, dressing up for parties, having my photograph taken, being fêted. I wanted to be able to erase him if he was not willing to be with me. But of course I could not.

After about ten letters from him I did write. He was in a place far up north called Meductic, about to cross over to Newfoundland. Frost had acquired two ill-fitting soldier's uniforms from somewhere through a touch of expensive bribery, and the two of them had travelled north dressed exactly in the garb they were escaping from. It was the simplest most effective plan conceivable. Who on earth would question soldiers as to whether they had yet enlisted? His letters arrived in my mail-box filled with news of the stories they had concocted at their excitement at being on furlough, their preparations for travel to Europe, their theories of war. Cars pulled up on the roads out of every town they exited offering them lifts, one man driving them two hundred miles to help them meet up with the rest of their squadron. Frost had cleverly failed to specify what kind of uniforms he wanted, and the pair of them were traversing northwards dressed as two air-corps pilots, lying their way through a thousand miles of fascinated queries about what it must be like to fly.

They slept in fields, their itinerary marked out in increasing detail as they edged deeper into Canada, the cars fewer and fewer the further north they reached. His letters were saturated with remorse for the speed of his departure, for the fact of it at all, and often I cried reading them, caught up in the conflict between yearning and rejecting. They were outpourings of his feelings for me, assurances that when we were reunited we would never be apart again, reiterations of the promises and vows we had made to one another in those five delirious days. He never made excuses for leaving, just passionately beseeched me to understand him always, and be with him always. Everything, he said, seemed to remind him of me – his conversations with Frost, the books he had brought, the loneliness he professed to be afflicted with, a woman balladeering at a piano in an inn they stopped at, the sight of children playing . . . He asked after my children often, and said that, as soon as we were together again and the war ended, we could make plans for them to travel from Italy to meet us.

His newest plan was that we should rendezvous in Argentina, that I should travel to Buenos Aires and he would join me. I stayed where I was. There he was in Canada with me down the coast in New York, and yet he thought it sensible that he and I each journey to Argentina to reunite. Still the letters came, filled with love and longing for us to be together. He mirrored everything I felt in my heart in his letters, but though I had been slow to write, when I did the letters were, reluctantly, as open and full of love. I had to decide to trust him, to accept that we would never operate within reasonable, ordinary boundaries, that I should not expect the proprietorial sensibilities that had prevailed in my other relationships. If I was to follow everything I felt, I had to abandon the usual expectations and accept the vulnerability that ensued. Else I too, like everyone in the world around me, would be caught up in the pettiness of everyday loves. And we were both worth more than that. Much more.

I did a lot of my own writing in those weeks, retrospective work on Italy now that I was freed of its weights. I also had the delicious experience of having my sequence of poems, Love Songs, finally published. There had been a great deal of work to do in preparing them for publication, and they did not exactly earn me new friends in the conservative wing – Amy Lowell came out for me again with her rusty cleaver – but I was delirious with excitement at finally seeing them all run together in a sequence, as they were written to be.

I knew they were good. I knew they had been crafted with a diligence and certainty of purpose that had not been applied to anything else in my life, and when they were published I simply thought rather highly of myself. I wanted Fabian there to share the feeling, the pride. At the same time I did not send a copy to one of his thousand postal bureaux.

He was progressing well in his bid to secure me for ever. I was happily carefree again, partly because I felt the poetry beginning to matter, partly because the children's letters were full of gaiety at having made a great number of new friends during their school term, but mainly because of what came to me of him through the mail-box every second day. I had resumed frequenting the Arensbergs', and was again being asked my opinion in newspapers as the glamorous Modernist. I think Marcel was the mad one, and Louise Norton had resurfaced downtown as the giggler. Walter was the rich one. It passed quickly, this idiocy, but it was nice being at the centre of things again, or at least feeling I was. Few believed that Fabian and I were still very much in love; the whispers were loud and deliberately so. I did not care. I came now to this circle as a supplement to my inner world, where he reigned utterly.

And then suddenly the letters stopped. One minute he and Frost were awaiting a whaling boat to Mexico, and the next, gone, all contact suspended.

For the first three weeks I didn't let myself worry. If he was travelling, then he may not have had time to write, may have posted his letters from a point *en route* that would take a long time to reach me, may indeed have decided to wait until he arrived in Mexico before he sent me any word of his journey. Then I began to worry obsessively, checking the mail-box five, six times each day despite having received my other post, haranguing Frost's maid daily about her master, sending stricken letters to the postal bureau in Newfoundland which had been his last contact address, even writing to the postal officer himself to find out the last occasion Fabian had been in to collect his mail. I asked about Frost too, and Arthur Cravan, whom he was travelling as in most places to suit the papers he carried. I received prompt replies that told me he had last been in on 27 September, the day after the date of his last letter to me.

As it goes with panic, it occupied me completely. Those days seem innocent now. New York filled with Christmas and I struggled with snowfall, slipping and sliding around the smaller unploughed streets as I went each morning to the library to work on the poems. It was an unconvincing distraction. And then one day in mid-December I received a visitor, a small Texan man who had been with Fabian just three days previously, and entrusted with bringing a letter to me when he reached New York. I brought the man in and gave him food while clawing at him for knowledge of Fabian, or Art Cravan as he kept calling him. Once I knew he was alive and safe, the familiar anger grew in me. He was in Mexico. I think the small man thought I was his married sister or something – when I asked how he was, was he healthy and free of illness, he bellowed a lewd laugh from his tiny body and proceeded to tell me what a man that Cravan was with women, they could not resist him in southern parts, and could he drink! Well, could he. A great man, he said, he was sorry he hadn't known him longer. How long had he known him? Oh, two long days and nights, he said, and winked, and said he must be on his way, he was in New York on important business.

When he left, I read the letter, desperately unsure what to think. I wanted to talk to someone, to ask them what I should believe, but Frances was in England and Mabel and I had not talked properly in over a year. I felt very alone.

His letter was very depressed. He said he missed me fearfully, that he was tormented by the idea that he would not see me again, that he could not bear to think that I did not understand how much he loved me. He said he was on the verge of suicide, but like me was far too afraid of letting himself go entirely. And then more protestations of love, and then the news, the reason for his lack of contact.

Frost was dead. They had been eating breakfast together in a ditch outside a town called Curling, when Frost was suddenly overcome with tiredness and needed to lie down. Fabian had jostled with him, saying they had only just awoken, and after another while walking they would be near the harbour, he could sleep for days on the boat. But Frost had insisted, and Fabian had written to me while he slept. He never awoke. Fabian had been unable to shake him, and when he could not find a pulse, had run back to the town and fetched a doctor, who said there was nothing he could do, and pronounced Frost dead.

They found he had died of a haemorrhaging to the brain. Fabian stayed in Curling for over a week, arranged a funeral, explained to the pastor and the concerned that military honours would not be required when they suggested the young soldier be given his full burial rights. He had left the town then, in shock still, he said, barely functioning. Functioning enough though to understand that he could not travel alone in uniform or he would attract attention as a deserter. So he dressed as a woman, and travelled north from farm to farm, through fields and woods, until he got to the harbour.

Frost dead. They had been friends since sixteen, had travelled to America together that first time and ridden boxcars to California, had worked together in the orange groves, sparred in the boxing clubs, come back to Europe and urged each other into lunacy throughout Paris and Berlin. And then Frost had returned to America, gained citizenship through his family, and settled down to paint at the bidding of his father's wealth. They were brothers far more than Otho, Fabian's blood brother, united in every mistake and triumph for more than a decade. To lose him was almost like losing a wife or husband or a lover we have made promises to in our hearts. I thought of the days and weeks that had followed Oda's death as I wrote to him at the Mexican address on the letter, trying as best I could to do all the things for him that I had ached to have done for me, whispered to me, in that time. And I cried that night, not for the insinuation of infidelity by the lecherous oaf who had delivered the letter, but for the acute impotence my life was seized by in not being able to be with him. My need for him.

I was scared by the doubt I felt, the idea that I could not breezily dismiss the suggestion of other women. There were two men, the one I loved, and the one who went upstate when we fought, who ran away to Canada within minutes of pledging his life to me. One was beyond reproach. One was beyond belief.

He was on his own now in Mexico, he was working in some kind of opal mine to earn the money to travel onward to Mexico City. I did not mention what the Texan had said at first. When I did he was desperately upset, and gratified. Every letter up until Christmas swore that he had been steadfastly faithful, that that part of his life was past now, that I was foolish to believe anything a brigand like that said anyway. They had met for just two days and swapped a lot of bar-talk. He had been drinking very heavily since Frost's death and maybe they had talked in that drunken swagger about women, but only in talk, if that. I was to trust him, he loved me, I was not to doubt him in any way but to think of all our time together and know that he loved me. The pride came from the idea that I should be so concerned; he was delighted that I was reacting so possessively. Had he heard a whisper of that ilk about me he would have been destroyed, he said, and it was balm to know that I felt as powerfully as he. I chose to believe him then, and I still do.

New York at Christmas is a jollying affair, unless you are a mother separated from her children, or a lover apart from her soul-mate. I was disconsolate that Christmas. Only my divorce from Stephen resurrected my spirits, freed me from his arachnoid grasp forever. I knew I wanted a life with Fabian, with the unpredictable insanity he offered me amidst his intelligence, his constantly questioning mind. I had never met a man so knowledgeable, so absorbed by literature and history and art, and scathing of so much that middle-brow New York was enraptured by – never met a man who thought so much like I did, and still made everything seem unpredictable.

I spent much of that Christmas with Walter and Lou, and the merry band of self-proclaiming atheists and pagans that Marcel assured me always came out at this time of year. There were many parties, many strangers, but not one of them as interesting, even fleetingly, as the one who had swept down on me on the night of the Blind Man's Ball. Bill came to me at the Christmas Eve Supper and asked had I any new work, he would love to see what I was doing now. I gave him a sheaf of work I thought matched my Love Songs for their clarity, poems I had played a great deal with, teasing out words that lent them an eclectic air of sobriety.

I got Fabian's Christmas letters all in one batch, as though sent on the same day. His Christmas Eve, while I flirted lightly at the Arensbergs', had been spent in a makeshift tent eating kidney beans softened in vinegar and drinking stale beer. He wrote that without me he was numb, that all his savagery and manias were flooding him until all he could think of was death, of dying alone, without me, that he feared Frost's death was turning him mad. He had taken a vow of chastity, that were he never to see me again he would not ever so much as kiss another woman. He said too that in some ways I had not known him at all in New York, and yet had known him absolutely for seeing beyond what he called his hideousness. Then he asked me to marry him, to come to Mexico and marry him, to be with him always. 'You know very well,' he said, 'that I can provide for all your needs and that I'd be the happiest man in the world if I had the chance to do it . . . I can't live without you, Mina, you must come or I must go to New York. I am desperate. Do you know letters take a month to arrive and you would only take four or five days – this thought makes me almost delirious. Please come. I forgot to tell you that I love you as much for your mind as your heart and I'll love you wrinkled, with your hair turned white, just as much as I love you now. You told me that I was the only man who had given the impression of a god. Come if you want a taste of the angel. Please come, if you don't you will leave me empty. Do you know what it is to empty a man? It is to leave him without genius. *Je t'aime, je t'aime, je t'aime*. . . be my wife, Fabian.'

It was as though I had known it was coming, and I did, I suppose – the plan made in haste, immediately discarded by me, that I should follow himself and Frost to Buenos Aires, the things said by the fire in those five days, the conclusion really to all that had come alive in each of us since that forlorn dawn in prison. It was not a sense of destiny that rose in me as I sat in my apartment thinking all of it through, it was a surge of quasi lust, a passion that made me want to hold him close to me always, something I had the chance now to do if I wanted it enough. And I did. New York was a place of sense, of protocol, of war and changing habit, where I had come and been happy and could now go from and be happier. War was war, unlikely to rearrange itself merely because I had fallen in love. I could not bring my children from Italy until its close, and all I had in New York had been upended by him from the moment I had known how I loved him. I wanted to feel fresh, to wake up vital and unsure, for the days to be unpredictable but always, always to awake in his arms and face the world with dual vision.

I wrote back that evening, and three days later Marcel and Bill saw me off on the journey that would bring me to him, each of them counselling me not to go, not to sacrifice New York for the sake of a love-affair. But it was more than that. I was not leaving for the sake of a love-affair, I was leaving to pursue what I had always pursued no matter what hue I had cast on it. I was leaving Mexico to chase my own happiness, that elusive thing that finally, finally, had settled in a place it truly belonged. In Fabian.

You, Jack, of all people, must understand the compulsion. Please write soon.

Your friend,

Mina

FABIENNE

My father reached Spain in 1923, with the clothes he stood in. Or perhaps he had belongings, picked up here and there as he traversed the South American continent trying to get back to Europe, to his wife and unseen child. He had no money, only his own resources and memories of my mother. So he came up with a plan.

The pilgrims stretch almost two kilometres and a hundred people deep, sending their prayers of thanks that they should be the village chosen from all those in Spain, from all across the world. In this border town they are too close to Portugal to feel entirely benevolent about the phenomenon at Fatima. Why Fatima? Why not Aliseda?

Now Our Lady has blessed them too and they scour the skies looking for her, seeing her halo form in the clouds, her shape, and then, gone, as though she had changed her mind. They see her at all times of day, but yet she does not appear to them properly. They try to hear her voice speak to them, but hear only the low cacophonous drone of hundreds of thousands of voices incanting her name, her prayer, over and over.

Only the mine-worker to whom she has appeared has been blessed with her words. It is to him that they throng, to the dirt track where he kneels night and day talking to the Blessed Virgin when she appears to him, while the crowds ripple with euphoria that she is among them, though they cannot see her. He falls down exhausted after she has come to him, speaking strangely in the minutes that he rests, and they are afraid to go to him in case they break her spell.

He is wondering how much longer this will have to go on. He had estimated a week, but underestimated the devotion and persistence of these people, and the phenomenal powers of the tiny village in spreading the news. At ten days the boredom of kneeling for eighteen hours a day almost wears him down, but still they throng, and still he stays, relaying the Blessed Virgin's message to her faithful, the human conduit.

She has come to him six times in two weeks on this path, told him that they are blessed, that Spain is blessed, that those who give her love will receive her love, that the world needs her light. It will change their lives that the Madonna has seen how they struggle.

Share your light, she tells them through the miner, for this can be a world of love again. The people who come from across Spain are in awe that this young man should be the chosen one, this small empty village, and it renews their piety that the Blessed Virgin should appear to such simple people, to a town not unlike the one they themselves have left behind long ago to find work in the city.

Those with wealth begin to collect money to build a church here where the man kneels, and soon there is enough for five churches. One morning the miner turns and rises and they see he is a tall man, broad, a man to entrust divine thoughts to for safe-keeping. He stands and addresses them, says Our Lady has bidden him to go northwards to spread her love and wisdom, and he must leave. She has gone, he says, but she may return. Their devotion has given her great joy, he adds.

He is given a large sum by the wealthy men so he can begin an order as Our Lady has instructed. Many people accompany him until near France he disappears. Eventually they give him up, some believing he has ascended to greater things, and they return. Their church is built, the shrine visited by thousands upon thousands in the years to come. His name is legend evermore.

Jack

New York, May 1946

Dear Mina,

So that was how you ended up in Mexico. Cravan was wild when he heard you were on your way, he could have lit up Mexico City for a year the way he glowed. You really loved the bastard, didn't you? And he was so damned crazy about you, it would have been worrying in another man, that kind of devotion. But I understood once I met you. There never was anyone like you, Mina.

I never had that kind of devotion. I had fans, and people all over who thought I was their hero, I had the worship and adulation all right. But never like that, never from one person I felt the same way about.

The other kind wasn't much use when the Feds turned against you. There I was in Paris, exiled from everything I loved, with only Lucille to keep my head from going crooked. Of course, I pretended I loved Paris. It was 1913, it was the place I'd always dreamt of. A person could be anything in Paris, nobody judged, nobody shouted nigger at you as they crossed the street. We had our big house, Lucille in her furs, her diamonds, I had all my cars shipped over and we roared around French society like we owned it.

And I hated it. It was tough on Lucille. She thought the stigma of abuse would end for her now that the trial was over and we were starting again. We left Paris for a short while to go to London, where I did my vaudeville show in the West End, and then toured with it. I did exhibition matches too, for the truth was that after three months of high-kicks and expensive parties, my money was low. Enough for another few months, but after that . . . Lucille thought I was doing the shows to keep busy, but I was doing them for a thousand English pounds a week. Even in England there was war in just trying to stage the show, with all the moral crusaders leaping out from the wings in full costume chanting the usual script.

I was a nasty nasty black crook. That was the sum of it. If all those lovely white people in America thought I was a bad bastard, then obviously I was. I must be stopped. I was, for a bit, but the promoter got his balls back when he realised how much publicity was being stirred, and he put me straight out on tour to milk it. I made a good haul from that tour. Strangely, the only bigwig to come out in my defence was the guy Cravan hated above all others, the Marquis of Queensberry. He said he was a malicious bastard who had destroyed his uncle. He talked all the time about that. Was Oscar Wilde really his uncle? I asked him a few times if it wasn't just another of his daft stories, but he swore to me it was true. I was never sure if I believed him.

I was damn near broke after a while, even with all the vaudeville money still in England – the problem really was that I had been living too high off my dollars. I'd never had it like that before, the normal way of doing it was to store up the cash and when I ran low, organise a big fight, make a wad more, then keep going. I'd kind of forgotten my new situation. Life wasn't normal any more. Nothing was. I had a tattered glamour in Europe, a vague idea I was a hero of some kind. I'd been done by jealousy back home, but in the end it faded fast. Nobody really gave a damn. I was a news story for a few months, Jack Johnson and his beautiful wife Lucille open the Motor Show, and pictures of me beaming with Lucille looking like she was going to fall out of a hot-air balloon.

I think Irene burned them all after we got married, but there was all this other stuff around too, newsreel of me and Lucille driving down the Champs-Elysées smiling and waving, of us at the theatre, at the Moulin Rouge, the Bal Bullier, in restaurants and opera boxes. Then the novelty wore off. I was still there, and hadn't gone off somewhere else, was still being Jack Johnson in Paris when what they wanted was Lillian Gish in a gondola in Venice telling everyone how she loved Europe. For the first time in my life I had no control. I was at the mercy of other people. That was how it felt, and damn it, I hated it. I really hated it. I just wanted to be back in Chicago getting speeding tickets again, planning a big fight to knock all those sorry bastards off their perch. But they had me. I was had, first time ever, I was had.

I got broke pretty quick. Money-wise, I mean. The other way never really happened, not completely. I got very down, very depressed and stuff, but they never broke me. If they had I'd be a bitter old bullfighter or something now, and I'm here, happy, telling it all to you. You're the proof they didn't get me. Don't think I'd be talking so freely if I thought they'd got me. Nobody did. They just winded me for a while, that's all.

But I came damn close to being felled by the exile thing at the start, the loneliness and betrayal I felt all the time, and it was Cravan that kept me from going under. That was why he was so damned important to me all my life. When I met him during that time in Paris, everything going on inside my head was just like a fight, like that breaking point I told you about when one of you faces into your own fear and you either rocket on through it or you're faced with it for the whole fight. And you lose. That was exactly how I was then, I was facing into the shittiest bit of my life I had ever known, I'd nothing left to prove, I'd shown them, and yet here I was, the one in exile with a prison sentence waiting for me at immigration the second I tried to get back into my own country. It was hard not to get self-pitying.

Cravan stopped me. Part by example, by his rushing around

the place getting on with things, all his schemes and plans going at once, falling over each other to string him up, but working out all the same. He made you get all fired up and want to be doing the same, to be racing around up to something all the time, not sitting in a big expensive sandstone house feeling all sorry for yourself.

It was when I got back from England that I met him. I was supposed to be fighting a guy called Battling Jim Johnson in Paris, more to build up a bit of revenue than anything else. A man called Cravan I was told was running the betting – if I wanted to place a wedge on myself to win, he was the man to go to.

We met in a bar in Montmartre where the lamps were made of sheep's stomachs with the guts washed out. It was seedy even by my standards. It was also his office. I'd expected him to match the place, be some fat little gluttonous pig handling used notes and drinking too hard for that time of day. But there he was in the corner of the bar that he lived in, this big, broad, blond man in a cream linen three-piece and two-tone leather shoes all polished up and perfect, writing hard at this bar table like his concentration was about to make him explode. He had it all placed round him, the inkpot, the piles of papers, the scribbled notes, photographs, telegrams, all this junk that made him look as frightening as the damn judge that sent me down. I looked round for the pig man but the place was empty. This had to be him.

As I went over in his direction he saw me, and leapt up and pulled out a chair before giving me this great bear hug and telling me wasn't it great that I was living in Paris now too, wasn't it a bitch of a city to get by in, what did I drink, how he'd seen the footage of the Ketchel and Jeffries fights, but his favourite was Tommy Burns because the bastards really didn't know what had hit them in that one. All the others was me battering the crap out of them, but Burns, he said, was the one that really screwed them, they weren't ready for that at all, which was my own favourite, which was the one I'd fight again in the morning, calling to the waitress for Pernod, for water, was I bruised about how quiet Paris was, didn't Jeffries really try his best, poor fool, wasn't Jack London really the most ignorant bastard alive . . .

I was floored for a second at first – most people I'd met, even ones that liked me, usually thrust out their hand and grinned a lot, but Cravan and me got right on into it, how the Tommy Burns fight had happened, all the chasing I'd had to do to get to the little bastard, told him about that whole palaver with the natty suit and the wicker case that wasn't on the fight film, all the quiet at the Ketchel fight, all the noise at the Jeffries one, how the Burns fight was my favourite because it was the first one, the one that let them know Jack Johnson had arrived and was after their blood, but it was the Jeffries one I'd loved fighting the most, that was the one I'd love to be able to do all over. We must have talked all day, people coming and going all over him all the way through. This is Jack Johnson, he'd say, best fighter that ever lived, and they'd look at me the way people used to do in Chicago and New York and San Francisco, like I was the greatest thing in the world and they were lucky to be there with me.

I've never connected with a man like I did with him. It was instant. The big welcome, the drinking, the energy of him. From then on in, Paris changed for me, it was a place with life and things going on all the time. I got to know so many people through him, made so many friends, drank so much, felt active and alive and as if America wasn't such a big deal after all, full of bigots and lynch-mobs, they could have America, Paris would do me fine. I stopped all the self-pitying moaning I'd plagued Lucille with from almost the moment we landed, though I think if she'd seen more of me after that she'd have appreciated it more. I began spending all my time at the bar – the Closerie, they called it – with Cravan, planning schemes we'd never do, but Lord, we loved making like we would.

Everybody who came in seemed to know him, wanted to

come and say hello, ask about people they knew, deals he was at, talk about that magazine of his. The circle of people he liked was small. He was a bad-tempered bastard when he wanted to be, and he'd no time at all for the idiots who hung around pretending to know about pictures and art. He really hated the ones who'd come looking for him in the café in their thick scarves and throw that magazine of his at him and shout that he knew nothing about art. They were art students usually, and he would be very calm and ask them why, what did they know? And just as they'd get all puffed up to tell him, he'd jump up and bellow this great list of barrack-room obscenities, the kind we'd use at fights all the time but not the kind you'd ever hear streaming out at top volume from a quiet bar in Montmartre. The fool and his entourage would go streaking off down the street like they'd just been set on fire, and he'd turn round with a big grin on his face and go back to whatever we'd been talking about. I used to love those ass-kickings.

Cendrars was his big buddy, they'd be everywhere together when I first met Cravan, but I think there was a bit of a row that cooled things a bit. Cendrars didn't like me that much, so I wasn't too bothered, but I think it had to do with a woman. There were plenty of them, Mina, that was why the transformation in Mexico was such a shock, there he was, his woman off in another country, the Mexican girls as sexy as women come, and he was playing faithful. I thought it was for show at the start, but after eight weeks I gave in. In between I'd had the most perfect woman in the world described to me forty times a day, her hair, her skin, her voice, the way she walked, her laugh, her humour, her brains. I had her poems read out to me, I had to help frame photographs of her for the Academy walls, go down to the post office to wait for her letters, to post his – Lord, Mina, if you only knew what I had to go through over you. That man was as faithful as I ever was when I knew him before, then suddenly he was all cracked up and in love. It was like he'd found religion. It was also the truest thing I'd ever seen. It made me very lonely. I wanted what he had. I wanted it to be just like that, like a car ran you over and instead of being dead, when you stand up you're a prophet, you're a miracle-healer. That was what he was like.

The Battling Jim Johnson fight was a con. Everybody knew it except Jim Johnson. Well, the crowd weren't let in on it either, but all we were in it for was the money. Cravan had got some Arab in Antwerp to believe that Jim Johnson was the hot ticket, and Jack Johnson the blow-in. This guy had wagered so much on Jim Johnson that Cravan was able to offer the best odds on me and still cream a profit. So everyone came to him to lay their bets, he skimmed his commission, threw down a load of money on me through one of his own rivals, and when I won, everybody was singing. Except the Arab in Antwerp, but after about six weeks it was safe for Cravan to surface again. He stayed with me while he lay low, with nobody knowing except Cendrars, and that was before their row. Even so I don't think he'd have been the type to rat on Cravan. Once the Arab's buddies were convinced Cravan had absconded to New Orleans things went back to how they usually were, Cravan in the bar working on his magazine, and everybody else hanging around to get in on his next scam.

I'd moved out of the big showy mansion by then. All those days of showing off were over, well, for a while anyway. Lucille didn't mind, she set to finding us a nice apartment with the big long windows she liked. I told Cravan he could move in with us if he wanted a place to stay for a while, but after the Arab thing died down he went back to his own place on the Avenue de l'Observatoire. I could even speak French by then, enough to get by anyhow, which I was all proud of. Lucille too, better than me, but with more of an accent. Still, financially we were going to be stuck again soon, even with the move. I started thinking about going on tour again.

I'd thought I'd be pretty invincible in Europe, but there's

bad bastards on every continent. This time they were French. The French Federation of Boxing Clubs were the chief guys in France and they went and decided that I was a criminal. They took my title away from me. Well, they couldn't, that was my outlook, I'd won that title fair and square and I sure as hell hadn't won it in their stupid country, so all I decided they could do was just not recognise it in France. Made me hate them, that really did. I got so anti-French you'd have been ashamed of me, Mina. But they tried to do way more than that, they tried to get the big brigade on my back too, the International Boxing Union, even got a proposal put forward that they had the right attitude and I was just a convict, not worthy of the title. See what I mean about hating them though? They really went all out to lynch me. The IBU didn't go with it, they threw it out, but it got nasty.

Cravan was officially Middleweight Champion of France still, nobody had taken it off him yet, so he said he'd go and see if he could persuade the French to back down and change their minds. Thing was, and he knew it better than anybody, the French bosses hated him almost as much as they hated me. I was a criminal, he was a charlatan, and the two of us could shove it, that was their view. They didn't think he deserved the title because of the way he'd got it, the first guy not showing up so Cravan didn't even have to fight for the title, then the second guy going down before a punch was thrown. It did sound odd, even to me, and there wasn't much I hadn't seen in that game, but he had the title, so let them weep. They hadn't managed to get anyone to take it off him, he'd had to go to Athens for a serious fight, and he'd won that, so it was their problem. But it meant that the pair of us were the bad guys to the French boxing authorities, and the less they had to do with us the better.

So we decided the thing that'd piss them off most was if we organised a big fight that they couldn't get a cut of, not a penny. We did talk about the pair of us fighting each other, but Cravan wasn't up for it then. Later, when it suited him, that was when that idea got legs and ran him all the way to New York.

But for this one we decided to open the field a bit, see what we could find. We couldn't use a Frenchman otherwise the bastarding authorities could weigh in on us, and anyway, there was only one Frenchman who had any class and that was Georges Carpentier. He was too light to fight me, he was a whole rung of weights under me. I liked him a lot. Him and Cravan went back years, and Carpentier used to drink in the Closerie with us every so often. He was one of the gentlest men I ever knew, and he was the only man in Paris to rival Cravan for style. Along with me, of course. The three of us turned some heads when we walked down the street together. Georges was the French bigwigs' golden boy, he could have bartered the Hotel de Ville in Paris for a summer spot in the Caribbean and the Federation would have convinced the government to let it go. So when he asked if he could referee the match, the insult really started to come full circle. So would the box office.

All we needed now was a contender to go up against me. Cravan was promoter on it, and every day we'd sit down and work out who'd suit us. There were plenty of options, but we shot a lot of them down instantly. There was Sam Langford, an old enemy of mine from back in Galveston days, a pretty good fighter, only one ever to come close to me, I reckon, but I'd beaten him over eight years before and I wasn't up for fighting a man my own race, not even in exile. There was no money in it for a start, no fears to play on, nothing to stir. People paid to see me laid flat on the canvas. If I'd learnt nothing else since Australia, I knew that. That was why I loved getting rich and spending my money right in front of them. I was spending the profits of hate. Of being hated. Nobody gave two cents if I beat Sam Langford or not. There was no chance to see me humiliated that way, even in France where the world was supposed to have its template for civilisation. Anyone thinking that should have seen them baying at the Jim Johnson match, and if they missed it, Cravan and I were going to give them another chance. That was why we chose Frank Moran.

Moran was from Pittsburgh, Belle's stomping ground, and if there was anything we were going to have in common, it'd have been her. She'd have been just his type. He was Irish, an all right fighter who'd had some great victories back in the States, and some fairly miserable defeats to boot. He was perfect. My drinking had made my belly soft, and I didn't plan on going mad on training just to piss off a few bigots in the French Boxing Federation. Just to make some headlines, stir some blood.

Cravan got a guy called McCarthy to put up a hundred and seventy-five thousand francs as the purse, and the pair of us tied ourselves into a juicy cut of the film rights. The French had been buying up fight footage from America the moment it had come available, and Cravan didn't have much trouble stirring up interest in some home-grown stuff of the Heavyweight Champion of the World defending his title against an Irish American, in Paris, with the French sweetheart Georges as referee. We also got a good percentage of the gate. He was a good promoter, Cravan, the classic kind, went in biased and came out rich.

There was plenty of interest in America too, all the agencies had their Paris men focused on the build-up, the training, the feeling in the camps. I had mine just outside the city, but as usual they were simply places to gather the reporters and spread rumours out of, do some sparring for an audience, shoot the breeze, build the image. I sparred Cravan mainly, he was good, whatever happened in Barcelona was between him and his finances, because he sure could have gone the rounds with me for a while.

The fight was scheduled for 27 June 1914. It was at this covered bicycle track called the Hippodrome d'Hiver, and it was the strangest venue I'd ever seen. The French really love their wheels, engines or spokes, it doesn't seem to matter a damn. It was sweltering and jammed, and we were flying it, the pair of us. Cravan had worked out how much we'd made off the door and was grinning like a newly minted millionaire. He'd had this massive purple satin tent erected over the stage, with the enormous camera lights toasting the scalps of half the crowd and threatening to fall over on top of everything, including the canopy. It was chaos even before me and dour old Frank ran down the ramp and up to Georges who was looking like he'd just stepped out of a Parisian outfitter's window, all tanned in a cream silk shirt open at the neck and cream slacks. I swear to you, Mina, he was a man a nervous husband would keep his wife well away from. She'd have been safe enough with Georges, he was famously loyal to his family, but she wouldn't have been able to stop herself.

There were plenty of swooning heiresses anyway. The elite had climbed down off the chandeliers for the night and were sitting in the expensive seats, all kinds of animal life, the Rothschilds, the Vanderbilts, Middle Eastern royalty – more jewellery than a Cartier window around some of the necks. Let's say it was a far cry from what I was used to. I was all for wealth coming to see me fight, but it made a strange spectacle to come running out of your dressing-room into the ring and find you can't even spot your wife because of the glare of diamonds sparkling in the film lights.

Moran was no match for me when it came down to it, and I felt like I was sunbathing as I swatted him round the ring. There'd been motion-picture cameras at every title fight I'd fought, but because this was my first indoor one, the heat and the brightness took me by surprise. Still, they were the reason Moran got to go twenty rounds with me. If the film money hadn't been bagged, I'd have just floored him in the second or third, given the crowd something to see first, then gone in and finished him off. I felt like doing it anyway, halfway through almost every round, out of boredom, but I held back and let him dance around me a bit, then tickled him with a nice slow uppercut, pulled back, danced some more, fought the urge to belt him and kept tickling under his chin till the bell went. Twenty rounds of it. I tell you, I should have won an entertainment award for keeping the crowd going like I did. If it hadn't been for them changing their minds about who they wanted to win every five minutes, I'd have fallen asleep. In the end I got cheered out of the ring, which made a nice change, and we all headed to the Closerie to drink ourselves into the following afternoon. They were good days, Mina. It makes me all nostalgic thinking back on them. They were good days.

It was after that fight that I introduced Cravan to racing in a big way. I'd always been crazy about it, but he barely knew the rudiments of driving, so I taught him, and after a few lessons we were taking my roadsters into the French countryside and racing each other. There were a few crashes, nothing serious, except that he became better at the whole caper than I was, and being the big oaf I can be, I took it badly and refused to go out in the cars any more. If he wanted to race, I told him, he could find a car of his own to put in ditches. So he did. Cendrars got him a beat-up Austin racer that lasted two outings, but by then he'd kicked me out of my sulk and I let him drive one of mine again. Didn't matter which car he got, he'd always beat me. He was the only man in the world I let do that after Barney Oldfield, and he was a pro, so my dignity didn't get bruised where he was concerned. But Cravan got away with it too, like he managed to do with most things. Times I think it might have been better if he'd had a harder time of it, you know – maybe he wouldn't have taken so much for granted that way. But that's just the old jealousies rising perhaps, who knows?

That magazine of his, *Maintenant*, it got him in a lot of trouble for a few bits of paper and some photographs all stuck together. He'd give it to me to read when he finished an issue, all proud of it as I would be of a title, like it was just the last word in genius. To tell you the truth, I couldn't see what the fuss was about. But, boy, did it land him in trouble. He'd write all the articles himself, big pieces about art and artists and art movements, and about that uncle of his, and a load of other things I don't recall. Like a gossip sheet in lots of ways, all the stuff about who was in fashion and who was in whose bed, and who had all the airs and who had all the money, and pages of poems and a few advertisements for the places we ate in and drank in and danced in. Gossip.

But people got mad. He'd get me to come with him and sell it, and that was stranger than the magazine. He had this wooden wheelbarrow that he'd fill with copies of it, then off he'd trundle with it to the racetrack, park it outside the entrance and sell it to everyone going in and out. Twenty minutes, and the barrow would be empty. Thing was though that because all the art and poetry crew thought it was very scandalous, they'd try and get it off him in the Closerie where he wrote it and put it all together, but he'd refuse point blank. Anybody that wanted *Maintenant* would have to be there at his pitch outside the racetrack on a given day by the third race, or that was that.

And they did. I reckon the first few issues must have been sold to a whole load of innocent fools thinking they were buying a programme of the race meet, but by the time I came along, all the art gang would turn up one by one for their copy and then for the next ten days they'd go on and on beating him over the head with it for telling all their secrets and not being nice about their friends. He didn't care. If anyone went on too long or too intensely about it they got the same treatment as the art students, only worse, because Cravan reckoned they really should know better. But because it was funny, and done as if he truly could not give a damn, nobody really took all that much offence.

Except twice. The first time was when he used the magazine to do a sort of review of this huge art exhibition all his friends were involved in. You kept mentioning it, Mina, that Salon des Independents. Did he tell you about all that fuss? All the people who'd come down to the Closerie to hang out with him had pictures in it, including that guy Frost. I met him. He was quiet, dull almost, but Cravan and him would get giddy together a lot. It's a pity he died like that. Well, he was in it, and all these other people who'd come down, Henry Heyden and Marc Chagall and Suzanne Valadon, and Van Dongen and Albert Gleizes. I didn't like Gleizes so much or Heyden, but the other three were nice enough when they were cheerful. Well, Cravan went to their big exhibition and then wrote the whole magazine about how awful the damned thing was, how pretentious and stupid and full of wind they all were. But he didn't do it prettily. He said he'd prefer to spend two minutes under water than have to look at Heyden's painting, he'd suffer less. Frost did nothing for him, he said, and as for Gleizes he just was completely talentless, which was a pain in the ass for him, but there he was. He sort of liked Chagall and he thought Van Dongen was great. All the rest, he said, couldn't paint a room for their egos wouldn't let them.

There was war over it. He was cast out of their arty circle, which he regarded as a bit of a triumph, and lots of people came and tried to take him aside to tell him what a nasty man he was. He didn't pay the tiniest bit of attention to any of them, and when Apollinaire's woman came down specially to tell him that everyone was very annoyed and he was a disgrace, he wrote another piece in the next issue about how she needed nothing more than to have her skirts lifted. That was when the second bit of trouble happened.

Apollinaire was his friend for a bit, but mainly he was Cendrars' friend and when Cravan and him fell out, off stomped Apollinaire. I was a bit like you with that Bill guy, Mina, I didn't know he was famous really, he just seemed like another big head who liked giving Cravan lectures about how to behave in polite society, which was a real red rag to a bull. So when the girlfriend Marie Laurencin got that said about her in the magazine, down came Apollinaire with two damned pistols and challenged him to a duel to protect her honour.

Cravan found it very amusing, but when the little guy insisted and stood there in that courtyard with his leather gun-case smoking himself into a frenzy of righteousness, he asked me what he should do. I asked if he'd ever shot a gun before and he said more or less, and must have taken it to mean go ahead, because he strode up to the little guy and asked him which gun he preferred. Apollinaire got a bit jittery then, when the bravado suddenly had to become real, but they chose their guns, cleared the friends and started pacing the courtyard. I still thought it was a joke, that the little guy would see Cravan had absolutely no fear of anything and back off, but he'd brought a troupe of friends, the offended woman included, and I suppose even if he wanted to, he couldn't have.

They went through the whole ritual. About eight of us watched as they stood back to back, guns cocked and held high at their chests, then paced one two three four five, and bang, shots went off, smoke everywhere and when we saw them, Apollinaire was on the ground and Cravan was casually placing the smoking gun back in the little guy's velvet lined gun-case, completely unscathed.

He'd aimed at Apollinaire's foot, and got it, and Apollinaire had aimed at his head and missed. There was lots of screaming and accusations of cheating but in fact the only other rational-minded person there was the little guy himself, who congratulated Cravan and said it was a fair contest. While Marie Laurencin screeched and the others ran about hysterically, the two men discussed the offending article, and Cravan explained that he only wrote what he did to make a name for himself and to infuriate all those he found pompous and self-inflating, that to be notorious made it very easy to bed a woman and get people to invest in you in a business like boxing or art. Art, they agreed, was in the guts, not the head, and that was why there was nothing as suitable as boxing if a man wanted to understand art. Then he invited Apollinaire to the next fight he organised, turned to the still screaming Marie Laurencin, and was apologising for any offence he had caused her when the police came and he was hauled away.

I drove Apollinaire to the hospital first, then went to the cop station, my first French one, where Cravan was getting lectured and shouted at, though God knows what they were saying to him. He didn't look too flustered, but when he saw me he explained they weren't going to let him out on bail because they didn't feel like it. So he got eight days in jail, Mina, for something that had nothing to do with him really, and it was only on the eighth day when Apollinaire got out of hospital and came down to drop the charges that he got out.

They were sort of friends after that, cagily enough, but a lot better than before. We met that Marie Laurencin in Spain again, where she was all over Cravan like a rash. She'd dropped Apollinaire by then. In the end he was far braver than any of us, he went out to war for France, got his helmet split in two by shrapnel as he sat in a trench reading, and came looking for her all bandaged up and not the best. That was just after Cravan and me had fought in Barcelona. He recovered though, but bad luck got him again, and he caught influenza and died two days before the Armistice. Everybody was talking about him for ages, like he was their hero now that he'd gone and died. I met him a few times with Cravan in the Closerie after the duel fiasco, he seemed on a level, I guess. I never read any of his stuff though. I might look it up some day if I ever get bored.

We used to go to the Bal Bullier a lot. It's strange to think you used to go there too a few years before, to think you might have been at any one of the tables we sat at. I used to bring Lucille on those nights because of the dancing – she really loved that place. It was like my club, only the ceilings were eighty foot high and the chandeliers would have killed a hundred dancing couples if they'd come loose. There weren't any sporting rooms either, otherwise you can imagine what my club was like. Everybody was happy. Cravan used to flirt with Lucille, make her giggle, give her outrageous drinks, not to undercut me on my own wife, just to keep her gay and laughing. He knew she was having a hard time of it with this whole exile business. She didn't much miss her mother, but she did miss all her friends, and with the war thing looking serious, we weren't sure she could go back to visit any more. That had kept her head straight when she got all depressed and cried in my arms at night. Don't worry, I'd say, we'll always have enough money to send you back on a visit if you want to go, and now it looked like that'd have to go out the window along with everything else.

The war was starting to worry everybody. Cravan arrived at the apartment one morning and said there was talk of drafting. Those official French papers of his were on his mind. He declared he was going to make a run for it to Spain, which had to go neutral because of all the trouble they were having themselves. If he left now, he said, he'd be home and dry by the time the conscripting started, but it could be declared any morning now and he wasn't ready to get snared by anybody's war. He asked if I wanted to come too. He reckoned that, with the war, the interest in anything whimsical like boxing would be over, everybody's eyes would be on the real fighting. He thought we could set some fights up in Spain, and at least have a better time than it looked like we'd be having if we stayed. I talked it over with Lucille, who was all on for it, and a week after Cravan escaped down to Barcelona, we arrived with our three cars and French furniture and all Lucille's cases of clothes and hats and jewels and mirrors.

Spain was good to us for a while. Cravan was sleeping at the apartment of some girl he'd met by the time we got down, and we moved straight into a place that had been arranged for us from Paris. By now the war was in full throttle and everyone I knew seemed to be ducking it. They all had their excuses, and they all probably believed in them too, but there was only one reason that people didn't fight and that was fear.

I was as afraid as anyone. As brave as the men I was surrounded with in Barcelona, all full of great political reasons not to fight when they had just the same one as me, they were just too damn scared of dying.

I didn't see Cravan too much in the first couple of weeks. He had some scam on the go with a Matisse painting that had caught up with him, but he found out where I lived and we got ourselves a new Closerie out on the Ramblas, and settled there every day to plot our next move.

We decided we'd open a boxing academy of our own. There were a couple in the city run by two-bit chancers in filthy gyms. With the Heavyweight Champion of the World, and the former Heavyweight Champion of France running the show, we couldn't lose. With Cravan's Matisse money and some of the cash I got from selling all the French antiques that wouldn't fit in our new apartment, we had the money. Through a friend of Cravan's we found an old hall in the centre of the city that we could have for a few months until the boss came back. We set up four sparring rings, got some equipment shipped over from London on the sly, and we were suddenly in business. All we needed were the students.

That was where Cravan came into his own. It was back to the wheelbarrow way of doing things. He got a whole series of advertisements done up and hawked the barrow up and down the Ramblas every day for two weeks giving them out, explaining it to everyone. He got posters made with my name in huge letters and I put them up all over town – every gable wall and billboard knew about the Jack Johnson and Arthur Cravan Professional Boxing Academy. From his barrow he announced the grand opening, and we put up a hundred posters outside every factory and sweatshop in the city. Then we just sat back and waited.

I didn't have too much Spanish then. I was still learning as I went along. The posters looked great, had my name on them, Cravan's name, the Academy's name, the date, the place. I thought all the other stuff was directions or something, hell if I read it. Then people started coming up to me, telling me how brave I was, how crazy – would we really do it? Were we both insane? Telling me to wish the big guy good luck and save some for myself, all sorts of weird stuff. I still didn't read the damn posters carefully.

Do you know what that bastard you married had set us up for? All over Barcelona these great posters plastered everywhere declared that Jack Johnson and Arthur Cravan would open their all-new Boxing Academy by performing the spectacular feat of walking from the roof of their Academy to the roof of the building across from it by tightrope. Tightrope, Mina! I blew up, yelled and bellowed and screamed like I hadn't done in years, not through the Feds, the fights, the moral outrage. But he was convinced we could do it, that it would be fantastic, a new challenge to rise to, and the publicity, Jack, that was what he kept saying, the publicity will make us a fortune.

Course I didn't do it, was I mad? I got some shit for it too, all these weak-limbed little bastards coming up and telling me I was scared. Like they'd ever want to take me on head to head. But that got me crazy angry with him, that people thought I was frightened. I was, hell, who wouldn't be, a two hundred-foot drop from the roof of an eight-storey building, damn right I was. I just didn't need the world knowing it.

But, Mina, it was majestic. We had our grand opening and we were thronged. The papers said next day that over four thousand people had shown up to see it. The crowds packed the street, people hanging out of all the street windows for a better view. Everyone thought they were going to see him fall, including me, but the more I tried to convince him out of it, the more he seemed sure that he had to do it.

He appeared up on the roof with a huge pole and a little Spanish guy from the carnival gurgling instructions at him while Cravan tested the tautness of the wire. At his first step out, he teetered so much the crowd seemed scared to exhale in case the air blew him off, but he steadied his great loping body in seconds, and placed another chalked step on the jumped-up sewing thread that was holding him above the small cordoned-off patch of cobbled stone beneath. It was when the hecklers started that I knew he would do it, knew that if the loud squawking voices of the nags beneath him did not throw him off, then his concentration was such that he could not hear a thing, was deaf to everything but the voice in his head urging on his feet. Still the Spanish carnival man gabbled instructions, but he was deaf to everything, Mina, I knew it because he was still up there, wasn't being scraped off the stones at my feet. Each step seemed to take an hour, each tremble in the long pole, in his hips, his elbows, made the entire crowd draw breath, their eyes fixated on the delicacy of every inch moved by the wide-shouldered giant balancing on the rope, wavering like a dog-hair on a silk-thread needle. But he was locked away in his own world, Mina, his own thoughts powering him so that he manoeuvred that great body of his every one of those forty-eight feet right across to the other roof, and what cheers and shouting and euphoria when he did it, when he stepped off that jazzed-up clothesline and on to solid brick and slate. Over four thousand people hollering and yelling, shouting for their new hero.

And so the great Jack Johnson took a back seat in Barcelona. It was Cravan everyone wanted to meet, to say they'd drunk with him. Hell, I got my adulation all right, but he was the hero, and, boy, did we make a mint from that Academy. Never mind boxing, half the people there came to learn tightrope walking, and Cravan taught them. We took over every one of those eight floors, Mina, drafted in every circus man and boxer we could lay our hands on. It was the talk of the city for near on a year, and I bet you even now there'll be people who could tell you about Arthur Cravan's tightrope walk.

In fact, once the Academy was up and running, neither of us had to do very much, just go in every couple of days and do the Champion thing, maybe get in the ring and do a few rounds with each other or with whoever was in it at the time, play the big guy, strut around a bit telling people how they were doing, how to do a perfect feint, how to put the power into an uppercut to the jaw, how not to fall off brush-shafts, stuff like that. Easy stuff. We kept the country's down-and-out supply of wasted ex-pros in work, the public got professional attention from guys who'd been the rounds, and everybody was happy. Most of all us.

So we'd loads of time to go riding round the Spanish countryside in my automobiles, racing each other, stopping off in new towns and checking out the women, the bars. A high life, Mina, the best. Every so often we'd end up in ditches or get in fights, but they were all easily sorted out. It didn't take too much money to live well in Spain then, and our demands weren't too hard to fulfil.

He was still up to something with those damn pictures though, trading Picassos he'd bought up cheap from some Portuguese guy, and selling them on to London. I don't know if they were the real thing or not, you never did with him, it was just business, and in our way of doing things, that was fine. I had more things on my mind, to be honest.

The driving around stopped after word came from an old manager of mine, one I could trust called Jack Curley, that the latest white hope had laid down a challenge to me, and wanted a fight. The money would be great. He was called Jess Willard. Even writing his name gives me the creeps, Mina. Anyhow, here he was, the newest hot thing off the Caucasian conveyor belt, a huge big bastard by all accounts, two hundred and sixty pounds and six foot six in height. Curley sent footage of his last fight where he won by knock-out, but he was the most cumbersome damn fighter I'd ever seen, a big lug with hands like shovels and smithie's irons for feet. I'd have been more frightened if Belle had showed up in a drunken rage. I asked around, sent telegrams to a few people back in America like Tex Rickard, and they all said the same.

I'd bury him within three rounds, less if the cameras weren't rolling. He was everything he looked on film, slow and thick and without a drop of natural fighter in his whole damned body. I sent word I'd take him on.

Things started heating up again after that. In America the Feds went nuts, said if I stepped foot on American soil they'd clamp cuffs round me in a second and drag my ass off to Joliet Prison. But there was no way the fight could happen in Europe, everything was war, war, war.

So they decided to set it up for Mexico, but the Feds tried to hatch a secret plot with one of the revolutionaries, Carranza, to arrest me the second I landed in Veracruz. Cravan, because he had all the Spanish and French and German it took to negotiate a fight in a war, took charge along with Jack Curley. It was Cravan who thought of Cuba. And it was Cravan that the Feds dropped in on in Havana to have the chat that changed everything. Everything.

He was just having a drink in one of the bars when two men came over and sat down beside him. They knew his name, or at least his fake one, Cravan, knew what he drank, where he and I had last got drunk before leaving Spain, even told him the last place the pair of us had crashed in my yellow roadster, a tiny town, knew stuff nobody in Cuba could've known. So we were being spied on. Well, there was a surprise. Didn't the Feds have enough to do on a war-torn foreign continent rather than trail boxers, but no, obviously not. Spying on me was clearly serious government business, no matter where the hell I went.

But here was the rub. My mother was very ill – would he care to pass that on to Mr Johnson. Mr Johnson didn't have a clue about that, I'd been sailing so damn long to get to Cuba that no one had been able to get to me yet with the news. She might not last more than a few weeks, and it would be a terrible thing for a son to miss his own mother's death. It was, Mina, it was the worst thing I've ever gone through. Worse than what followed.

Things hadn't changed much in America, they told a bemused enough Cravan, everybody still hated the nigger just as much, and they needed to get themselves a white champ soon to get him out of the spotlight for good. Would he please tell Mr Johnson that the US Government was ready to deal.

Well, when Cravan came back and told me, it was my mother I was worried about for a while. Then I got a telegram sent the minute she had got mine to say she was poorly but nothing to get concerned over. Then I got one from my brother saying she was dying, had a few months to live at most, and she was desperate to see me, but she understood the circumstances. Then I got another one from her saying not to listen to my brother, that I was to stay out of the US and defend my honour, and my family's honour, and not to risk getting jailed for anything.

It sounds confusing now, but it wasn't then, not at all. She was dying and if I had to serve time to be with her, I would. I'm not sentimental about much, Mina, only the important things, and they didn't come much more important than this. I talked to Lucille about it, and she said that, if that was what I wanted to do, she would stand by me all the way through it.

Then I got to thinking what they meant about the deal part. They sent Cravan a note at the hotel telling him where to meet them to discuss matters in more detail. They warned him not to bring me. No deal could be visible, it had to stay underground. I felt like I was watching vaudeville, but Cravan and I decided to see what the story was with them and their secret operations. He went.

It was simple as pie. No side-of-the-mouth stuff this time. I lay down for Willard, a white man got the title, and I was allowed back into America to see my mother, pocket thirty thousand dollars, get my sentence reduced to a fine, and given the key back to my old life. It was a clean sweet compromise all round.

It was the hardest decision I ever made, Mina. Truth was, Europe scared me now it was at war with itself, and nothing there was like it was at home. The novelty had long worn off, both for me and for Europe. I was banned from England, stripped of my title in France, and if it hadn't been for meeting Cravan, I'd have gone mad long before. Every time I got to the edge, he'd come and shake me out of it, say nothing about what he could see was going on in me, just come and do it, fix me up, get me through another week, another month. He was my crutch, the best friend I ever knew, and the only really good thing to come out of that sorry exile. I don't know how many times I talked late at night to him about throwing in the towel, drunken talk, self-pitying weak man's talk, but real, and heartfelt. I wanted to go home, to drive down Chicago's highways in my classy automobiles and get waved at by people saying there he is, there's Jack Johnson. I wanted to open up my club again and have it full of all the friends I'd known over the years just like before, all the energy and music and bourbon and claret and duck with plum sauce and my Rembrandts up there on the wall, and the chandeliers hanging like they did in the Bal Bullier, and people clinking crystal tumblers and playing craps and having fun. Having fun at Jack Johnson's club, at the Café du Champion.

And here was a way to do it. Hell, I knew I was good, I was the best, even at thirty-seven I'd floor that fool Willard, but I wasn't going to be this good for ever. I wasn't invincible, I felt like I was, I acted like I was, but I'm a bright man, Mina, I knew the score. I'd seen men fold and get nothing for it, only humiliation. Here was my way of getting my old life back. I could do it, and I could because everybody knew it was no contest. They knew I'd floor him. That's why the Feds were there, they were petrified of the effect of me winning again, and they knew I would. Everybody knew. If I went down and then resurfaced in the States almost immediately, jail sentence forgotten about, then everybody would know that too, and how it had come about. I would retain my dignity because everyone would see right there on the fight footage how I'd won America back.

And so Cravan met up with them and told them it was in the bag. All he needed was a contract to bring back to me to prove they'd do as they said. What fools we were to think we could take the US Government at their word, that a contract was worth anything more than the law they'd used to bring me down. What fools we were, Mina, all-round fools.

Or rather what a fool I was. Cravan was doing my bidding under duress. He said he could get me in, we could work out a route and he'd sneak me into America with forged papers, over the Mexican border, most likely, or over the Canadian one, but not to trust them. I should have listened, he'd scammed enough people in his time to know a liar or two when he saw them and he saw them, but I just rolled on in my dreamland, all the way home to Galveston, to Chicago in my head, paying no heed to anything but the voices in there that said do it, dive, dive, dive.

There were fifty thousand people at the stadium just outside Havana. The crowd were excited but as if they were at a favourite nephew's birthday party rather than the battle for the Heavyweight Championship of the World. They weren't used to this kind of thing, I reckoned. The cameras were all set up, and on the hills behind about ten thousand people sat like obedient ants to try and see the fight for free. I looked at the guards and decided I knew exactly why the crowd was so damn quiet. They'd have scared a tribe of rabid mercenaries into subservience.

Lucille knew and Cravan knew. After that I didn't know or care who was in on it. I assumed somebody had had the decency to tell Willard, but with the Feds you never knew. I sure as hell didn't care. All I knew was that the film guys didn't know, and I was getting a cut of their business. It was going to go at least twenty rounds of the forty-five scheduled.

And it did. Willard standing like a joke for the first ten, his back so straight I thought he'd ironed it for the occasion, his left arm locked erect to try and hold me off, his right swinging like it felt it had to do something to bring a bit of a breeze into the ring. It was going to be damn near impossible to make this look realistic. All I had to do was walk round to his right, ram a left-hook up under his jaw, then follow in instantly with a right uppercut at his left temple above the static arm, and he was out cold. For ten rounds I danced around him imagining this, thinking of all the alternatives, how I could lead in this way and follow up with that, and whack, he'd be on the canvas, or else go in with a feint and cream him with a surprise right just on the side of the jaw, and down he'd go. I fantasised for ten full rounds about how I'd do him, each time thinking of my mother dying to stop me from following through. God, Mina, a more frustrating hour I can't imagine than that one. It was like I was boxing a schoolkid who'd won his sports day and got to fight me as his prize. Even the crowd could sense it, see something was up that I wasn't going for him.

I came on in the eleventh and decided to stop waiting for some semblance of a fight to come to me. I started beating him up a little, alley-way punches, the kind that make a half-decent fighter wake up and get angry that such lousy shots are being put past him, but not our Jess. He just shuffled along on the edge of the ring with his left arm rigid and his right swinging, his big cud lip sticking out like a signpost over his jaw saying hit me hit me. I started doing a bit of punchbag on him, the kind of blows that wind you, rib-tickling numbers, but don't put a man down, and he took them like he didn't know where he was.

I had to keep thinking of my mother to stop myself just going all out and spreading him on the canvas. This was new territory to me, Mina, I'd barely ever lost a fight in my life – in my whole career I'd lost three fights out of hundreds. I didn't know how to lose. I didn't have the instinct, the experience, I couldn't recognise any of the stuff my head was telling me to do, and that is why it went to plan, because I made my body listen to my head, not my instincts, not my gut. In those places I didn't know how to go down, but the rational corner of my brain guided the rest of me through it. Freedom, it kept saying, freedom. Pictures of my mother flashed through, of Chicago, of the club, and all the while I was puttering about on Willard's face like I was lathering him up for a shave.

We went on like that for another fifteen rounds. By the time round twenty-five came I was so damn bored I decided that the next round would be the one. Twenty-five rounds was all a movie man could hope for, even of this kind of stuff, and I was ready to go down. In my corner before the twenty-sixth I asked Jack Curley to take Lucille back to the dressing-rooms. I didn't want her to see me go down. I also knew that it would hint afterwards that I knew exactly what I was going to do in the next round, evidence that I was in control without proof that I could be done under. Cravan held the bucket for me to spit into, and as I brought my head up I whispered to him under my breath, Gonna do it now. He started whispering furiously back but I was up now, in the ring, boxing the shadows in the noonday sun, ready to do it, to throw the title.

Willard lumbered out and the bell rang. The bell ringing caught me. I started thinking, This is my last round ever as World Champion, this is it, so when he did punch the side of my head I was surprised. I turned instinctively with a right uppercut and then just as the blow was about to hit him I killed it, just rubbed his face instead. You could see the surprise on the big lug's features, trying to work out what I was doing, and I realised then that nobody had told him, nobody had told him a damn thing. He thought I was just having a slow day and would come in and kill him any minute now. The Feds were so sure of what a cheap-rate boxer he was, they hadn't deigned to let him in on the fact that he'd won it before he even got in the ring. They'd known I'd control the whole bout, that Willard wouldn't have an ounce of say anyway, so they let me roll with it. They were so sure of him, and so sure of me. Let them, I thought. I'm getting what I want out of this, nothing else counts.

It was hard-going getting him even to hit me, never mind

throw a punch that I could pretend to be floored by. Dance, dance, dance was all he wanted to do, long puny white arm still locked at the elbow, right still circling in the heat, whole of his face open as a walk-in closet, and me there fighting the urge just to belt him and be done, trying to make him throw something respectable so I didn't go down to a feather punch. I started taunting him, asking had he left his balls behind, to hurry up and hit me, he was going yellow in the sun, and it worked, he came in with a left to the jaw that wasn't too serious, then a lightbelt in the stomach and another left in my side. I let him at it, he wasn't hurting, and if I counter-punched, I had him at a perfect angle to blast a left uppercut to the side of his head and knock him out, which of course I couldn't do. I didn't trust myself not to, so I acted like he'd got me and decided that, whatever came down next, no matter how weak, I'd dive on it. Nothing went through my head but that thought, all ideas of this being my last round as Champion banished by the need to concentrate so hard to go through with it, to go down. Next thing I saw a right coming through headed straight for my jaw at about one mile an hour, but it was enough to look real, and when impact came, I tumbled over on to my back. Down.

The sun glared right in my face and burnt the eyes out of me – I thought they'd never start the damn count. I shaded them with my hand, then remembered I'd to look groggy like all the sorry bastards I'd ever felled, so I let my knees slide down and my hands fall limp by my side, killing the urge to leap up and say, Ha, got you, now let's make a real fight of this. The canvas was scalding, all that Havana sun beating down on it – I thought my back would start blistering if the count didn't wind up soon. I felt like I was watching myself, I'd my eyes closed for effect now, but I could see what it all looked like, the referee standing over me, Willard with his thick lip standing looking stupid, Cravan looking sickened, the crowd all delighted . . . but when I got up, Cravan just seemed angry, Willard bewildered and the crowd not really sure what the hell was going on. Cravan helped me to my corner, not looking me in the eye at all, and the crowd picking up now, the black man down, waving white flags all round the place in triumph.

I didn't know what I'd done till I had to go out through the crowd to the dressing-room. They were so crowing, shouting and yelling, booing me, every insult I'd ever heard coming back to me in screeches, and I'd nothing to lean on. This wasn't new, all this hatred and caterwauling, but I'd lost what lifted me above it, that majestic knowledge that I'd won and there was nothing they could do to change it, nothing. I was Champion, I was the winner here, the one who walked away with everything while they just went home to their hovels feeling weakened and furious. I was the conqueror, I had the glory between me and them.

And I didn't any more, I didn't have anything, I just wanted to turn round and race back into the ring and fight round twenty-seven, the one where I laid every punch on Willard that I'd held back in the twenty-six rounds before it, every last one, pummel the bastard into the canvas and all these imbeciles with him, but I couldn't. Cravan held me and kept me going to the tunnel, kept me from making a fool of myself, I suppose, but then he'd tried to do that once and for all before the match and I decided I knew better. Well, Mina, what did I know? What I know now of course changes everything, but what I knew then should have been enough. I should have fought like I always did, paid attention to nothing but what was going on in that ring, and I didn't. I went soft. I went soft and lost everything in the time it took to dive to the tune of the weakest knock-out punch in the history of boxing.

The contract was worthless, of course. They never had any intention of letting me back in, or of commuting my sentence. My mother died a few months later. She had sent me a letter which I got after that long sickening journey back to

Spain. She said she knew what I had done, that was all, she knew, just as she knew she would never see me again, but she loved me and was as proud of me now as she had ever been. I never forgave them for the way they got me. I don't have it in me, nor do I want to. I want to carry this for ever, and if I'd had children I'd have wanted them to carry it for ever too. I was cheated of everything I ever fought for, and that is an unforgivable thing to steal. It was hard not to fall apart after Cuba. In Spain at least they had the grace to lament the loss of Jack Johnson's title to Jess Willard, but in America I knew they were in the throes of delight that the black man had been beat. Money from the movie rights still comes in every now and again, for everybody loves to see the mighty fall. But I lost everything in the twenty-sixth round of that fight in Cuba.

Cravan kept me together. He distracted me with his scams, art deals and forgeries, with the Academy, with all sorts of things he thought of to keep my mind occupied. A lot of drinking mainly. We shifted right back to the world as it had been when we left for Havana, except now I no longer had any currency. I was what I had always made other people – defeated, with a long bleak future ahead of me.

The Academy kept going, despite everything. The Spanish didn't care that I was no longer Champ, they kept coming to the club with my name on it. Cravan and Cendrars made up and Cendrars came down to Spain to live. He had only one arm now, he lost the other in the war that was raging north of us. We drank a great deal. Cravan was passionate about getting out, getting to America. He needed to get there with a ferocity I had never seen in anyone, as though without the chance to make it in New York his own limbs would fall off one by one. He had reason to panic too, for he was officially English, Swiss and French, and France and England were coming after their conscripts. People shirking their loyalties would be caught.

There was paranoia everywhere, spies believed to be inveigling their way into every group of foreigners, so that every newcomer was treated with suspicion. It was a nasty time, Mina, though Italy doesn't sound like it was a whole lot of fun then either. By the time Cravan suggested we fight each other in a big bout, we were climbing walls, the pair of us, for the same reason, though we gradually stopped discussing it. We both yearned for America, he for the country that was his to explore, and me for the country that I knew so well, the life I had led so happily before all this, before Lucille's mother, before Belle's revenge, before taking flight, before Cuba. I had money, if nothing else, and I did not need to fight that bout in Barcelona. But he did, and that was how the fight came to happen in that old derelict mill in Barcelona, and how he escaped all the way towards America. Towards you.

Take care, Mina,

Jack

FABIENNE

It is 1932, and my father's money is low again. He works unremarkably as a calligrapher by day, but wants the thrill of real money again. Neither bourgeois living nor banality suit him, he feels. He thinks the time has finally come to avenge his uncle's ghost. He sets to work. He writes exquisite pieces of prose entirely in his uncle's voice, the same handwriting, and sends them in a distressed state to several self-referential book-dealers in the city. They are, he tells them, the lost writings of Oscar Wilde, found in a trunk in a Paris hotel. He has the advantage of knowledge. He knows, as do a very few easily contacted verifiers, that his uncle lost an array of luggage in Paris in 1888, the year after his own birth, and that all but one trunk had been recovered.

Inside it had lain a draft of The Decay of Lying, *notes for* The Soul of Man, *poems, set sketches for* Lady Windermere's Fan, *doodles, drawings, musings. A treasure chest to all the assorted dealers and book-traders and dandified aesthetes who nourished the cult worship of Oscar Wilde. And so when Mr Dorian Hope offers these gems, there is much excitement in the little world of letters. Much scepticism too. There have already been forgeries proffered, but the men involved are thorough. They engage Wilde's son, his biographer, Wilde scholars, all manner of self-confessed experts and professionals to authenticate the contents of the mythical case, the one they have for so long dreamt of finding.*

This forum of wisdom takes the documents one by one and excitedly confirms their authenticity. Notes scribbled in the margins exhilarate them for they contain notes of hotels frequented, journeys made, family dilemmas detailed, thoughts on the funeral of a loyal valet, things, in short, that only Wilde and his family would know. Greedily the auction begins.

What was being sold was the appearance of authenticity. The papers he knew were a masterclass in forgery, his knowledge so intimate, his details so accurate, for he understood that the key to his art was in the detail. Too easy to fabricate a perfect document in the precise script, but it is the notes, the barely legible addenda that ease his plan to fruition. And he appreciates that those you choose as your victims are those who most eagerly yearn to believe that what they see is real. They will investigate the story spun, will tease out the infinitesimal details given with apparent disregard, research flippant references the seller reveals in his correspondence. Every detail, every postmark and date and name and place dropped into the whole affair must have unerring accuracy in its appearance. Then the illusion is complete, for it has impeccable provenance. In this case, what better provenance than the secrets and stories of the family vault.

He never shows himself to anyone, executes the entire affair by having his post routed through Rome to give a reason for his consistent unavailability in person. He monitors the experts as they monitor his craftsmanship, and when the bidding begins he almost turns up to watch it himself. It is decades before the counterfeit is uncovered. By then the contents of the lost suitcase have passed through many hands, have acquired a status unequal to their value, which is high. He knows it for it is what he lives on in Rome for eight more years. Revenge on the establishment for his uncle's demise, revenge and wealth magicked together with the flick of a forger's pen and a litany of lies.

It is another excuse to postpone the search for his lost wife and child, another distraction, another new life to escape to. But he thinks of them. He thinks of his child and yet his courage never rises enough to return to them. This is why I never saw him. He thought our hatred would be more than he could bear. He thought we could not forgive him. We never got the chance.

Mina

New York, May 1946

Dearest Jack,

Thank you wholeheartedly for the photograph from Barcelona. You look most dapper with your cigarette holder. Is that Lucille in the hat with her eyes closed beside you? Fabian looks so like himself, sombre and pensive but as if he is about to start the whole company in a fit of giggles. Who are all the people crowded in around your dinner table in their suits and tuxedos? They look an odd bunch, some seem like alley-way hooligans squeezed into dress-suits, others have that millionaire half-smile as though they are patronising the photographer with their presence. Who is the man with the blackened eye crouching at Fabian's knees? Who are they all?

The Oscar Wilde stories were true. I thought the same as you at first, it seemed a little outlandish, but Wilde was his uncle. Fabian's father was the brother of Constance, Wilde's wife, so while he was no blood relation, there was enough genuine connection for him to flaunt when he chose. He wrote a big piece in *Maintenant* thirteen years after his uncle's death declaring that Wilde was utterly alive, recently returned from Sumatra, and had just visited Fabian at his home – while they finished off a bottle of cherry brandy, Wilde declared the woes and secrets of his missing years to his nephew. Some bright spark working for *The New York Times* in Paris saw it, and filed it as a front-page story a few days later. It got picked up all over London and New York, how Wilde's own nephew had seen him in Paris, had interviewed him, and he wasn't dead at all. What trouble that caused. But the connection was very real, Jack, he was telling the truth about Wilde. That was in 1913 while I was in the throes of my Futurist alliance.

It has been strange reliving so much again. With you, I have an excuse. When I write to you I feel my nostalgia has purpose and my regrets have bearing. Nothing seems quite so pointless when there is someone listening who knows what I mean, or wants to. I am increasingly envious of the freedom you have enjoyed, Jack, the ability to glide away from anything that might encumber you. And yet you have known as much trouble as I, more perhaps.

I don't mean to devalue our friendship, not at all, for when you write to me it is your life that enthralls me, not the details of my own. I love your letters, your stories, all the energy of your life is contagious – it makes me want to find a new enthusiasm at the close of every letter. And I feel such anger at the hatred stirred for you, this imbecilic, dangerous loss of rationality that has made you redirect your fury into the ring each time. You are lucky to have boxing. Poetry has its moments but it is a poor relation for unloading hurt. Other times it is my clearest voice, but not one I pay very much heed to. Nor does anyone else, my days of praise and glory ended a long time ago. It is Bill who became famous, quiet, gentle Bill, and my tormentor Marianne Moore. Mina Loy disappeared between the cracks, and truth told, she really doesn't care. I don't. Of the things that are important, famous successes are not ones I care about. It is the private ones that count if there is a need for success at all. I do not believe there is. My only source of it is in my children and I failed two of them so greatly that they died on me. I found a marriage of the purest love, and that disappeared too. I do not dwell on thoughts like these often, I doubt I would get up each morning if I did – I would find a noose instead. But they occur, and they are painful as all truths are, yet they slip back into the shadows and let me get on with my life.

I thought I had lost him, you know, once before, when we lived in Mexico City. I think it prepared me, made me think that there could be a time when he wasn't there. But nothing ever prepares you, and I suppose when he lived I thought we were immortal, that we could brave anything together. He became very sick with amoebic dysentery – the doctor said there was nothing he could do, that it would depend on his constitution and his body's will to fight. For weeks we lived in a fever together, he hallucinated most days and nights, and I too in a sane way, caught in the room with the stale blistering air feeding the disease and making everyone around us stay away, coming close only to convince me to hand him over to a sanatorium. In Mexico! As if anyone would give the person they loved most in the world to the squalor of a Mexican hospital. I willed him to live and he fought off the fever despite what they all predicted, fought it off and after five weeks of it I got him back again, both of us fired anew to make everything we could of our new country, our new life. But I was so scared of losing him even then, he never knew how afraid I was or how close he came to dying. Death was his greatest fear, and after Frost died so suddenly he was desperately scared that I would be next.

When he recovered we began discussing the idea of leaving the claustrophobia of the city. There were a lot of reasons to go, not least a rumour that a list of draft-dodgers was being sent to Mexican officials, and deportation orders were threatening to come ticker-taping their way across town. Fabian was spectacularly conspicuous, with his fights and the Academy and the extravaganza with you. I suppose it was the same pressures that were being put on you. I am glad now that I know why you had to leave so abruptly, why too you were arrested in the first place, why it was when he met you that you couldn't go back to America. I had no idea it was such a backward country, Jack. I have lived in it all this time and thought always that it was the most progressive, open environment in the world. And yet they could legitimise what they did to you. You were courageous to go back. I'm not sure I could have.

In all honesty, there was another factor too. There were a few smaller-scale fights after you left, local heroes or big-headed draft-dodgers against Fabian, all easily dealt with and further honing his mythical-god status around the city. There were six or seven conquests, I think, and they brought more trade than he or his broom-boys could handle at the Academy. Then an opportunity arose that he could not let go. A guy came to town who all the Mexicans went mad for. He had been their boxing hero a few years before but had got into trouble and left. Fabian said he was an old opponent of yours – Black Jim Diamond, and you'd stuffed him. That was what he said anyway.

This guy wanted Fabian to fight him. A gang of other people wanted a man called Tom Fowler to do the job. It was such an easy decision, for Fabian was still convalescent at the time, far too weak to take to a ring and slug it out with a professional boxer. But he hated Fowler, who he said had tried to thwart your bout, and he decided he would fight Black Jim Diamond himself.

There is not a lot of point in telling you how it turned out, Jack, there is only one result when one opponent has to get out of bed to show up. He was stronger than most men even when sick, but nowhere near the fitness of the old timer, and it went three very miserable, very wearying rounds. I was furious with him still for over-riding my opinion, but we had no time for that – he had bet heavily on himself to lose and we left Mexico City at first light the next day for Salina Cruz. So while I pretend there were real reasons for leaving, I suppose it is to hide the fact that we skulked out of the city as though we were criminals, racing to Salina Cruz as if to paradise.

It was a happy journey once the shock of our speedy exit

had dissipated. In our letters while I was in New York and he in Mexico he had written to me that above all else we had to go voyaging together, that he was only truly himself when he travelled. '*Je suis presque frappé d'imbécillité quand je reste longtemps dans le même endroit*,' he wrote. I know all of his letters word for word. When she was a child, Fabi used to read parts out and ask me to say which date, which place he sent it from. I would indulge the game only momentarily, for it was far too hard a game for a child to endure when the voice she read was that of a father she had never seen. Too hard for me also, I could not sustain it at all. It was a perverse ghost story when I closed my eyes, Fabienne reading his words aloud as though they were details of the newest fashions, no idea that it was those words that impelled me to join him, that gave her life.

Salina Cruz was all that I had dimly expected of Mexico. I had thought of the country, not the city, and now here I was. We had soldiers on the roof of our carriage fighting off bandits as we travelled through chilly hilltop villages all the way down through the suffocating heat thousands of feet below the city, the jungle swallowing our train and then spitting us out again on to the dry plains that led to the coast. I thought I had seen a great deal of Mexico *en route* from the US border but our escape from Mexico City was a proper adventure. We had to climb off the train and sleep in ditches each night with the soldiers protecting us by firelight – the train would not run at night when the rebels could clamber aboard in the dark and hijack it. For some reason the soldiers thought a stationary train and unconscious passengers easier to protect. It was a romantic sort of danger, we were caught up in the air of vigilance and caution, but as we huddled together at night the sense of fear was utterly negated by the sight of the soldiers standing in the crescent of light beyond the fire. Probably we would have been petrified if we had believed the stories of machete massacres that roped the circle in low voices, but we didn't. We didn't pay any attention to anyone, only to each other and the infant we had learnt I was carrying a week before the fight. I was almost two months pregnant, the doctor said, and if our flight from Mexico City was precipitous, Fabian had spared no thought in making it as comfortable for me as possible. He bought fruit and tortillas for us as the train slowed through towns, and gave me the bulk of the food when there was little, kept me wrapped in the warmest clothes at night, gave me the coolest seat in the hottest regions, and the least draughty in the coldest.

It was exciting to arrive there. A lot of panicked draft-dodgers had also come down when their own escape-route to Buenos Aires, which was Veracruz, was closed off to them. The Allies it seemed were searching all Gulf ships for deserters before they left Veracruz port, and so everyone flocked to Salina Cruz in order to escape to Chile and Peru. We lived sociably there, a new experience for us, as before we had only ever been interested in the world we invented together. Now we enjoyed dancing and dining with others – artists and revolutionaries and anarchists, all self-professed and completely fallacious titles, but, with the exception of just a few, they were fun and light-hearted and asked no questions about anyone's past. They also helped us to settle in a hotel where most foreigners lived, and it was there, after almost three months of frivolity, that we formulated the plan that would get us back, first to New York, then to Europe.

There was a fast traffic in departures from the port, with the rumour abounding now that the monitoring of deserters and those without proper papers was about to spread to Salina Cruz. We were in an awkward position. I was perfectly able to travel anywhere, but my pregnancy meant that if I was to move it would have to be very soon. Fabian, like three of the men we had become good friends with, was unable to travel anywhere legally. His papers, forged and real, had been lost, confiscated or abandoned since he had left New York in his soldier's uniform almost eighteen months earlier. A known police informer had been making enquiries about how to acquire Arthur Cravan's famous services as a forger for a friend of his who needed to get out of the country. There was no way he could fake his own documents, nor anyone else's as long as he was under surveillance.

Meanwhile my pregnancy grew more and more pronounced. We knew what we wanted to do, and that was get out of South America to New York in time for the baby's birth. There we would settle until the end of the war, and then we'd travel all three of us to Florence and pick up Giles and Joella, before settling the family in Paris. We also intended travelling to Lausanne to show our baby to Fabian's mother, who lived there still. She did not even know of her son's marriage, as it turned out. This was our dream, and we planned it in the tiniest detail as we wandered along the coast together each day. From this we devised our plan of escape. I was to travel as safely as possible because of the baby, and so a berth was booked for me on a passenger ship going to Chile. Fabian and the other three men were going to sail to Chile and meet me there, while other friends planned on travelling overland. We would all meet and work out our route to New York from there.

He built his own boat, and, Jack, for all the know-alls and interferers who gently tell me he deserted me that fact is all the evidence in the world that I need to reaffirm his fate in my heart. That and the weather reports of the storms. His plan, you see, was that he would buy the shell of an old boat, one that had been hulled but could be rebuilt, and we did that, we did it together one morning, filled with excitement that our plan was in progress. He would make it buoyant, then sail it to Puerto Angel up the coast. Once there he would exchange it for a more seaworthy boat, armed with the collection of money we had gathered from the other three men, and then sail back down the coast to Salina Cruz, load up the provisions and the other three, and altogether they would sail to Chile to meet me and the others. So simple. So incredibly simple.

I still had eight days until my ship left port for Chile. The boat was taken to a stretch of beach opposite the hotel, more because the tide did not come up very far than for the proximity, but it meant that each day I could join him. And so for five days we awoke and went out to the boat, where I sat in the shade of some trees and sewed and read and wrote and at mealtimes I cooked little meals that had us starving for real food within hours. He worked a few feet away on the beach, hammering and swearing and battering that little tub into a miniature yacht, complete with working sail. We tried shouting to each other but he was fractionally too far down the beach, so we devised our own communication system with bits of salvage. A certain piece banged hard with some wood meant, I love you, another banged with iron meant, Food is ready, if it was me, or, Shall we eat? if it was him. Yet another knocked against the tree under which I sat meant the baby was moving, and for that he would bound up to me. He would bang out his messages every few minutes on the rim of the deck, or off the hull, until we had a noise and an implement for every endearment and caress we had ever shared. Some days it seemed as though we went out each day and did almost nothing but play with our toys, thinking up the most inventive noises for the sweetest memories. I was surprised he didn't knock a hole in the bow with our efforts.

And yet the boat got done amidst it all. It looked a mess, but on the fifth day he ran up to me and declared it ready for testing. We were both so excited that I suggested he take it out there and then in front of me so we could see if it worked. He kissed me and stroked my hair and then ran off all full of excitement using the low tide to manoeuvre the boat into deeper water. Then the tide swelled up and caught it so he had to swim after it and hurl himself on to the deck, then he turned and waved to me, and I still wake at night with that image grafted on to my dreams, wishing with everything I am that I could unsay it, that I could make him come home . . . such a simple conversation, Jack, so easy not to have spoken, to have hugged him, for us to have walked up to the hotel and taken refuge in our future, excited, used our baby as an excuse for someone else to go to Puerto Angel, squired some other innocent fool to take that beaten-up busted wheelbarrow out to sea . . .

But it was he. It was he that sailed away.

I thought he would be back within an hour, maybe two. I was surprised when the boat left the bay, at first going left, then right, then left again, as though it were trying to turn around. It sailed out further and further until it was indistinguishable from the gulls skimming across the mouth of the inlet. Then he sailed out of sight, gone.

By nightfall I was anxious, but people had gathered with me, Bob Brown and his wife Rose were the ones who took care of me then. Everyone said I was crazy to worry, that he had hit a good wind and availed of it. They said Puerto Angel was two days up the coast, and I shouldn't expect him back for at least another four days, more if the weather turned.

The weather did turn. Gales struck up in the bay and out to sea the fishermen fought for hours to keep afloat. I questioned so many through Rose in the week that followed. I wanted to know if anyone had seen a small schooner in trouble, if a boat that size could have braved those winds and a sea so violent. They would look at Rose as if what they thought was untranslatable, but in the end they would say it, would say, No, a boat that size would not survive, the sea around Salina Cruz was an impossible nightmare even in calm waters – a little boat would not have a chance.

Of course I would not believe it. My sole means of survival in those earliest days was by incanting his name over and over, believing that he was down the coast somewhere, that he was invincible and would somehow navigate his way to safety, and to me. I would go out at dawn each morning and stand in the place where he had kissed me last, watching every gull and curlew swoop and dive, every trawler and cargo boat arrive and leave. I stood for years in my mind, convinced that the very next boat would be his, the conviction so strong that I hit Bob Brown when he tried to carry me in, shouted or ignored all the do-gooders who came to entice me back into the hotel when dark came, who brought me food and tried to make me eat, who invoked our baby as a reason to sleep.

Eventually I would relent, when my eyes could see no more, not even darkness, and I would lie on our bed where his scent was strongest, going through in my mind all possibilities, thinking of new questions to ask the next day of the fishermen, the hotel manager, anyone who knew the coast, the tides, the waters . . . always waking with a fresh theory, a new notion as to where he could have been blown off-course, a new explanation for the fact that I was utterly alone and needed him with me so much that the thought that he might never be again made me bang the bedstead with my rings, my bracelets, books, the lamp . . . trying to get through to him, to send him a signal that I knew he was all right, that I loved him. When they stopped me I collapsed. I was hallucinating, feverish, being buzzed around as people treated me, desperately afraid that I would lose the baby, that it would die in my panic.

She didn't die. She is all I have left of him. When the passenger ship came into port, they put me on it, Rose Brown trying to get a berth on it to accompany me, but she was unlucky. Rather, I was. I was still in a waking delirium then, and when after a few days at sea I came out of it, it was to the shock of my circumstances, to the fact that I was sailing alone towards life without him, that he was dead, that I was completely alone but for the child I carried.

The journey seemed infinite, a litany of strangled languages, shouting, noise, strange coasts with mythical names, frantic ports where the steerage passengers climbed off to earn their livings in a new place, while those who had tired of its novelty replaced them in the innards of the ship. I watched distractedly. I saved knowledge for Fabian, saved descriptions and colours and details of the fights that broke out in harbours as papers were checked, tickets torn up, tempers lost. The acute pain of not knowing where he was threatened to rend me in two, and so I struggled in that month at sea with the desire to put a stop to it. I am certain that I wouldn't have, even had Fabi not kicked and squirmed in me, primed for life. I both knew he was dead and believed he was alive – he would return to Salina Cruz in my absence, would journey on to Valparaiso where I would be docking, where we had planned to meet once he and the others departed in the new Puerto Angel boat. The other three men had not shared my faith. They had set off on foot towards the border. I never heard of them again, I never found out their fate. I hope they escaped.

I was unable to concede that he was gone. What I knew was that he was dead. I knew this. But it was the unthinkable then. Now occasionally it is the consolation. Figure that out for me, Jack.

I still truly believed there was a chance that in the month my damned ship had been cruising the Pacific picking up bananas and dropping immigrants off in Peru, he had made his way back from wherever he had been blown off-course, back to Salina Cruz or Puerto Angel, and was now either *en route* to Valparaiso to explain everything to me, or was already there waiting for me with the Browns, who had risked the bandit convoys and gone by train. And so I strained to see his big blond head and his broad shoulders towering over the Chileans at the harbour when we docked, and broke down when all I saw was Rose Brown.

There had been no news since, not even a shipwreck found. I had thought that news of his battered boat would be the worst news I could find, but already at that point I was becoming desperate for any news that might give me an answer. Still at the forefront of my mind were my theories, all the possible places he could be. Washed up along the coast with amnesia, concussion . . . jailed by officials in any one of half a dozen countries if his luck ran out . . . in custody at one of the land borders . . . being beaten and tortured by bandits . . . all perfectly sensible reasons for him not to be at the docks in Valparaiso, or the beach in Salina Cruz, or the port in Puerto Angel.

Rose Brown had sent along the coast for word of him. Descriptions, details of his attire, his build, his languages, his past identities – and I was outraged, for it was as though she were citing information about a wanted man, an escaped criminal, a traitor. We had to be careful, I explained, for officials mustn't know, in case he was stranded without papers and needed to escape over borders. She said she didn't think that was likely. She was worried now about getting me somewhere permanent to have the baby. I was more rational than I had been in Salina Cruz, but nonetheless stupefied with grief and bewilderment. She began making plans around me, over me, and in retrospect I owe her a great deal for her kindness, though at the time I thought she was making me abandon all hope of being there when Fabian arrived.

I don't know if grief truly is easiest borne when occupied. I wish I had been able to sit down and think clearly in those weeks, unfettered by the need to make decisions, plans . . . I wish I had had time to understand what was going on. I felt on edge with frustration, trapped in my body so I could not travel freely to look for him, constricted, so I could not make plans to investigate prisons after the birth, and utterly crippled by loneliness and panic that I really might never see him again. I have never known such aching loneliness as in those first months. People talk blithely of being in despair at not getting to the post-box in time for the last post, of despairing of ever finishing their latest painting, their latest money-making scheme, their latest voyage. Despair is not quotidian. It has no way into life unless it enters through loss or tragedy. Anything else is merely discomfort or misfortune.

Despair is what constituted every hour of those months. I couldn't make sense of it, of the fact of being with him, our whole lives bound up together, planned in such detail, and then, within seconds, a kiss, a dash in the water, and he was gone. Utterly, completely lost to me. I hated him for it, I had such vengeance planned for when he returned. I would threaten leaving him, divorcing him, would treat him with contempt when he tried to explain that it was not his fault. But of course these thoughts were the fleeting ones, the ones that crawled in at night but were gone by morning when the decisions had to be made. They were merely the comfort of anger. I needed one logical explanation, and from that point onwards I could think of the child, of our health.

He was being imprisoned. I didn't know where, but he had got to shore somewhere and been arrested for not having correct papers, for being a deserter even, and was as alone as I was now, utterly powerless in letting me know what had happened. I knew exactly what to do. He would want me to go somewhere safe, somewhere our baby could be born healthily, somewhere he would know to come to. And so in my desolate clarity I decided to go home, to return to England, to my mother to have my child. He would know where to come.

God knows it was insane. I hated my mother, and she me. She was ashamed of me, of my unfeminine interests such as art and men and poetry. She had never read a word of my writing but damned it from a height, which was fine for had she seen it she would possibly have institutionalised herself with the dishonour of having a daughter as coarse and dreadful as I. As it was I was merely scurrilous. I had written to her from Mexico of my marriage, and heard nothing in return. My father at least would have cabled me his congratulations, but he was dead now, never having made the trip to Florence to see the house his money bought, the marriage his money sustained or the grandchildren his money educated. He understood me. She was ashamed of him too.

She had always thought of herself as a woman of aristocratic demeanour who had married beneath her. My father was one of London's most prestigious, elegant gentlemen's couturiers, Jack, but to my mother he was merely a jumped-up tailor with a medium level of wealth. I found out something after her death that made me warm to her more; like me, she had been pregnant before her marriage. Like me, she chose the respectable route of least resistance. And yet, had she known of my reasons for marrying Stephen, she would have been utterly hypocritical. She had little room for compassion – understanding was entirely beyond her realm. But it explained in part why she resented my father so much; and from life with Stephen I knew how easy it was to indulge in it.

The trip to England was unbearable. I wrote to everyone I could think of, people we had known in Mexico City, in New York, to Frost's family, even to the people in the Academy whom he had been running from since the Black Jim Diamond fiasco. People he had mentioned in passing in Paris, in Berlin, in Barcelona, in London. And you. But by far the most important letter I sent then was the one to his family in Lausanne, explaining what had happened, my suspicions that he was trapped in a prison somewhere in Argentina or Chile or Mexico. I told his mother that there had been high storms on the day he had left, but didn't finish the point – for my own sake, I recall, far more than for hers. I told her about our wedding, and about the baby I was carrying, and about my plans to have the child in England. I gave her my mother's address, and said I desperately hoped to hear from her soon. I also sent a sealed letter to Fabian at her address, a heartpouring missive filled with all the tenderness and love and joy I felt at the idea that he should read it, should have reached Europe and now be able to join me.

I never heard a word from her. Nor from him, of course, but she had not the grace to write and acknowledge me, or her prospective grandchild. Later I visited her, brought Fabienne to meet her, but despite the infant's obvious physical resemblance to her son, there was nothing more than an icy politeness. It was clear that she did not regard me as her son's wife, even after I showed her our marriage certificate, nor Fabienne as her son's child. She made my own mother seem like one of the Three Graces.

Fabienne was born a few days after I arrived in England. Our baby was born on 5 April 1919. I never felt such sadness. Around me my married sister clucked and sang, all the house in tumult at the infant's birth, but I had no heart for any of it. She was my fourth baby, and the dearest, which I know is a callous thing for a mother to say, but truly she was born out of love, and I loved her deeply. But I felt such desertion. I felt abandoned, whether he was dead as some tried to tell me, or had absconded as others said, or was simply imprisoned as I believed, he was not there. He was not there. He should have been wherever I was, should have been there to see his daughter, to share this life, and I was alone, fussed and fêted, Jack, but so alone.

I wrote again to Fabian's mother and told her of her granddaughter's birth. I suspected, in my raging paranoia, that she knew more of him than I did, that her silence was a guilty one. I asked her for his address, but she merely cabled back informing me she had none. There was no mention of Fabienne, not a single acknowledgement. Even his family were leaving us out in the wilds.

Once I had recovered from the birth, I desperately wanted to go back and see if he had perhaps appeared in any of the places he was meant to – Salina Cruz, Puerto Angel, Valparaiso, Argentina, even Mexico City or New York . . . but first I knew I had to go to Florence, to Giles and Joella.

There were many shocks when I returned to Italy, but by far the worst of them was the discovery of Giles' abduction by Stephen. Stephen had just swooped down and stolen my son from his home, from everything he knew, his school, his friends, his sister, his nurse, and, as it turned out, the language he spoke. Joella gabbled away in Italian trying to explain how she had allowed Stephen to do this, and seemed utterly bewildered when I asked her to speak in her mother tongue. I of course had perfect Italian, but I did not want to have a perfectly Italian daughter. It had been three years since she had seen me, and yet she behaved as though I were a visitor she had mildly expected to drop by. We had written frequently to one another when I lived in New York, in English, and I had told her of all the things we would do together when she and Giles arrived to join me. But she had not known of my sudden move to Mexico, nor of my marriage, the infant . . . she had known none of it. I suppose the shock of losing first her mother, then her brother, and now discovering a new sister, must have been great. Still, I did not expect an over-courteous Italianate to greet me, and certainly not with the news that my son had been robbed from me.

She had written many, many letters, but it was almost two years since I had left New York bound for my new life. It seems a harsh fact on the page, not to have been in contact with one's own daughter for so long, but the first time I truly had time to absorb anything of my new life was when it folded around me. I seemed to journey endlessly to an accompaniment of platform squeals and naval whistles – all I had time to do was think as the panic lessened. Guilt formed at some point, an embarrassment that I did not know how my own children were when my mother asked, though I covered it up, and never so acutely as when I discovered my son no longer lived in the home, on the very continent, I had left him. I railed against Giulia at first for allowing Stephen to take him, but what legal rights had she over his own father? I suspected it had far more to do with my success in acquiring the divorce than any paternal longing. Had that really been the case, Joella was as vulnerable to his right-invoking child snatching as Giles. But it only required the upkeep of one child to make the point.

Giles died. I think I told you already. I got a letter from Stephen in the Bahamas that was twenty-nine days old, telling me Giles had died the previous night. A growth was found on his chest, and not one of Stephen's island doctors could stem our son's deterioration. I knew nothing of it. No one wrote to say, Your son is dying, come quick, or even to let me know he was unwell. And it was my fault, Jack. I was so angry that he had gone away with his father I blamed him for his not being there when I returned for him. I would not write, would not read the letters he sent, would not listen to Joella's beseeching. I exiled him to the Bahamas for his audacity in bending to his father's will. He paid for my hatred of Stephen, and he died without me, without knowing how deeply I loved him, how desperately I wanted him back by my side, the man in our new family. He never saw Fabi, never even knew of my remarriage, isolated instead in a place far from everything he knew, and everyone. His death is the only thing that ever put Fabian's loss in perspective. I grew able to talk about my husband, but to this day no one ever mentions my son. His death is my most unforgivable deed.

His disappearance from the villa in Florence gave the place an air of expectancy. Everything seemed ready to start, as though awaiting his entrance. My own seemed only to confuse things. Joella was very happy to see me, but she was growing up a stranger to me, filled with Giulia's twee little notions of womanhood. She was twelve years old and her time was spent doing the household accounts, cartwheels, sewing, and reading dreadful love stories in Italian. She went to an English-speaking school, but all she ever seemed to do was gabble in Italian. Everything seemed to be breaking down, Fabian gone, Giles kidnapped, and Joella becoming the child Giulia had always longed for, no longer mine.

I left Fabienne with them and took the boat to New York. I had to find Fabian, and nothing else in my life would work until I did. I wanted a family, not this disjointed alienating pretence. I wanted to settle in myself, and give my full attention to Fabienne. If Fabian could be found and Joella reclaimed, it was not too late for everything we had planned to become real. I would work on retrieving Giles as soon as we four were settled. I was obsessed. Everything would fit when I found Fabian, all I had to do was go back to where the misunderstanding had begun and unravel it. My children would come back to me, my baby would grow up happy, I would regain the greatest love I had ever known. All I had to do was find him.

I got help in New York from people I had known, like the Arensbergs, the Browns, Bill Williams, but the journeying I did alone. People thought I was mad and in my alleged best interests, told me so. I returned to Mexico and Salina Cruz, to the place where he had last kissed me. The town was in disarray, the rebels causing chaos in every enclave that had not supported them wholeheartedly in their rise to power. I asked questions everywhere, but no one had seen him or anyone like him. I travelled up the coast to Puerto Angel for the second time, but he had never got there. From there I took a ship to Iquique, from there to Callao, from there to Valparaiso. I looked in holding wards and prison cells, had ambassadors and consuls search inmate lists going back to October 1918 when he vanished, had them introduce me to intelligence agents and police chiefs alike, grilled known spies about the rebel movements in Chile, Argentina, Mexico – about possible sightings, possible explanations, places he could be, then searched those out, and nothing, nothing came up. I travelled on to Santiago, to Buenos Aires, all the time being treated like a lunatic harridan chasing her henpecked husband across the Americas.

I was sure he had been arrested. All sorts of theories clasped on to my need for an explanation and that particular one took nineteen prisons, camps, unofficial 'holding zones', before I gave up and accepted he was not there. That journey was the hardest of my life, Jack. Not so many months before I had come off that same train and found him there awaiting me in the bustle and noise, and from there our whole magical adventure had begun, everything yet ahead of us, me finally meeting you, the wedding, our travels, our baby conceived. And now I was utterly alone, he was not there to meet me, to hold me, to rub my neck of its travel-weariness and kiss it, kiss me, take me to see his Academy, to meet you, to the bullfight, the boxing match. Gone – our whole future together and all his dizzy plans for us.

I thought you would have been one of the ones who would suggest he had run away, who saw only the side that took care of himself. Now I know that you saw almost everything in him that was exciting and gentle, that you knew him as he was, not as he professed to be. I wonder now would we have had so much to say to each other, to reflect upon, had we started corresponding then. I think not. Besides the obvious effect of the lives we have lived in the twenty-eight years since, I don't think I would have had the ability to engage with anyone at this level. I had no desire to share my thoughts, to ruminate aloud on the past before I knew him. I was incapacitated by grief in a way that I do not think anyone can understand unless they lose the other half of their soul in the same savage mysterious way. I will never know exactly where he died, never be able to hold his corpse in my arms, to bury him and have my place of pilgrimage. Perhaps this is it. Perhaps you are my way of standing at his grave and talking, perhaps you are my exorcist, Jack.

In Buenos Aires I saw my first ray of sunshine when an intelligence officer told me that a German fitting Fabian's description had recently arrived in Necochea, down the Argentine coast. I was so sure, so absolutely, stupidly convinced it was him, for he had perfect German from the years in Berlin, and had often said the safest face to put on in Mexico was a Teutonic one. I rode to Necochea with so strong a sense of going to meet him, I even felt angry with him again, I was cross that he had me traipsing the world for him. But the predominant emotion was of unleashed relief, as though all the grief I had refused to give vent to had been melted down and reconstituted as elation, as euphoria. I had no sense whatsoever that there could be an error, that this man was not him.

And of course it was not. The man was very kind and very sympathetic but ultimately a squat professorial medicine man, with nothing in him resembling Fabian but the colour of his skin. With nineteen prisons scoured and over two hundred people wrung out with questions, I knew he was dead. I knew it in Necochea, as though it was the single clearest thing that could be seen from where I stood. What I had stared at from the deck of the steamer between Salina Cruz and Puerto Angel was not merely endless waves of ocean spinnakering out into Polynesia, it was his grave. It was where I should have mourned. He was dead, and I would not see him again. That was all. It was over.

It hasn't been over at all, of course. The grief still flicks its residue in my eyes each morning when I wake, or sometimes later, as I arrange my hair or dab my pulses with scent. The ache of loneliness never changes, not even in the best of company, when Marcel calls, or even Frances. It gnaws me so acutely as though I am cheating when I do things and he is not there to see, to share them. Sometimes I have convinced myself that it was not love, it was only as important as the patter of Bill or Walter Arensberg and I am a fake in my melancholy. But that is the sort of ludicrous self-delusion that the brain chews to bits within seconds, a fickle attempt to dupe my loneliness into accepting the attentions of those who could take it away. But I have met no one, have no interest. It is not a deliberate celibacy, it is simply that I grow so bored when in the company of others. Even my children, even them.

As I write, Joella and Fabi are in their homes preparing their belongings for the move to Aspen, Colorado. It is each their second marriage – perhaps my habits are catching. Joella is remarried to an Aspen man – they introduced Fabienne to a young architect there who has bought up the town with grand plans to expand it, and they fell in love, properly in love, not like poor Fabi's first encounter with a far older

German gentleman. This suits her far better, it makes her wear her youth happily, not adopt the dreadful failed wisdom of the divorced woman that she threatened to wear about her in the weeks after her divorce. She is like a true first bride now, besotted and gay but appreciated for all her worth. She got all his intelligence, Jack, and a little of mine, but she is his daughter really. She has his wicked joyfulness, sees it in everything, and like her father she neutralises cynicism in all who meet her, and it is for this that her new husband loves her. I feel it will last. I hope so.

And so my daughters are leaving. I will officially be alone again, but for a few friends and my thoughts. It will be a pleasant time, I believe. This life here suits me, I have no one to preoccupy me. In the mornings I will read, in the afternoons I will go out in the neighbourhood and collect objects and interesting details that lie around. Then each evening I will be free to compose my collages unless interrupted by Marcel or other old friends come to look for a dinner companion. It will be as I want it.

The girls are incessant in their exhortations to come with them. They will have large houses, they say, I will be near my grandsons. Fabienne, to my great sadness, cannot have children. It upsets her a great deal that she will be childless all her life, and though I cannot even hint it, I too have yearned for the day when our grandson or granddaughter was born. I have wanted it since she herself was a tiny child, the thought of his vigour and vibrancy, of all the things I loved in him, becoming infinitely delivered to the world. But they are to die with Fabi, and nothing can be done.

These days, Jack, they have made Fabian into a fool. Dada this and that, when he would have had no truck with any of it. He despised the hijacking of art into orthodoxy, he thought it all utterly foolish and self-indulgent. Now Marcel has pitched him as a Dadaist hero as though it were the finest epitaph he could have. There are better kinds. I allowed Marcel to print his 'Notes', the long poem he began when Frost died, his mistress on those long nights when I was not yet there, just before we married. I have written a lot to try and make sense of his loss. Many poems that begin as ideas and mutate, but they have been gathered now, published as a book. No one has noticed it, no one besides my friends, my family. I don't mind. I never wanted to be like Bill, that is for him to enjoy. People read as they choose. If they choose not to read me, it is because they don't want to, or do not know I exist. Either way, Jack, I am not bothered unduly.

I feel there are so many things I have not said. I have not told you much of my life in Paris after I came back from searching the prisons. When we moved there I learnt the rudiments of business – I designed lampshades, Jack, and sold them in an exquisite shop. Peggy Guggenheim put up all the money, and I all the talent and skill, but the giddy woman ran away to buy revolutionaries for some poor patronised war, and I ran the shop alone in the end. I moved here a decade ago.

How far things have gone, Jack, and yet how much they remain the same. No place is his place, and in the end, that is all. Do write soon, Jack, I cherish this correspondence more than you can know, it lends freshness to everything around me. I have found reliving the past after such a time has made the urge to grasp the present irresistible. Write soon, dear Jack, I will look forward to your next missive greatly.

As ever,

Your affectionate Mina

FABIENNE

He is recruited through his own foolishness. An overheard conversation in a bar about the art of forgery. He could have been arrested if talk like that fell on the wrong ears, but fortunately they fall on the right ones. He is given an address and a name. It is not an order, but he senses exactly what is going on and a responsible vein twitches in his arm. He goes.

It is 1941, Toulouse. They are having serious difficulties in getting access to zones they must enter if they are to operate. They need a gifted forger to replicate passes, papers, documents of all kinds. The Gestapo are not fools. New documents are introduced and cancelled so quickly they cannot keep up and vital access is destroyed. They have seen the passes my father has made for his friends in Toulouse, regarded them with awe. They have checked him out and found that, whatever he is, he is not the enemy. Exactly what they know intrigues him. They call him Benoît, but have traced his life only to Rome and London, believe him English. He shows them his papers, but they are not interested. Forgery is, after all, why he is here.

He agrees to help, and is given a selection of genuine passes to replicate by morning when the originals will be returned. They are VAP passes which enable commercial travellers into restricted zones in Paris, and are needed to ease escapes from the capital to Toulouse. This cell has the responsibility for getting shot-down US and British airmen away from their parachutes, over the Spanish border and on to escape-boats to England. He thinks it will be an adventure. In truth he has wanted to join for months. But for once he has had to wait to be asked. Why else speak so loudly in a bar of such a dangerous subject unless to attract the attention of the man behind?

It is the sleuthing and subterfuge that attract him, but after a year he is up to his neck in everything the underground entails. The adventure still thrills him as he escorts his wards through south-west France and over the border to Spain, each one carrying the identity of a man whose language he cannot speak. He provides the displaced airmen with their new papers but adds the details that kill the doubts in Gestapo minds when they stop the masquerading foreigners on trains, the ID proffered legitimising the airmen as Frenchmen commuting to livelihoods. He gives them useless IDs like library cards and sports-club memberships in amongst their proper passes and official papers, documents that give these anxious American and British airmen the extra edge that could save their lives. He rises in the organisation swiftly, and rises too to the responsibilities it bears upon him. Their cell evacuates four hundred and six airmen to safety in total.

He travels to Paris one August day in 1942. It is his job to pass on a list of informers who are not yet uncovered so that they can be manipulated to the highest extreme. Included too are the newest codes to pass on to London for radio communication. All the information is scrawled minutely on cigarette papers, wrapped around needles, and inserted into his rationed cigarettes. He must deliver the packet to a guard at the Gare d'Austerlitz.

He is wearing his most effective persona, his quiet, pensive priest disguise. His papers are all in immaculate order. It is a dangerous liaison, the station swarming with Gestapo and Vichy's men. The guard comes up and shouts at him to move aside, that he is not permitted in the zone he is in. He drops the cigarettes and shuffles off in a priestly fashion as though obeying the station guard's order. He sees the guard pick up the cigarettes as though it were he who had dropped them. The task is completed. He moves on. In the confusion of the station and the marching Gestapo he takes a wrong turn and suddenly he sees them. Thousands and thousands of them, in dresses and tunics and skirts, the platform before him thronged with little girls, bruised and filthy, terrified, the stench of urine and unwashed skin travelling through his nostrils to the pit of his stomach, as they are moved forward on to the cattle carts of the train, the weeping sound droning through the air like a low air-raid signal, blood dried on some of the faces, so many children huddling into each other, moaning, crying, wetting themselves, so many that the guards can barely move as they wade through them, striking the small uplifted faces with the butt of their guns if they try to reach up and grab hold of the soldiers' arms or lapels.

Something in him breaks and he runs into the waist-high swarm scooping up as many children as he can, trying to deposit them on the other side of the barrier, telling them to run, screaming the words as he tries to turn back and reach for more, grasping dementedly at the children, shouting at them not to get on board, not to follow the guards, to follow him, waving towards the exit with toddlers swinging from under his arms, but the Gestapo are on top of him, dragging him away to the room where they beat him unconscious as the train is loaded up and whistled off to its destination, five children lighter in its load for his efforts.

They wait for him to come to before they begin again, and when he reaches prison, the torture proper begins. They electrocute his genitals, lock him in a freezer for eighteen hours and then position six electric fires around him as he is tied to a chair, his blood thawing. He is sent for execution four times, blindfolded, stood against the solitary wall while the instructions are shouted to shoot. Four times he is 'reprieved' with a split second to spare. They cut off the index finger on his left hand. He has nothing to say. All he can think of is her, is of the life he discarded, the child he has never seen. He wants nothing but the chance to start again. He yearns for his child so desperately he is unable to speak. He never forgets what he has seen.

When the war ends he is freed. He learns that there were four thousand and fifty-one children he did not get across the barrier in time, four thousand and fifty-one children who completed the journey to Auschwitz that August day, the children of Drancy. Over and over he relives the moments before he moved, the moments in which he stood transfixed, when he did not act, and thinks how many more he could have lifted from the crowd. This thought accompanies him all the way to Mexico, back to the place he saw her last. He knows it should be New York where he goes, but he is too certain that he must do it right, cannot waste his chance. He thinks of Jack. He writes. He waits.

Jack

Chicago, June 1946

Dear Mina,

I never did get your letter from Buenos Aires. I don't know where you sent it, but I never got it. As for the photo, hell, most people in that were just hangers-on and dolled-up greaseballs. Only faces I recognise myself are Lucille's and Cravan's.

So, Bob Fowler popped up again. Cravan must have gone mad – he hated Fowler with a passion because Fowler had spread rumours about the Academy being a cover, that it was in fact a training camp for foreign spies. The idea was to try and spike our business so the pair of us would clear out and leave the old pro's boxing game in Mexico for him to monopolise. You'll be glad to hear I punched him out cold in Mexico City when I went back.

I didn't hold a grudge about the Barcelona con. I knew he'd only done it because he was desperate. It was just something he'd do, there was no malice or badness in it, just need. A lot of it. He was withering in Spain, he needed a new world to interest him, not the dreary, war-doomed paranoia of Spain in 1914. I was jealous as hell if truth be told, I wanted everything he had. I hated Spain by then too, I was terminally bored, Lucille was driving me nuts with demands for distractions, and I was sick to death of whining Americans who thought the only conversation I could possibly want was about how awful America was, how disloyal and ungrateful she was to her heroes. I'd been having that conversation since the day I landed, hell, I had so many variations on it I could have turned it into a musical, but it was my line, not some two-bit piss artist's who'd decided war made him an exiled genius. If I was bored of it after what I'd gone through, what must have been going on in their self-pitying little minds? The only interesting characters had been Cravan's buddies, Francis Picabia and his wife that you were talking about in New York, and people like Cendrars. They'd all left for America, everyone had that could, leaving me to the mercy of fools. I had to get out.

So when he wrote to me from Mexico saying there was a fortune for us to make there, I didn't need too much persuading. I took the next ship leaving, which was two weeks later. Lucille decided she'd had enough by then. She said if I was leaving Europe, I either came back with her to Chicago, served my time, and start a new life with her when I got out, or I went to Mexico to Cravan and made a mess of my life on my own. That she could even say it like that meant she'd lost all her faith in me. I didn't want a woman like that around me. She'd no belief in me any more. And that was that. She went back to Chicago, and I went to Mexico, and that seemed like marriage number two was trounced, though at least she had the manners not to top herself when it was over.

So I was a free man when I got to Mexico City, even if the law didn't technically agree. I was ready for everything that Cravan could throw at me. He was drinking less, and for the first time ever he seemed completely to lose interest in women, it was just Mina, Mina, Mina the whole time, while I kept up the side for both of us. He was very different to how he'd been when I'd left him, but he was still himself in all the ways that counted. He organised that bullfight for a start, that was lunatic, best fright I'd had since my mother had died, I really thought I was a dead man that day. That was a good day for us, wasn't it? I've never been as carefree, never seen Cravan as happy. It was because you were there, you had finally come.

We fought a few fights, exhibition jobs, before you came that earned us some serious money, and I realised Cravan was right, the place was crawling with chances for two pros to make money, especially when one of them was Jack Johnson. I don't think I'd really accepted I'd lost the title, even then, two years on. It just felt like I hadn't retained it, and to me there was a big difference. One was failure, the other oversight. And anyway, I had kept it in all but name, it was the set-up that went wrong, not me. Any fool watching the fight footage could see I had that match in the palm of my hand whole way through. Everybody knew Willard was a dud champion. I had retired until my affairs were in order. I would definitely be back.

Cravan agreed, and that was when we decided to set up the Academy in Mexico, exactly like the Barcelona place, right there in the city centre. You saw it, Mina, it was a great joint, wasn't it? Always full, and we'd some pretty promising youngsters in there too, some real talent. Never heard anything about any of them since though, they probably got caught up in all that revolution that cut the place up. Did for me too in the end. But it was a club and a half, that place, even better than Barcelona by the time I left.

We were still doing the exhibition fights round the country, or the bits closest to Mexico City anyhow – we weren't much up for all that bandit business, to be honest. You are a far braver woman than I am a man, Mina, for all the fighting I did. You have balls – courage like nobody I know, man or woman. I wouldn't have gone poking around those kind of prisons if they'd had Lucille or Etta or Irene locked up, hell, if they'd my whole family, I'd just have sat back and waited for it to sort itself out. I wouldn't have fancied those jails one bit.

The only problem with the Academy at the start was that it wasn't drawing in much money. In Mexico nobody had the access to money they had in Barcelona, where the jobs were bad but they paid. In the chaos of Mexico, good guys were revolutionary heroes one minute and governing with machetes the next, bad guys were out scaring the shit out of people one day, and helping to fix their roofs a day later. For all the war in Europe, it had stability compared to this place. One second America was their greatest buddy and of course they'd arrest Jack Johnson for them if he tried to fight for his title in Mexico, then America was an evil tyranny and I was turned into a hero for daring to stand up to them. But it was all factional and day-to-day stuff. When it came down to it, nobody could be trusted and nobody got paid. We were coaching for free pretty much, and enjoying it, but it couldn't last for ever. When word came down that the Mexicans were trying to barter me in return for American favours, I knew I had weeks left.

That fight was my idea, Mina. I wanted to cash in on my name while I was still allowed to stay there, so you two could start off your marriage with money. He wouldn't take any off me. We got such a crowd to the bullring for it, took it those fourteen rounds before he got me. Maybe I fell, maybe I dived, I don't know. It was a hot day, the sun kept catching my eyes. Whatever happened, he fought better than Ketchel and Burns, just a bit short on Jeffries and Sam Langford, but a damn good fighter when it was seriously put up to him. It was a pity he had to lie down for the bet on Black Jim Diamond. You'd beat that barrack boy yourself, Mina, it must have been awful hard for Cravan to dive to him. Suppose he'd seen me do it for far bigger odds though, maybe that took the sting out of it a bit.

It was one of the best nights of my life that night. You and him were something else together. Then up the next day for the ceremony in that little church. We couldn't get photographs, could we? I remember that annoyed me, I was scared it'd all seem flat, all of us there and me darting off the next day like I had to. It was dangerous enough staying that long, but I never told you that then, I wanted to be at that wedding more than I wanted to be at any of my own. It's why I got married again, you know, I wanted to see if I could have one more go at getting what you had. But it doesn't work like that. What I have now suits me, but it's not what was in that church that day in Mexico with all the wild flowers and the sun streaming in through the stained glass and the padre speaking so slowly because we were foreigners, and then it was done, finally Cravan could be shut up once and for all, he'd got his dream, he had you there in his arms, his wife. God, it made me feel lonely leaving, lonely just looking at the two of you, the understanding there, the acceptance, the optimism in you both for all that was ahead.

After that he was made up in Mexico as far as I could see. He'd beaten me, and my name talked loud in those days. The US marshalls were licking their lips at the border and I was prey again. I'd signed over all the Academy dealings to Cravan before the wedding, and sailed for Europe. Did you get my note that time? I really hated the Feds for the pressure they put on me then, but Cravan had a new life to begin, a real one, without me.

Spain wasn't so bad after I'd had a break and shed Lucille. She was a nice girl, but I married her for all kinds of reasons, and being head over heels in love wasn't one of them. Without her there, I travelled all round the country fighting exhibitions and getting treated like I was King, and I got such a fondness for that place in those couple of years. It wasn't like before, milking people because they hated me, wanted to see me lose. In Spain they really loved me, Mina, really wanted me to win, even in silly exhibition fights they'd chant my name to a crescendo and roar for me. It was a tough time in Spain then, all their crops were dying, everybody seemed to be on the move all the time, I just felt as though I was joining their trail. But of course I wasn't, I had money from diving to a fool, though at least I'd stopped hanging around with ones as well.

He had gone to such trouble for you coming into Mexico.

He'd moved into a better apartment because he said it had a view you'd love, over the noise of the market, and he'd planted a ton of arum lilies in pots on the balcony, and he had your pictures all over the Academy. God, Mina, he was so excited. Everything we did and saw that was fun or interesting we had to remember it and do it when Mina came. I was deluged by you, stories and pictures, what pictures, what a beauty, and poems and more stories, more plans for your future together. He made me come with him one day looking at cathedrals and churches and cloisters, to decide where you would get married. In the end it was simpler than that, it was the little place on the hill you fell for.

But I still don't think you fully understand the change you brought on in him, Mina. The man who conned me out of my share of the purse in Barcelona didn't think of love – he was the man who when Lucille asked if I was faithful told her that she should get out and enjoy herself a bit too. Women loved him, you knew his charm, and he was as lackadaisical about them as he was about everything else except that damn magazine.

When he'd escaped like that from Barcelona, that was Cravan. But he was a different person in so many ways from the man I fought in Mexico. The new Cravan was calm, settled in himself, focused, he drank less, he was disciplined, got up every morning and went to the library where they had all these French novels, and he read, and he wrote, and he talked sense half the time which was the biggest shock. Part of knowing him had been knowing his codes, his gestures, this great vocabulary of manoeuvres that made him seem insane if you didn't know him, that energy and excitement that caught you by the balls, a dart of thrill sometimes that wasn't erotic at all, but chilling, because you were catching his energy like it was cholera. That was why you ended up in a deserted mill amidst a hurl of burning timber and pews, why you found yourself in a bullring with eight thousand people cheering your escape from a maniacal bull with horns to tear your liver out. That was why you ended up caught in the crossfire of duelling antique silver pistols or hoisting fake Matisses out of windows late at night, why you held your breath with over four thousand people as he walked the tightrope, why your car ended up in the ditch as he went waving by you, because all the time you were caught in his energy and it was the most exhilarating place in the world to be. And God, he loved you, Mina Lloyd, you and no one but you, you changed his life around, don't ever doubt that you did, or that he loved you with everything in him. I've had love, I've had it in every state, in every position, I've been jailed for it and fined for it and closed down for it, and it hasn't been worth a single second I wasted on it. What was there between you was the purest understanding and acceptance a person could hope for. Every second I spent hearing about you, Mina, seeing you together, made me feel lonelier than I've ever known possible, made me feel that for all the titles in the world I missed out something I could never have.

Which is not to say I'd change a thing, well, not a thing up until that twenty-sixth round in Cuba. I'd sell my soul like Robert Johnson if I could have that moment back and die unbeaten at the top. But there it goes. Everything happens for a reason, I guess. It's an easy philosophy, but it suits my kind of life. Otherwise you'd be so damn bitter the whole time you'd be consumed by getting even, righting wrongs, sorting out the people who did you down. You forget all your glory that way. That's how I keep things under control, Mina, I just think of the days when I was King, when there wasn't anything could be done to stop me. I remember what it felt like throwing those punches on Jeffries, on Stanley, on Tommy Burns, every fight I won I have here in my head to replay over and over like pornography. That's what keeps me hard and able. They tricked me out of the title, but they can't trick the whole world into forgetting the days when Jack Johnson ruled it.

I went back in the summer of 1919. As a pawn, and a lug for even thinking they could be trusted after the other fiasco, but the Mexicans had decided that the Americans were just cheating bastards who'd never accept a favour from them in case they'd be beholden. They invited me to come. Seriously. I was telegrammed in Barcelona by Carranza himself and told there had been a dreadful mistake made in the past and they would like to rectify it by having me back as a guest of the new government. I must have missed you by a couple of months, you were off having your baby by then. I'd sent word to the old Academy address, and telegrammed your apartment beside the market to say I was coming back, but I heard nothing. When I got there, the Academy was all boarded up and no one knew where he could be found. In fact no one could be found at all of our old friends, the people he introduced me to when I landed there before.

If I'd known what had happened, I'd have come with you to look for him, travelled with you, done something to help. But I didn't know, nobody knew there, I had no idea, and I didn't find out until I went back to America. The news didn't travel up to Mexico City. You know how closed off the country was. I just assumed you had gone off together to Europe to get your children, like you'd told me you were going to when the war ended. I thought you both were gone. If only I'd known. So many lives lived between us, Mina, so many disguises to get us through.

The Americans were on my back still, watching me all the time, checking out everything I did. I had fun with them though. I opened up the Academy again, started giving a few exhibition fights, some lessons, to try and get back to fighting-weight. Willard had been neutered in front of the world not long after he got the title, which was always a good bet, and now Jack Dempsey had it. I wanted Dempsey. I wanted that title back with the true Champion, and to do it, I had to get fit.

So I combined training with coaching to take the boredom

out of it. The Feds had a great idea, they'd send their undercover man in to take lessons off me, become my buddy, and find out my plans. You could tell the kid was a Fed from the way he punched. He didn't. He'd obviously been a fan of Willard. Well, I pumped him so full of stories and adventures and secrets and conspiracies he was soon coming to me every day to perfect his right hook. How I was in Carranza's pocket, was one of his closest advisers on American relations, how we were plotting a revolution from right there in Mexico City to take over America, instigate an uprising starting with California and Texas and work our way north-east. The kid must have run home and told mama everything, because suddenly two of his friends wanted to take lessons too. It got amusing.

I did what I should have done in Spain, I opened another club. It wasn't a great club, not like the Café du Champion, but it was popular and I enjoyed being back in the game again. It made me want Chicago though, made me want old familiar faces, my own craps table, some good strong bourbon, James P. playing stride piano, a familiar girl on each knee. I wanted home, a final blast of homesickness before I threw in the towel for real. The crunch came when some different rebels overthrew Carranza and I was blacklisted for being part of his administration. Me and my mouth. The new regime came in and trashed the club on me, and banned me from fighting anywhere in Mexico. I was tired. I was forty-one and bored with travelling the world like a circus boy, bored with ships and wars and revolutions. I wanted America, I wanted everything I had lost back again, and after these years of playing it tough and acting like I didn't give a damn about my country, I wanted my old life back. I went to my three least-promising pupils and told them. After they crawled out indignantly from their Trojan horse, they agreed to take my request to the top. The top came back. They would meet me at the border at Tijuana, a black cop would arrest me, there would be no handcuffs, and they would have the reporters I had specified there to take down my side of the story.

And so it went ahead. Wearied of all the pretence and effort of exile, I gave myself up. I just wanted home. On 20 July 1920 I walked into America for the first time in seven years, and was arrested. The time had come. I was ready.

There were over four thousand people at the station at Leavenworth to welcome me back, Mina. They had banners and letters and were yelling out my name loud enough to drown out bombs. It was some homecoming. Somebody even had the loan of a great big Chalmers limousine just like the one I used to have for me to drive myself up to the jail myself, all slow with people cheering all along the roadside as if I was coming back from stuffing Dempsey. That was all I got asked, When you gonna fight Dempsey, Jack? When you gonna fight Dempsey? And my answer was, in one year and one day. I meant it. When I came out of that prison, Dempsey would be made to return the one thing that would never be his as long as I was alive. It felt so good being back, Mina, my own people hollering for me, treating me like a hero again, letting me know they would always be on my side. I felt real, like the whole European thing had been one long vaudeville tour and now I was headed home.

Only thing was, instead of my nice big house on Wabash Avenue and Lucille there waiting for me, I had a nice big jailhouse instead, and I didn't expect there to be many with Lucille's charms inside it. She had written to me, told me she was glad I was home, said maybe we could keep in touch now and work something out when I got out. She wasn't filing for divorce. I liked the idea of her being true to me, but truth was, Lucille and I were long over, over the second she doubted my ability to keep my dignity and fight on. But it would be nice to get letters, I thought. I wrote back and said, Great, a second chance.

There was a sort of awe given to me in Leavenworth. I don't know if it was because I was Champion of the World, or because I'd escaped the law for seven years, but I had their respect from the start, and that helped things along nicely.

That place was good to me. I even get nostalgic about it, which is crazy, I guess, soft about your old prison, but I do.

It was generally agreed by everybody that I wasn't an ordinary prisoner. The other guys thought it, the Feds thought it, and most surprisingly of all, the chief warden thought it. He was an old buddy, Dickerson, he'd been Governor of Nevada when I'd fought Jeffries in Reno and he'd had a mad interest in boxing. He'd come down to my training camp seven or eight times to chew the fat, play craps with the boys, watch me train. He didn't care what anybody thought of him, just as long as his wife loved him and Nevada kept voting him in. It was a relaxed kind of place, he suited it down to the last turnpike and piece of scrub. Somehow though he'd ended up playing keymaster to a bunch of crooks. Maybe Nevada hadn't liked him so much after all.

I got treated like a king in that prison. Any music I wanted, any book, any magazine, any newspaper. They knocked two cells together to give me a decent bit of space. I had a double bed and blankets enough to wrap up an orphanage, I had lamps and bookcases and a reading desk and a phonograph. I was allowed to pay to get my meals brought in from outside, and the best cigars. I wanted for nothing.

For all these privileges they asked me to take over as physical education director of the penitentiary. That was just like running one of the Academies, Mina, sparring and punchbags and big exhibition fights where they'd bus in prisoners from the jails all round to see Jack Johnson fight. I couldn't have asked for it better. I trained everybody in that place so well they could have taken on Dempsey themselves when they got out. Trained myself too so I could do just that. I was in top shape. All the papers were saying I was easily the measure of him, would flatten him before anybody else would. When Georges Carpentier came over from Paris to fight Dempsey, they let him in to see me, to go over old times and discuss Dempsey's form. Georges lost, which in a way I was glad about, better to have to floor that thick-necked tent boy than suave old Georges.

The sentence ended. I was almost sorry to go, well, only for as long as it took to say goodbye. When I came out it was like the crowds that had given me my send-off had only gone home to get their friends, because there were thousands and thousands there to greet me, to celebrate that Jack Johnson was a free man again, raring to go. I was driven in an open-top roadster like a debutante with muscles, driven all the way to the station, and when that train pulled into Chicago we had a near riot, I was lifted out and carried over people's heads. I made a speech on the steps of City Hall, told them all that Jack Johnson was back in business, and that business was chasing down Jack Dempsey's puny ass till it was mine. Did they cheer, Mina, what a racket, like I'd just announced the Prohibition was over and there'd be free bourbon for everyone.

It was so damned good to be back in Chicago, still to be a hero to the people who'd stood by all the times things got hard for me. There were the bastards too, but the ones who turned up to welcome me home, they were the ones I'd been fighting those fights for. Well, they were now I could decide they were. At the time though I guess I was fighting to beat those bastards for my own glory, for my own revenge. I just beat them because I wanted to be better than them. And I was, I always was, with or without that title I was better, the only Champion to have changed a thing. Those crowds got the best of me, that was what I gave them, and they knew it. That was why they risked losing their jobs to come out and welcome me back, let me know I was still their undefeated hero. That's why I loved Chicago so damned much – New York had nothing on it.

But Dempsey was just a piece of shit like all the rest before him. I never got my chance to shove that smug ugly scowl of his down his throat. He drew the colour line, little bastard said the only challengers he'd meet to defend his title were white ones – as if anybody believed that title was his until he'd beaten Jack Johnson, shown everybody he deserved it. But he knew. The smirking little low-life knew I'd beat him, just like everybody knew, and he was scared, hid behind his title like it was Mama's skirt, refused to come out and stand up in the ring with the only real Champion anybody'd ever seen. I taunted him and teased him, declared outright that he was a coward, a sniffling little brat who'd won his title off a fool, who'd won his in a fix, but nothing happened. He just stamped his big lug feet and said he couldn't fight a black man and that was that.

And it was. Fool nearly got killed a while later by Luis Angel Firpo before Gene Tunney came along and battered his balls all the way back to Manassa. I trained Firpo, he came to me looking for advice on his technique and I trained him in the final few weeks. Closest I ever got to Dempsey. Firpo nearly got him too, savaged him, punched him so hard he went out through the ropes into the crowd, but he was shoved back in again and the referee decided Dempsey should get to box on. The bastard won it a few rounds later, but he was in some shape after it. If I'd been wearing those gloves, he'd have been humiliated, and he knew it well. Still, it was good to see him bloodied round the ring with my punches, even if they came from another man's glove.

I couldn't have boxed any of them. I was banned, refused a fighting licence. All the weak-kneed imbeciles on the state boards followed right on through till I could barely fight my own shadow without breaking the law. There are some things a man just shouldn't have to deal with when he's earned his respect. And I'd earned mine. Whatever they hated in me, I'd won that title and I'd defended it. If they had a problem with my lifestyle, well, hadn't I just served a year in prison for pissing people off with how I lived my life? I was due respect, and due some mannerly treatment from the likes of them, stuffed shirts and breeches who'd pass out if they ever had to throw a jab at anyone. These were the fools regulating the careers of men like me. It was insanity.

I never got to fight again. Not truly. Exhibitions, illegal bouts, silly fights on the Mexican border, but never a real fight, a title fight, again. I never knew it then, but my career ended in that twenty-sixth round in Havana. Other fighters lost their title and came back, but not me, I was denied that the second the Feds got me by the balls and wrested that title back into white hands. People keep asking me to tell them what I think of the new black kid Joe Louis, and they get all righteous when I don't fawn all over them right there on the spot. He's a good kid, fights tough, and you can see he has it in the head, in the eyes, but he leaves his left side wide open to a panel-beating. I said that ten years ago, and sure enough, Max Schmeling went in and creamed him from the left in '36. He's still fresh though, still winning, despite that glass chin of his. But there was only one man could be the first. First black man, sure, but first full-stop too. They did a poll there a few years ago, who was the best heavyweight ever, canvassed all the sports reporters, coaches, managers, spars . . . and it was me they chose, Mina. Jack Johnson won the day. I might be getting old now, but that's a lively bit of recognition to be carrying round in your head.

I married Irene twenty years ago last August. We had a bit of a party, but the big one will be the twenty-fifth. Longest marriage of the lot by a long shot, but I'm calmer now. I'm not as testing. It doesn't take so much patience to be with me these days. They've been quiet enough times. I'm still fit as ever, do my routine in the yard every morning, still going to the gym and sparring, still picking up tickets wherever I head, but mainly we've just settled down. I've read a lot – I always loved books but there were so many interruptions on the road all the time it was hard to finish the sports pages, never mind anything else. That Dumas is some man, but it's Victor Hugo that really gets me. I love that stuff. I went looking for your poems, but I couldn't get them, it's not much of a bookstore for poetry. Most moving thing I ever read though was that Joyce story, 'The Dead'. All that sadness, Mina, it makes you wish you could fix things like they're supposed to be, not just leave them there broken and end up with the wrong fate. I think we should meet, you and I. There are things I want to tell you that can't be put on a page. Things you need to see a person's face to tell them. Will you? I don't mind how you want to do it – I'll come to New York, or if you wanted to come and see some high-life here in Chicago that'd be something special. I can come to New York any time suits you. My most pressing engagement here is playing craps with a bunch of blind men and sobered drunks. If you fancy coming west, I'll pick you up at the train station whatever day you say.

Write soon,

Jack

Mina

New York, June 1946

Dear Jack,

I agree, I think it would be wonderful to meet. What is it you are so eager to tell me? You make it seem so exciting. Would you like to come to New York, or shall I travel to Chicago? I don't mind the journey, it would even be an adventure compared to the simplicity of my everyday life. I am finishing a collage at the moment.

There's a professor in your direction who wants to meet me and discuss some complex theory he has about my poems. The girls have been trying to convince me to go and meet him – he has besieged me with letters ever since he got my address from Marcel. He's offered to come up, but I could see him in Chicago too if I did make an adventure of it. I can only assume he will be dreadful, all theorists are, even if it is about my work. Particularly so in fact. Sometime towards the end of this month would suit perfectly, Jack. I'll have finished this collage and got the girls and the grandchildren off to Aspen . . . it would be perfect. Do you agree?

Write and say which you prefer,
Until then,

Mina

PS. I think it will be quite strange after so long, and such intimacies, but, Jack, I cannot wait, I truly can't. Write soon.

10 June 1946

He is excited by the prospect of the rematch in New York. Everybody he knows thinks Joe Louis is the business, best fighter on the go, they say. Nearly as good as Johnson when he fought Jeffries, say the ones in the know. But he disagrees. The kid might have it in the head but he leaves options wide open to his opponent. And if you have it in you to be the best, you don't do that. You leave no opportunity for anyone to catch you on a weak spot. You train yourself into protecting all the possible angles, so you can concentrate on the attack. The way Louis fights, Jack reckons he is in for a long hard beating one of these days. He wouldn't mind doing the job himself if somebody would let him.

That job's been entrusted to Billy Conn. It's been a long time coming, this rematch. First time out was four years ago, then the war came and made dutiful soldiers of the pair of them. That time Conn had him, was winning easily, but he had to get clever and tried for a knock-out. Any fool could see he wasn't that kind of a fighter, even Louis, who picked himself off the ropes to come in and floor the white kid. Gone are the days when they need a Great White Hope. The title stays with Louis, and then the war comes and distracts everybody all over again.

So now it's the rematch. He is tired. A three-week tour of Texas just ended, singing a little, playing the bass-viol, a bit of graceful sparring with the shadows on the theatre walls. He hasn't toured in years, but he did this one for old times, going to all the towns he knew as a kid, winding up in Galveston, seeing all his old friends. Irene gets to meet his sisters and brothers for the first time, see all his old haunts, get an idea of who he was before she fell in love with him. But she is too tired for the New York trip. She suggests he takes Jack Curley with him instead, try out the new Lincoln Zephyr he just got sent, custom-made to all his quirks.

He is frustrated on the road, tired. It is too early in the morning to be awake and he just wants to get the journey done, get some rest, get to the match then hit home to Irene after he's seen a few people in New York. He could look up Mina, he has brought her address, but he decides to leave it as planned in Chicago for ten days' time. He wonders how he will tell her.

He accelerates past ninety but as they come round the bend a truck comes into view and he has to slow. A straight patch comes up so he puts his foot down to get past it and then the road is clear in front of him for as far as he can see, just pure North Carolina highway eager for a bit of speed. The old familiar feeling comes over him, the exhilaration in his belly that coils and uncoils as he eyes up the road ahead. Curley is singing to himself, well used to this, and Jack has his foot down hard on the accelerator when suddenly the car goes loose on him, he can't get the steering wheel to take grip on the tyres, so by the time he sees the telegraph pole the car is doing a hundred headlong into it and the brakes won't stop him. It spins on its back for what seems like an eternity to the truck driver, who pulls out the small guy first from the passenger seat, then tries to get to the other guy who seems folded right up into the front of the car, his hat still on and blood all over.

Eight hours later as Jack lies in Raleigh County General, North Carolina, Joe Louis takes to the ring to fight Billy Conn. It is all over in six rounds, Conn backing off at every punch, lacking the guts to go in and bring the fight to him. At the end Louis is triumphant, holding up the belt to the crowds screaming his name, waving and cheering and shouting for the Champion, yelling, Joe, Joe, Joe. Jack is dead by then. Internal injuries, the doctors tell Irene – nothing could be done to save him. Jack Curley walks out five days later, and Irene cannot forgive him for being the one alive.

My mother is pottering at her collage when I call in. I give her the newspaper, open and folded at page four, point to the headline in the bottom right-hand corner. She blanches, sits down quickly. She does not understand. Quickly I postpone my plans for the evening and stay with my mother all night. In those moments I do not understand the nature of her shock as I do now, nor its force. All I know is that the two have exchanged some letters in the past few months, and that they were to meet in a few days' time. Fleetingly I have thought it odd, but never asked, never listened when she told me.

It hits Mina as if it were Oda all over. Not Giles. Not Fabian. She feels as she did when Oda died in the night, as if, of all the people in the world it had to happen to, she had been picked because she had done something wrong. She is certain it is her fault, that she caused it, that Jack would have lived for years had he never contacted her. My sister and I are more alarmed by the effect of Jack Johnson's death on our mother than anything that has happened to her before. She pretends to be acting as normal, but it is clear there are things she cannot even begin to explain to us, no matter how we try to engage her. She resumes her life, will not hear of accompanying us to Aspen. Her life goes on.

In the Miahualtan Mountains Ernesto Guavez awaits his post with such fervour that the postmaster begins to think he is a spy of some kind. He receives a letter written in early June telling him that Jack and Mina are meeting three weeks later in Chicago, Mina's choice. Jack promises to send word of her reaction as soon as he leaves her, even if it is just a postcard. For two years the postmaster puts up with questions about the postal service, about the likelihood of letters getting lost, about the chances of a letter being misdirected away from this godforsaken outpost. Then Guavez disappears, the questions stop. No one ever sets eyes on him again.

A NOTE ON THE AUTHOR

Antonia Logue was born in Park, Co. Derry in 1972, and brought up in Brussels. Educated at Trinity College, Dublin, she now lives in Castletownshend, West Cork. *Shadow-Box* is her first novel.

A NOTE ON THE TYPE

This book is set using Bembo. The first of the Old Faces is a copy of a roman cut by Francesco Griffo for the Venetian Printer Aldus Manutius. It was first used in Cardinal Bembo's *De Aetna*, 1495, hence the name of the contemporary version. Although a type cut in the fifteenth century for a Venetian printer, it is usually grouped with the Old Faces. Stanley Morison has shown that it was the model followed by Garamond and thus the forerunner of the standard European type of the next two centuries.